Sins
of the
Past

Susan Tuttle

Published by: WriterWithin Publications

Copyright © 2014 Susan Tuttle

A WriterWithin Publication; All rights reserved.

Cover design by Aaron Kondziela:
www.aaronkondziela.com

ISBN-10: 1941465005
ISBN-13: 978-1-941465-00-4

DEDICATION

For my son, Aaron Kondziela, computer guru
extraordinaire and amazingly gifted artist and
musician who can do whatever he sets his mind to do.
He's a true 21st Century Renaissance Man. And he
designs the world's best book covers. Thanks for being
who you are!

CONTENTS

Acknowledgments	i
Chapter One	1
Chapter Two	13
Chapter Three	23
Chapter Four	32
Chapter Five	46
Chapter Six	59
Chapter Seven	69
Chapter Eight	86
Chapter Nine	110
Chapter Ten	121
Chapter Eleven	141
Chapter Twelve	159
Chapter Thirteen	174
Chapter Fourteen	180
Chapter Fifteen	192
Chapter Sixteen	212
Chapter Seventeen	223
Chapter Eighteen	237
Chapter Nineteen	247
Chapter Twenty	258
Chapter Twenty-one	273
Chapter Twenty-two	289
Chapter Twenty-three	303

Chapter Twenty-four   313

Chapter Twenty-five   327

Chapter Twenty-six   345

Chapter Twenty-seven   359

About the Author   368

Books by Susan Tuttle   369

Sins
of the
Past

ACKNOWLEDGMENTS

Even though writing is a solitary occupation, no author produces a book in a vacuum. Many thanks go out to my wonderful critique partners, who make sure my work is the best it can be: Ginger Lasher, Anna Unkovich, Lynne Diane Smith, Dennis Eamon Young, Richard Sudden, Evelyn Cole, Claire Gordon, Jim Leonard, Christine Taylor, Mark Arnold, Lorie Woodward.

And of course, Debra Davis Hinkle, a great writer and critiquer in her own right, without whose computer expertise you would not be holding this book in your hands. She dragged me kicking and screaming into the twenty-first century, and convinced me I, too, could conquer today's technology. And so I designed and laid out the interior of this book, all by myself. Thanks, Debra, you're the best!

CHAPTER ONE

He read through the last two files yet another time, sighing aloud and hoping for lightning to strike. Nothing happened. Whatever was amiss wouldn't come clear. Growling, he kneaded the bridge of his substantial nose. *This wouldn't have happened a few years ago,* he thought, shoving files aside. *This goddamn pencil-pushing, paper-rattling, desk-jockey job is killing me.*

He snorted in disgust and glared at the nameplate perched on the edge of the dark mahogany desk: Mitchell James Lawson, Coordinating Liaison. Him, a bureaucrat, for pity's sake. Once the Marshal Service's top field agent, Mister too-valuable-to-be-pensioned-off Lawson now slowly lost his mind in the Freaking Bureaucracy of Idiots, collating facts and figures for the National Incident-Based Reporting System (NIBRS).

Nothing but busy work tailor-made for the company screw-up. He wasn't a real agent, he was a paper agent. A paper agent in a paper city in a paper world. He'd like to strangle the bastard who invented the frigging stuff.

He wanted to be a Marshal still, not an FBI bureaucrat. He wanted to be out on the streets not in a paneled office. With his .357 magnum where it belonged, snugged beneath his armpit, not stuffed in a drawer. He wanted the danger back, the excitement, the anticipation of the unknown. What did he have to look forward to here? Eye strain? Paper cuts?

It's your own fault, buck-o, he reminded himself, glaring at the miniature Alp of folders on his desk, his punishment for taking two weeks off. *You're the one who screwed up. You misread the situation, not someone else. You played it wrong and got shot for your efforts. No one to blame here but yourself.* The proof was in his daily life—hours of safe, dull, boring work in a safe, dull, boring office.

And now his elephantine memory had holes in it.

He shook his head. Maybe a break would help. Mitch growled again and shoved away from the desk. He thrust himself out of his chair and turned toward the window. Pain shot up his left side from knee to hip. His leg buckled and he stumbled up against the desk. Like a churning mudslide, the mountain of files cascaded onto the gray carpeting, sweeping nameplate and pencil holder with them. Grimacing, he stood massaging the pain in his hip, shaking his head and staring at the mess littering the floor. *Can it get any better than this?* he asked himself as he waited for the pain to abate. *Can it just fucking get any better?*

The door opened and his secretary, Kelsey of the velvet voice and fuck-me heels, wiggle-hipped across the carpet. She set a steaming cup of the decaffeinated, half-herbal brew she deemed coffee on the newly cleared desk. She looked down at the file-strewn floor and shook her head.

"Mr. Lawson. What happened here?"

Mitch shrugged. "Earthquake."

"Funny, I didn't feel anything."

Mitch grunted.

"It epicentered on me."

"So I see." Kelsey smiled and stooped to retrieve the folders.

"You don't have to do that."

"I know, I just can't help myself. It's a conditioned response, like Pavlov's dogs salivating." Kelsey handed Mitch a stack of folders, which he set on the glossy desktop. Then she reached for more. "The price of having kids."

"My sister's the same way," Mitch said, shuddering slightly at the way Kelsey's voice stroked down his tingling nerves. She knew exactly what the sound of her voice did to most men, and he knew she used it to her advantage. That she was also one of the most efficient, intelligent secretaries he'd ever met, was for Mitch mere icing on the cake. "She's always wiping or picking up something, no matter who drops it. And cutting up everyone's food. Thank God I dodged that bullet."

"There are rewards, you know." Kelsey stood up, put the last of the files on the desk and looked at Mitch, who took a step back.

"No, I don't. And I don't want to. I am quite content being a carefree bachelor, thank you very much."

"And using Maureen's boys as surrogate kids. Best of both worlds, huh?"

"Absolutely," Mitch said. He winked and moved to the window, hoping, as he opened the blinds to the rain-swept dusk, that his slight limp wasn't noticeable. He might have ended a mere desk jockey, shuffled over to the FBI, but he'd be damned if he'd show any of the weakness that had caused his fall from grace.

"What I came in for, Mr. Lawson, is to remind you that it's getting late. Are you leaving anytime soon? Or are you going to ruin the entire value of your vacation in one day?"

"No, and yes," Mitch said, looking out at the rain-blurred lights.

"I thought so." In the window's reflection, Mitch watched Kelsey cross her arms, tilt her head and study him, her auburn locks a fiery contrast to his sand-colored hair. "Is there any possible way I can make you go home at a reasonable hour?"

"Only if you promise to come with me and talk to me all night. You know how I love your voice. For relaxing, it's even better than that Bahamian beach." Mitch turned and grinned at her. "Pure heaven."

"If I come, my five-year-old will have to come with me. And he never shuts up—he even talks in his sleep. You'd never hear a word I'd say."

Mitch shook his head. "You're a hard woman, Kelsey McGuire. You should be kinder to me, considering my advanced age."

Kelsey laughed and Mitch almost purred with pleasure. "Nonsense. Forty-seven is the prime of life, Mr. Lawson. And I don't believe," she picked up the coffee cup and walked over to give it to him, "that you went to any Bahamian beach. I think you went to Ireland and kissed the Blarney Stone—again."

Mitch chuckled. He set the cup on the window ledge and turned to watch the city outside glimmer through the rain into an iridescent sheen as full dark fell, absently twisting his onyx ring round and round on his finger.

"Look at that, Kelsey. Isn't it amazing? So beautiful."

"Like an enchanted fairyland wrapped in velvet," Kelsey murmured.

"You know," Mitch sighed, "I think I'll miss this the most when my time comes, the way the city lights up at night. Those lights look like warm glowing jewels. Or beacons of hope maybe. An oasis of welcome in a cold and indifferent world."

Mitch fell silent, his mind wandering back to the file that had caught him up short. Kelsey looked up at him, her face solemn. Mitch frowned and shook his head.

"But there weren't any welcoming beacons that day," he said. "No comforting, man-made incandescence, not on a sunny summer afternoon. A hell of a time to die, wasn't it, when everything else was so alive? Odd that Webster didn't detail the stolen items, the things the guy died for—"

Mitch froze, his recalcitrant memory finally displaying the appropriate pages to his mind's eye. A premonitory shiver went down his spine. He could hear the traffic on the street below, feel the thud of his own heart, as again he saw the victim's name, the impersonal, abbreviated description of the crime, the lack of evidence that had quickly stymied the local police investigation. He scanned Agent Webster's oh-so-logical conclusion. Another innocent victim unfortunate enough to be home at the wrong time. Logical, yes. But wrong. Dead wrong, if Mitch's memory hadn't totally failed him. And it hadn't. Though it had been years, he knew damn well that it hadn't.

"Mr. Lawson?" Kelsey asked, frowning. "Is everything all right?"

Mitch whirled and strode to the desk, shoving files around until he found the one he wanted. Then he turned and pointed at Kelsey.

"Don't leave until I get back," he ordered. "And don't let Dan Jeffers leave, either. I'm going to need him."

He left her staring open-mouthed at his retreating back and took the stairs up two flights to the Bureau Chief's office. Mrs. Marlin, Oscar Henry's sixty-something martinet of a personal assistant, stood up as Mitch thrust open the office suite door.

"Is he still in?" Mitch asked, not slowing to hear her response. He could see light behind the frosted glass panel in the door to the Chief's office.

"You can't go in there, Mr. Lawson," Mrs. Marlin grated in her two-pack-a-day voice. "He's in a meeting. Mr. Lawson. Stop!"

Mitch didn't break stride. He moved down the short hall and shouldered his way into the inner sanctum. Ignoring the man sitting in the visitor's chair, he marched up to the Chief's desk and dropped the file, open to the pertinent page, in front of Oscar Henry.

"Yes, it's all right, Mrs. Marlin," Henry said into the phone, his deep voice gentle and soothing. He glared at Mitch. "I certainly cannot expect you to stop a runaway train. I will deal with it. You go on home and we'll talk about it in the morning."

Henry dropped the receiver on the cradle and held up a finger when Mitch started to speak. He gave the page a cursory scan and raised angry, deep-charcoal eyes to Mitch's face. "You remember Joe Islington, don't you, Mitchell?" Henry waited until the two men shook hands, then turned to Islington. "Will you excuse us a minute, Joe? I need to hand this young man his head."

Smiling, Islington nodded, stood and quietly left the room.

"Oscar," Mitch said, but Henry cut him off with a gesture as elegant and sophisticated as his attire. It was hard to believe he'd once been a defensive tackle for the NFL.

"What makes you think you can barge in here whenever you want, Lawson?" Only the raised pitch of Henry's normally soft, drawling voice attested to his anger. "I don't know how you did things in the Marshal Service, but here there are rules. And they apply to you, too. You need to calm down and follow protocol. Do you think Islington won't take the tale of your impertinence back to the White House? I have enough to deal with, without adding failure to control my employees into the mix."

Mitch, despite the urge to kowtow in the face of the Chief's disapproval, leaned on the desk and shoved the file closer to Henry. "It's one of mine, Oscar," he said, his voice filled with fury and pain. "From the Program. This shouldn't have happened. Go on, read it. And then tell me to calm down."

He paced while Henry, his thick, strong fingers turning pages in their methodical way, read through the file. At last he looked up at Mitch and nodded.

"This is disturbing, to say the least. How long has he been—"

"Fifteen years."

"And how long since you last—"

"Eleven years."

"You're sure it was—"

"Yes, I'm sure. And so are you. We both know who did this." Mitch ran his hand through his hair and growled. "He was well hidden. It shouldn't have happened!"

"These people have long memories," Henry reminded Mitch. "Nothing is ever forgotten, or forgiven. Have you any idea how he was found?"

"Not yet, but I will," Mitch growled, his eyes flashing. "That Webster is an idiot!"

"Cut the boy some slack. He was working without the insider information you have." Henry closed his eyes a moment, then nodded. "I'll assign Lacey and Parrett to the follow-up. They're two of my best."

"No!" Mitch whirled and leaned over the desk, suppressing a grimace as pain again flared in his leg. Startled, Henry raised his brows. "This is my case, Oscar. I'll do the follow-up. Give me two weeks and Dan Jeffers—"

"No. You are not a Marshal anymore. And you're not a field agent, Mitchell."

"I'm still better than those two put together, Oscar, and you know it. Just one week—"

"Absolutely not. You don't have status."

"This is my case, damn it!"

"Not anymore. Protocol states—"

"Fuck protocol!" Mitch spat.

"Mr. Lawson," Henry intoned, his hardened voice one of warning. He began to rise, his huge dark palms pressing on the desktop. Mitch held up his hands and struggled to contain his anger. He shook his head, stepped back to lean beside the window and crossed his arms. The Chief subsided to watch Mitch through narrowed eyes.

"I'm sorry, Oscar. That was out of line." Mitch looked up to see Henry incline his head, accepting the apology. "But damn it, this is personal. It's my case, has been from day one. *I* coached him, *I* made sure they placed him well, *I* promised he'd be safe. And now he's dead." The muscles in Mitch's jaw worked as he ground his teeth. "I *have* to do the follow-up, Oscar. I *need* to do it." Mitch glanced out the window, frowning, his voice pinched from more than just physical pain. "I have to know if it was me, if I screwed up again, if did something that let him be found, even after all this time."

Henry cleared his throat. "I very much doubt you did, Mitchell. You were too good at your job to make a mistake about something so important."

"Yeah, right," Mitch muttered, the muscles in his jaw working.

Henry waited a beat before continuing.

"It was probably one of a thousand things you had no hand in, or control over."

Mitch lifted one shoulder.

"Maybe. But I have to know. Do you understand, Oscar? I have to find out or it'll haunt me. Destroy me. And don't tell me I'll get a copy of the report. Lacey and Parrett could overlook a clue or misinterpret evidence. I'm the only one who can do this because I'm the only one who knows it all—both what's in the original file, and what isn't. Not even the other Marshals know it all."

Henry shook his head. Mitch gave him a grim smile, seeing the denial in the Chief's face. He straightened up, looked Oscar Henry in the eyes.

"The follow-up, Oscar. Please. Let me do it with official sanction."

"You'd do it without?" Henry sounded surprised.

"If you force me."

Mitch waited while Henry studied the determination he knew was etched in his eyes, his face, his whole body. After a long moment Henry sighed and nodded.

"I'll give you two days, Mitchell," he said. "That's all."

"I need more than two, Oscar."

"Really? Lacey and Parrett could do it in two, and you just told me that you're better than both of them put together. Is that not correct?"

Mitch heaved an irritated sigh and crossed his arms.

"You're enjoying this, aren't you?" he growled. Henry's lips twitched. "What about Dan Jeffers?"

"Only if it's absolutely necessary. He has his own work to do. And I want a full report on this from you at lunch on Thursday. One o'clock. Don't be late. We'll review your sorry excuse for a budget at that time, also. And Lawson," he added as Mitch turned away from the desk. Mitch paused but didn't turn around. "Don't ever back me into a corner again. You will find it most unpleasant when I come out fighting. And I will, you can bet on that. Once has always been my limit."

Mitch turned his head and nodded his understanding. Not until he'd crossed the room and his hand was on the doorknob did the Chief speak again.

"On your way out, wake Joe Islington and send him back in here, will you? The White House is waiting for my answer. And you owe Mrs. Marlin an apology for your rudeness—an abject one, asap. It would be prudent not to wait until morning. I think flowers would be a nice addition."

"Understood, Chief," Mitch said, smiling.

He'd lost the smile by the time he entered his office suite and dropped the file on Kelsey's desk.

"Jeffers?" he asked. "We've got work to do."

"Waiting in your office," she said, and blinked at him. "I see you got what you wanted."

"Yep. But I owe Mrs. Marlin some flowers. I hope there's a florist still open."

Kelsey grinned and shook her head. Picking up a pen, Mitch jotted notes on a piece of scratch paper from her desk and handed it to her.

"Pull those files before you leave, Kelsey. And order something in for Jeffers and me, it's going to be a long night. Make it Italian, lots of cheese. The hell with my arteries. And I'll need to talk to the idiot who wrote up that file, what's his name, Webster? I'd like to know who trained him, he's a poor excuse for a field agent. Then make a reservation on the first flight out tomorrow—no, tonight if possible—and get me full background on the local-yokel detective in charge of this case. Let's hope he's got more intelligence than our boy's shown. Call them both after you make the plane reservation and let them know when I'll get there." He took a deep breath and raked a hand through his hair. "Unless I'm very much mistaken, the sins of the past finally caught up with this one. And the payment sure wasn't pretty."

CHAPTER TWO

They barely spoke after the first awkward greeting, all the long way back from the Buffalo, New York, airport. Sabrina Compton kept her head lowered and her eyes closed, marking their progress by the late-October smells of the journey. Car exhaust and hot pavement near the airport. Suburban flowers and dried grass when they passed the golf club. Dusty brick, hot metal and restaurant fumes as the city closed tight around them. Her hands clenched tighter the closer they drew to their destination, until at last she could no longer feel the nails digging into her flesh. She was grateful that Anne Bradley, driving, respected her pain and kept silent, contenting herself with surreptitious glances at her passenger.

Sabrina, never very strong, looked fragile now, her skin pale and translucent, stretched tight over protruding bones. Sunken cheeks narrowed an oval face framed by a thick cloud of shining black curls. Her natural quiet shyness had pulled in upon itself. Sabrina appeared tiny, petite, in the seat next to Anne, much less than her five feet six inches. As though a strong gust could blow her away. As though a wrong word or sideways glance would shrivel her into nothing. Time, elongated by the unnatural stillness of Sabrina's body, stretched on until it seemed the journey would never end. But it did, all too soon for Sabrina. It felt like mere seconds to her before Anne pulled into her own driveway, which lay alongside the Compton's.

"Well, here we are," Anne murmured, shifting into park and twisting the key to silence the engine.

Sabrina took a deep breath, raised her head, and looked across to her house.

She couldn't believe it. The house, gleaming white with Williamsburg blue trim, stood with a proprietary, almost smug air on its raised lot, bursting with a sense of its own largesse. It looked exactly the same, as if nothing had happened, nothing had changed. She stared at the center entrance Colonial that had sheltered her for over six years, and tried to breathe past a throbbing suffocation. Multi-paned windows sparkled in the late afternoon sun. A deep gray Mansard roof cradled the structure like a comforting hand. Someone had cut the lawn—Anne's husband, Donald, Sabrina was sure—and trimmed and watered the geraniums that lined the front walk. That would have been Anne. The cheerful red flowers pulled her gaze to a matching front door, where the grapevine wreath she'd decorated with summer ribbons and wooden geese still hung, the trailing ribbon ends beckoning in the soft autumn breeze. *Come in*, they urged. *Come in, get warm, make yourself comfortable.* It was the last thing Sabrina wanted to do.

"Do you want me to go in with you, Sabrina?"

Sabrina blinked, startled by the sound of the words. She'd forgotten Anne was in the car. She looked at her companion, at the brown doe-eyes large with concern and the familiar wind-blown, salt-and-pepper hair, and tried to smile. Anne had been her next-door neighbor and occasional confidante for the last six years. It had been Anne, strong, capable, motherly Anne, who had gone where Sabrina couldn't, who two months ago had packed the suitcases that now lay in the back of the SUV. Sabrina took a deep breath, and shook her head.

"No. Thank you, Anne," she said, abandoning her attempt to smile. "It's all right. I'll be all right, really I will."

She opened the car door and got out, wondering who she was trying to convince, Anne or herself. Tears blurred her eyes and she bowed her head as she burrowed in the depths of her purse for her keys. Anne got out, opened the tailgate, and liberated the two suitcases.

"I'll carry these over for you," she offered, but Sabrina shook her head.

"No, please, Anne. They're not heavy. I'll take them. You've done so much for me already." Her voice shook only a little.

The two women stared at each other, reading in each other's eyes the words for which they could not find voice. Then Anne nodded and stepped back. Sabrina bent, picked up the suitcases. Her keys bit into the palm of her right hand. She winced a little at the pain, but did not shift her hold. The ache helped to steady her.

"Donald will want to talk to you, there are things you need to go over with him. Come for dinner tonight, at six. It's only chicken, nothing fancy. Please, Sabrina," Anne begged, and Sabrina knew the older woman had seen the refusal flooding her face. "You shouldn't be alone, not this first night. Please."

Sabrina held herself very still until the wave of dizziness passed.

"All right. At six," she managed to say, not meeting Anne's eyes.

She turned away and marched across the drive and the fresh-cut lawn that separated their homes. *You shouldn't be alone*, she thought, tears clogging her throat. *Do you hear that, Charlie? She's right, I shouldn't be alone. But I am. Aren't I, Charlie? Aren't I?*

She climbed the steps and set the bags down, her shaking fingers barely able to fit the key into the polished brass lock. A playful breeze danced with her shoulder length curls. It pulled glistening black strands across her face when she turned to look back at where Anne Bradley stood watching. Sabrina shivered and caught at the errant locks as she turned away from her friend's blurred figure. She knew that Anne would wait until she had entered and closed the door behind her, and the knowledge moved her hand to turn the key and crack open the door before her mind could absorb the meaning and deny permission for the movement. Then she took a deep breath, lifted the suitcases, and nudged the door wide with her knee.

It swung easily, silently, on well-oiled hinges, a welcoming arm flung wide in invitation. Just as it had opened that afternoon two months before. Only then she hadn't had suitcases in her hands, she'd had packages. Bags and boxes filled with surprises for Charlie's birthday, her cheeks blushed with excitement, not autumn's chill kiss. Excitement that had died an early death, giving way first to puzzlement, then pain and despair, and finally the empty hopelessness that was now her only, and constant, companion.

"No," Sabrina whispered, shaking her head, refusing entry to the memories. Her heart hammered as she stepped into the slate floored foyer and shoved the door shut with her foot. The thud echoed dully around her, warning of a place long empty. No one awaited her homecoming. She stood still a long moment then set down the suitcases. She dropped her keys and purse on the marble-topped wrought iron stand against the left-hand wall, her eyes avoiding the cracked mirror that hung above it.

Tea. She needed tea. It would calm her, bring a semblance of normality to the day. She moved down the hall to the kitchen, keeping her gaze straight ahead and away from the archways that led to the dining room on the left and the sunken living room on the right. Her feet paused at the stairway that led to the upper floor, her hand clutching the banister, her vision blinded by a past she loathed. She shook her head and moved on. She would have to go up there eventually, but not now. She couldn't face it now.

Fading daylight dimmed the usually cheerful kitchen. Sabrina's reluctant fingers pushed the light switch on the wall inside the doorway and she stood blinking in the sudden brightness, her body trembling, only her large, dark eyes moving as she looked around the blue and white room. The broken dishes were gone, utensils replaced in cupboards and drawers, the blood on the floor and tabletop washed away.

A sigh shuddered from deep within her as she pushed her hair away from her face and walked to the stove. She lifted the dented copper kettle and took it to the sink. She let the water run a few minutes, to clear the pipes of stagnation and rust, then filled the kettle and set it back on the stove, lighting the burner beneath it. She opened cupboards while the water heated, searching for tea bags and a cup.

Nothing seemed in the right place. Had she been gone so long that she couldn't remember where she kept things? Surely two months wasn't long enough for that. Or had it all simply been put back according to another's system of order? *Anne*, she thought, at last finding the tea bags in a lower cupboard, the metal canister bent and wobbly on the shelf. Only three cups remained, each chipped, one with a handle missing. Four saucers sat beside them in the half-filled cupboard. But it didn't matter now. There was only one to cook for, only herself who needed tea. Chips were all right, for her. Sabrina stared at the flawed china cup and let herself float into blankness, a technique she had perfected these last few months to keep from thinking. The whistle of the kettle recalled her to the kitchen.

She made the tea and carried the cup into the living room. She couldn't bear to stay in the kitchen, where she'd first seen the blood. She set the cup on the coffee table and looked around. This room had also been tidied. Broken knickknacks removed. Books replaced on shelves. The afghans she had knitted thrown over the wreckage of couch and chairs.

Tabletops and mantel were free of the dark powder that had peppered their surfaces when last she'd been in this room. Sabrina smiled sadly, and shook her head.

"Anne," she sighed. Here, and in the kitchen, and the rest of the house most likely. Cleaning the mess, tidying as best she could, knowing that coming home was trial enough, making things as normal as possible. Dear, sweet Anne. How would she have ever gotten through it all without Anne?

She wandered around the room, adjusting placement of the things that had survived. Her mother's silver candy dish she moved from the right to the left side of the television. The heavy crystal vase Charlie had given her for her birthday three years ago, chipped now on the rim, went from the end table beside the couch to the one between the chairs. The Victorian pottery candlesticks, their pieces fused back together with clear glue that had globed on the pebbled surface, she removed from the coffee table and put one on each end of the mantel. Anne had set the picture there, in the center of the mantel, the portrait they'd had taken on the cruise two summers ago, Charlie's arm warm around her, their faces turned to each other, love shining clear in their eyes. Sabrina touched it with tentative fingertips. The bent filigree frame wobbled, threatened to collapse. The glass was missing. Slow tears dripped down Sabrina's face.

"Oh, Charlie!" she whispered, her heart breaking.

What would she do without him? A whole lifetime of emptiness, devoid of her love, her anchor, her purpose for being. She blinked her eyes clear and gazed at the beloved face. Broad and ruddy-complexioned, it was bisected by a bumpy arching nose to each side of which sparkled greenish hazel eyes. Silver stranded the dark hair, mostly on the left side. Lips a trifle full, quick to smile, to laugh, to enjoy life. A strong body only three inches taller than hers, wide and solid, built for bear hugs and home cooking, long walks, swimming pools, velour shirts and bulky-knit sweaters. A man to have and to hold, forever. Except forever had ended two months ago. The day she went shopping.

Sabrina reached out and laid the photo face down on the mantel shelf. It still hurt too much even to look at his picture. She turned away to continue her circuit of the room and found herself in front of the bookshelves that lined the front wall, framing the windows. Padded seats invited beneath sparkling panes misted by lace curtains. Sabrina refused to allow herself to think. She let her hands dictate as they began to rearrange books which had been put back however they had come to hand. Charlie's texts and research volumes on economics belonged on the right, his classics, from translations of Plato's 'Republic' to Hemingway's 'Old Man and the Sea,' on the center shelf. The history and geography books he loved so well she placed back on the left, her own meager selection of biographies immediately below. There was so much here of Charlie, her intellectual university professor husband.

Shouting and laughter caught her ear. She paused in her work and knelt on the window seat, parted the curtain. A triangular-shaped park separated the two sides of Larchmont Avenue. Her house stood near the wide base of the triangle, the third house in from the cross street, Devereaux. Children often played in the park, their high spirits adding a spark of animation to Sabrina and Charlie's quiet life. She smiled now as she watched the lively game of touch football that had developed among the trees as homework had been wound up and freedom regained. A man, tall and solid, with sandy hair and windbreaker collar turned up against the chill, played with a tri-color beagle, tossing a stick along the base of the triangle for the dog to fetch. Sunlight slanted like a knife, piercing through the trees, sparking flames of color amid half-turned leaves. It picked out the children's wind-rosed cheeks and flashed off a ring the tall man wore.

For a moment, the world was normal. Life was as it should be. Innocence and trust had not yet died, crushed beneath cruelty and change. Sabrina watched the tall man throw the stick. The dog ambled after it, grasped it tight in its teeth, then abruptly collapsed on the ground and began chewing on it, ignoring the man who threw up his hands in comic despair. Sabrina laughed and turned to Charlie, the words dying on her lips as once again the empty room, her empty life, engulfed her. Charlie was not there, would never be there. Charlie was gone. She was alone.

She couldn't breathe. She dropped the three books she still held onto the window seat. The noise jump-started her lungs. She breathed in a ragged breath and walked to the couch. She could feel the wounds the afghan concealed when she sat, but the impression passed swiftly by, making no mark upon her mind. She stared at the cooling tea, letting the silence of the house cover her. It clung tight, muting the sounds of life and gaiety outside until they ceased to exist. The sun lowered, the light fading into indistinct murk, but

Sabrina did not move, did not light a lamp. She sat still and quiet, as empty inside as the house around her, her mind blank, her gaze unseeing on the tea, until at last the telephone rang, shattering the brittle silence.

CHAPTER THREE

Sabrina jumped as the shrill sound clawed at her. The darkness of the room confused her mind. It took a moment before she realized that it was the telephone, a moment longer before she could force her shaking hand to move. She reached for the lamp on the end table, sliding her hand up the smooth ceramic body to the switch, her questing fingers finding a jagged scar marring the once-sleek surface. Light sprang on at her touch and she stared at the ill-repaired break, the insistent bell ringing on beneath the hand that had dropped onto the telephone. Finally, Sabrina shut her eyes and lifted the receiver.

"Yes?" She sounded frightened, even to herself.

"Sabrina? I was getting worried, it took you so long to answer. Are you all right? You sound rather rocky."

"Yes, Anne. I'm all right." Perhaps if she said it often enough, it would turn out to be true.

"Donald's home, dinner's keeping warm and the bar's open, so come whenever you're ready. You can tell us all about California."

Sabrina could hear Anne's fierce determination to keep the conversation light, breezy, and she appreciated it though she couldn't summon enough energy to smile.

"About five minutes. I just want to be sure the house is locked up."

"I'll have the wine ready," Anne promised, and broke the connection.

Sabrina sat staring at the receiver in her lap, wondering who had had it fixed. She didn't remember calling the telephone company herself. Probably Anne or Donald, she decided. A recorded voice warned of a receiver off the hook, prompting her to hang up. She sat a moment, unable to move, her hand still on the receiver, panic thudding her heart in her chest. She licked her lips, looked at the over-turned picture on the mantel, then slowly stood, picked up the cup of cold tea and walked into the kitchen. She rinsed the cup, left it in the sink and checked the back door deadbolt and chain to satisfy herself that it was secure. She returned to the front hall for her purse and keys, stopping on the way to turn on the dining room lights.

This room, too, had been cleaned and dusted, though a half-empty china cabinet and shredded chair seats told their own tale. The chandelier, without its crystal globes, threw harsh light onto a once-glassy oval cherry table. Sabrina left the lights burning, crossing to the living room to add two more lamps to her attempt to banish shadows. She returned to the hall and ran a comb through her hair, her eyes barely registering her image in the mirror. She put her hand on the doorknob then looked back over her shoulder at the staircase, blue-gray carpeted steps disappearing up into the murk of night. *I'll go up after dinner, when I come home*, she promised herself, trying to still her racing heart, her trembling hands. *When I come home*. Then she grasped her keys tight, pulled the door shut behind her and ran across her front lawn and the two driveways to Anne and Donald Bradley's well-lighted brown house.

It was a good dinner, chicken fricassee, one of Anne's specialties, with old-fashioned homemade biscuits, peas, a cabbage salad and a Jell-O mold. Sabrina pushed her food around on her plate while Anne and Donald caught her up on the latest news of the neighborhood. The Walkers had moved, the new people would be coming in sometime in the next week, a mixed-racial couple with three children, very nice, Anne had met them two days ago when they had been painting in the house. Joe Masterson had finally gotten his promotion. They were in Hawaii, celebrating. The Devlins built an addition, a family room with an indoor hot tub. "Just imagine," Anne said. Claire Thomas' little girl had fallen out of a tree in the park and broken her arm, and their own daughter, Donna, was pregnant, due in six months, their first grandchild. Sabrina listened, smiled, nodded, but said very little, absorbing in silence the comforting warmth of her friends.

Anne, at fifty, was plump, energetic and barely five feet tall, though she filled whatever room she was in with her good cheer and practicality. Donald, fifty-two, was gray and spindly, his limbs long and loose as though he had never outgrown that gawky teenage stage all boys go through. He was mild mannered and soft-spoken, the most unlikely law professor Sabrina could imagine. But he was well-respected by his colleagues and worshipped by his students, despite— or perhaps because of—his tough, inflexible mode of teaching. And he was as staunch and loyal a friend as his wife.

"I don't want to put a damper on this lovely evening," he said now, seating Sabrina in a comfortable armchair in the living room. Anne passed around coffee, then quietly left. "But the sooner this is finalized, the better. There are some papers you have to sign. I'll explain them if you wish—"

"No." Sabrina shook her head. "There's no need, Donald. I'll do whatever you say I must."

She bent over the clipboard he gave her and signed her name on the lines he'd X'd, legal lines on legal papers that pigeonholed her tragedy into a neat legal niche. Donald Bradley kept silent until she had finished and handed back the clipboard.

"I went over everything very carefully, Sabrina. I'm sure it's all been pieced together properly. He named me executor in the will, you know, and—"

"Will?" Sabrina looked up, startled. "What will?"

"Charlie had me draw it up about four years ago."

"I didn't know, he never said anything to me." Sabrina shivered, despite the warmth of the room. "I never thought much about things like that."

"Many people don't, which can make situations like this very difficult." He smiled. "But not Charlie. He loved you very much, Sabrina. He wanted to be sure you would be well provided for. He bought mortgage insurance. The house is paid off, you needn't worry about having to sell it. And he had life insurance with a death benefit of five hundred thousand dollars. You're the sole beneficiary. With careful investing, it should last you quite some time."

I don't want money! Sabrina screamed silently, staring into the crackling fire. *I want Charlie!* Donald leaned forward, shuffled papers, then sat back on the couch with a document in hand.

"There were some stocks, a couple of CDs, and of course the checking and savings accounts—about sixty thousand dollars all together. He left it all to you, with three exceptions. A small bequest to the university's economics department, and two even smaller bequests to two women: Maria DiGesare and Carla Piccolo. I have no idea who they are. Do you?"

Sabrina sat stunned, the crackling fire over-warming the air as she stared at Donald Bradley, his words echoing in her head. She finally shook her head.

"No, I don't. I've never heard those names before."

"Could they be relatives of some kind?"

"I don't think so, Charlie said he was all alone. He never talked about any family. He said I was all the family he had." She began to shake. Pain seared her heart. Tears crowded into her throat. "All the family he ever wanted."

The pain defeated her. She bowed her head, her clasped hands pressed tight against her mouth. Tears darkened the skirt of her dress. Donald set the legal papers aside as she struggled for control. Then he drew a handkerchief from his pocket and offered it to Sabrina.

"Thank you," she whispered, blotting her eyes. "I'm sorry."

"Don't be silly. It's my fault, I should have waited a few days, not rushed at you like this the day you got back. I guess curiosity got the better of my good judgment." He patted her arm. "You need to rest. We can finish this later in the week. Come on, I'll walk you home."

Sabrina nodded and rose. She thanked Anne for the dinner and the older woman held her tight a moment before draping a sweater over her shoulders against the night dampness. Donald walked close by her side across the two driveways and her front lawn. Sabrina hunched her shoulders as she walked. The feeling was back, the one she'd felt most of the time she was away, the sensation of eyes staring at her, boring into her back, watching every move she made. She shivered, cold despite the wool sweater. She asked Donald to unlock the door for her, knowing her shaking hands could never manage it themselves, and turned her back to her lighted windows, letting her gaze search around the darkened park, empty now of laughing children though the tall man still lingered among the trees. She couldn't see the dog. Or anyone standing watching her. Then her door swung wide and Donald escorted her in, away from the night, the park, and the sandy-haired man.

"Are you sure you don't want Anne or me to stay with you tonight?" Donald's earnest eyes stared into her wet face. Sabrina glanced at the shadowy staircase, and sighed.

"Of course I do," she admitted. "I'm terrified of being here alone. But I am alone, and I have to face it.

The longer I put it off, the harder it will be. It's been too long already." She removed the sweater from her shoulders and held it out to Donald, certain her sad smile left her eyes untouched. "Thank Anne for the use of the sweater. I forgot it would be so cold at night now."

"Bravery is one thing, Sabrina. Foolishness is something else." Donald took the sweater, draped it over his arm. "Don't push yourself too fast. We're only a phone call away, you know."

Sabrina nodded, unable to speak past the lump in her throat. Donald kissed her cheek, squeezed her hand for reassurance, then let himself out into the damp darkness, cautioning Sabrina to lock the door behind him. She twisted the deadbolt knob and slid the thick chain into its slot, the cold of the wood radiating into her palms. Empty silence folded down around her. Her heart began a slow, thudding tattoo in her chest. She turned, looked at the suitcases, then lifted her gaze to the stairs, up to the dark into which they disappeared. She had to go up there and she had to do it now. She would never find the courage if she waited until morning.

She moved slowly, as if in a dream, walked to the bottom of the stairs, pushed the light switch up. The ceiling fixture in the upper hall sprang on, throwing soft light down the steps. Her left hand clutched the banister as, step by step, Sabrina pulled herself up, her head bent, her eyes tracing the path her feet trod. The stains were still there, though faint. Permanent discolorations in the carpet fibers. She reached down, touched one with trembling fingers. They came away clean, dry. She stared at them a moment, then drew in a deep breath and continued on, up the final few steps and into the hall where she paused, fighting the urge to turn and run.

Straight ahead the bathroom door gaped open. Light from the hall gleamed on the bath's mosaic floor tile. To her left stood their bedroom door, closed, and to the right the two spare rooms they had fixed up as a sitting room for her and an office for Charlie. Those doors were also closed. Sheets and towels no longer littered the hall. The linen closet drawers and doors were shut tight. Sabrina looked at the two doors on her right, shook her head, and moved to the bedroom she had shared with her husband for six wonderful years.

She'd been right, Anne had cleaned up here, too, scattered clothing put away, drawers returned to dresser and chest, bed remade with fresh sheets and blankets. She had never slept in that bed alone. It looked immense to her now, endless, cold and barren. Her hands clenched into tight fists that dug her nails into her palms, and she backed away, gasping for breath. She turned to her sitting room and threw open the door, praying that it was just a dream, that Charlie would be there in her rocker, waiting, as he often did when she went out, for her to come home to him, to the safety of his arms.

The room was empty. Neat, dust-free and sterile. Not a trace of life. Not a trace of Charlie. A cry of despair echoed the tears that slipped down her cheeks as Sabrina edged along the hallway wall to the office door. Her trembling hands inched toward the knob.

"No!" she whispered, her shaking voice flattened in the vacuum of the hall. "No, don't."

But her hands did not obey. They grasped the knob, pushed open the door, fumbled for the light switch. Sabrina stood in the doorway, staring at the room, the floor, the great blotches on the rug where Charlie had lain.

"Oh, Charlie," she moaned. "Why, Charlie? Why?"

Her legs collapsed. She slid down the doorframe and curled onto the rug, her fingers reaching for the rusty-red stains beside the desk. The present faded. The past two months vanished like smoke in a high wind. Sabrina again relived the warm, brilliant summer day when her perfect life had come to an abrupt and horrifying end.

CHAPTER FOUR
Three Months Earlier

 Sabrina smiled with pleasure as she turned the corner and caught sight of the house. Seven years three months married, and still just the thought of Charlie sent her heart racing. And she'd only been gone three—she glanced at her watch —no, four hours. Thinking of him the entire time, as usual. She had to laugh at herself. She felt and acted just like a teenage newlywed.

Oh, but Charlie was so special. She sighed, pulling his prized vintage Nash Rambler into the drive. He had rescued her from obscurity, from the aching loneliness that had held her enthralled, and set her on a pedestal so high that nothing and no one else was visible to her. Except for Charlie, who she had placed on a pedestal even higher than her own. And there they dwelled, filling the rarefied air with their all-consuming love.

"Oh, brother!" she muttered, rolling her eyes at the sophomoric sentimentality of her thoughts. But it really was true. Charlie had worked a miracle in her life.

Sabrina Steves, an only child and an old maid at twenty-seven, had been almost paralyzed by fear—fear of being alone and abandoned, a fear that had been realized with her mother's death two years earlier. She was shy and insecure, tortured by recurring dreams of isolation and rejection, with no family, few friends, and not even a full-time job. She added occasionally to her more-than-adequate inheritance by substitute teaching in local private high schools. At last, after suffocating beneath a pall of loneliness for too long, she decided to sign up for evening adult education classes at the University. But as usual her fears kept her hesitating until the last minute, and the course she wanted had been filled. Sheer desperation forced her to accept the only class still open: economics, about which she knew nothing, and in which she had little interest.

It was taught by Charles Philip Compton, assistant dean of the University's economics department. He was fourteen years her senior and reminded Sabrina of her father, who had died when she was nine. Like Edward Steves, Professor Compton was a big man. Not tall, but broad and solid, a sturdy rock to which to cling. Sabrina sat in front of him for two hours, two nights a week, absorbing the sound and feel of his rich full voice, mesmerized by his precise movements and the immediacy of his presence, without once comprehending what he spoke about. Though she did try to understand. The subject was simply too foreign to her nature for her to grasp. She got a 36 on the midterm she'd spent hours studying for.

She stared at the paper, humiliated, barely hearing the professor wish everyone a happy Thanksgiving. The others around her gathered up books and coats, laughing about the foibles and idiosyncrasies of their families. Sabrina kept her eyes lowered as she folded the test paper away, wishing she had a family to complain about. She hated holidays. They only increased her sense of loneliness and isolation. She sighed out her unhappiness, wondering what the professor thought of her now. Knowing she would not—could not—return the next week, could not bear to repeat the humiliation, she rose to follow the rest from the room.

"Miss Steves, may I speak with you a moment?"

Sabrina froze, turned fearful eyes to Professor Compton. He walked around to the front of his desk and perched on the edge, folded his arms on his chest. His eyes crinkled up and almost disappeared when he smiled.

"You didn't do so well on the test, did you?" he asked gently. Sabrina shook her head. "Did you study?"

She nodded.

"I-I guess I don't really understand this stuff," she said.

"Why?" He frowned with genuine looking concern. "Is it something I'm doing, the way I'm teaching?"

"Oh, no." Sabrina shook her head. "No, it's me. Economics just isn't very... interesting. To me." That sounded like an insult. Sabrina felt her face flush, then she bit her lip and looked down at the books she held.

"Really?" Compton said. "Then why did you take this class?"

Sabrina shut her eyes. What could she say? She could never tell him the truth. She glanced at the door, but she was too frightened to simply bolt out without answering. She wanted to cry, but bursting into tears would be even more humiliating than the 36 on the test. Tension mounted. He was waiting for an answer. She never knew just where she got the courage. Perhaps it was the knowledge that she would not be coming back that prompted her to take a deep breath, lift her head and look directly into his beautiful hazel eyes.

"I waited until the last minute to sign up and this was the only class still open."

"Really?" He blinked, obviously startled by her answer. "What did you want to take?"

"Early American Poetry."

He laughed until tears leaked from his eyes.

"Oh, you poor thing. You must be bored to death. Poetry and economics are poles apart, aren't they? Well, I do thank you for your honesty. It's refreshingly creative." He picked up his books. "Come on, I'll walk you out."

Sabrina smiled and hunched her shoulders, waiting in the hall while he turned out the lights and locked the door. They walked a few moments in silence. Professor Compton held the outer doors for her.

"I'm curious," he said as they walked quickly through the cold night to the parking lot. "Why did you bother taking this class? Why not just wait until next semester and get the class you wanted?"

"I-I wanted something to do," she replied.

He glanced at her, Sabrina acutely aware that he knew 'wanted' meant 'needed.' What she didn't know then was that a tiny pain flared in his heart, memories of loneliness, isolation and unmet needs. She stopped beside a rusty blue station wagon.

"This is mine. Thanks. Have a nice Thanksgiving."

"Yes. You, too." He hesitated, seemed loath to let her go. "Have you got your turkey all ready for tomorrow?"

"No." A tiny smile, a tinier shrug. "I don't bother, not just for me. It seems pointless." She couldn't pull her eyes away from his.

"You're all alone?"

His eyes consumed her, darker than the night surrounding them. Sabrina nodded, swallowing hard. The softness of his voice pricked tears behind her eyes.

"So am I," he said. "I hate being alone, don't you?"

Again, she nodded. His eyes pierced through her, stopped her breathing. She offered him her whole life on the dark platter of her silent eyes.

"Would you have Thanksgiving dinner with me?" he asked, his rumbling voice soft, tentative. "I'd like that, very much. Please."

Sabrina, terrified, agreed. She gave him her address. He took her to a restaurant, and from the very beginning only the two of them existed. They had very little in common. A penchant for French pastries and fine wines. A love of Colonial architecture and furnishings. A deep enjoyment of classical music and an orphan status in a family-oriented society, though Sabrina did have one distant cousin in California to whom she wrote occasionally. Nothing else. Charlie probed the depths of the nation's economy in his classes each day, at night reading philosophy and history for enjoyment and the classics for edification. He rarely watched television or went to movies. He loved chess, backgammon and crossword puzzles. Weekends were devoted to research for treatises and papers. Sabrina read little, preferring short stories and poetry, and biographies of famous women. She did not play, or even understand, chess or backgammon, and had little patience with puzzles. She enjoyed knitting, and cooking unique new dishes though she rarely bothered for only herself, and spent happy hours before the television watching light adventure shows and classic western movies. She dreamed about traveling, about walking foreign cities and wind-swept beaches. Charlie shuddered at the thought of leaving his familiar, comfortable office chair.

Yet their love grew, reveling in the commonalities and feasting on the differences, slowly blossoming like a rare flower that glows with color and fills the air with sweet perfume. Charlie worshipped Sabrina, laid his heart at her feet, and in doing so brought the world alive for her, placed warmth in her shy dark eyes and animation in her timorous heart. He became her rock, her lifeboat, her hostage to loneliness, her security against fear. He made her life worth living. As did Sabrina for Charlie. She completed him, imparted joy and peace and contentment to his quiet, ordinary, myopic world. She gave herself to him totally, immersing her being into his until their two spirits, indeed, became as one.

Day by day their love and devotion grew and deepened. At the last, neither knew where the one ended and the other began. They married in May, and bought a house the next year, close to the University and beside that of a colleague of Charlie's from the law department. The warm, inviting center entrance Colonial became a fortress, a world apart from which they set out to explore the magic of life each day, and to which they returned for safety every night. It cradled and nurtured their love, standing as an oasis of solace for them when sorrow laid its pall across their shoulders. It was a symbol of their love, that house, but in the end it betrayed them brutally. On a fine, carefree, mid-July day, a week before Charlie's forty-ninth birthday, it betrayed them.

Sabrina gathered up the bags and boxes filled with things she'd bought for Charlie, and skipped up the front walk. She couldn't wait to see him, to feel his arms strong around her, his lips firm against hers, and smell the special fragrance that was Charlie alone. Spicy aftershave and mellow pipe tobacco, mixed with the rumpled, professorial aroma of books. She would tease him with the bags. He loved surprises, and she knew the sight of her full arms would improve his mood. He had grumped and grumbled around all morning, unhappy with a piece of research for the paper he was writing. She always laughed at him when he acted that way. He grumped, she laughed, he kissed her and she kissed him back. And his work was always excellent and well-received. But he wouldn't be working, now. It was almost five. He would probably be in the kitchen, watching the clock, waiting for the wine to chill and worrying about his bank balance. Or waiting for her in her sitting room, enveloped in misty pipe smoke and rocking slowly in her grandmother's chair.

She had reached the steps and juggled the bags around to get at her keys before she noticed that the front door was ajar.

"Oh, Charlie!" she said, laughing. It was the third time this month her absent-minded professor husband had left the door open. Good gracious, how she loved him. She pushed the door wide and stepped into the foyer.

"Hi, Charlie, I'm home!" she called, dropping her purse and keys on the marble stand. "And I didn't spend all your money, only most of it!"

Before shutting the door she glanced in the mirror, giving herself a conspiratorial grin, listening for Charlie's bellowed reply. Dead silence met her ears. The glass of the mirror was cracked, the wound spiderwebbing out from the lower left corner. How had that happened? Her smile faded into puzzlement. She forgot about shutting the door. She turned and stepped toward the kitchen.

"Charlie? Where are you?"

No answer. Could he have fallen asleep? Sabrina didn't think so, he rarely took naps, not even after doing yard work or after a rare, sleepless night. She walked by the dining room archway. A glitter caught her eye. She turned and froze in shock.

The room was a shambles. The hutch drawers had been pulled out and emptied onto the floor. The china cabinet doors gaped, the contents smashed and scattered across the rug. The upholstered chair seats had been slashed to shreds, the tabletop gouged, the crystal globes from the chandelier shattered across the once-pristine surface. Glass shards glittered like tear drops in the afternoon sun.

Sabrina blinked, wondering if this was a dream. Her mind refused to acknowledge what her eyes saw, refused to wrap around the reality spread out before her. She shook her head and backed away, unable to breathe, clutching tight to the bags she held. Slowly, fearfully, she turned to the living room and gasped aloud.

Couch and chairs had been sliced to ribbons. Stuffing spilled out in untidy eruptions. Shelves were bare, books scattered onto the floor, pages torn and bindings broken. Drawers had been pulled open and emptied, lamps overturned, figurines and vases smashed, flowers shredded across the rug. Abruptly, her mind cleared. Reality hit her like a fist. Sabrina began to tremble. Her heart pounded.

"Oh, my God!" she choked. "Charlie?" Where was he, oh, God, why didn't he answer? "Charlie!"

Her legs felt stiff and uncooperative as Sabrina edged down the hall to the kitchen. She stopped in the doorway. Again she saw wanton destruction; cupboards and drawers agape, dishes, utensils, pots and pans, food from the pantry, the refrigerator, smashed and scattered on counters and floor. And something more, there on the table, and on the pale blue tile below.

Slowly, dazed, Sabrina walked over to the table, her stare locked on the knife that lay in its center, on the red stains that surrounded the blade. Glass crunched beneath her feet. She reached out a trembling hand, touched the jellied blotches. Her fingers dragged a deep red streak across the white porcelain surface.

"No," she moaned, staring at the blood on her hand. "Oh, no!"

She backed away. The packages fell from her suddenly nerveless arms. Her mind froze in horror and she stared uncomprehendingly at the wreckage around her. This wasn't her house, it couldn't be. Then her gaze snagged again on the bloody knife and her bloodstained hand. A gasp. A whisper.

"Charlie!"

Then a scream.

"Charlie!"

She whirled and ran for the stairs, shock blurring her vision, numbing her body. Her feet grew awkward. She tripped halfway up the flight, cracking her head on the banister and her ribs on the hard stair edge. She lay a moment, dizzy and panting, then forced herself up, crawling on her hands and knees. Dark spots spattered the steps, spots that stained her hands red when she touched them. She pulled herself to her feet at the top and stood panting, unable to move, terrified to look further. The open bathroom door beckoned. She stumbled closer, over sheets and towels dumped from gaping linen closet drawers and shelves, to find the medicine and sink cabinets emptied, pills and glass littering the tile floor. There was blood here, too. But no Charlie.

Sabrina shuddered and pushed open their bedroom door to find more carnage. Both dresser and armoire had been emptied, clothes flung out of the closets. Bedding lay shredded amidst the ruin of mattress and springs. And blood. Blood on clothes, bedding and jewelry. And still no sign of Charlie. Oh, God, where was he? She called his name in a voice choked with panic as she turned and lurched across the hall.

Her sitting room, too, had been ransacked, the remains of her knitting project tangled in a heap on the floor, furniture slashed, closets emptied, her library books shredded. A wave of cold despair washed over her as she looked at Charlie's office door. She knew what she would find, what she would see, when she opened that door, and for an endless moment denied reality by refusing to move. Then she reached out and slowly pushed the door wide. Her fingertips left dark red blotches on the white paint.

The desk had been looted, the files shredded, books and papers torn apart. But Sabrina did not see the room, she saw only Charlie. She stared, frozen, at her husband, her beloved husband, who lay face down on the floor in a pool of blood, hands bound tight behind his back, ankles roped together. Blood oozed from slashes all over his body. A bloody gag was still wrapped across his mouth. His eyes were open, but he was very dead. The back of his head had been blown away.

Sabrina couldn't breathe. A buzzing grew in her ears, and the edges of her vision turned white. She shook her head. It wasn't Charlie, it couldn't be, it had to be someone else. No one would do that to Charlie, not her Charlie. But it looked like Charlie, she could see silver streaking the blood-matted hair. She recognized the shirt, she had given it to Charlie for his birthday last year, and those were his sandals, the ones he'd bought in Mexico City.

"Charlie?" Her whisper wavered unsteadily. She took a few wooden steps closer.

He didn't answer. He lay still and silent in his blanket of blood.

"Charlie?" Louder, her voice trembling, horror rising to choke her.

Charlie lay on, unheeding. Sabrina knelt down, reached out to him, touched his face, his back, his hands with her hands, her stained fingers, a comforting touch to take away the hurt, put back the lost life, heal the body so brutally torn apart.

It didn't work. Charlie was gone, and not even her fathomless love could bring him back. Her hands lifted, red hands dripping with still warm blood.

She screamed.

Screamed over and over until the horror consumed her, crushed her, twisted her, gave her life that was no life in a world that did not exist. Donald Bradley found her there an hour later, when he came home from work to find her front door gaping wide and receive no answer to his worried call. She sat on the floor of the upstairs office, Charlie's shattered head cradled in her lap, her bloodied hands stroking his cheek while she murmured to him of the things they would do when he woke up. She had no awareness of Donald's presence, or of Anne's. She did not hear or see the police arrive, or the doctor that Anne summoned. She sat cradling her dead husband and talking to him, her eyes as blank and glassy as his, until the coroner's ambulance came to take Charlie away.

She fought them then, screaming like a mad woman, clawing like an animal until at last the doctor sedated her and took her to the hospital. Two days later she sat wrapped in numbed unreality, answering the homicide detective's questions with a dreamy air, her voice and movements filtered through strong tranquilizers. She heard the words she spoke and wondered who said them. She heard the sounds she made, and wondered what they meant. She watched incuriously as they rolled her fingers in sticky black ink, took her fingerprints for comparison. The unreality, aided by the drugs, persisted through the wake and the funeral. At the graveside she turned to Anne and asked her why Charlie was not there with her.

The protective numbness did not wear off until the police took her back to the house, walked her through destroyed rooms patinaed now with fingerprint powder and asked her to reveal what was missing, what had been stolen that had been searched for so thoroughly. She could find nothing. Everything was still there, though smashed and scattered, even her jewelry. Sabrina clasped tight to the antique locket she wore, the one that had belonged to Charlie's grandmother, the locket she'd worn the day she'd gone shopping and hadn't taken off since. Her protection shredded away as she followed the detectives through the house. She broke when they reached the office and sobbed bitter tears of despair as she stared at the outline of Charlie's body still visible in blood on the rug. She couldn't stop shuddering as she forced herself to inspect the room.

"I don't think anything's gone, unless it's something that Charlie wrote, his notes, something like that. I wouldn't know how much of that he had here."

She turned away and walked to the door, pausing to look back from the hall. A memory quivered and she frowned, her eyes again searching through the mess.

"I don't see the picture." She looked up at the detective. "Charlie had a picture of me on his desk, in a brass frame. It should be here, somewhere."

Charlie had a picture. The past tense stabbed at her, destroyed her control. Her body tremored. She looked back at where Charlie had died and fainted into the detective's arms. She left for California three days later.

Once the crime scene had been released, Anne and Donald Bradley slowly set Sabrina's house back into order, cleaning up the broken glass and hiring a crime scene cleaning service to scrub fiercely at the thick reddish stains on the rugs. Donald collected and patched together Charlie's personal and financial papers. They did not find the picture with the brass frame.

CHAPTER FIVE
Present Day

 Sabrina woke with lights blazing above her. Darkness at the windows. Her eyes burned and her head throbbed. Her throat felt swollen. Her hair stuck to her face when she sat up, fine black threads spiderwebbing her anguish into a visible pattern of despair.

She looked at her wrist. The hands on her watch stood at two thirty-three. Sabrina shuddered, wiped shaking fingers over her stiff, tear-stained face and pushed herself to her feet, an old and defeated spirit encased in thirty-five-year-old flesh. Another night barely half-gone, endless empty hours to be gotten through somehow. Wrapping her arms around her body, she stared down at the obscene stain on the rug until at last the picture of Charlie's broken body faded from her mind. Exorcism, of a morbid sort. She turned away and left the room, automatically darkening it behind her. Light spilling out from the bedroom across the hall drew her and she walked over to lean on the doorpost and contemplate the space that embodied the silent vacuum of her life. Slowly, her eyes closed. She shook her head. She could not imagine walking into that room, her former oasis of safety and love. She could not fathom pulling back the covers and sliding into the empty wasteland of her once-conjugal bed. Its vastness terrified her. She knew her battered spirit was no match for the ugly void leering at her. She would dissolve completely, become as nonexistent as the love they had shared.

She kept her movements deliberate and calm, refused entry to the thoughts that lurked at the edges of her mind as she turned off the overhead light and shut the door, wondering if she would ever be able to face that room alone at night. She went into the bathroom and splashed water on her face, not noticing the stains her makeup made on the pale yellow towels. She pulled a sheet and blanket from the linen closet and, with a desolate sigh, went down the shadowy staircase into the echoing silence of the living room.

Sleep evaded her, as she'd known it would. The emptiness here, in this house where love had blossomed and had so brutally ended, felt entirely different from the emptiness she'd endured in her cousin's home, and in the lonely string of motel rooms in which she'd tried to hide from her memories. That emptiness had merely been empty, a vast, echoing darkness of absence and loss. This emptiness, however, was full to overflowing, crammed with the very essence of blank, unfeeling despair, leaving hardly any room at all for her. Sabrina felt she might drown in the overwhelming reaches of darkness before dawn once again emptied the light of a now-meaningless life back into her existence. Would Charlie be waiting, his arms and lips warm with welcome, if she did drown in the dark?

She lay staring at the unfamiliar shadow patterns spread on the ceiling, and felt time slow to a crawl. The emptiness was too full, and too cold, for her to even glimpse Charlie. There was no warmth here anymore, not for her, despite the abundance of heat radiating from the furnace. The chill numbness that filled her soul was impenetrable and everlasting. She felt as dead as Charlie, for all that her body still dwelled above ground. Dead, and lost to him forever.

She lay still for what seemed an eon, then turned her head and looked at the suitcase gaping open on the chair near the black maw of the fireplace, her clothing neatly draped on the chair's high, wounded back. *Maybe I should unpack*, she thought. But that meant mounting those steps again, recreating movements that so tortured her memories. It meant opening the bedroom door, stepping into the room's desolate embrace, treading the bitter arctic tundra at the core of her being. She couldn't do that, not at night with dark emptiness imprisoning her from within. The lights in the ceiling were no help. She barely saw them. She needed the cold warmth of daylight for a protective shield. She would have to stay where she was.

Again she sighed, rubbing at burning eyes with weak, sleep-starved fingers. She counted backward from ninety-nine, reviewed her repertoire of knitting stitches, tried to remember the order of the articles she'd read in a magazine on the plane. But sleep still eluded her desperate, groping efforts. Finally she rose, took a small bottle from her purse, and went into the half-bath tucked beneath the stairs opposite the dark, whisper-filled kitchen.

The hands on her watch now stood at three-thirty and Sabrina slumped with discouragement. She'd hoped it was later, prayed that dawn was near. It certainly felt as though hours, if not days, had passed since she first lay down on the couch. She turned on the water with a weary twist of her wrist, then opened the small bottle and spilled out a mass of blue-green capsules into the palm of her left hand. She stared at the doctor-prescribed sleep inducement, miniature in size and very mild. She had fought taking them at first, fearing the nightmare-riddled world of dreams until she discovered the drug somehow kept the horrors at bay. Just one of the tiny capsules ensured six to eight hours of oblivion.

How many would grant me permanent relief?

It tickled into her mind, that unspeakable thought, its sinuous fingers of darkness rich with deceptive, luring promise. A vision of Charlie waiting, smiling, arms spread, love ready, flashed into her mind's eye. Sabrina lifted her head and stared at her reflection in the oak-framed mirror above the rose marble pedestal vanity. A face drawn and haggard stared back, eyes blurred with despair, cheeks sunken, skin sallow. Pain and sorrow had aged her prematurely. She looked years older than thirty-five. She gazed long into her dark mirror-eyes, looking beneath the glassy overlay of blank despair to the fear and longing deep within her soul. Her heart lurched. If she emptied the bottle, swallowed the twelve or so pills that lay in her hand, she could be with Charlie forever.

Shock flooded her, a cold, icy wave that poured over her head and shoulders, penetrating the marrow of her bones. Sabrina gasped, blinking. She looked down at the small capsules in her now-shaking hand and couldn't breathe, had no awareness of any reality other than those enticing, ocean-hued capsules.

"No," she whispered, an echoing plea in the darkness for she knew not what. Her head jerked back and forth in negation of the terrible longing that turned her inside out. "Oh, no. No."

She tipped the sleeping pills back into the narrow amber bottle, all but one which she swallowed quickly, and cupped her hands beneath the flow of icy water. The glass that had once stood in the tiny white ceramic alcove in the wall, shattered in the rampage that had destroyed her life, had not yet been replaced. Sabrina dried her hands on an embroidered hand towel, set the bottle of pills carefully on the scalloped edge of the sink and left the half-bath without a backward glance. She returned to the living room and straightened her makeshift covers, willing herself not to think. Then she smoothed down the silken floor-length nightgown she wore. Emerald green, Charlie's favorite color on her. He'd bought it for her for Christmas, ten endless months ago. Tears sparkled in Sabrina's hopeless eyes as she climbed onto the lumpy, uncomfortable couch and lay motionless in the darkness, staring at the unfamiliar ceiling with burning eyes, waiting for the drug to whirl her away from reality. It didn't take long. In fifteen minutes she was fast asleep, oblivious to the strange, ominous movements of a shadow that eddied and swirled from window to window, a lurking darkness startlingly human in shape.

She woke at ten-fifteen the next morning, still groggy from the sedative, to a beautiful late-October day brilliant with sun. Russet and orange leaves left their perches to play tag with the crisp fall breeze, applauded by still-green spectators that clung tenaciously to swaying branches. White puffed-cotton clouds high above spied jealously on the multi-colored earth below. It was what Sabrina had come to think of as a Charlie-day, the kind that lured him irresistibly out of his den into the life-renewing vitality of nature, even if it was only an impromptu city picnic with his wife in the pseudo-park across the street. He had often declared that fall was God's favorite season. "After all," Charlie had often declared, "He had lavished all His considerable artistic talents on it, hadn't He?"

Sabrina, wrapped in a deep sea-green terry cloth robe, sat a while on the front window-seat watching echoes of her former life through the misty lace curtains before rising and wearily making her way into the kitchen. She put the kettle on to boil then opened the refrigerator, though she knew that nothing resembling breakfast remained within, not after two months. It was mere habit, a reflex action that moved her unconsciously into a routine long-familiar. To her surprise, milk, butter, bacon and eggs lay within on the glass shelves.

Bless you, Anne, she thought with a small, grateful smile accompanied by a sigh. She'd lived too long already on coffee, sedatives and nerves. A decent meal was the best medicine for her at this moment. She soon had bacon and eggs crackling in the pan, their comforting aroma wafting gently around her. Sabrina finally began to let go, to relax. The torturous tension of her homecoming dissipated into the golden brightness of the new day. Warm sunshine streamed through the windows, puddling around the oak-inlaid white lacquer table, spotlighting the snowy Formica counters. The only jarring note was the absence of Sabrina's glass canisters which once held flour, sugar, pasta and spices, and the coffee maker that had perched in the corner. She sat at the square table facing the hall, the back door behind her and the sun on her left, her chipped plate and handleless tea cup centered on a blue flowered placemat. She ate slowly, willing herself not to think, not to acknowledge what—who—was missing. She did not want to add to the ponderous weight of yet another lonely meal, a meal that itself added to the three-hundred-some already past. How many thousands more to come?

She sighed and forced down the last of the eggs, finished her tea and set the dirty dishes in the sink, deciding to wash them later, after she'd showered and dressed. She took the suitcases one-by-one up the stairs, but could not bring herself to open the bedroom door. She brought them, instead, into her ravaged sitting room, laying them open on the floor, extricating the personal items she would need. The clothing didn't matter. The summer apparel she'd fled to southern California with was of little use for late autumn in the East. She might as well just leave it packed, and dig her cool weather clothes out of the sitting room's closet and chest where she kept them stored.

Wondering what had survived the murderer's insane rampage, Sabrina moved to the twin closets that flanked the room's rear window and turned to the door on the right. Hers. Charlie used the left-hand one to store his off-season suits, slacks and shirts. She wouldn't open that door yet. Not for a long while. She gritted her teeth, stretched out her hand and pulled open her closet door.

A shocked gasp escaped her lips, rang in the silence. A red mist swam up to obscure her vision. Charlie's clothes hung amid hers, a legacy of Anne's sympathetic helpfulness, dark tweed and brown serge sandwiched in between feminine cashmere and delicate silk. An almost visible aura of staunch maleness radiated out to engulf her, smelling of vain promises of a lifetime that had lasted only seven years.

Sabrina began to tremble. Anger rose to mask the unbearable pain. She could hardly breathe. Fury froze her lungs. Wasn't it enough that whoever had done this had taken Charlie from her, destroyed her life, denied her a future? Did every tiny piece of her existence have to be invaded, too? Was she to be allowed nothing, no insignificant enclave left whole in which to hide? She wouldn't allow it! How dare he? What right had he? It was her life, not his. *Hers*. And Charlie's. She'd show him, that bastard. She'd destroy him the way he had destroyed her.

Sabrina marched out of the sitting room and down the stairs to the living room telephone, rage crackling around her like static electricity. She snatched up the receiver. One trembling, wood-stiff finger jabbed at the buttons. She didn't have to look up the number, it was burned indelibly into her brain, despite the fact that she'd used it only twice before leaving for California. It was answered on the fourth ring.

"Buffalo Police Department, Homicide Division. Ser—"

"I want to speak to Detective Raymond Burke," Sabrina's steel-hard voice cut in, words enunciated with clipped precision. "Now. About my husband's murder. This is Sabrina Compton."

"Yes, ma'am. Just one moment."

Sabrina shut her eyes as the desk sergeant plunged her into a blank silent void of waiting. She counted, slowly, her clenched hands aching with strain, the numbers mounting to twenty-seven before the compact, red-haired detective's gravelly voice vibrated through the line. She could hear papers shuffling in the background.

"Burke here, Mrs. Compton. I'm glad you're finally back, I—"

"I want to see him," Sabrina snapped. A moment of silence met her demand.

"Him? Who, Mrs. Compton?"

"The man who killed Charlie. I want to see him."
I want to touch him, I want to hurt him, I want to kill him!

"Mrs. Compton—"

"You have no right to keep me from him, not after what he did," she argued against his tight condescending tone. "I want to see him. Now. Today."

"Mrs. Compton," Burke said with a weary sigh, "we don't have the man who killed your husband. We have not made an arrest in this case, not yet."

"What? How can you just let that man walk around free? What kind of police are you?" Sabrina felt like she was suffocating, smothered beneath incompetence and indifference.

"Please, Mrs. Compton, calm down. There's no need to get so upset—"

"No need?" Sabrina cried, her voice rising to a shout. "What do you mean, no need? There's more than enough need. My husband was murdered over two months ago, detective. Three months! Do you expect me to be *pleased* that you haven't caught the killer yet? Am I supposed to laugh and smile, pretend this is just a social call?"

"Of course not, Mrs. Compton. I just—"

"You just what? Don't care? Can't be bothered? Are too lazy? What the hell's the matter with you? Why are you sitting at a desk? Why aren't you out there doing something? Or wasn't Charlie rich enough? Is that it? He wasn't important enough to rate some *real* police work?"

"Now listen, Mrs. Compton, there's more to this than you're aware of." Burke's exasperation and anger rang clear beneath his forced calm, but Sabrina didn't hear it. "If you would just shut up and let me explain —"

"Explain?" Sabrina's voice grew even louder as she spoke. "I'll let you explain, all right! You can start by telling me why this happened in the first place! You're supposed to protect people, aren't you? Isn't that what police are for, protection? Then how could some maniac just walk in here in the middle of the day, tear the place apart and torture and kill my husband? What the hell were you doing, playing golf? Eating doughnuts? Why didn't you do your job? Why didn't you stop him?"

"Mrs. Compton—"

"Don't 'Mrs. Compton' me, you incompetent jackass!" Sabrina shouted. "You're a joke, not a police department. You couldn't protect us, and now you can't even catch the killer. My God! How can you sleep at night?"

"I know this has been difficult for you, but I'm not going to sit here and listen to any more of this crap." If he had hoped to jolt her back into sanity, it was a vain hope. The detective's icy voice merely whipped Sabrina's frenzy higher. "If you don't calm down and stop shouting at me, I'm going to hang up, Mrs. Compton. I've—"

"Don't you *dare* hang up! Do you hear me? Don't you dare, you no-good—"

"Good-bye, Mrs. Compton."

The detective's receiver crashed onto the cradle. Sabrina stood shocked, her mouth gaping open, her now-dead receiver still pressed to her ear. Hatred shuddered through her, a rage so bitter she tasted bile in her throat. Gasping audibly, she re-dialed, savage jabs of her finger that sent painful shocks up into her wrist. She could barely force the words out when the desk sergeant answered.

"Get Detective Burke on this phone," she ordered. "Now!"

"He's not here, ma'am. He's gone out, just now." Sabrina growled at the obvious lie. "He won't be back until quite late. He said—this is Mrs. Compton, isn't it?"

Sabrina felt as if ice water had been thrown in her face. She lost her hold on present reality. Her emotions shut down abruptly, leaving her marooned in a limitless void.

"Yes," she whispered after a pause.

"He said to tell you not to call back. He'll call you when he has the time, or when there's anything new to report. Don't call him. He'll call you, Mrs. Compton."

Sabrina couldn't bring herself to speak. She set the receiver in the cradle and stood staring at the phone, her body quaking, her mind completely blank. She couldn't breathe, couldn't move. Then her hands rose and pressed against her face, releasing her from the inertia. Her body moved though she was still trembling, her mind still shut down. She turned, mounted the stairs, selected clothes from the sitting room closet and chest, shut the bathroom door behind her. She turned on the water, adjusted the temperature, and shed both robe and nightgown, all with no awareness of her movements. Then she stepped into the shower and emotion overwhelmed her, released by the power of the streaming water. It welled up from her toes, anguish and fear and anger, filling her full to bursting. It overflowed, a keening wail that wove around and into the drumming of the water, burning tears that burst out to mix with the needle-sharp spray. She hit the tile wall, battered it with her fists, screaming her pain out in great sobbing gulps until at last she sank to her knees and hugged the tattered remnants of her life to her breast while the water beat upon her bowed back. The hot water was gone when the storm finally ebbed, leaving her dry and empty inside. Sabrina finished her morning ablutions with water almost as cold as her heart.

CHAPTER SIX

Homicide offices all looked the same to Mitch Lawson—motion, purpose and quietly tense anger beneath a thin veneer of off-handed casualness and levity. Protective mechanisms, he knew, that enabled ordinary, everyday, moral people to deal daily with the savage cruelty and painfully immoral reality of murder. They all sounded the same to him, too, their hushed clatter more self-important and intense than that of regular precinct offices, voices muted-seeming even when raised in alarm, haste, or frustrated rage.

But it was the smell that really set homicide offices apart. Even blindfolded, Mitch would know where he was just by the smell. It clung to painted walls and tile floors, to the desks and the clothes of detectives hard at work. It was the stench of death, the odor of bodies violently robbed of life, though no bodies ever passed through those office doors—no dead ones, at least. Still, the smell was there, as real and offensive to Mitch's nose as fish rotting in sun-baked seaweed. The smell of blood, cold, congealed, rusting blood. A smell of endings, of mortality arrived too soon, emanating, somehow, from the reams of paperwork that sudden, violent death required. Rising from the forms, and the carbon and the typewriter keys, from the computers and printers, the manila folders and filing cabinets that held the shattered lives and dreams of humanity.

They always depressed him, homicide offices, for they reminded him with unnecessary clarity of the dozens of bodies he'd inspected over the years, the flower-saturated funerals he'd attended, the mourning survivors who had left their bewildered cries echoing in his soul. Not that he needed reminding. Mitch had never been very successful at laying to rest the ghosts he'd acquired in this job. There were times, more often now that he'd retired from the field, when he wondered why he felt so damned responsible for all those deaths. That certainly didn't make sense. But then, to him, little in life did.

He sighed and rose, sliding his hands into his back pockets, letting his thumbs peek over their corners. He wandered away from the desk, acutely aware of Andy Webster's puzzled brown eyes watching him from his place nearby. Mitch knew the short, stocky young agent resented this intrusion into his territory, his ego still smarting from the dressing-down Mitch had given him earlier and the silence Mitch had maintained about his interest in the case. Mitch didn't care. He wasn't here to babysit, he was here to find answers that didn't seem to exist.

He shook his head and rubbed a hand hard over his face. His back hurt. The chair, sized for a smaller man, was too low for him, uncomfortable and awkward. He towered over both Buffalo's field agent and the local detective in charge of this case, looking even bigger than he was with his suit coat off, his shirt straining across his chest, sleeves rolled up and holster straps wound around his shoulders. The case file and impounded evidence lay scattered on the desk behind him where Mitch had left them. So far, he'd learned little more than what had been contained in Webster's simplified report.

He stopped at the window of the small fourth floor office and stared at the way the surrounding downtown buildings thrust solidly up from a patchwork of concrete lawns. The disparity in Buffalo's architectural styles was gently compelling, imparting a feel of comfortable familiarity. Foreshortened figures hurried to and fro, secretaries, bankers, lawyers, shop clerks, all buffeted by the chill autumn wind on their way back from a late lunch to an afternoon of work. A cart vendor on the corner still did a brisk business in apples, pears, bananas, oranges and grapes. Mitch thought of the greasy doughnuts he habitually ingested in his Washington office. *Seems people here are more health conscious*, he thought, watching hurrying workers carry off their afternoon treats. *Friendly, too.* Mitch saw faces smile, lips move, hands rise in greeting as people passed one another. Cars even stopped to let pedestrians cross the street, something he'd not seen happen in years.

He liked this place. From the moment he'd landed at the airport the night before, he'd felt a warm sensation envelop him. It remained with him despite the reason for his being there and the presence of a glacial and antipathetic Agent Webster. It refused to dissipate when he entered Police Headquarters and was not quite fully submerged even beneath the oppressive miasma of the homicide department. He felt, amazingly, like he had come home at last. As though he'd lived here all his life. As though it wasn't his first trip to Buffalo, New York. It disconcerted him. He wished he didn't have the job to do that faced him still. He wished the answers he needed had been in the police file.

The office door opened with a muted click, hinges squeaking faintly over the soft clatter of busy typists in the next room. Mitch swung around to face Ray Burke, in whose glass-and-wood paneled office they stood. Burke, a twelve-year veteran of the homicide department, was compact, wiry, and snake-quick in both mind and movement. His graying red hair, reddish complexion and bright blue eyes attested to the reality of the Irish ancestry his name proclaimed. He had dealt calmly and capably with Mitch's federally-backed intrusion, taking him and his baby-faced companion step-by-step through a frustrating investigation that had turned up not one lead in over two intensive months of work.

Indeed, Burke had shown much less hostility and irritation than the local field agent had, and little of the curiosity that kept Andy Webster's eyes narrowed and alert. Mitch had requested that Burke leave the two F.B.I. agents alone in the office with the files and the meager evidence the Buffalo detectives had collected, though Mitch had been aware that Burke had not gone far. He'd kept careful watch through the glass in the door, until Mitch had walked to the window and Burke obviously concluded that the personal inspection was over.

Burke smiled, the mischievous glint in his eyes jarring with the hard glaze of professionalism on his round, snub-nosed face. He had wrapped his out-sized hands around three Styrofoam cups of steaming coffee, and had a small white bag tucked beneath one arm.

"Thought you could use this," he said, dropping the bag on the desk amid the gruesome relics of Charles Philip Compton's life. He held out the trio of cups to Agent Webster, who took the middle one, then offered a cup to Mitch. "It's thick as sewer sludge and doesn't taste much better, but it hasn't killed anyone yet. Not that I know of, that is," he added as Mitch took the cup into his own huge hand.

"Let's hope I'm not the first," Mitch said, taking a slurping sip, wincing slightly as the scalding liquid slid down his throat. His shoulders lifted with pleasure. This was coffee the way he liked it, thick and rich and hot enough to burn his insides. Buffalo moved up another notch in his estimation. Any place that could offer coffee this good was close to perfect.

Ray Burke moved around to his chair, sat, and opened the bag he'd brought. He looked up at Mitch, who had perched on the corner of the desk.

"Like I said before, there's not much to go on. It's hard to believe someone could do something like that, and nobody see or hear a thing." He took three still-hot cheese Danish from the bag. "Here. Empty calories, my specialty. Eat 'em while they're still warm, they're best that way." He handed out the Danish and sank back in the seat, speaking around the food in his mouth. "We figure the killers were in the house maybe three hours, all the time beating on that poor guy, cutting him... Hell of a way to go."

"What makes you think there was more than one?" Mitch reached out, turned the lab photos of the body around, and squinted at the gruesome images while he ate, passing them one-by-one to Webster who, Mitch could see, tried his best to gaze as dispassionately at them as did his superior.

"Nothing concrete." Burke shrugged. "It's just hard to believe only one man could do that much damage. And Compton was no featherweight, for all that he wasn't very tall. He went a good two hundred pounds, most of it solid muscle. It'd take more than one man to bring him down."

"Unless he was caught off-guard," Mitch mused, finishing the coffee. He licked sweet stickiness from his fingers. Not a bad lunch, all told. Better than the tasteless faux food they charged you a small fortune for on the plane. Webster had abandoned his pastry in the face of the photos. Mitch reached over and confiscated it.

"Off-guard..." Burke mused. "That could be. There was no forced entry. Wife said the front door was ajar when she arrived home. But she also said he was absent-minded, had left the door ajar before. So, either he opened it to whoever killed him and let them in, or he simply forgot to close it when he took in the mail or whatever, and they just waltzed in unannounced. Somehow, I can't imagine the killers being stupid enough to stand out on the doorstep and ring the bell. Not in the middle of the day, for crissakes. And a warm, sunny summer afternoon at that. Kids playing, people out watering lawns, walking dogs, enjoying the weather. And a park right across the street. If that's what happened, it's just plain dumb luck that no one saw them."

"Him," Mitch corrected. "One man. And luck had nothing to do with it."

"You sound like you know who did it." Burke frowned, a note of suspicion in his voice. Andy Webster's head rose. He stared at Mitch, his face, his body, death-still.

"I do. I just can't prove it."

Mitch picked up the bloodstained wallet and looked again at the snapshot inside of Compton and a woman he assumed was the wife, taken two months before the killing. The past fifteen years had wrought startling changes in the man Mitch had known, turned the stylishly thick wavy black hair thin and graying, added lines to the cocky, pretty-boy face and softened the cruelty of his full, mobile lips. The years even molded a slight stoop into a body that had strutted once with invincible confidence. Gone, too, were the neatly trimmed beard and mustache, the flashy gold jewelry, the hand-tailored silk shirts open halfway down a hairy chest. The man in this photo looked every bit the aging, absentminded, mild-mannered professor he'd become. Mitch could have passed him on the street and not recognized him, though a vague sense of deja vu would probably have nagged at him until he remembered of whom he'd been reminded.

"This the wife?" he asked, turning the picture to face Burke.

The detective nodded, his eyes hard and speculative on Mitch's face.

"Not quite his usual type," Mitch said. "Looks fragile and clingy. He always liked gutsy blondes. And she's a bit young for him, isn't she? When did he marry her?"

"Seven years ago. She took a night class from him, that's how they met. We thought about the age thing, checked into it, wondered if maybe she had a friend on the side who got a little impatient. But there's nothing. She's clean. They were happily married, if you can believe that in this day and age. What the hell's going on? You sound like you knew Compton."

"I did, once. A long time ago." Mitch handed Webster the wallet and took a last look at the crime scene photographs before sliding them back into their envelopes. "Don't waste any more manpower on this, your killer's imported talent, long gone by now. We know who he is, though we've yet to find anything concrete to link him to any one of his jobs. Any idea what he was looking for so thoroughly?"

"None. Nothing seems to be missing that we can figure, but the widow's not exactly reliable, emotionally speaking. We haven't gotten a coherent sentence out of her since it happened." He glanced at Andy Webster, frowning. "How can you be so sure you know who did this? There's nothing to go on."

"That's exactly how I know," Mitch replied, pulling Burke's eyes back to him. "This guy never makes a mistake, never leaves anything behind but a mutilated body. His trademark, you might say. But the method is always the same. He works mostly in daylight—I guess he likes to tempt fate. And he uses a different gun each time. He enjoys making his vics suffer. They all look like Compton when he's finished with them. We've got twelve files like this, all with his name on them. And those are just the ones we spotted. God knows how many we haven't. It was just luck I happened to run across this one and recognized the signature. He's never left such a mess before, though. That's really got me puzzled. I wonder what he was looking for that was so all-fired important."

"I wonder if he found it," Andy Webster said in a quiet, deep voice.

The three men looked solemnly at each other, then Ray Burke sighed. Mitch rose and shrugged into his suit coat, the motion pulling Webster to his feet.

"So, what's your next move?" Burke asked.

"We'll meet you at the University in the morning, say nine-thirty. I want to have a look at his office, see what I can find. Then we'll go talk to the grieving widow, see what she knows. The answers are here, somewhere, and I'm going to find them."

"You won't get much from the Compton woman except tears and four letter words," Burke said, his tone sour as he picked up the files and evidence envelopes. He dropped them on the civilian aide's desk for re-filing as he walked the F.B.I. men out. "She's something else, I'll tell you. We hadn't heard a word from her since just after the funeral, then she called here yesterday, ranting and raving like a banshee because we hadn't made an arrest yet. I wouldn't go near her unarmed, if I were you."

Mitch gave a sympathetic chuckle, then shook hands with Burke. He'd endured his share of antagonistic, belligerent civilians over the years, people who expected the police to work miracles, and even blamed them for 'allowing' the crime to happen in the first place. Their work was hard enough without having to suffer unreasonable, and sometimes physically abusive, citizens. He walked beside a suspiciously quiet Webster until they reached the car. He slid into the passenger seat with a sigh, wondering if this child-agent really was old enough to drive.

"Listen, find me a place where I can get a car, will you?" he asked as they pulled out of the parking ramp. "I want to do some sightseeing."

Webster didn't offer his chauffeuring services, he simply grunted assent. The wind off Lake Erie bounced the silver Taurus around as they threaded their way through the welter of one-way downtown streets. Not until they gained Gennesee Street, heading for the rental agencies near the airport, did Webster speak, his voice stiff with suppressed anger.

"So this was a contract hit. I figured it had to be big-time to bring you all the way up here. What the hell would a university economics professor have done to rate a contract hit?"

"You'd be surprised."

"Are you gonna tell me?"

"Nope," Mitch said, and Webster's eyes narrowed. "It's need-to-know."

Webster growled. Mitch sighed. He leaned back and closed his eyes, letting the junior agent suffer in silence. He knew why Compton had been killed. It didn't really surprise him. What did surprise him was that he'd been found. And that the house had been torn apart. Why? It never should have happened, not the searching, or the killing. Because Compton shouldn't have been found. He shouldn't ever have been found.

CHAPTER SEVEN

Huge and old, Forest Lawn Cemetery spread out in the heart of the city, a rolling treed landmark full of serenity and peace. Sabrina pulled through the wrought iron main gate, her heart hammering loud in the hushed afternoon silence. She glanced at the stone administration building to her left, wondering if she'd be able to find the grave by herself. She hadn't exactly been alert or aware the last —the only—time she'd been here. But she drove slowly by, not stopping, unable to make herself face saying the words. *How do I find Charles Philip Compton's grave?* Though she knew he was dead—oh, dear lord, how well she knew it—still she could not bring herself to give that fact the reality of words.

She continued on, steering Charlie's dark blue Nash Rambler past the statue of Red Jacket, Forest Lawn's most famous resident. Elevated far above her on a round stone pedestal, the sculpted Native

American looked away to his right as though accepting in stoic silence the brevity of man, the immutability of death. Sabrina could feel the man's innate dignity radiating from the age-greened bronze.

Sabrina, despite reluctance that bordered on fear, was impressed by the beauty surrounding her. Stone monuments in gray and white created a Lilliputian cityscape amidst manicured lawns and wind-molded pines. Red geraniums and mums of russet and yellow glistened in the brilliant sun, peeking from beside headstones and nodding in the freshening autumn breeze as if possessed by the life left behind by the people buried below. Tranquility and stillness filled the air, the cemetery's wrought iron fence a staunch guardian that kept the bustle and noise of the surrounding city at bay. Stone benches, many occupied by young and old alike, beckoned the weary and heart-sore to rest a while in comforting sunshined silence.

But Sabrina did not stop. She drove slowly on, straight ahead, uncaring now of her destination, past a beautifully designed gazebo-like structure on her right. Within the round room life-size statues of a grief-stricken mother and father attended their adult son's realistically carved deathbed, their sorrow and devotion sculpted into glittering white stone for ages to come. Family names caught her eye as she passed, chiseled facets limned with shadow and light. Sanford, Carleton, Gerasse, Benedict, name after name on cross, slab and plinth. Husbands, wives, children and lovers, their travails ended now, their hopes and dreams bequeathed to other bodies that soon would join them in sleep. Sabrina began to tremble. Her heart fluttered wildly in her chest. How could Charlie be here, in a place like this? How? Why?

The roadway curved, forked. Sabrina steered to the right, past an intersection and around to where water glinted beneath the cloud-dotted sky. **Mirror Lake**, a rustic wooden sign proclaimed in sedate, burned-in letters. Ducks and gulls floated on the water's surface.

Sabrina pulled the car to the side of the road where it divided to circle the small body of water. Her shaking hands were barely able to extract the keys from the ignition. She opened the door and got out, shutting it gently in the wind-swept afternoon, loath to intrude on the pervasive silence. A monument-studded hill rose beside her to the right, discretely labeled *Section One*. Headstones ranged in neat rows facing the car, generations of people once called Flack, Horton or Jacus. She left the Rambler to their eyeless scrutiny and crossed the road. A sun-warmed bench further to her right, near the tiny lake's northern edge, drew her near.

She sat and watched the birds until her heart had calmed and her shaking stilled, soothed by the waterfowls' presence, the feeling of life that surrounded them. Sienna, gray and white, the birds glistened in the sun, floating with effortless unconcern on the dark, sparkling water. A dozen ducks, accompanied by fresh-water gulls, broke away from the crowd to approach the bank where she sat, obviously expecting food. Iridescent green heads glimmered blue in the sun. White rings circled their necks like collars. Sabrina had never seen male mallards so close up before and she stared in fascination, intrigued by the way pale gray feathers arrowed down their dark backs, leading her eye to their perfect, pointed white tails. They stared expectantly at her, poised a mere three feet away. She wished she had something to give them, almost opened her mouth to speak an apology. Finally, uneasy beneath their pleading gaze, she shook her head and raised her eyes.

Further out on the lake a lone large white bird kept its distance, its orange beak brilliant against the dark water. She looked to her left, traced the curve of the shore around the oval lake. Willows swayed in the breeze, soft green foliage turning autumn-yellow on the branches' upper reaches. Further along, where the bank curved a minuscule peninsula out into the water, three teenagers sat on the sun-kissed grass surrounded by a mass of birds vying for the seed they offered.

Sabrina sighed, feeling a pall of isolation drop over her. She let her gaze continue on to the right, around another jutting peninsula, until she reached the small lake's southern end and her gaze snagged on the stone mausoleums that stood half-hidden by the now-leafless, decorative trees lining the shore. The sun's rays glinted sparks from stone and marble, reminding her sharply of where she was, the sole purpose of such a place. She had almost forgotten beneath the magical spell of the duck-strewn lake. She shivered then, despite the warm sun on her back, and shut her eyes, knowing that eventually she would have to move and find the place where Charlie lay.

She saw a statue standing out in the water near the southwestern shore when she opened her eyes. Curiosity tugged at her. She rose and walked to it, a circle of three age-greened bronze women, nude, clasping hands, one bending down with a hand to her raised foot as though she rubbed her instep. A bronze plaque set in a stone pedestal on the shore informed her that it was a fountain sculpture by Charles Cary Rumsey, a local artist of world-repute, who had died in 1922. It was entitled, *The Three Graces*.

Sabrina tried but couldn't remember enough mythology to understand the artist's interpretation of the Graces. Charlie would have known, but Charlie was not there to ask. Sabrina, feeling empty, turned around, crossed the road, and, with the lowering sun in her face, climbed the hill that overlooked the lake, threading her way between the headstones. She turned at the summit and looked down on the water, an enclave of peaceful beauty centered in an oasis of quietude. She wished Charlie's grave was here, in sight of the lake. He'd enjoyed nature so much, he would have loved this spot.

She sighed and looked at the engraved obelisk beside her. It soared skyward, four narrow sides converging to a point far above her head. Her breath stopped when she read the words chiseled into the gray stone.

Fannie E. Hathaway

D. June 28, 1842

Aged 5 years

Her vision clouded with shock. Blood roared in her ears. She stumbled to her left on numb legs to read the side of the monument facing away from the lake, forcing herself not to think.

Kate Hathaway Sexton

B. March 1, 1851

D. August 20, 1926
Beloved mother of Henry Hathaway Sexton
B. September 24, 1879
D. April 22, 1947

That was better. Sabrina's heart began to slow. Kate had been seventy-five when she died, her son almost sixty-six. Taken by old age or disease after a life of dreams fulfilled and wishes come true. That was as it should be.

She decided to ignore the notation about little Fannie Hathaway and moved around to the front side of the obelisk. There were Kate and Fannie's parents, Isaac T. Hathaway who died in 1880 at eighty-four years of age, and his wife, Eliza, who followed Isaac four years later at age sixty-seven. Though she'd been twenty years younger than her husband, still Eliza had spent a rich and long life with him. Fannie had been born in 1837. Her parents had probably married a year or two before the birth. That gave them forty-four or forty-five years together. Not a mere seven, but a lifetime. Sabrina wondered if they knew how lucky they had been.

Another young death marred the last side of the monument. Sabrina stood in silence, her gaze solemnly tracing the words.

Capt. Henry C. Hathaway, U.S.A.
Co. 1 12 NY Cavalry
Died October 3, 1864 at New Bern, NC
Aged 21 years
"He died for his country"

Dead in the prime of his youth, of bullet or bayonet, a casualty of war. The Civil War. It seemed so distant in time and space, not real, a fairy tale concocted for history books. But Sabrina felt a shock go through her as she re-read the date, and Henry's age. She thought again of Fannie. Long lives, yes, for Isaac and Eliza, but not sorrow-free. Not death-free. *He died for his country.* Sabrina could not take her eyes off the words. Somehow, they lent this death a purpose and dignity. A reason, something acceptable to live with. He died for his country.

What did Charlie die for? Sabrina wondered, turning away, pacing slowly along the crest of the hill toward where her car waited. *Where was the purpose, the dignity, for him? How do I accept the unreasonableness of what happened? How do I go on?*

Tears blinded her and she paused to wipe them away, only to find herself staring at another tall, narrow obelisk. Unable to stop herself she walked around it, reading the inscriptions, horror growing in her breast. Jason Parker, who had died at sixty-two in 1876, had had two wives and four children, three sons and a daughter. Only one son, the third child, had survived childhood to die at the age of sixty-nine in 1920. Little Millard Fillmore had died when he was only eight, Emeline Younglove at age two, and William Edwin, Jason's firstborn, had lived only a year and a month. The mother, Emeline Austin, followed the baby a year later.

Sabrina stared at the names, Emeline Austin and William Edwin, painful memories washing over her. She felt again her elation when the doctor confirmed her pregnancy, relived Charlie's joy and excitement when she told him on Christmas morning, saw again the pride shining in his eyes, the new spring to his step. She remembered the way her body had changed, her belly rounding out with new life, the butterfly feel of the tiny child's movements there within her. Then there had been gut-wrenching pain, the placenta inexplicably separating from the uterine wall. Blood had cascaded down her legs as she fought desperately to stop it, to save her baby, barely managing to save herself.

She'd given in to despair when the doctor told her there would be no more children, ever. The damage had been extensive, an emergency hysterectomy the only way to stop hemorrhaging that took her to the brink of death. It was only Charlie's love that had brought her back, his comforting presence, strong arms and warm lips giving her the strength to put the tragedy behind her and go on, to build a full life for the two of them alone. She wondered now, staring at Emeline's name, Emeline who had not survived the death of her child, where her own son was buried. If he was buried at all. She hadn't wanted to know, had left it to Charlie to handle, had never even asked what had been done with their seven-and-a-half-month-old fetus. It was enough that he was gone, gone so swiftly he might never have existed at all.

She turned away and descended to the car through the ranks of Flacks and Hortons and Jacuses, glad now that Charlie was not here among these old bones. No lake, no matter how beautiful, could ever compensate for the memories the dates on those stones dredged up. She unlocked the car, slid behind the wheel and sat staring at the lake, noting idly a young couple strolling hand-in-hand near the edge. An old woman, accompanied by a middle-aged man, feed the flocking birds. A man sat on the bench she had quitted, legs crossed, reading a newspaper, the sun sparking golden glints in his sand-colored hair. He sat in quarter profile, square jaw and jutting nose limned against the dark water of the lake. Sabrina watched the breeze dance with his fair locks, saw him struggle to turn a page, blinked when the sun sparked on a ring he wore, while she sorted through her disjointed memories of the funeral. But it was no use. Nothing would come clear except pain and despair. She knew only that the grave was somewhere in section ten. She sighed, started the car and made a U-turn in the road's fork, deciding simply to drive around until she found the right area.

It didn't take long. She drove straight ahead, ignoring the cross roads, heading for the fence separating the cemetery from Delaware Avenue. The road began a gentle curve to the left, and from the corner of her eye Sabrina saw a signpost on the right: *Section 10*. She pulled over and stopped, scanning headstones and names, searching for something familiar. But the names she saw—Nash, Schierer, Hart, Ross, Fumerelle, Steele, Smith—struck no chord at all. Then her eyes lifted and her heart lurched. She remembered the traffic signal at Forest and Delaware, remembered watching it change from green to amber to red to green while the interminable, incomprehensible graveside service droned on. She recalled now her anger at the movement of cars, remembered wondering why life seemed so oblivious to death, to this death above all. Yes, she remembered the traffic signal—and a headstone shaped like an archway.

She could see it clear in her mind's eye now, an open archway, like a gate to the life beyond this world. She remembered staring at the empty space between the stone sides of the arch and feeling as blank and invisible as it looked. Charlie was here somewhere, near the traffic signal and a strangely shaped headstone. All she had to do was force herself to get out and look.

Sabrina climbed out of the car and moved onto the grass, her gaze sweeping over the open, level area of Section 10. Suddenly, she saw it, an open stone archway ahead to her right, half-hidden behind a solid headstone chiseled with the name Porter. With trembling steps she drew closer, able now to see the name carved into the base supporting the arch: S. W. Arsdale. And there, just beyond, brown earth still mounded and raw-looking even after ten weeks, was where she had left Charlie.

Sabrina stopped, not sure she could go any closer. She wondered for the first time what would have happened had Donald Bradley not found, attached to the will, documentation of the grave plots Charlie had purchased shortly after their marriage. The Bradleys had handled everything else—the funeral home, the service, they even chose the casket and the clothing Charlie would be buried in—but Charlie had himself provided his own final resting place. And hers, providing for his beloved wife in all ways as a good husband should, though he had not discussed this particular purchase with her. Who could have known how very soon he'd have need of it?

Sabrina, still reluctant, moved slowly forward, drawn by the rose-brown headstone gleaming in the slanting sun. That was odd, she didn't remember a headstone—not that she remembered much of that awful day—and she knew it was too soon for one to have been set up. Not until spring would the earth be settled enough. But here one sat at the head of the plot, its brown face polished, top slightly arched, rough sides still showing chisel marks. And in the center, in square Roman lettering, cut strong and deep: Compton.

Below the name the face had been divided into thirds. The center space marked where Charlie now lay.

Charles Philip Compton
Born July 23, 1940
Died July 14, 1989

An economy of words, curt and impersonal. They felt like a knife in Sabrina's breast. Her gaze moved on. To the right, her name had been carved: Sabrina Steves, Beloved Wife, the rest left blank, waiting for life to run its inevitable course. How many long, empty, endless years? She looked away, to the space on Charlie's left, and discovered at last their unborn son.

Daniel William
Our only child
Lost before birth, April 1985

She couldn't breathe. Her heart stood still. Pain lanced her breast. A desolate moan pushed through her open lips to echo on the clear autumn air, and Sabrina pressed a hand hard on her mouth. She sank to her knees, overcome by the brutal reality of the chiseled words. All her life, all her reason, all her purpose lay here before her, side by side beneath six inaccessible feet of cold, hard earth. Why had she been left behind?

What sin had she committed to deserve this? All she had wanted was someone to love, someone with whom to share life, someone to help her make sense of living. She had waited so long for Charlie, for Daniel. Why had she been given them, only to have them taken away again? What point was there to life if love had no place in it? If all it came down to were terse, emotionless facts chiseled into cold, unfeeling stone?

She didn't know how long she sobbed, but when at last her tears slowed and Sabrina became aware of her surroundings again, little had changed. The sun still shone brightly, though a little lower in the sky. The breeze still tugged at her soft shoulder-length curls. Birds sang with uncontrolled joy in nearby trees, their melodies underscored by homeward bound traffic on the street outside the fence. An old man held a young boy's hand a few yards away and watched her curiously, turning away when Sabrina wiped her face and fumbled in her purse for a tissue. Not until she stood and looked again at the headstone Charlie had selected did she see the line inscribed across the top: *To live in the hearts of those we love is not to die.*

She gasped and shook her head, stepped back from the grave. *Oh, no, Charlie,* she screamed silently at him. *You're wrong. Dead is dead. That's all it is, just dead.*

Pain beat at her, crowding tears back into her eyes. Sabrina stumbled toward her car. A dark gray four-door sedan sat behind it, the passenger door open. A man sat sideways on the seat facing the graves, his feet planted flat on the ground. His head was lowered as if in sorrow. The wind played with his light, sand-colored hair. But Sabrina barely noticed him. She jammed the key into the ignition with shaking hands and drove away, half-blinded by tears she could not stop. The road curved left, joined the main artery, and led her quickly through the gate and onto Delaware Avenue. She was forced to stem her tears in order to concentrate on the thickening traffic, and by the time she reached the supermarket on Kenmore near Englewood, a mere four blocks from the house, she felt in control again, capable of picking up a few groceries. She was wrong. Halfway through the meat department she realized she had chosen enough for two, all of it Charlie's favorite cuts. Two boxes of a whole grain cereal which she didn't eat but which Charlie could not live without sat in the cart along with the grapefruit, oranges and avocados he loved so much, the tomato juice he drank each evening before dinner.

She almost screamed, feeling trapped by smothering panic. She turned and fled the store, leaving the half-filled cart blocking an aisle. Dusk was falling when she pulled into the garage. It took all her courage to unlock the front door. She found a note taped on the hall mirror.

'Sabrina,' she read, 'there's a faculty dinner tonight we can't miss. God, how I hate these things! I left a pot of stew on your stove, salad in the fridge, along with a bottle of wine. Enjoy. Brought your mail over, too. I'll help you go through it tomorrow if you'd like. We'll probably be out late, so I'll call you in the morning. Sleep well. Anne.'

On the table below the mirror sat three neat stacks of mail that had accumulated while she'd been away, minus the bills that Donald, as executor, had opened and paid from the estate. Sabrina saw catalogs and magazines, most with Charlie's name on them, on the left, and cards and letters of condolence addressed to her alone in the center stack. Other personal correspondence, again mostly addressed to Charlie from people who most likely did not yet know of his death, made up the last pile. Sabrina gathered it all into her arms and took it with her into the kitchen to sort through while she ate.

The envelopes spilled out across the table when she set them down and she stared at them, gleaming white in the overhead light as if possessing a life of their own. Silence clamped around her, an empty silence that only Charlie's presence could banish. She looked at the stew on the stove and shut her eyes, shuddering. She knew she wouldn't—couldn't—eat a thing, not tonight. She put the pot away in the refrigerator, took out the wine and poured herself a glass, hoping it would relax her enough so she could at least sleep. Then she sat at the table and began opening the cards.

The first four were sympathy cards, sent from out-of-town by Charlie's former students. Two contained money, one a notice of Catholic masses to be said for the repose of Charlie's soul, though he had been a Methodist. *I could use some for the repose of mine*, Sabrina thought, carefully noting the names and addresses for later acknowledgment. Unaware that the piles had mixed together, Sabrina opened the next envelope without looking at the addressee on the front.

It was a card, not for her but for Charlie, sent by a former colleague who now resided in Tempe, Arizona. Joe Snyder, ignorant of the murder, had mailed it four days after Charlie's death, intending it to reach Buffalo in time to celebrate a birthday that had never arrived.

Shock flooded over Sabrina like an icy wave as again she relived the excitement of shopping for that same birthday, excitement that had ended brutally in horror and death. The card dropped from her nerveless fingers, its confetti-sprinkled front an obscene slash of gaiety amid the colorless cards and envelopes of mourning.

A shudder rippled through her, brought on by the impact of a day crammed with pain and memory. She pushed away from the table and backed out of the kitchen. Panic lifted her chest in huge gasps. She ran down the hall, hands clutched tight in her hair, trying vainly to outdistance reality. She started up the stairs without thinking, out of habit. Halfway up she stopped, blocked by a vision of blood and gore. She stood swaying, unable now to move either up or down. Finally she turned and sat where she was, leaned her head against the wall while great sobs tore from deep within. She couldn't bear being in this house, touching things that shouldn't exist, dealing with a life that no longer had meaning. She didn't know who she was anymore, what was real or what was safe. She longed to crawl away to where she would not have to deal with the end of what once had sustained her.

Away. She wanted to go away. Sabrina's head lifted. Her mouth gaped open in surprise. Why hadn't she thought of it before, gone to the beach house in the first place instead of looking for the impossible in California? It was just what she needed, a place sheltered and secluded, a private oasis where she could lick her wounds and gather strength. She'd not even need to go upstairs and pack since she left a complete wardrobe there for quick getaways. And though there would still be traces of Charlie there, it would not be the same as here because the beach house had been hers before Charlie came into her life. It wasn't a place they had built together from their love, like this one was. Maybe there, with the comforting sound of the ocean bringing her shattered spirit solace, she could learn to face the remnants of her life and extract the good that surely must lie dormant beneath its torn and bloody surface.

She wiped her face with trembling hands, then rose and descended to the telephone to call a cab. She didn't care when the next plane left. She'd rather wait hours in the airport than spend another intolerable night in his house. She could call Anne tomorrow from the beach. The cab arrived twenty minutes later. Sabrina ran down her front steps with a heart lighter than it had been for ten endless weeks, since the late afternoon of July fourteenth.

* * *

He watched the garage door close behind the big old car, saw lights flick on downstairs as she progressed through the house. The upper level remained dark, as he'd figured it would. She'd need more than one day to be able to face the memories up there with equanimity.

He glanced at his watch in the fading light to find the hands standing close to seven. She'd fix dinner, now, then maybe read for a while and bed down early. On the couch? Probably. He waited another twenty minutes to make sure she wasn't leaving again, then drove away, heading for a nearby restaurant and a meal of his own. He ate slowly, lingering over coffee brewed strong and hot the way he liked it, reading the local paper with undisguised interest. It was almost ten when he returned to the house on Larchmont Avenue, feeling well-sated and pleased with the world. As pleased, at least, as he could feel with unanswered questions eating at him.

The house was dark, as he'd expected. Her kind of woman—wispy and ineffectual—was so predictable. She was either asleep, aided by pills or liquor, or lying awake staring into the darkness, startling at every sound. Either way, she wouldn't be going anywhere else, not tonight. Not in the dark. He might as well go back to his room and get some sleep. He could sure use it after last night. He didn't think it would be much longer now. A day or two at most and this case could be closed. He could go home, turn his attention to more interesting things. This was already beginning to bore him. And he got nasty when he was bored. Real nasty.

Out of habit he checked the weapon nestled beneath his arm, then started the dark gray rental car and drove away, giving the darkened house one last glance. *Until tomorrow, Sabrina Compton,* he promised. *I'll get my answers from you tomorrow.* Well satisfied, he drove on past street lamps that threw his jutting-nosed profile into relief against the darkness and glinted through the car windows onto his fair, sand-colored hair. He thought again of tomorrow, and smiled.

CHAPTER EIGHT

Sabrina arrived in Charleston, South Carolina, at eleven-fifteen the next morning, thoroughly exhausted from a restless night in the Buffalo airport. The sky was overcast, the air humid. The mid-sixty degree temperature, though below average for the time of year and cool for the local residents, felt more than warm to Sabrina. Her navy wool-blend skirt, heavy white cotton sweater and loose-fitting khaki jacket, perfect for the northeast's cool, breezy fall, only added to her discomfort. She had forgotten how different the weather would be nine hundred miles south of Buffalo, just as she'd forgotten how very much alone being alone could be. She had forgotten a lot during her seven years with Charlie. She wondered now if it were possible to survive the relearning process.

She fell sound asleep in the cab despite the cloying warmth, or perhaps because of it, waking with a start when the tires bumped onto the bridge leading to James Island. She sat up, blinking, half-blinded by a stubborn sun trying to burn through misty clouds. Fort Sumter stood its ground out in the harbor, weathered gray stone staunchly awaiting nineteenth century frigates long since rotted in death. Sabrina could almost hear the boom of cannon, the tromp of military feet, the click and rattle of musket and bayonet.

It was here in April of 1861 that the shots were fired that began the Civil War and tore apart families across the then-settled states of the nation. Sabrina thought again of Captain Henry Hathaway, who at twenty-one had died for his country. At New Bern in North Carolina, the monument had told her. Sabrina turned her eyes away from the fort and wondered how far New Bern was from Charleston, if Henry's parents had ever made a pilgrimage to the place where their son had died and was buried. If so, where had they found the courage? Where would she ever find the courage to return home, to go on with a life empty and meaningless? Her head began to throb. Sabrina leaned back against the seat and bit her lips to stem burning tears.

The sun lost its battle with the mist and retreated behind thickening clouds. The ocean looked leaden beneath the heavy skies, the usually-colorful landscape flattening out in the pale half-light. Dunes humped to either side of the cab as they crossed James Island and approached the bridge leading to Gaffe Island. The cab crossed the bridge then swung left around the island's northern tip, where tufts of sword-sharp grass clung with tenacious determination to the sandy soil. Sea birds, disturbed from restful contemplation by the passage of the car, rose into the air on self-righteous wings, screaming raucous imprecations at the noisy interloper. Sabrina lowered the window and let the hot moist breeze play with her hair as she breathed in the comforting aroma of salt, sand and seaweed. For as long as she could remember, coming to the beach house transported her to another time and space, leaving behind all the cares and worries of everyday life. It was no different now. The pall of misery that enveloped her slowly shredded away, despite the moody weather and uninviting expanse of dull rolling water, until only tiny wisps remained clinging to her heart and mind.

The cab jounced along the eastern shore of Gaffe Island, the endless stretch of the Atlantic on their left. The land on this end of the island was high. Twenty-foot cliffs and sandy dunes undulated down to where gray-green waves caressed a shell-studded beach, while on the southern end of the island a mere two feet of height separated ocean from land-anchored homes. The single looping road that serviced the long, narrow isle wound around outcrops of rock, through stands of Palmetto trees and past numerous houses, some almost as old and weathered as Charleston itself, others new confabulations of cedar and glass.

Within a few minutes, Sabrina could see ahead on their right, between the road and the beach, the E-shaped outline of the four-story Gaffe Island Inn. Sitting cater-corner on its elevated lot, it stretched window-studded arms out to the southeast, exposing the majority of its rooms to a spectacular ocean view, a view more than adequately reflected in its seasonal rates. Sabrina's heart began to thud, her gaze tracing the Inn's weathered, once-white-washed siding as the winding road carried the cab around behind the hotel, blocking the ocean momentarily from view. Not much farther, now. A quarter mile at most and she would see her house, her haven of safety, her refuge from the horror that life had become.

Please, God, don't let it have changed, she prayed, leaning forward in the seat, tense, terrified, her breath held. The road twisted again, threaded through rustling Palmetto trees before breaking into the open once more. And suddenly, there it was. Sabrina's beach house, perched on the edge of a sand-clad hill, solid and secure against the gloomy sky, accepting as if by right the obeisant kisses of the ocean upon its shell-strewn feet below. Sabrina, scarcely aware of her actions, got out of the cab and paid the driver who pulled slowly away, leaving her to the sound of the waves and the birds and her own heart pounding in her chest.

She stood motionless a long time, staring at the house, absorbing the feel of the small blue-and-white Victorian cottage built by her great-grandfather as a wedding gift for his bride. The two-story high structure faced the ocean and boasted gingerbreaded porches on both front and back and a one-story addition along the south side that housed a comfortable eat-in kitchen and carriage-house/stable turned garage. The living room occupied the entire first floor of the main structure, a large but cozy room liberally sown with overstuffed furnishings, dark wood and hurricane oil lanterns that shed a warmer, more homey glow than the electric lights her grandmother had had installed. Above lay three bedrooms and a bath, complete with claw-footed tub and Victorian brass fixtures. Three generations had lovingly enriched each room's appointments— handmade quilts, needlework samplers and candlewick spreads, to which Sabrina had added knitted afghans in shades of soft greens, pinks, beiges and blues, the colors of the ocean and its mystical environs. A repository of love and loving, the small, neat cottage had gifted Sabrina's family with shelter and solace for over a hundred years. This was where Sabrina and Charlie had spent their honeymoon, returning every few months throughout the seven miraculous years of their marriage. If Sabrina was to find Charlie anywhere, it would be here, in Amelia Feldon's bridal cottage.

She walked trance-like up the back porch stairs, her footsteps echoing in the oppressive heat. Whatever breeze had toyed with the sand and waves earlier had died now, leaving a void that sea-soughing and bird voice could not quite fill. Sabrina felt inordinately aware of the blood flowing in her body, the breath passing in and out of her lungs, as she ran her hand along the wooden porch railing, its surface cratered by time and oddly cool to the touch. She closed her eyes, stilled her mind and listened to the welcome whispered by the house, the beach, the ocean foaming gently sixty feet away. It clasped her like warm, comforting arms, enfolded her in an embrace at once joyous and questioning. *Why have you come alone?* the house murmured, a question echoed by the sand, the waves, the birds. *Why are you alone?*

She drew in a deep breath and walked to the door, rummaging in her purse for her keys as she moved.

Time slowed. Her actions elongated. Opening her purse, reaching inside, withdrawing the keyring, inserting the key into the lock, twisting it until the latch disengaged and the door swung inward with a mellow squeak seemed to take hours. Sabrina stared into the dark house, unable to make her feet move. Perhaps this wasn't as good an idea as she'd thought it would be. Perhaps even here there was too much of Charlie. Perhaps it would be better for her to go back to Buffalo.

But to do that she'd have to go in the cottage and call for another cab, a cab that would take her back to the airport, to a plane that would return her home. And then she'd have to face that shattered house again, the unbearable silence, the stains on the carpeting, the cold barren void where her life should be. That she knew she could not do, not again, not for a while at least. She knew, too, that wherever she went there would be emptiness and longing. And pain—she'd learned that well out in California, in the myriad faceless motels that had given her body the rest her spirit could not find. It had to be better here, among familiar, nurturing possessions that had not been violated, had not been torn apart, had not witnessed what should never have happened. It simply had to be. There was nowhere left for her to turn. Nowhere.

She shook her head, walked into the cottage and shut the door, cutting off the sounds of the world outside. The long hall, windowed only on each end where the front and back doors stood, was dark and gloomy. Little light spilled in from either the multi-windowed living room or the kitchen. The air felt musty, dank after standing so long closed away from life, and cold after the clinging heat of the cab ride.

Sabrina shivered and felt for the light switch on the wall near the door. Nothing happened. The hallway remained dark, despite her repeated flicking of the switch. She frowned and peered through the murk at the brass and frosted glass fixture hanging from the ceiling halfway down the long, narrow stretch of hall. *The bulb must be out,* she decided, trying the switch one last time. Still, her heart beat fearfully as she groped her way past the staircase on the right, beneath which nestled the original access door to the garage, now enclosed into a storage niche, and on to the kitchen archway beyond, visions of death and destruction dancing before her eyes.

Not a thing was out of place. Windows lined the front wall of the kitchen, affording a majestic view of Atlantic sunrises while breakfasting, though today the mass of clouds above allowed in not much more light than reached the hallway. Sabrina dropped her purse on the round, glass-topped wrought iron table and shivered again, glad now that she had dressed for Buffalo and not South Carolina weather. She pushed the switch on the wall near the door and again nothing happened. No warm, welcoming glow radiated out from the pierced-tin shades of the wrought iron chandelier suspended over the table, or from the converted gas wall fixtures mounted on either side of the ancient iron range. Her heart began to thud. Panic nibbled at the edges of her cope-ability. Her hands shook and her body felt weak and unresponsive. What was wrong? Had the doom that had spread over her life extended here, too? Was there no place where she could simply hide and be comforted like a child? Did God really hate her?

She clenched her teeth to keep from screaming, and abruptly the reason burst upon her, as bright as the lights that would not light up. Relief made her legs feel wobbly. It was the electricity. She had not called ahead to have it turned on. It had never occurred to her, Charlie had always taken care of that. Even when a sudden impulse would grab hold of her to pick up and spend a few days at the beach, he somehow always knew, had already called to have the cottage prepared before the idea even hit her. He knew her so very well. She hadn't thought that the lights would not be working because they always had been. She just hadn't thought about it.

She sighed then groped in a kitchen drawer for matches and lit the hurricane lamp that stood in the center of the table, smiling at the mellow glow it shed. She remembered all the times that she and Charlie had ignored the newly-turned-on electricity and ate by lamp light, read by lamp light, made love by lamp light, just as her mother and grandmother and great-grandmother had done. No more. Now the lamps would be her only companions, their warm glow as cold as the emptiness of their promises. Her smile faded and, clasping the lamp with trembling hands, she made her way carefully across the hall to the living room, gliding smoothly in her circle of illumination, its misty circumference a barrier that isolated her within a bubble of barrenness. She'd not willingly seek the soft shine of lamplight, not anymore. Lamplight was for sharing. She'd call and have the electricity turned on, today if possible. Gritting her teeth, she set the lamp down on the mahogany piecrust table in the far corner, beside the telephone.

But the telephone did not work, either, another of Charlie's little chores that she hadn't remembered. These things had simply worked whenever they arrived, and Sabrina, who before she married Charlie had come to the beach house only twice after her mother died, had had no real conception of the preparations that needed to be made days before leaving Buffalo. Indeed, she would have floundered long before now had Charlie not come into her life, for she had merely been going through the motions, existing each day in a vacuum, untouched by reality and the world around her. She would have drowned, as surely as if she had walked into the fathomless sea outside the windows.

She stood, now, staring at the ancient black telephone, at the arrow-slim line of its upright stance, the funnel-shaped mouthpiece, the earpiece dangling from its hook, and willed herself not to cry. She tried to look at it logically, and forgive herself. It was understandable that she would forget such things as turning on utilities, since she'd never really had to do it before. It would take time, that was all. There was no need to cry at every mistake, every failure. If she did, she would never survive, never have time to learn. She'd be too busy wiping away tears. She had to be strong, for Charlie's memory, if nothing else. She had to be strong for Charlie.

And she would be. In a little while. As soon as she could stop shaking. As soon as her mind began to work once again. Sabrina sank down onto the high-backed flowered chair that sat next to the telephone table and held herself very still, afraid even to open her eyes lest she lose control completely. She had no heat, no lights, no phone. She felt completely isolated, cut off from all contact with other people although she knew very well that there were neighbors just a few hundred yards away. But the thought of rising, walking out of her house and over to someone else's, terrified her. She would have to tell them what she wanted, and that she did not know. She would have to explain that for which she could not find words.

She sat very still, trying not to think, not even to breathe. The world faded. Even she disappeared, lost in an abyss of nothingness. All she could hear, all she was aware of, like a broken record deep inside her, was *please*. Just the one word: *please*. Over and over: *please, please, please*. Until at last the tiny, desolate voice softened, echoed slowly to a stop. And she returned.

She could hear birds and the ocean, see the misty glow of the oil lamp beside her through her closed lids, feel the chair's age-smoothed fabric beneath her body. How long she had been gone she did not know, but she felt ancient now, and very, very tired, as though she had fought a battle for life itself and won, coming away with a prize that suddenly had no value. She shuddered, wishing the nightmare would end and Charlie would come home to her. It had gone on long enough.

Blinking, Sabrina looked around the murky room, trying to remember what it was she needed to do. Finally, it came to her. If she was going to stay she had to somehow get the telephone and electricity turned on. And she'd need food, too, more than the few 'emergency' canned goods that sat silent in the cupboards. She felt cowed by the enormity of the tasks facing her, and thought with longing of the cab that had pulled so unconcernedly away. If only she had a car, these mountains would subside back into the molehills they really were.

A car. Sabrina gasped, her hands flying to her face. Oh, dear lord, she really must be thoroughly exhausted from her sleepless night not to have remembered the car. She rubbed her eyes hard and flexed her shoulders, allowing herself to laugh at her own stupidity. Of course she had a car. It sat waiting in the garage, a 1937 Oldsmobile that had been her grandfather's, dark gray and black with a real wood dash, wide running boards, and pearl gray mohair seats. Their 'beach car,' Charlie's pride and joy next to his cherished Nash Rambler. She could still remember riding in the back seat when she was just a little girl, her grandparents in the front, her parents following behind in their own year-old automobile. Dressed up for church on Sunday in a ruffled, crinolined yellow dress and shiny black maryjanes, white gloves on her hot, sweaty hands, clutching her 'special treat' ice cream cone on the way home, licking as fast as she could lest it drip on Granpa's like-new seat and she not get another the next time they visited.

That was before her father had died, so endlessly, so agonizingly, and soured her mother. His illness and death had ended vacations, abolished joy and laughter, and made life a burden to be suffered in silence, without the beach, without her grandparents or the car and its promise of sweet, sticky ice cream treats. Her grandfather had died two years later, just as her mother had begun to pull out of the depression into which she'd sunk, and Gramma had come to live with them. Without the car. Without the ice cream cones.

Sabrina was fifteen when her grandmother joined her husband, and eighteen when her mother first fell ill with the same monstrous disease that had taken her man. Eight years later, still bitter that the beach house had been left to Sabrina and not her, Judith Steves gave in to the cancer, leaving her daughter numb and guilt-ridden. It seemed now, to Sabrina, that all her life had been spent in the cold embrace of death. It had set its mark upon her years ago, and jealously guarded its treasured possession.

Perhaps that was why Charlie had had to die. She had begun to truly live for the first time in the warmth of the sun, the glow of love, and death could not allow that to continue. Deep within, Sabrina adjudged that what had happened, all those deaths, were really her fault, punishment for some grievous sin committed in the long-ago past. She just didn't know what sin it was.

She rose and went into the kitchen, retrieved her purse and keys, unlocked the kitchen access door and stepped down into the dark garage. Barely able to see in the gloom, she whacked her shin on the car bumper while groping her way to the outside door, which she opened out to provide as much light as possible. The car looked the same, felt the same, even smelled the same as she unlocked the driver's side and slid behind the wheel. Her hands stroked the lap belts that Charlie had installed, the only concession to modern safety he would allow to mar the classic car. But when she tried to start the engine only a dull click and total silence echoed on the sultry afternoon air.

The battery was dead. Not a spark of life remained to so much as tease her with false cranking. Sabrina sat clutching the wheel, refusing to give in to panic, and thought hard, ordering herself in her school teacher voice to go over the things Charlie used to do when they arrived at the house. How did he start the car? How did he cope with a lifeless battery?

Her movements precise and calculated to keep her mind in one piece, Sabrina slid out of the car and looked around the garage. Spare tires, two bamboo rakes, old broken porch furniture, tools, gardening paraphernalia and left-over cans of paint for both inside and outside the house spilled out from the old horse stalls on the left, leaving barely enough room for the car. On a shelf along the back wall she discovered a battery charger, a piece of equipment she didn't remember ever seeing before. Had it not been labeled clearly with a metal tag, she would not have known its purpose.

The green metallic box looked to be three feet square. A heavy metal clamp dangled from each side on thick coated wires, one black-handled, the other red. A gauge on the front would indicate when the battery was properly charged. It didn't seem complicated to use. All Sabrina had to do was raise the car's hood, somehow clamp the charger onto the battery and wait. There was nothing to it. Nothing at all.

She turned to the huge old car and ran her hands along the pointed hood, poking fingers into the grill, afraid to push or pull on anything too hard for fear of damaging it somehow. The gleaming gray hood remained solidly shut, not budging even an inch. Sabrina shook her head, feeling herself begin to shake. Damn it, why hadn't she ever watched Charlie work on the car? It was such a simple thing, raising the hood. Why couldn't she do it? Suddenly, she remembered the station wagon she had owned before she married Charlie. Inside, beneath the dash, there had been a handle to pull that popped open the hood. Relief washed through her. Her pent breath gusted out audibly. She smiled at her own silliness and opened the car door, slid again onto the velvety bench seat, and searched for the release handle.

She found none. Anxiety began to close her throat as her trembling fingers fumbled in vain over and under the smooth wooden dash. *Oh, dear lord, what am I to do, now?* she cried silently, gasping for breath. The garage tilted. Her vision darkened. Panic swooped down to enfold her in its steely talons. The car doors leaned in toward her, as if to crush her to death, and Sabrina flung herself from the car. She stumbled a few steps on the cold dirt floor, banging up against the shelves lining the rear wall, and found herself staring at the battery charger, at the electrical cord and grounded plug she had missed seeing before. Even had she been able to raise the hood, the charger would have been useless without a live electrical socket to plug it into. It was completely useless, just like she was.

A low rumble of thunder drowned her despairing cry. She backed away, toward the steps leading to the kitchen, tears streaming down her face. It was hopeless, she couldn't do it. She couldn't live on her own, without Charlie. She was too stupid, she couldn't cope, it wasn't worth it. Oh why, why hadn't she died with him? Why?

Wrapped in misery, Sabrina huddled on the steps, sobbing wretched, heart-broken tears. Rain began to spatter in huge drops outside the garage, splatting on the shingle roof with a lonely, hollow sound that underscored the isolation she felt. She cried for Charlie and for herself, terrified by the thought of facing the rest of her life alone. It had been hard enough before she knew Charlie, before she knew what love and togetherness really was. But now it was impossible. Sabrina found herself wishing her heart would literally break in two and release her from the hell that life had become.

"Sabrina? Is that you?"

Sabrina gasped, startled by the deep voice. She looked up, swiping at the tears on her cheeks, to see a murky shape darkening the open garage door. She tried to find her voice but couldn't, tried to stem tears that would not stop flowing.

"Sabrina?" The shape moved closer, toward the steps where she sat, the shadows parting to reveal a man of sixty or so, broad and solid of body, scant of hair, weathered and salty of skin—Geoffrey Simmonds, who owned the house next to hers, two hundred yards down the beach. "I saw the light in the house, I thought you might need some help. Are you all right?"

The concern in his face, the worry in his eyes, were Sabrina's undoing. She could find no words in answer. All she could do was shake her head, her lips pressed tight to keep her sobs from echoing into the air. Geoff Simmonds dropped onto the step beside her and folded his long, strong arms around her quivering body.

"It's all right, Sabrina," he said in his soft drawl. "Don't cry. Whatever's wrong, we'll fix it together. It's all right."

He had come to the funeral, all the way to Buffalo, it was one of the few things that Sabrina could remember clearly about that day, Geoffrey Simmonds' soft brown eyes red with unashamed weeping, his big hands enfolding her icy fingers, the quiet, solid reassurance of his presence so very far from home. He and Charlie had been great friends, spending long hours together over both chess and cribbage boards, taking Sabrina for lazy cruises on Geoff's twenty-six-foot sailboat, and sharing fine wine and cheese on both hot summer nights and cold winter days. The burly, balding sixty-one-year-old retired investment broker lived on Gaffe Island year round, as did most of its inhabitants. Divorced for fifteen years, he had three grown children and seven grandchildren who visited him occasionally. He was warm and amicable, almost a father figure to Sabrina. She considered him a part of her family. She and Charlie had always looked forward to the time they would spend with Geoffrey Simmonds.

Through her tears, she told him now of her flight from Buffalo, her arrival at the beach house to find herself without electricity or a car, her inability to do even as simple a thing as lift the hood on the Oldsmobile. Her tears dried as she talked, leaving her feeling empty and desiccated, as though she really didn't exist anymore. It was only echoes that were left, wispy vestiges of what once had been. She sighed, a deeply hopeless sound.

"It really doesn't matter about the hood," she said, her body slumping with exhaustion. "Without electricity, the battery charger's useless, even if I did know how to hook it up, which I don't. I haven't the slightest idea. I haven't the slightest idea how to do anything."

"What you need, my dear, is some sleep," Geoff said. "You'd be amazed at how much one can learn while one is sound asleep." He smiled and put an arm around her again. "And I think something to eat would be appropriate, also. You haven't eaten for quite a while, have you?"

"No. I haven't really been hungry. It just seems like too much effort to eat."

"Then it's settled. You'll come back to my place and I'll feed you. Then we'll run into town and see about your electricity. No arguments, now," he cautioned, rising and pulling Sabrina to her feet, stilling her protest. "I've got three kids, remember? I'm an expert in squishing excuses. I haven't lost an argument in years, especially not to someone your size. You go blow out that oil lamp and make sure your doors are locked, and I'll pull the car up closer so you don't drown in that downpour out there. It won't last much longer," he cast his sailor's eye at the leaden clouds, "but there's no sense in getting any wetter than you have to. Hurry along, now!"

He squeezed her shoulders gently and sauntered off to retrieve his car. Sabrina watched until he was out of sight, then turned, mounted the steps and reentered the cottage, following Geoffrey's instructions with a somewhat bemused air. *Imagine him driving over here,* she thought, carefully blowing out the oil lamp. Geoff Simmonds had never driven to her house before. Whatever the weather he always walked down the white sand beach, letting the tide play with his toes. He must have known about the lights and the car, just as Charlie would have, she concluded.

A small, grateful smile curved her lips, the burden of despair lifting. There was someone to help, to guide her, at least until she got her own feet under her. If she couldn't have Charlie, at least she had that. It was better than nothing. As she checked the lock on the back door, Sabrina decided that she would stay on at the cottage for a week or two. Maybe longer. She could call Anne from Geoff's house. The hard knot of tears that choked her began to dissolve when finally she ran down the steps to where her rescuer sat waiting in a low-slung little MG Midget.

* * *

The night turned cool after the rain. A gentle breeze slowly dried the wet sand. Phosphorescent ocean swells rolled with lazy abandon, glittering into myriad points of light as they shattered like glass on the moonlit shore, an echo of the twinkling stars in the heavens above. The half-moon, released now from its cloudy prison, glinted on darkened windows, picked out objects in sharp, monochromatic relief—driftwood flung up on the sand, dark rock poking through sparse sea grass, a lone figure motionless on the top of a dune.

Sabrina still wore the wool-blend skirt but she was barefoot now, her ankles and feet coated with cool, gritty sand. She huddled into a bulky sweater that fell halfway to her knees and wrapped her arms around her body for warmth. Stray wisps of her midnight-dark hair danced in the breeze, swaying in rhythm to the tranquil dance of the ocean. She held an almost-full glass of pale wine from which she sipped occasionally, although she gave the impression that she had no awareness of the action. She stared unblinking at the faint luminescence of the deepest water. Moonlight glittered on the tears that tracked slowly down her hollow cheeks. But for the lifting of her hand, the parting of her lips when she drank, she could have been made of stone herself, or sand.

A warm glow illumined the window of her living room, thirty yards down the beach. Soft lamplight melded with the serenity of the rain-washed night. Sabrina's tracks across the sand stood stark in the moon's glow, oval pools of inky blackness cutting across the diaphanous gleam of nacre-studded sand. She stood enfolded in wave-filled silence, surrounded by darkness and the echo of a life that had ceased to exist. She saw, from the corner of her eye, the stocky figure striding through the sand, his movement sure and steadfast on the unstable surface, his bare feet obscuring her marks as he drew closer and climbed to where she stood. But she did not turn, or speak, or acknowledge his presence in any way. Her gaze stayed on the undulating expanse of water. A deep breath lifted her chest, and she once again sipped at the dwindling wine, finishing the last taste. Beside her, Geoff Simmonds watched the ocean swells in matching silence, his hands thrust deep into the pockets of a dark brown windbreaker. Long minutes passed before Sabrina spoke, her voice soft with anguish.

"He's so close, Geoff. I can feel him, waiting for me. For the first time since that day, I can feel him. Oh, God, how I miss him!"

Geoff looked at her, his face quiet, watchful. He didn't speak. Sabrina looked at her feet buried in the chilling grains of sand and let her gaze move down the dune, across the beach, and back out to the rolling depths of the Atlantic.

"I've been standing here, trying to move. If I walked out there, just let the water close over my head, I could be with him. Forever. It would be easy. So easy." She sighed. "But I'm such a coward. I can't make my feet move. I want to go to him, but my feet just won't move."

Geoff reached out and silently gathered her into his strong, warm embrace. He held her, comforting her with his loving touch. Sabrina could feel the words he did not speak, had no need to use, and they eased the pain in her soul, lifted the ache from her heart. After a few minutes, she raised her head and smiled sadly at her friend.

He returned the smile, then took her hand and led her down the dune, back toward the welcoming light shining from her window. They walked in the water, letting the cool waves break gently on their feet. Water droplets glittered like diamonds in the moonlight. When they reached the steps leading up to her front porch, Geoff gave her hand a comforting squeeze.

"It's never easy, Sabrina, but it does get easier," he told her, his candid eyes gazing into hers. "You're not the same woman you were before you married Charlie. You don't have to drift just because he's not here. Remember that. And sleep well. Take a vacation from what happened, and sleep well for a change. Tomorrow is another day." He smiled.

"And another day is a new beginning," she said, completing his favorite adage with an answering smile. "Thanks, Geoff. I will sleep well, now. Good night."

He kissed her cheek and turned away. Sabrina watched his rolling gait until he disappeared into the darkness, her stare again seeking the ocean vastness before she mounted the stairs. *Grief and despair are funny, they do strange things to your mind,* she mused as she climbed, subconsciously counting the fifteen high steps the way she always had since she was a little girl. She knew very well that if she had walked out into the ocean and drowned herself, Charlie would not be waiting for her at all. He'd be too angry at her, and she'd only end as alone as she was now. But she had come so close to convincing herself that it was right, that he wanted her to join him in death. Not until she spoke the words aloud to Geoff did she realize the self-pity inherent in them.

At the top of the steps she turned and looked down at the beach, sweeping her gaze over the sand and waves and on to the glittering heavens cupped above. The night smelled clean and new, with just a faint hint of salt and seaweed in the freshening breeze. Sabrina took a deep, cleansing breath, reveling in the serene beauty surrounding her. There was just enough of Charlie here for her to feel comfortable and safe. Not overwhelmed like she had in Buffalo, or cast adrift the way she'd been in California, but consoled and calmed, able to touch him, to caress his memory without shattering into a million pieces. Perhaps it was the soporific murmur of the waves, the gentle whisper of the wind, the eerie plaintive call of the seabirds. Perhaps it was the house itself, a place of love and warmth, a place not empty but filled with the ghosts of those who went before her, that gave her a feeling of safety, an anchorage in the storm of her life.

Or perhaps it was just time itself that had begun its inexorable work within her, healing her despite herself. But whatever the reason, somehow she did feel stronger standing here with the sound and the smell of the ocean rippling around her, the feel of the aged wood porch beneath her bare feet. She felt stronger even with the lapses into despair and her reliance on Geoff, capable of sleeping through the night, capable of wanting to wake up in the morning. Geoff was right. She didn't have to drift anymore. She was not the same woman she was when she had married Charlie. And though he was gone now, she didn't have to turn back into that Sabrina. She could remain who she was.

I'll stay here, she decided, entering the cottage and locking the door securely behind her. *I won't go back to Buffalo. This will be my home from now on, my safety, my refuge.* She smiled, lifting the lamp and carrying it carefully up the stairs. Tomorrow she would have electricity and a telephone that worked. Even now she had a car that ran, thanks to Geoff Simmonds' jumper cables. She would move slowly, take each day as it came and rebuild her life from within the protecting shelter of this house. It would not always be easy, she knew, but as long as she remained within this sanctuary, where the horror could not touch her, she could do it.

Her smile fading, Sabrina paused at the top of the stairs a moment, opposite the bathroom door, staring down the hall at the door to the bedroom she and Charlie had shared. Large and filled with dark mahogany furniture, it faced the murmuring ocean, greeted the rising sun each morning. They had often made love with the sun's first, tentative, delicate rays sheening their bodies with gold. Deep inside, Sabrina could feel her carefully built serenity begin to crumble, and she willed herself to be very, very still—her mind, her heart, her soul itself, still and dead in the misty warm glow of the lamp. At last she turned her head and looked at the closed door to the middle room, the one they used for storage. It also held two single brass beds. Sabrina rejected it, not wanting an empty bed beside her to further erode the uncertain peace she had just discovered.

She finally turned and entered the room that lay beside the head of the staircase. The smallest of the three, it contained a high, double four-poster bed of age-darkened cherry, a small dresser, and a tall gleaming wardrobe. The single window overlooked the street at the back of the cottage. This, now, would be her room, her sanctuary from memories and pain.

Sabrina braved the memories she feared to take a nightgown and clothing for the next day from the master bedroom and carry them into the small bedroom. She ignored the vestiges of Charlie in the bathroom—his shaving gear, toothbrush, cologne—and, shivering with cold, splashed icy water on her face and brushed her teeth with her usual thoroughness. She hesitated only slightly before shaking a sleeping pill into her hand, knowing that without it, despite her hopeful resolutions, she would not sleep well this first night, if at all. It took only fifteen minutes after she'd ascended to the upper floor before she climbed up into the ancient bed, using the bed-step that stood waiting to assist sleepers in reaching its great height. The colorful quilt, a Dresden Glass Dish in rose, blue and gold, made by her grandmother when her mother was very small, Sabrina had carefully folded over the maple quilt stand in the corner. The sheets felt glacial. She was glad to have two wool blankets atop her. Slowly, her ears alert to unfamiliar sounds drifting through the open window, her lids drooped until at last she fell fast asleep, alone in the same bed she had slept in as a child, the bed where she would wake alone in the morning.

To a new day and a new beginning.

Alone.

CHAPTER NINE

The day started out bad and deteriorated from there. The motel forgot his wake-up call. HIs alarm didn't go off. Mitch made it to the airport with barely five minutes to spare. He left the rental car in the hands of an airline ticket agent and raced for the gate, his empty stomach growling and gurgling acid.

It took him less than five minutes to regret making the flight. The plane bucked like an enraged bronco while lighting flashed inches from the windows and rain pelted the fuselage like enemy salvos. Mitch declined to purchase the proffered breakfast—as did most of the other passengers—not sure exactly where his stomach was but certain it was nowhere in the vicinity of the airplane. He did, unfortunately, accept coffee, which a particularly violent lurch caused the flight attendant to spill down the front of his white shirt before he could lay a hand on it. He spent the remainder of the trip sitting in a chill puddle and cursing the day he was born.

The flight arrived late and heavy fog at the Charleston airport kept them circling for an hour and a half. They landed just before eleven and Mitch debated whether to grab something to eat in the terminal before picking up yet another rental car, or risk starving to death somewhere on Gaffe Island. He chose starvation in the end. The sooner he talked to the Compton woman, the sooner he could get back to his paper mountain in Washington. He shook his head in disgust as he threaded his way through the crowded terminal toward the Avis counter. He must be crazy. All he'd thought about these last five years was returning to the field, and now that he was here all he could think about was getting back to the office. Of course, this wasn't exactly what he had in mind for a field assignment, but lord! Beggars shouldn't be choosers, or regretters. Should they?

The Avis people couldn't supply him with the full-size car he requested. He had to settle for a compact, and the thought of accordioning his oversize body into its minuscule interior didn't improve his mood any. Before he got in the car he took it out on the telephone, punching in his office number with savage, right-handed jabs. Even Kelsey's dulcet purr didn't do much to mitigate his angry frustration.

"You're not still in Buffalo, I hope?"

"No," Mitch growled. "I'm not."

"Then you just overslept, right? You're on your way in?"

"Not quite." Mitch plucked at his shirt, pulling the damp cloth away from his sweating skin. "Actually,

I'm in South Carolina. Charleston. I'm sweaty, wearing day-old clothes and a cup of coffee, very unhappy and waiting for a rental car."

"You're where? You have a lunch meeting with the Chief at one, Mr. Lawson. Something about the budget you butchered? And a report? He's been down here twice already this morning, looking for you." Mitch opened his mouth, but Kelsey spoke right over him. "I promised him you hadn't forgotten, that you probably got in really late last night and just overslept. He growled, you know how he does when he doesn't believe you, then he said you better be back in town, your two days are up, you're not getting any more, the field office and the Marshals can finish what needs finishing and he wants you in his office at one sharp, for lunch. Barbecued, I believe he put it. Then he added something about being an idiot. I'm not sure if he meant you or him. I think you're in trouble, because you're certainly not in Washington. Shall I get you the next plane out?"

"Tell the Chief," Mitch snapped, "to stuff his meeting. I'm not leaving until I get what I came for. And get off my case, Kelsey. It's not my fault the merry widow's afflicted with wanderlust. Damned woman can't seem to stay put. I was right, it is our boy, Biaggi, though just try to prove it. And I'll be damned if I'll trust this to a field office. Or the freaking Marshals. What the hell would they know about a fifteen-year-old case? *My* fifteen-year-old case?"

"They could read the file," Kelsey suggested softly.

Mitch saw red. It was all he could do not to yank the phone off the wall.

"Whose side are you on, Kelsey? And what the hell could they learn from the file, anyway? There are unanswered questions they'd never know to ask, not unless they knew what *isn't* in the file. And I'm the only one left who knows that, because what's not in the file is in my head. This is my case, has been from day one, and I'll be damned if I'll let some piss-ant junior flunky still wet behind the ears screw it up. You can tell the Chief that if he doesn't like the fucking way I do my job, he can do it himself. I'll be back when I'm done here, and not before."

Kelsey's eloquent silence thrummed through the wires straight to Mitch's recalcitrant conscience. He rubbed his eyes hard, and sighed.

"I'm sorry, Kelsey. Really. It's not your fault, it's mine. I've had a hell of a morning, and the day's not promising to get any better. I should be back soon, God willing. Another day or two is all, unless the Compton woman takes off again. And I'm not taking any bets. According to the detective in charge, she's a real nut case. And there's only a snowball's chance in hell that she knows anything, or is even sane enough to tell me if she does."

Kelsey laughed, which inexplicably made Mitch feel better.

"Apology accepted, though you better return bearing gifts. Expensive ones. I'll think of something to keep the Chief from awaiting your arrival with barbecue skewers in hand. Where are you staying?"

"I don't know yet, I just arrived. Somewhere on Gaffe Island—a prophetic name if I ever heard one. I'll let you know later, unless I have to camp out on the beach or something, which wouldn't surprise me, the way my luck's been going. Give Dan Jeffers an update, will you? I may still need him. Call my mother, tell her I'm out of town for a couple of days, and I think I've got a date tomorrow night with Alicia. Cancel that. Oh, and Maureen too, let her know, she'll have to take the boys for hockey registration if I'm not back in time."

"Yes, sir!" The vocal military salute reverberated in his ears. "And I'll water your plants, feed the gerbils, wash your socks, get your gro—"

"Ahh, don't give me any smart talk, Kelsey, I'm not in the mood. Just do your job and let me do mine, ok?"

"Oh, it *has* been a bad day so far, hasn't it?" Kelsey sighed. "It's okay. Calm down and don't worry. I haven't let you down yet, have I? You just go do what you have to do, and get back as soon as you can—at least while you still have an office to come back to. And Mr. Lawson," she added, a sly note creeping in beneath the sultry softness, "try not to chew up the Compton woman too badly."

Mitch hung up, chuckling, then made a face as he picked up his overnight bag. Having something small enough to stuff under a plane seat eliminated frustrating waits at baggage carousels, but it also meant he'd have to suffer his coffee-saturated shirt and suit again tomorrow. To say nothing of the dearth of underwear in the half-empty case. Things like this had never happened to him before when he was out in the field, not that he could recall. Everything always went smooth as glass. He just wasn't living right anymore, that was it. Or he was getting old. There was always that. Getting old. Shit.

Mitch folded himself behind the wheel of an obstinate, mustard-gold Chevy Metro. His head brushed the roof and his knees bumped the steering column. He man-handled the toy car into and through historic old Charleston, seeing little of its quaint picturesque streets through temper-narrowed eyes while, with quick sidelong glances, he consulted the road map sprawled beside him. The car stalled at every red light, and wallowed whenever he stepped on the gas. The windshield washer fluid tank was dry, the wipers streaked the rain-soaked glass, the left turn signal worked only when it felt like it and the air conditioner didn't work at all. He got lost three times before finally locating the James Island Bridge.

Sweat streamed down his face and darkened the back and sides of his suit coat by the time he crossed over to Gaffe Island. Opening the window to the humid, damp fog did little to alleviate the smothering discomfort or the claustrophobic feel of the car. Mitch drove along with wet palms slick on the wheel, singularly unappreciative of the eerie, captivating fog-shrouded seascape spread out around him. He located the Compton woman's quaint gingerbreaded Victorian cottage on the first pass, then pulled off the side of the road just beyond the short driveway. He wrestled himself out of his sopping coat, yanked off his tie, and adjusted the side-view mirror to reflect the two-story house behind him, across the street. He could barely breathe in the sweltering weather. Sweat stung into his eyes as he watched the Compton place for signs of life and his mind roamed back over his second, and last, day in Buffalo.

They had met that morning as prearranged, Mitch, Burke and Webster, at ten in the faculty parking lot of the University's Main Street campus. From there they'd walked to Professor Compton's office. The field agent still radiated antagonism over Mitch's close-kept silence, as well as the way Mitch had dismissed him after renting his own car. The silence had grown overbearing by the time the three men reached the economics building. They discovered the professor's office had been cleaned out and re-assigned six weeks earlier, Compton's possessions consigned to four cardboard boxes which had been shoved in the back of a closet until the widow deigned to claim them. The new Assistant Dean of Economics, a short, thin, nervous man of thirty-six whose books and papers now filled the small space, hovered anxiously outside the door, which seemed to make Webster uneasy. Mitch, backed by years of practice, ignored everyone and everything except the task at hand.

He paced the room thoughtfully, absorbing its feel and gazing long out the tall, old-fashioned windows at the serene, tree-lined academic walks below, watching graduate students stride to and from classes, as Compton often must have. Mitch sat behind the desk, his hands shuffling papers, wishing Compton's chair still remained. This one was even lower than the one in Burke's office. Finally, he had pulled out the abandoned boxes to paw through the books, papers and personal mementos left behind, not an easy task considering the jumbled condition they were in. He didn't learn much, but he did discover how Compton had been found. Mitch had carried the thick, oversize leather-bound book with him when the three policemen left at two-thirty, leaving assistant dean Mark Adler hopelessly behind in his work.

They'd stopped for a late lunch before attempting to beard the widow in her den. Rush hour traffic congested the streets by the time they'd finished, the brisk air filled with revving engines, tooting horns, and children's laughter. It was a nice street, Larchmont Avenue, full of flowers and families, puppy dogs, station wagons and backyard pools, a quiet, peaceful enclave within walking distance of Compton's office. Mitch had stood on the front stoop and watched a touch football game unfold in the park across the way, wishing he lived in a place like this, where the world didn't intrude and life was lived in harmony and safety. Then Ray Burke moved, descended the steps, and Mitch abruptly remembered why they were there —because the world had intruded, because the safety was a sham. Because Charles Philip Compton had been brutally and viciously deprived of his peaceful, serene life.

They'd checked the garage and found the car within, Mitch's pounding heart not slowing until the next-door neighbor informed them that Mrs. Compton had left once again, this time for South Carolina. Mitch began to wonder about her, what sort of woman she was. He picked up telltale clues in the empty house when Anne Bradley let them in. He concluded that Charlie's wife was woman of quiet, somewhat old-fashioned taste, who liked greens and blues and earth tones in muted shades. She was also a woman who liked to cook, judging by the culinary apparatuses in the kitchen, and a woman who left pieces of herself scattered in each room—hand-knit afghans and sweaters, dried flower arrangements, nostalgic prints on the walls. And yet it was obvious that the whole house revolved around Compton, each room laid out for his comfort and convenience. Mitch decided that his estimation in Burke's office had been correct. The Compton woman was weak and clingy, living not for herself but through her man. A shadow-person who had folded when tragedy struck, a woman who all but ceased to exist upon Compton's death. No wonder she couldn't face this house.

His imagination had restored the house to the condition in which Sabrina had found it that fateful July day. His professional eye detected the faint trail of blood ascending the stairs. Graphic descriptions from the police report replayed in his head as he entered each room. Still he had trouble sympathizing with her pain and fear, simply because he had no patience with clingy, dependent women. They made him feel unaccountably guilty, their helplessness evoking a like helplessness within himself. As if he were somehow responsible for their vulnerability, for the pain and anguish they suffered. That made him angry, a deep burning anger that ate at him like acid, made him snappish and even more intolerant, until in the end he felt that these women deserved the awful things that happened to them. They caused such things to happen by their very powerlessness to stop them.

He didn't really believe that, not deep down, but the doubt and hesitation he sensed within himself frightened him, made him even more irate. He usually avoided weak, clingy women. He wasn't looking forward to enduring the Compton woman's tears and self-pity, not at all. It only irritated him the more that he'd had to follow her to South Carolina, waste another day because she was the helpless, dependent type. He'd really like to strangle her. She should have stayed home, where she belonged.

Activity in the car's mirror pulled his thoughts and eyes to the present. The garage door opened, folding out to the side, giving Mitch a dim view of the long, narrow interior—two box-stalls on the left and a pre-World War II car that appeared in mint condition. The Compton woman emerged with a barrel-chested man who looked to be in his early sixties. They spoke for a few minutes, the woman's eyes dark on his sun-tanned face, then he embraced her warmly and walked off around the side of the house, disappearing down the hill to the beach. He walked with a rolling gait, the way a sailor might.

Mitch stared at the Compton woman, studying her face, her clothing, her body language. She seemed thinner than she had in the pictures Mitch had seen, her bare arms stick-like and her skin sallow against the yellow tank top she wore, her hipbones noticeable beneath the red and yellow print skirt. She had wedge-soled sandals on her feet. Mitch raised a brow at the lost, wistful way she watched the man walk away. Then she squared her shoulders and re-entered the garage. She backed the car into the short driveway, got out to fold the door closed, and climbed once more behind the wheel. Mitch grabbed his map, spreading it out across the steering wheel, letting a corner stick out the open window, and bent his head as if in study. The big black and gray car, an Oldsmobile built around 1934 or '35, Mitch estimated, slowly picked up speed and passed him, the dark-haired driver merely glancing at the 'tourist' bent over his map.

Mitch waited until she was almost out of sight—a near-fatal mistake given the fractious nature of the car he drove—then started up the Metro and jerked after her down the road, wondering about the man with whom she'd been so chummy. Burke had said she was clean, no sign of any extra-marital involvement. But maybe he was wrong. Burke hadn't known about the beach house, he'd been totally surprised when Mrs. Bradley had told them about it. His jaw had dropped clear to China, joining Andy Webster's. Mitch had merely shook his head, disgusted at the lack of quality in police investigations today, both local and federal. Maybe this man went with the beach. Maybe that was why he hadn't shown up anywhere before now. Maybe the widow's grief wasn't all so disconsolate. There just might be more method than madness to her interminable flights from tragedy.

Maybe, just maybe, the Compton woman wasn't as clean and angelic as she seemed to be. Maybe she really did have the answers he needed. Mitch's eyes began to sparkle. This might not turn out such a bad field assignment after all.

CHAPTER TEN

Sabrina braked carefully on the damp pavement, stopping for the red light at the edge of town. She looked at her watch. Twelve-forty-five, was that all? It seemed she'd been up for days already, and here it was only just after lunchtime. Early to bed and early to rise might make you healthy, et. al., as the old saw promised, but it also made for a very long day to be gotten through. She'd already walked the beach, cleaned half a year's accumulation of dust from the house, dragged out the old wicker front porch furniture and made lists of what she needed in Gaffe. Whatever would she do to fill the endless afternoon hours?

The small town hadn't changed, its sleepy Southern look unaffected by the fog which the sun was beginning to dissipate. Light glinted off cars parked along the curbs. Heat shimmered on the pavement, distorting Sabrina's vision, making her stomach roll and reminding her that she hadn't eaten lunch. She scanned the street for a parking spot as she inched past ancient, salt-weathered clapboard shops, most needing paint and roofing tiles, until she neared the grocery store, owned and run by the same family for over eighty years. It had once been the Island's only general store. Now it was the largest and most successful place in the Main Street shopping district, though its hand-painted sign looked as weathered as all the rest.

Sabrina spotted an empty space nearby and pulled the Oldsmobile slantwise into the curb between yellow marker lines. She sat a moment, staring at the old hitching rails that still lined the sidewalk, hearing echoes of Charlie's voice. *We ought to put reins on this thing. I always feel guilty that we don't tie it up when we come to town.*

She got out of the car before tears could rise to drown her and fumbled in her purse for the lists she'd made. The grocer, the butcher, the florist, the library. And she'd need to eat, too, she'd treat herself to something special, celebrate her arrival at the beach. She'd linger as long as possible, waste as much of the afternoon as she could, not leaving until evening hours lapped close to her heels. She looked to her left, planning where to start, barely noting the ugly gold sub-compact car that pulled into a newly vacated space three stores from where she stood. She had turned away, heading for the library, before the tall, solid sweat-caked man behind the wheel emerged into the heat-soaked humidity of downtown Gaffe.

"Well, gracious me! Where have you been, Sabrina Compton? I expected you early last month."

Caroline Lydia Gardiner McMasters, white-haired and reed-thin, clad in a lace-trimmed, ankle-length summer frock hand constructed over a century ago, and known to one and all as Miss Caroline, Gaffe Island's sole librarian, waggled her ancient, aristocratic-looking head.

"I found those books your Charlie asked about, I knew we had them, in the basement storeroom just as I thought they'd be. No one's looked at them for years. They've been waiting right here, all dusted off and ready to go."

Papery, age-trembling hands set three thick volumes on the old oak counter. The tarnished gold edgings of the books gleamed softly in the strengthening sunlight that filtered through the beveled glass of the library's carved doors. Sabrina stared at the tomes, at the handsome, worn tooled-leather covers, unable to speak.

Why had she come here? What was she to do, now? She had forgotten that Charlie had asked Miss Caroline to locate the oldest books she could find on the history of Gaffe Island and Charleston Bay. He always went as close to the era as he could when reading history. It was less distorted that way, he asserted. More accurate, unfiltered by time, tradition or judgment. He'd been fascinated by the name of Gaffe Island, the canny play on sound given its proximity to the ocean—gaff being a support for a sail or a fishing hook, and *gaffe* the French word for a blunder. He wanted to know who had named the island. Had it originally been spelled with an 'e' or had that been added later, by some clever wit?

"Is something wrong, my dear?"

Miss Caroline's cracked voice startled Sabrina, made her jump. She caught her breath with a tiny gasp. She blinked, shook her head and backed slowly away, unable to take her eyes off the ancient volumes beneath the librarian's equally ancient hand.

"No. Nothing's wrong. I-I need a couple of books for myself. I-I'll just go see what I can find."

She turned away, burying herself in the depths of heavy oak stacks, fighting a desire to scream. What could she do? How would she ever manage to get out of this horrible place without falling completely apart? All she wanted was peace and safety, a refuge filled with restful silence, not painful memories and agonizing explanations. Perhaps she should simply take the history books, as though Charlie waited for them, for her, at the house. It was by far the easiest thing to do. It would give her time to gather strength, to learn how to face the unacceptable, to find words that would not pierce her like a knife with every repetition. Sabrina rubbed her arms and tried to let go of the tension that stiffened her shoulders and knotted her stomach. That was what she would do. She would smile and take the books and leave explanations for another day.

Her decision made, she finally was able to concentrate on the task at hand. She perused titles until she found the section she sought. At random she reached out and snatched two volumes from the shelves: Carol Burnett's life story, *One More Time*, and *Shelly: Also Known As Shirley* by Shelly Winters. She stared at the dust jackets, wondering if she should put them back and try to find something more appealing. She usually read biographies of historical figures, the lives of people long dead, whose trials and tribulations could not touch her here in the present. But she found, when she looked again at the shelves, that she had no more energy for selecting books. What she had in her hands would have to do. They would, at least, get her out of the library.

She walked around the ornate shelves to the checkout desk, where Miss Caroline marked return-date cards with careful precision. She smiled at the librarian and handed her the two books, but did not speak, bending her head to rummage in her purse for her library card. When at last she found it and looked up, her gaze snagged on the thick, old volumes of local history. She knew she couldn't bear to even touch them. With birdlike movements, Miss Caroline recorded the two autobiographies Sabrina had chosen, then reached for the first of the history books. Sabrina's heart lurched. She spoke before she knew she had opened her mouth.

"I-I won't be taking those, Miss Caroline." Her voice shook, its tone rich with suppressed tears. "I don't need them. Charlie isn't... didn't come with me, this time."

"Oh, my. I am sorry to hear that. I do so enjoy it when he stops in to see me." Her canny green eyes, bright with curiosity, narrowed in thought. "I assume he had to remain behind because of his teaching, this is such a busy time for him, isn't it? I'll just keep these set aside, for the next time." She paused, startled, when Sabrina shook her head. "Oh, dear, there isn't something wrong between you, is there?"

"No. No, we just— I-I mean—" Trembling violently, Sabrina picked up her two books, hugged them close to her breast. "Charlie's dead, Miss Caroline," she said, her words spilling out in an uneven rush. "He was killed. In July. Just before his birthday. That's why he's... not here. That's why I won't need those books. Not ever."

Sabrina turned and half-ran to the beautifully carved entry doors, unable to bear the look of incredulous shock on Miss Caroline's soft, wrinkled face, the dentured mouth that gaped open. She knew that if she lingered even a moment longer, there in the place where the awful words had been spoken, where they echoed on still, she would burst into hysterical tears or begin screaming like a mad woman until they had to take her away, sedate her into senselessness as they had before. She could not bear the humiliation. But more than that, she didn't think she would ever be able to regain control if she once again lost it. Pain and grief would devour her and she would cease to exist, as surely as Charlie had. The thought alone was attractive enough to terrify her thoroughly.

A tall, sandy-haired man in a rumpled suit pushed the library's door open for her as she neared them. Sabrina barely glanced at him. She muttered a thank you and fled out into the cloying heat of the afternoon. She needed to put distance between herself and the words she had spoken and so she moved swiftly down the street, almost running, not stopping her headlong rush until she reached her car. She did not hear the cawing scream of gulls overhead, nor feel the give of sun-softened pavement beneath her feet. And she didn't see the man step from the library to stand staring after her in frowning concentration.

She tossed the two books on the car's front seat, certain now she would not read them. The memories attendant on their acquisition made it too painful even to look at them. Then she shut the door and stood with her hands pressed to the roof of the car, her eyes closed tight, gasping as the almost-scorching heat seared through her skin, percolating into her blood and bones. She plunged for safety into its cauterizing feel and let it boil away the panic and tears, bake hard the fear and anger, until her heart shriveled, her trembling at last stopped, and once again she felt desert-dry and empty inside. Her eyes, when she finally opened them, watered in the brilliant sun. She straightened slowly. Her hands fell from the hot metal roof. They ached dully and her palms had reddened. She wondered idly, caught in an emotionless void, if they would blister. Not that it mattered. Nothing mattered, anymore. Not one damned thing.

She moved back onto the sidewalk and approached the grocery store, pausing near the raised wooden fruit and vegetable bins that flanked the door in front of the shop's mottled glass windows. Heaps of autumn color iridescing in the sun's rays beckoned to passers-by, enticing with promises of freshness and flavor—tomatoes and broccoli, potatoes, apples, grapes and winter squash. Sabrina stared unseeing at the displays. After a blank moment she moved on, walked further down the street, past the grocer's door, past the butcher shop, the drug store, the imported china shop, the barber's spinning red-and white pole. There she stopped and glanced across the heat-shimmered street to where the florist's windows exhibited a less flashy fall format than that of the grocery. White, yellow, rust and orange mums and asters nestled amidst the cool greenery of fern fronds and the delicate tracery of baby's breath. Here and there, the pinks and reds of carnations and fall roses peeked out, lending a piquant, saucy note to the larger flowers' sedate, placid aura. Charlie had loved flowers, fall flowers most of all. The vibrancy of their colors, he'd said, echoed nature's last defiant shout in the face of monotone winter to come.

Holes opened in her brittle blanket of protection. Sabrina turned her head away and took a deep breath. She needed more time, time to mend and strengthen her protective emptiness before she could continue with her tasks. She glanced at her watch. It was one-thirty. She would eat first, linger over a lonely meal she no longer wanted until she felt able to withstand the onrush of memories that came with every step she took in this quaint little town. She would buy the time she needed by enduring a solitary and barren repast. Then she would quickly finish what she had to do, and return to the cottage to another meal just as solitary and barren. Perhaps she would have that carved into her side of the headstone Charlie had chosen: *Here lies Sabrina Steves Compton who, but for a brief moment, lived a life solitary and barren.*

She pressed her lips tight together, crossed the street and entered a small, moderately-priced cafe that catered mostly to local residents. The Lamplighter Inn, which sat on a small rise overlooking Gaffe's harbor and the Atlantic beyond, boasted a Southern-style menu, picturesque decor, and huge windows affording an ocean view, but the service was slow and the quality of the food was mediocre for all that it touted down-home 'authenticity.' It was also crowded most of the time with noisy tourists who didn't seem to mind paying inflated prices. Sabrina wanted a quiet place to disappear into and a good meal served quickly. If she chose to linger, she preferred it to be because she wanted to, not because of lousy service. Besides, she didn't feel up to the six-block walk down to the harbor, and was definitely not in the mood for quaint decor.

She stood just inside the café door a moment, letting her eyes adjust to the dimness, dismayed at the late-lunch crowd filling the tables. Only two were unoccupied—one large, round table which could seat eight in the very back corner of the cafe, and one small square table for two in the sunlit front window. Sabrina edged her way to the window past intervening tables of talking, laughing people, feeling as though she were stepping into a spotlight and hoping she would meet no one she knew, nor be recognized by anyone passing on the sidewalk outside. The last thing she wanted to do was talk to anyone. She sat with the window on her right. Through the wavy glass she could see across the street to the shops she had just passed, her antique car parked half a block away, and the library just beyond. The empty chair across from her beckoned and she longed to change her seat, to put the library out of sight behind her. But that would put the sun in her face, making her lunch even more uncomfortable than it already promised to be. She kept her place, her head bent and her stare on the menu in her hands.

The slowly westering sun streamed in the window and beat on her neck. It caressed her back with warm, comforting fingers and limned the table's place settings with a glowing halo. But Sabrina couldn't relax, despite the sun's efforts. She studied the menu, feeling like a deep-water fish caught in clear shallow waters, a lagoon ringed by thousands of grinning, staring faces. She wished now she had brought one of the biographies in which to bury herself. She glanced at the other patrons, wondering if they wondered why she sat alone. That was what she always wondered whenever she saw a solitary diner, especially after she had met Charlie. Before Charlie, it hadn't embarrassed her be to be alone. She had felt lonely and wistful, invisible at times, but never embarrassed. Now it was agony, torturous and humiliating. She hated how they must pity her, knew just what they all must think. *Poor woman, look at her, all alone. How terrible to be unloved, and unwanted. How terrible.*

The waitress, one of only two circling the crowded room, was a heavy-set woman in her mid forties with richly hennaed hair and too much makeup, especially around her eyes, which were bright blue and quite lovely. But the pink uniform straining across overly-abundant breasts, Sabrina was sure, would keep other people's eyes from noticing the waitress'. She looked harried, and more than tired. Her name tag read *Marie.*

"You alone?" she enquired, her curt tone radiating disapproval. Sabrina nodded, lowering her eyes and feeling her face flush with discomfiture. "What d'you want? I hope it's not the clam chowder, we're out of it."

Sabrina ordered a crab-and-shrimp salad, cornbread muffins and iced tea in a low, apologetic voice. Marie returned Sabrina's tentative smile with a grimace of boredom and turned away. *Damn,* Sabrina thought as she shifted her gaze to the window to watch shoppers and tourists wend their way up and down the street. *Why did I order all that? I don't want to be here, I don't want to eat, I want to go home. God, please, I just want to go home.*

The salad, when it arrived a few minutes later, was delicious. Sabrina found that she was much more hungry than she had thought. She ate slowly, savoring each bite, and gradually her unease lessened. Real whipped butter came with the cornbread muffins, which were hot and crumbly, just the way she liked them, and the iced tea surprised her with its strong, robust taste. It had been made fresh and not sweetened. Two thick half-slices of tart, juicy lemon lay on the plate for her to squeeze into the golden brown liquid. She licked the sour juice from her fingers, feeling like a child, knowing her mouth puckered at the taste and not caring. Spearing a large piece of shrimp and letting her gaze wander aimlessly around the sweltering street outside the window, she smiled to herself and thanked God in His heaven for the gift of this delightful, delectable lunch. It looked, felt and tasted special, which was just what she needed today.

The restaurant around her emptied while she ate. She finished the salad and buttered the last of the three muffins, finally letting her mind consider again the tasks that still awaited her attention. The florist was next door to the cafe, she'd start there, and hope the heat wouldn't wilt her mums and carnations too badly before she got back to the cottage. Then she'd go to the butcher, leave her order for him to pack, and finish the grocery shopping before she picked up the meat and headed for home. That way she wouldn't have to worry about anything spoiling, or melting too badly.

She glanced at her watch. It was two-forty-five now. The refrigerator should be fairly cold by the time she got home. Looking out the window again, she picked up the iced tea to take a final sip.

She froze, frowning. A man had crossed the street from this side to the other and stood now in front of the china shop's windows, munching a hot dog. He looked strangely familiar to Sabrina. Her heart thudded as she studied the sunlit sand-colored hair waving down onto his collar. He was tall and solid, a big man difficult to miss even in a crowd. He turned, studying the artful display of tableware in the window, presenting his hawk-nosed profile to her view, and Sabrina gasped, set her glass down with a sharp crack. She *had* seen him before, she knew she had, but where? She blinked at the ice melting in her glass, haunted by the golden glints in his hair, the sharp curve of his bird beak nose. He had turned away when she looked up again, moving to the door of the shop to open it for a customer who carried out two heavy-looking packages, holding it wide and acknowledging the woman's thanks with a rakish tilt of his head. He did not go in.

The library, Sabrina thought. He had opened the door for her when she had run out so abruptly. That was where she had seen him. She remembered, now. But still that profile nagged at her, and the glints in his hair. She could swear had seen him somewhere else, too, though she hadn't been anywhere else since she arrived on Gaffe. She puzzled over the strange sense of deja vu that plagued her as she paid her check and stepped out of the deli, turning left to the flower shop and purposely ignoring the man across the street.

She didn't see him when she emerged ten minutes later with an armful of white and yellow mums and pink carnations. She thought he must have gone on to wherever it was he'd been headed for. Then she crossed the street, angling toward the butcher shop, and saw him again. He stood at the outdoor vegetable bins, sorting through crisp, red apples which he placed in the paper bag he held. Old Jeremy Swann, who had worked at the store ever since Sabrina could remember, stood nearby, watching close and keeping count. The man looked up, smiled at the chubby, bald shopkeeper, hefted the bag in his hand and then looked casually up the street, his gaze meeting hers for a moment before they moved on, seeming unconcerned. Sabrina felt a chill touch her spine. She *had* seen him before today, she knew she had. Panic began gnawing at the edges of her mind. Who was he? Why was he still there, loitering on the street as though waiting for something? For her?

She shook her head and stepped into the cool interior of the butcher shop, trying to force her heart to slow. She was getting paranoid, she knew, letting her imagination run away with her. She'd done the same thing out in California, imagined someone watching her, following her. She'd even called the police twice. No one had been there, of course, it was only her shattered nerves playing games with her. She had hoped that familiar surroundings would calm her, the police had assured her of it once they'd heard the story of the murder, it was one of the main reasons she had returned. And now here she was doing it again, thinking an innocent tourist was out to get her. She had to get hold of herself or she truly would end in a mental hospital, and what good would that do? It certainly wouldn't bring Charlie back to her, or make his death any easier to bear. If only she could remember where else she had seen that man.

Still Sabrina couldn't stop trembling as she forced herself to concentrate on selecting meats, ordering enough for two of each cut as she had since she had married. She couldn't help herself; it simply hurt too much not to. Then she asked the butcher to wrap everything and set it in his cooler until she came back from the grocery store. She left with his cheerful agreement still ringing in her ears. Her heart, despite her resolve to stop being foolish, lurched as she stepped out into the bright sunlight. She squinted as she scanned the street but found no trace of the tall, fair-haired man.

She walked into the grocery store feeling a strange sense of relief and wandered up and down the narrow aisles, her mind only half on the shopping, her restless gaze pacing the hands on her watch as they inched slowly around its face. She took as long as she could, lingering over her choice of products, and managed to waste a full hour among the canned and boxed goods filling the shelves. Her watch hands stood at four o'clock when at last she sighed and headed for the checkout. She'd have enough, between her butcher order and what was in her cart, for about a month's worth of silent, lonely meals. She'd certainly have more than enough time to gather strength before she'd have to face another harrowing day in town.

The bill came to fifty-seven dollars. Sabrina wrote out a check and carried the bags and her flowers out to the car, assisted by one of the young teenage boys who worked at the store after school. She tipped him a dollar, her smile fading when over his shoulder she again caught a glimpse of the tall stranger. He stood in front of the barbershop, smoothing his hair with a square-fingered hand as if contemplating having it cut. She shuddered. She still had to get her meat from the butcher, and doing so meant walking closer to that man. What if he moved, came toward her? She barely heard the freckle-faced boy thank her, or saw his frown of concern at her pale face. She stood frozen by irrational fear until a car horn tooted behind her, startling her out of her fog. She blinked, sank onto the seat of the car and, pleading sudden illness, asked the boy to fetch her meat order for her.

The man was still in front of the barbershop when the boy returned and set the bag of meat in the spacious trunk with the other groceries. Sabrina gave him another dollar, turned the key in the ignition and began to edge back out into traffic. The man turned and walked swiftly to a small car parked not far from where she was. Sabrina moaned. Was he going to follow her all the way home? If he did, what would she do?

Sabrina, heart thudding and hands shaking, circled around the block and pulled onto Main Street, heading back the way she had come. Her gaze kept straying to the rearview mirror, making her progress dangerously unsteady, but she didn't see any sign of the mustard-gold car behind her. Within a few blocks she began to relax. *Maybe I should see a counselor or something*, she thought, trying to unclench her hands from the wheel as she passed beneath the town's sole signal light. *I can't keep scaring myself like this or I'll end up a local legend.*

Traffic was heavier now, as businesses closed for the day and residents headed home, adding their cars to those of tourists returning to Gaffe Island's three hotels after a day in the sun. Sabrina took advantage of the pause caused by a left-turner to snug tight the lap belt she had forgotten in her fearful anxiety. She smiled sadly, remembering Charlie's intransigent insistence on its use at all times. Then she pulled down the visor to shield her eyes against the glare of the lowering sun. To her right, the Atlantic sparkled like shards of glass. Heat shimmered on the dark ribbon of road before her, and the Palmetto trees to her left waved languid fronds in the almost-breathless atmosphere. Sabrina's flowers sat wilting beside her in the oven-hot interior of the car, despite the open windows. For most of the twenty-minute drive to the cottage, she worried about the groceries locked in the sweatbox of a trunk, dismissing her afternoon's aberration from her mind with resolute determination.

She stood a moment to watch traffic go by when she pulled in the drive and got out to unlock and open the garage door. Two small, yellow cars passed, but Sabrina could not make out either of the drivers with the way the sun glared on the windshields. She watched until both disappeared over the slight rise on which the Gaffe Island Inn sat. Neither showed any inclination to slow down or stop. She breathed a shuddering sigh of relief, pulled the car into the garage, locked the door securely behind her and carried the groceries into a kitchen that now flooded with light when she pushed up the wall switch.

She left the flowers soaking in water while she put the food away and planned her dinner—baked breaded chicken breast with a delicate Swiss cheese sauce, fresh cauliflower and an endive salad with vinaigrette dressing. After she put the chicken into the oven and washed the salad greens, she gathered vases from the living room and filled them with water, humming as she cut stems and arranged flowers with deft assuredness earned through years of experience. She carried two vases back into the living room and took another up to her bedroom, returning to pour herself a glass of white wine and put a record on the old wind-up Victrola. Al Jolson's voice crooned mellow in the background as she wandered out onto the front porch to watch the birds and the waves.

She almost screamed.

He was out there, the tall man whose hair matched the sand in which he stood, not thirty yards away to her left, on the dune overlooking her house, the very hill on which Sabrina herself had stood the night before. He was looking her way, not at her or the house but down the beach to where a group of raucous seagulls fought over their evening meal. Sabrina couldn't breathe. Shock flooded through her. Her head reeled and the edges of her vision turned white. The wineglass slipped from her hand and shattered on the top step of the porch. Her lungs refused to work. She groped behind her for the screen door, moving slowly, trying not to attract his attention. Once inside, she shut and locked the inner door and stood clinging to the age-smooth frame until the faintness passed and she could breathe again.

She moved to the window and parted the drapes with shaking hands. He was still there, sitting now, facing the house, reading something he held in his hands. Sabrina didn't think it was a newspaper, it wasn't big enough. Nor was it small enough to be a book. A map, maybe? She gasped, seeing a sudden image of a man in a car bent over a map, just outside the house when she'd left for shopping. A man in a dark yellow car with a map. She wasn't crazy, he had been following her! And she was alone here. Alone, and at his mercy.

She looked around the living room, fighting panic. Her gaze caught on the telephone and a wave of warmth flooded her. She had a lifeline. Thank God they had been able to turn it on so quickly. She snatched up the receiver, her shaking fingers barely able to turn the dial.

"Gaffe Island Police, Sergeant Markham speaking."

"Please, help me," Sabrina pleaded, trying to speak clearly through the choking fear. "There's a man outside, he's been following me all day. I don't know what to do!"

"All right, ma'am, just calm down," the sergeant drawled. "Most likely he's a just tourist, thinks the beaches are all public property. Happens all the time. Nothing to get all riled up about."

"No, he's not just a tourist. Please, I'm alone here, and I'm really scared. He's sitting out there, on the beach, watching the house. He was out there earlier, too. He followed me into town and back again."

"He approach you, say anything to you?" the sergeant's lazy, indolent voice asked.

"No," Sabrina answered, shutting her eyes in despair. Sergeant Markham thought she was just a hysterical woman who wanted attention. She could hear the amusement in his voice. How could she make him understand? "Please, I need help. I'm not just imagining this. My husband was killed two months ago—murdered. They haven't caught the man who did it."

She peered through the drapes again. The man on the sand dune turned the paper over, opened it out. The sun glinted off his hand and it hit her. She knew where she had seen him before. At the cemetery in Buffalo, on a bench beside the lake. She almost dropped the phone.

"Oh, my God! Oh, please, please don't let him hurt me!" she pleaded, backing away from the window. "He killed Charlie, I know he did!"

"Hold on, ma'am. Don't go all to pieces on me." Sergeant Markham sounded more alert now, less amused. "Where is the guy? Is he moving toward the house?"

"No. No, he's j-just sitting in the sand, w-watching the house."

"All right, you stay put. Keep the doors locked and stay away from the windows. We'll have a car out there in a few minutes."

Sabrina gave the sergeant her address, and a description of the man, feeling even more frightened when she hung up, terrified that the police would not arrive in time. She could not keep her eyes away from the front window. Despite the sergeant's advice she kept parting the curtain and peering out, expecting to see the man stalking toward her. But he remained where he was, sitting on the sand in his suit, sleeves pushed up and arms propped on his knees, his gaze sweeping over the rolling expanse of blue-green water spread out before him. Every few minutes, he turned his head and casually studied the house where Sabrina crouched in terror. But he came no closer.

Ten endless minutes later, a Gaffe Island patrol car pulled up. Two uniformed policemen got out and approached the man sitting in the sand, who rose slowly, his stance wary and alert. Sabrina watched from the front window, her hand pressed to her lips. The tall man listened quietly to the policemen, nodding his head, his lips moving in answer, his eyes lifting to stare at her house. Then he opened his suit coat and, with slow, precise movements, took out a slim wallet.

He handed it to the older of the two men, who studied it intently. The cop turned to look at Sabrina's house. After a moment, he sent the younger uniform back to the patrol car and led the tall stranger down the dune. Sabrina gasped in shock, stepping away from the window. He was bringing that man to her house. He was bringing Charlie's killer straight to her.

CHAPTER ELEVEN

Sabrina moved toward the front door in dazed disbelief, her hands clenched knuckle-white on the large gold antique locket she wore around her neck, the locket that had once belonged to Charlie's grandmother. She hadn't taken it off since the day Charlie died, not even at night when she slept. She stood in the dim hall, watching the men's shadowy forms through the translucent curtain on the door as they climbed the porch steps, crunched across the remains of her wineglass and stopped before the door. It seemed to take them hours. A sudden sharp rap rang out—hollow, insistent, official sounding. Sabrina jumped. Her heart lurched in her chest.

"Mrs. Compton? It's Sergeant Markham, you spoke to me at the station," the shorter of the two figures called in a lazy drawl now tinged with annoyance. Sabrina blinked, recognizing the deep, nasal voice. She took a hesitant step closer to the door. Sergeant Markham's next words froze her motionless.

"Open the door, please, Mrs. Compton. I need to talk to you."

Sabrina shook her head, her lips open in silent protest. Open the door, was he crazy? That man was out there with him, the man who'd been following her. No way would she open the door, not even with Sergeant Markham out there.

Markham hit the door another blow with his fist and again Sabrina jumped.

"Come on, Mrs. Compton. Open the door," he ordered. "Now, Mrs. Compton."

Sabrina edged to the door, the sergeant's banging fist echoing a hollow counterpoint to the thudding of her heart. The last thing she wanted to do was open the door. But she couldn't resist the authoritative demand in his voice. She reached out, snapped open the lock and cracked the door a few tiny inches to peer through the narrow slit.

Markham's dark eyes stared back, his aging, heart-shaped face filled with vexed displeasure. A man of fifty or so, he looked smaller, narrower, than his voice sounded. His belly rounded out over his belt-buckle. A hat partially hid his mostly gray hair. The only notable feature on a forgettable, nondescript face was his flat nose, which turned up into a point at the tip. Wide hands with short, spatulate fingers toyed with a slim, brown leather wallet.

The tall stranger stood to Markham's left, easily a head taller than the police sergeant. Sabrina could barely breathe. Close up, he looked even bigger, more powerful, than she had thought he was. Her eyes lifted, were caught by his. She stared, mesmerized by fear at the glacial antagonism that radiated from those blue depths. She could see him analyzing her, dissecting her. She felt like a small helpless child who had been caught stealing from an evil omnipotent giant.

"Mrs. Compton," Markham snapped, startling Sabrina. She had forgotten the policeman was there. "Is this the man you called about, the one you said killed your husband?"

"Yes," Sabrina whispered, shuddering. Why didn't he have his gun out? "Yes, it's him, he's been following me for days!"

"Well, ma'am, he may have been following you, but I doubt he had anything to do with your husband's death. This here just happens to be Mister Special Agent Mitchell Lawson, of the great, almighty FBI."

He held up the slim wallet. Sabrina, stunned, reached out, took it into her hand. Her eyes lifted once again to the tall man's cold glare. It took Markham's disgusted voice to pull them away.

"Go ahead, look at it, Mrs. Compton. Open it up and look at it."

Sabrina looked down, opened the wallet. She saw an identification card complete with official seals and a picture in the lower right-hand corner, a picture of the tall man who stood before her. It was a surprisingly good likeness. There could be no doubt of who he was, or who he worked for. 'FBI' was stamped at the top in large blue letters. Sabrina stared at the card, totally mystified, not looking up even when Markham spoke again.

"Special Agent Lawson, here, has informed me that his mission is Official Government Business. Nothing that the local-yokel police need concern themselves with." Markham's displeasure at this unexpected turn of events reflected in the sour drawl of his voice. The sarcasm made it clear he resented not being consulted by the federal law-enforcement officer, and felt foolish at the embarrassing position Sabrina's frantic call had placed him in. "So, if there is nothing else you need us plain ole cops for, Mrs. Compton, I'll just mosey on back to the station."

Silence fell. The two men stood waiting for Sabrina's reply. She stared on at the ID card she held, frozen by a suffocating sense of unreality, completely unaware that Markham had spoken. Or stopped speaking. An FBI agent, following her? How could this be happening?

"Mrs. Compton?"

Sabrina jumped at the sharp sound. She looked up, blinking, dazed, and flinched when she met the sergeant's angry dark glare. Did he blame her for not knowing this was a federal agent?

"Is there anything else you need me for? Ma'am?"

It seemed he did blame her, there was accusation clear in his tone. Sabrina tried to speak, but nothing happened. No sound emerged. Numbly, she shook her head.

"All right, then," the sergeant rasped, looking at the man beside him. "I'll leave you to your Official Government Business, Special Agent Lawson."

The tall marshal turned to watch the sergeant stomp down the steps and stride around the house to the waiting patrol car, his blue eyes quickly scanning the beach and ocean beyond. But Sabrina barely noted the policeman's leave-taking. She couldn't take her eyes off the man still on the porch, the man with whom she was now alone. She saw the alert poise of the muscular body, noted the confident assuredness with which he moved, glimpsed a strap of the shoulder holster he wore as the freshening breeze tugged at his open suit coat. Even in the shadow of the porch, his pale hair caught what light there was and braided it into the curls the humidity had coiled up on his head. After a moment of silence, he turned back to her and ran his icy gaze up and down her body. He held out a huge hand for his ID wallet.

Sabrina looked down at her hand to see the wallet clutched open in her fingers. She hadn't realized she still held it. She placed it in his palm, taking care that her fingers not touch his. She kept her eyes on their hands, away from his piercing gaze.

"I have to talk to you, Mrs. Compton. There are some questions I need answered." His voice, though soft and low, carried with it an unmistakable air of authority. This was not a request, it was an order. "May I come in?"

Sabrina turned to look at her living room, the inviolate space that meant safety and peace for her. She couldn't let him in here, it was the only thing she had left in her life that was still whole. She turned back, trembling, to where Mitchell Lawson, Special Agent for the Federal Bureau of Investigation, stood watching her closely.

"No. No, I'll come out," she said.

He didn't nod, he merely moved away from the door, giving her room to step out of the house. Her head didn't even come up to his shoulders. Sabrina felt infinitesimally small beside him and totally vulnerable as she walked on wooden legs across the porch and sank onto a white wicker chair. She clasped Charlie's locket with her right hand. Her left she kept clenched in her lap. It took all her courage to look up at where Lawson stood watching her in silence. She tried to force herself to speak, to demand what it was he wanted, to berate him for frightening her so. But she couldn't do it. The words would not come.

Silence stretched until Sabrina thought she would scream. Finally Lawson sighed, looked down at his sand-covered shoes, then crossed the porch to take the chair on her left. He settled back, propped an elbow on the rough wicker arm and ran an index finger over his thin lips as he studied her with calculating eyes.

"Just how much did your husband tell you, Mrs. Compton?"

Sabrina stared at him, the question bouncing on the warm breeze. She shook her head, puzzled.

"Tell me? About what, Mr. Lawson?"

"Agent."

"Excuse me?"

"It's Agent, not Mister. Special Agent Lawson."

Sabrina narrowed her eyes at him.

"Really? And what makes you special, Agent, your rudeness or your arrogance?"

Lawson didn't answer, he merely sat staring at her as her heartbeat ratcheted up. His index finger tapped an arrhythmic beat on his lips. Sabrina sat still, fascination and terror warring inside her. Finally Lawson broke the silence, his voice an order as cold and hard as his eyes.

"Answer the question, Mrs. Compton."

"What question?"

"What did your husband tell you?"

Sabrina shook her head, completely bewildered.

"Tell me? About what?"

"About who he was. About what he had or what he knew that he shouldn't have. About whatever the man who killed him was looking for."

"What are you talking about?"

"Listen, Mrs. Compton," he said, crossing his legs, his eyes boring into her, "I know all about your husband. You don't have to continue the innocent act with me. He's dead, there's no one to protect, anymore. You know something, you have to, you lived with the man for over seven years. He must have told you something."

"My relationship with my husband is no business of yours," Sabrina said, her courage bolstered by the anger that was kindling in her breast. "I have no idea what you're talking about. And you have no right to follow me around, to terrify me, and then sit there and accuse me of knowing why Charlie was murdered. If I knew why, I'd have told the police when it happened. And if I knew who did it, I would have gone after him and killed him myself!" Sabrina rose, her trembling legs barely able to hold her. She could feel her eyes snapping with rage. "I want you to leave, Agent Lawson. Now."

"Sit down, Mrs. Compton. I'm not through yet. Sit down!"

Fear shuddered through Sabrina. She sank back onto the hard wicker seat, feeling like a mouse crouched before a deadly snake. Mitchell Lawson uncrossed his legs. He leaned forward and rested his forearms on his knees.

"Do you know who Charles Philip Compton was, Mrs. Compton?" he asked, his deep voice now a soft caress. His hard blue eyes stayed riveted on her face.

"I-I don't understand," Sabrina stammered. "What kind of question is that?" Lawson didn't answer, he merely stared at her until Sabrina was forced to look away and break the tense silence. "He, he was my husband," she whispered, tears trembling in her voice though none shone in her eyes.

"And?"

"And a professor at the University, an assistant dean. I don't understand!" she cried, looking back at him. "You said you know all about Charlie. Why are you asking me this? What do you want from me?"

"I want to know what he told you about himself, Mrs. Compton. About his past, his family. All of it."

"Charlie didn't have any family, Agent Lawson. He said they were all gone. He was all alone, like I was." *Like I still am*. The thought pierced through Sabrina like a knife. She bit her lips and bowed her head. The breeze drew strands of her hair across her face.

"What about his enemies?"

"Enemies?" She looked up, astounded, her right hand pulling the strands of hair out of her eyes. "What enemies? Charlie taught economics at the University, Agent Lawson, we led very quiet lives. There's no reason anyone would want him dead. What happened was insane, the act of a madman. Charlie didn't have any enemies."

"Didn't he?"

The loaded question vibrated between them, Mitch Lawson's low voice almost drowned by the waves slapping on the sand. Sabrina stared at him, horror growing rising within her. Her mouth dropped open as the ominous meaning in the words broke over her.

"Oh, dear lord!" she whispered. "Are you telling me that it was because of Charlie, because of something he did, that someone *wanted* him dead? I don't believe it. It's not true, it can't be. Why? Charlie hadn't done anything, he was just a teacher."

"He wasn't always a teacher, Mrs. Compton. Fifteen years ago, he was the furthest thing from a teacher you can imagine."

Sabrina opened her mouth to protest, to deny Lawson's words, but the look in his eyes stopped her. There was knowledge, there, and truth—cold, hard, uncompromising truth that would destroy forever what little she had left to hold onto. Shock flooded over her like an icy wave. She shook her head.

"I don't want to hear this," she pleaded in a trembling voice, gathering herself to rise. Mitch Lawson reached out and grabbed her wrist, holding her where she was.

"I think you'd better. I still haven't gotten what I came here for."

Sabrina shook her head and looked away from Lawson as she settled back in her chair. Lawson did not release hold of her arm.

"Sixteen years ago," he said in a deceptively soft tone, "a man walked into the FBI field office in Scottsdale, Arizona, and made a deal. He'd tell everything he knew, and in exchange he'd get immunity from prosecution and a new identity. It was worth the bargain despite the lowlife that he was, because among his other talents, Anthony Albert DiGesare was also an accountant who kept the books for the local Mafia. He laundered their money, paid their hit men, and kept track of the profits from their drug, prostitution and gambling operations. He knew all the big boys, all the deals. He also knew where all the bodies were buried, mainly because he moonlighted as an enforcer who disposed of embarrassing 'problems' out in the desert to earn a little extra cash. He helped put a lot of important men behind bars before he disappeared into Wit Sec, the Witness Protection Program. We gave Tony DiGesare a whole new identity and a whole new way of life, far away from Scottsdale."

DiGesare. The name stabbed into Sabrina. She could hear Donald Bradley's puzzled voice: *Carla Piccolo and Maria DiGesare. Do you know who they are?*

"No," she choked, twisting her arm in the hard fingers holding her. Tears beaded up in her eyes. "No."

"Yes, Mrs. Compton. The man you called 'Charlie' didn't exist fifteen years ago, not until Tony DiGesare finished his testimony before the Grand Jury. That's when DiGesare 'died,' and Charles Philip Compton was born. I should know. I was a Marshal back then. I was in charge of the case. I got to know Tony very well. I'm the one who gave him his name. And found the teaching job at the University for him. The man you married, Mrs. Compton, killed at least seven men for his former employers before he came to us and broke the *Omerta*, their code of silence. Their type never forgets that kind of betrayal. It took them a long time to find him, but they finally did."

"No!" Sabrina screamed. Her eyes filled with horror. She wrenched her arm from Lawson's grasp and flung herself from the chair, stumbling backwards toward the door, suffocating beneath the impact of his words, her hands pressed over her ears. "You're lying. It's not true, it can't be true. I won't listen to this, I won't!"

"Mrs. Compton, please."

Lawson stood and reached for her, his soaring height terrifying her even more. Sabrina slapped at his hands, blinded by tears of pain and rage.

"No. Leave me alone. Get out of here. You're a liar. A liar!"

She whirled and fled into the house, slamming and locking the door behind her. She could see the vague outline of the Marshal through the curtain on the window and she stood frozen in the hall, wondering if he would break down the door and come after her. Tears ran down her face but she didn't notice them. She was too busy trying to breathe, trying to keep her shuddering body from collapsing on the floor. Centuries passed in the few minutes before the tall, solid figure turned away and descended the porch steps. Sabrina cried out in relief, closing her eyes and pressing a hand to her lips. Her weakened knees buckled suddenly and she clung to the wall to keep from falling.

How long she stood propped against the wall she didn't know, but the shadows were deeper when at last she pushed herself upright and groped her way into the living room. Darkness pooled in corners, lapping out to ensnare nearby pieces of furniture. She lowered herself onto an embroidered settee that sat across the room below the side window, her fingers tracing the raised pattern of the faded threads. But her gaze did not follow their path. Her blank stare wandered around the spacious room, passing the pot bellied stove to her right, the maroon horsehair sofa against the back wall, the open roll-top desk with its myriad pigeonholes on the wall across from her, to the left of the archway, passing them over and over, without seeing a thing.

Gradually, her trembling stopped. Sabrina sat statue-still, fighting to keep the memory of the tall sandy-haired agent's voice at bay. It was a losing battle. Whisper soft at first, growing louder and louder, the deep, insistent voice jabbed at her, refused to let her shut out the horrible knowledge it carried.

"No," she moaned, clapping her hands over her ears. The voice echoed on in her head. "Oh, no. It isn't true, it isn't."

She shut her eyes, her body folding in upon itself in agony. In the darkness, beneath the pressing, importunate cadence of Agent Lawson's words vibrated those that Donald Bradley had spoken. *Carla Piccolo and Maria DiGesare. Who are they?* Carla Piccolo and Maria DiGesare. Anthony Albert DiGesare...Maria DiGesare...Tony DiGesare... DiGesare... DiGesare... DiGesare...

Sabrina screamed, a lamentation of sheer anguish. Her eyes snapped open and her head rose, her hands slipping from her ears to fold together before her face, fingers loosely intertwined, thumbs resting on her parted lips. Her breath panted in hot gasps that misted her fingers with warmth she didn't feel. What she did feel was her life slowly dissolving. The small oasis of strength and safety she'd so painstakingly begun to rebuild on memories shredded away beneath reality's ferocious assault. It was true, what Mitchell Lawson had told her. She knew it as certainly as she knew that she was alive, alive and alone and unloved in a world where love held the only meaning. Every word he had spoken was true, each one an exploding bullet that tore her apart.

It had been a sham. Her life with Charlie, her love, Charlie himself—a sham. It hadn't been real. She had loved a man who had never existed, lived a life that had no reality. She had given her heart, her soul, to a figment of someone else's imagination, to a pretend person who had given her pretend love in a pretend world created by a cold, heartless U.S. Marshal.

Nothing. That was what she had come from, that was what she had had these last seven years, and that was what she was left with. Nothing.

Sabrina looked down to stare at the large gold filigree locket she wore. It had been Charlie's grandmother's. But since there hadn't really been a Charlie, how could there have been a grandmother? He had given it to her on their wedding day, clasped it around her neck with gentle, loving hands. But if he hadn't been real, how real was the wedding? How loving the gentle hands that had killed seven men at another's whim?

Her trembling fingers lifted the locket, pressed the catch to open it. And there in her palm they lay, the pictures taken just a week before they married— Charlie, his hazel eyes laughing, his face full of love and devotion; and herself, smiling shyly, her newly-awakened joy of life shining like the new-risen sun. Pictures set therein by Charlie's own hand. She stared at his beloved face, the face that had given her the strength to live through each endless day since his death. She looked at the thick hair she'd loved to play with, the gentle lips that had kissed her breathless, the laughing eyes that spoke their love so clear in her heart. She could feel his hands on her body, the pleasure he had bequeathed at night, hands that had bequeathed not pleasure but death to other bodies on other nights. A criminal. A trusted member of the Mafia. A murderer. Her Charlie.

Tears spilled over, tracked down her pale, gaunt cheeks. Sobs rose from deep within. Sabrina's fingers closed abruptly, snapping the locket shut. Her body rocked in desolate anguish as she mourned the sham she had loved so dearly, the reality that had never existed. How could Charlie have done this to her? How could he have betrayed her love like this? How could he have said he loved her? How could he have loved her at all, when he didn't even exist? He hadn't loved her. He had destroyed her, killed her as surely as he had killed those others. Killed her by giving her hope. Killed her by letting her believe in love. Killed her on the day he had married her. Dear lord, how she hated him. She despised him, detested him.

"I hate you, Charlie! I hate you!"

Sabrina screamed her rage and pain into the lurking darkness. She jerked savagely on the chain. It snapped it in two as she surged to her feet and ran from the room. She threw the locket from her as though its touch seared her skin. It hit the top of the old roll-top desk, skidded across the time-polished oak surface, and slid between the ponderous piece of furniture and the wall and came to a stop, caught on a nail six inches from the floor. Sabrina flung herself onto her bed. Her heartbroken sobs were kept lonely company by the plaintive cries of gulls, the melancholy susurration of waves and the mourning of the night wind, until at last she slipped into the tenuous comforting oblivion of sleep.

* * *

He sat concealed in a dark pocket, far enough down the dune so that his outline was not visible against the star-filled night sky. Moon glow frosted his pale hair with silver and buried his features in bottomless shadow, all but his arching nose, which jutted into the light whenever he turned his head to scan the deserted beach and rolling ocean. There was no sound save for the gentle slap of waves on wet sand, a comforting sound that lulled the senses into a state of nostalgic reminiscence.

But he was not lulled. He sat coil-taut and cat-alert, unaware of the chill radiating from the dune where he crouched, unmoved by the slight breeze that danced with his moonlit hair, his eyes and ears vigilant in the silent, still dark of the night. It was late, well past midnight. He had been there, watching, for more than three hours. In all that time he had caught no sound other than that of the water and an occasional car passing on the road a hundred feet behind him, out of his line of sight. He had spied no movement on the ebony-colored beach beyond the hypnotic undulating ocean. Not unless he chose to count himself—his head turning with calculated precision, eyes eagle-sharp despite the darkness. Hands lifting, bringing the field glasses to those same watchful eyes that waited for his quarry with unwavering attention. For long hours, there'd been nothing more to see.

When at last she did move, she unknowingly aided his observation by turning on lights, both upstairs and down. The powerful lenses brought her almost close enough to touch as he trained them on the north side of the house, peering through the half-open curtain covering the living room window. From that angle he could see past the living room archway, across the hall and into the kitchen. In the narrow hallway, at the extreme right of his range, the bottom of a staircase was visible.

He saw her descend the last three steps, moving as though ill. Her shaking hand clutched the banister with whitened knuckles. She paused at the bottom and looked over into the living room. To the silent watcher, it seemed that she stared directly into his eyes, her own eyes twin pools of dark pain-filled despair. Then she frowned, turned away and paced slowly into the kitchen to disappear for a moment. When again she appeared she carried a casserole dish, the charred contents of which she scraped into a garbage bag. Once more she vanished into the inner reaches of the kitchen, returning to sit in silent sorrow at the glass-topped table, her gaze locked on the darkened beach and ocean outside the windows.

He studied her profile, approving the way she had trained her dark hair to sweep back from a low forehead. He was glad it was long. He was partial to long hair, liked to run his fingers through it, twine it around his fisted hands, pull it across a woman's face until she could barely see. It frightened women, the way he played with their hair, and he liked his women frightened. They were prettier when consumed with fear, more exciting. He smiled, watching Sabrina Compton sigh and push herself to her feet, remembering the way fear had widened those exquisite dark eyes, paled that lovely ashen skin, parted her luscious full lips. He would more than enjoy getting his answers from her. Her terror would repay him for the inconvenience this case had already caused him.

She only half-disappeared this time, reaching out to the stove to lift the teakettle and pour steaming water into a china mug. She lifted the mug, darkened the kitchen and walked slowly into the living room, where she set the mug on a tall, round end table beside an embroidered settee. After a moment of indecision, she moved to a mahogany cabinet and turned the bronze handle on its side, setting a record down on the spindle and carefully placing the needle at the beginning of the spinning disc. He wondered what tune she had chosen to share the darkness with. He could see tears glittering in her eyes when she returned to the settee, and a melancholy smile on her lips. Swinging her legs up and bending her knees to fit onto the abbreviated length of the ancient piece of furniture, she leaned her head on the padded side wing and let herself drift.

He watched her let go. The tension in her body gradually eased and her shoulders settled against the embroidered fabric. Her hands relaxed as her eyes slowly closed. He marked the moment when she fell asleep, for her face sagged slightly and her lips opened as her head sank lower toward her chest. Her hair slid down to half-cover her face. The untouched drink sat cooling on the end table. The lamp beside the mug shed a soft halo of light onto her slender body.

He took a deep breath and lowered the glasses, cast his gaze again around the night-shrouded beach. The first faint glimmer of dawn pulsated almost imperceptibly on the ocean-bound horizon. The stars overhead seemed dimmer now, somewhat faded after their unbridled display of twinkling light. There would be nothing more to see tonight, no answers to be gained from mere observation. Not until they stood face to face would he get what he wanted. And he would get it, that he knew. Because she knew. Despite her caution, the carefully contrived pose of the innocent grieving widow, she knew. She had the answers. And she'd give them to him, one way or another.

He slung the glasses around his neck and rose, methodically erasing all trace of his presence as he made his way back to where he'd left the rental car hidden behind a tall hedge. He spared the pretty blue Victorian cottage one last glance before he drove away.

Another day or two, that was all. When the time was ripe, Sabrina Compton would open up like a clamshell thrown into boiling water.

CHAPTER TWELVE

Sabrina woke to warm morning sunshine flooding in through half-parted living room curtains. Her head throbbed, her neck had cramped and her body felt stiff and awkward when she tried to sit up. The hands on her watch stood at nine-fourteen.

She yawned and flexed her shoulders, massaged numbed legs and rubbed her hands over her face, sighing in exasperation at herself. She was definitely too old to camp out on a small settee. Her body obviously went into a state of mutiny at such foolishness. She should have gone back upstairs and gotten into the bed she had cried herself to sleep on top of earlier. Her mind shied away from the reason for the tears, skirted around the memory of the tall fair-haired FBI Agent whose words had shattered the little that had survived the murderer's rampage. She shook her head to keep her mind blank, turned off the lamp and picked up the cold tea. She dumped it in the kitchen sink, sighing when she saw the charred state of last night's casserole dish. At least she had woken up before the house burned down, though she doubted the casserole dish could be saved. She ran hot water into the dish to start it soaking, then attempted to eat a poached egg cradled on rye toast. Only half of it went down.

Sabrina could not stop thinking about what Mitchell Lawson had said, despite her determination not to give credence to what he had told her. She sat toying with the food, staring out at the sunlit beach, haunted by echoes of Charlie's face, Charlie's voice. But it hadn't been Charlie, it had been someone she didn't know, someone she never knew. Charlie didn't really exist. She didn't want to believe it, she couldn't believe it, and yet she knew Lawson had been speaking the truth. Finally, she pushed the plate away and looked down into her dark coffee.

It was all so insane, everything that had happened since that terrible day in July. They were just ordinary people, she and Charlie. Or so she'd thought. Things like this didn't happen to ordinary people. Unless, somehow, they did something to deserve it. Sabrina shut her eyes and let her mind search back, seeking the trigger, the sinful act so vile and craven that it merited such punishment as her life had thus far been. Though she could not find it, she knew it had to be there, somewhere in her past, a fatal sin that sent ripples of evil vibrating around the world until at last they came back to their source.

She catalogued them one by one, the sins of her past. Dripping ice cream on grandfather's car seat.

Tearing her new yellow dress. Losing the money her mother had given her to buy a quart of milk. Breaking grandfather's favorite pipe. Liking her father more than her mother, though she had truly loved them both. Stealing Carol Allen's rainbow barrette when she'd been eight, and lying about it when she had been found out. Cheating on her math exam in seventh grade. Skipping school to go to the movies. Sneaking out at night, twice, to meet Patrick McShane in the woods for a session of petting that, even with its youthful innocence, still made her blush.

None of that seemed quite evil or depraved enough to have caused the horror and betrayal she had endured. Sabrina sighed and shook her head. The pain and death had been going on since she was seven, when her father had first fallen ill. Perhaps it wasn't anything specific she had done. Perhaps the sin was just that she existed at all. Maybe that was sin enough.

I won't think about it, she decided, clenching her teeth. *I don't believe any of what that man said, and I won't think about it any more.*

Her lips set into a tight line as she washed the dishes, scrubbing ruthlessly at the burned casserole until at last it came clean enough to be usable. Sabrina took a broom and dustpan out onto the porch when she finished, the kitchen shining spotless behind her, and swept up the glittering remnants of her wineglass. Then, that task done, she cleared the porch of sand the wind had carried through the night, straightened the cushions on the wicker furniture, and swept away three large spider webs that bridged gaps in the gingerbread. She marched around the house, shivering slightly in the brisk breeze, and set her broom to work clearing off the back porch, also. She studied the aged siding as she worked, wondering if she should consider painting. But it barely showed signs of weathering. Charlie and Geoffrey Simmonds had painted only two summers before. If she chose to paint now it would be simply for something to do, not because it was necessary.

She re-entered the house a little after eleven and mounted the stairs to the second floor where she spent half an hour transferring clothing from the front bedroom to the back one she now used. Then she showered and changed out of the rumpled skirt and tank top she'd slept in. The temperature was not quite as warm as the day before, and the fitful gusting breeze made it feel even cooler than it was. She donned a lime-green safari-style shirt whose loose sleeves rolled up to just below her elbows, and a pink, green and white Hawaiian print skirt. Three or four pair of slacks did hang in the closet, but she usually wore skirts, even at the beach. She felt more comfortable with the easy, free swirl of fabric around her legs. And more feminine. Charlie had laughed about it, declaring she had been born a century too late, clothing-wise, but he had loved that quaint, old-fashioned side of her passionately. He had never bought her a pair of pants in the seven years they'd been married.

She glanced in the full-length upper hall mirror, and froze. This was Charlie's favorite outfit. Sabrina could almost see him standing behind her, hazel eyes shining with loving admiration. She gasped, and shook her head. She didn't want him here, he wasn't real! She fled down the stairs and stood in the center of the living room, her nerves fraying. She had come to the beach hoping to find Charlie. Now, she couldn't stand even thinking about him. How could this be happening? Where was she to go to find peace?

She began to straighten cushions and afghans that didn't need straightening, merely for something to do, moving methodically around the room and keeping up a running commentary in her mind about the furnishings so that she would not be able to think about Charlie, who was not Charlie. A photograph of Charlie, a duplicate to that which graced her mantle in Buffalo, sat on a piecrust table in the room's back corner. She laid it face down with a shaking hand and a thudding heart. Another picture, this one of Charlie alone, sat atop the roll-top desk. She slid it into a pigeon-hole and rolled the cover shut again, standing with her hands frozen on the worn oak knobs while she worked savagely to control herself.

She would not cry, she would not scream. That was over. She would merely remove all trace of Charlie's presence from the would-be sanctuary that was no longer the inviolate asylum she required. If only she could remove him from her mind and heart as easily. Calmer, she moved on.

She finally reached the settee on which she had passed the small hours of the night. It had somehow gotten pushed up against the side window, pulling the curtain askew. She adjusted its placement and knelt on the hard cushions to rearrange the folds of the curtain. Her gaze swept out over the shell-studded beach as she worked. Gulls soared above, towing puffy white clouds across the deep blue of the sky. The ocean's surface, whipped by the playful breeze, peaked into frothy bands of marshmallow-white foam, rearing up to form curling waves that broke into glittering shards on the sand. *Another Charlie-day*, Sabrina thought, letting her gaze drift farther to the left, to the dunes that followed the curve of the shore. *So much for banishing him from my life.*

And there he was.

"No," she whispered.

Shock flooded her like ice water. He was standing in the same spot as before, hands jammed into his back pockets. The wind blew his fair curls every which way, brilliant sun and flying sand narrowing the blue eyes that stared at her house. He had changed his clothes. Today he wore beige cotton slacks and a blue, gray and beige striped crew-neck sweater. He didn't even pretend to be enjoying the view or reading a map. His gaze was locked on Sabrina's cottage.

Anger rose to quell the fear the first glimpse of him had aroused. How dare he come back here. How dare he intrude on her life. Sabrina slammed out of the house, her teeth clenched with hatred, her blood roaring with rage, determined to confront the man who had caused her such damage.

He didn't move toward her. He stood on the top of the dune, hooded eyes watching her long, angry strides eat up the beach separating them, her sandaled feet sinking into the deep sand. His motionless stance, the eyes that coldly analyzed her every movement, only made her more irate. She was breathing fire by the time she'd toiled up the shifting sand to where he stood.

"Just who the hell do you think you are?" she yelled. "You have no right to spy on me. Go away!"

"Good afternoon, Mrs. Compton," he replied. His neutral tone grated on her nerves. "I was hoping to see you."

"Well, you've seen me. Now get out of here, leave me alone."

"Please, Mrs. Compton, we need to talk—"

"Talk?" Sabrina's hair whipped around her face. "You did more than enough of that yesterday. You've completely destroyed what little I had to hold onto, aren't you satisfied with that? What more do you want from me?"

"Mrs. Compton—"

"*Don't call me that!*" Her sharp screech launched nearby gulls into the air. Tears of rage blinded her. Her hands clenched into fists that longed to smash into his sharp-nosed face. "I'm not Mrs. Compton, I'm not *anybody*, thanks to you. I don't want you here. Get off my beach, stay away from my house. Go away and leave me alone."

Sabrina whirled and stomped down the dune, leaving Mitch Lawson looking stunned in the face of her vehemence. Halfway down her foot hit a buried rock. Her ankle twisted, sending bolts of pain shooting up her leg and pitching her onto the soft, shifting ground. She landed on her face and slid almost to the bottom of the dune. Gritty sand cascaded around her. The sudden, unexpected fall dazed her. She lay still a moment, trying to recover her bearings. Then she sat up and wiped sand from her face with shaking hands as Lawson slid to a stop beside her.

"Mrs. Compton. Are you all right?"

Sabrina turned her head away.

"Leave me alone." She tried to snarl at him, but her voice still trembled from the shock of the fall.

"Please, let me help you," he said, reaching out a hand. Sabrina jerked her body back, away from his touch, her arms rising to fend him off.

"No!" she yelled. "Don't you dare touch me. Leave me alone."

Lawson took a step back and watched while Sabrina finished brushing sand from her body. She threw him a scathing glance, then gathered herself to rise. Pain shot up her right leg and she sank back with a groan. Mitch Lawson crouched beside her, his eyes inspecting her swelling ankle. Sabrina slapped his hands away when again he reached out for her.

"Don't touch me. I don't need your help."

"Don't be ridiculous, of course you do. You've hurt your foot, you can't walk on it. You can't even stand up. What are you going to do, crawl all the way down the beach to your house? In that skirt?"

"If I have to," Sabrina replied, her voice truculent, her eyes glaring fire. She looked toward the cottage, perched a mere hundred feet away, and knew with a sinking heart that she could never make it. Just flexing her foot sent bolts of fire up her leg. She couldn't imagine trying to crawl through deep, shifting sand. And with a skirt on, no less. But she'd be damned if she'd let this Special Agent bastard know how helpless she was, or give him the satisfaction of helping her. She'd rather sit out here in the open until she died.

She took a deep breath and forced herself to her hands and knees, gritting her teeth to keep her pained groans from echoing over the rush of the breeze. She moved forward two crawling paces before pain defeated her.

"All right, that's enough," Lawson said, stepping around beside her and scooping her up from the ground as easily as if she were a beach ball. She fought his hands, his strong embrace, bunching her fists to hit at him. Before she could, his deep growl stopped her cold.

"Cut the crap, Mrs. Compton, and just be still. The sooner I get you home, the sooner I can be on my way."

Sabrina looked at him, a glare of frustrated anger, but the tall, strong FBI agent wasn't even looking at her. His glacial blue eyes scanned the path he took, lifting to the cottage every few moments as though to judge the distance still left to go. Sabrina let herself relax in his arms, secretly grateful for his help and strangely touched by the feel of his arms strong around her. It had been a long time since she had felt a man's embrace. If he'd been nothing else, and it seemed he hadn't, Charlie had been a very physically affectionate man.

Lawson strode across the soft sand with confident feet, hefting her weight easily, walking as though he held nothing in his arms. He was not even breathing heavily when he reached the fifteen steps to Sabrina's porch, and despite her anger Sabrina found herself studying his face as he climbed effortlessly to the front door.

It was a nice face, rugged and well-worn and showing signs of a fading tan. A small scar slanted on his right cheekbone, an inch or so above where the faint line of his reddish-blond beard began, a line not visible from a distance but all too noticeable to Sabrina, whose eyes were only inches away. It looked like a heavy beard, and probably quick-growing, judging by the amount of stubble visible so early in the day. *Like Charlie's,* Sabrina thought. She wondered if Mitch Lawson also shaved twice a day. *Probably not,* she decided, remembering how dark the shadow was on her husband's face. Then she remembered who Mitch Lawson was, the way he had so callously destroyed her husband's memory, and her heart hardened. Her body stiffened once again in the arms holding her.

"Open the door for me," Lawson said, stepping up onto the porch. Sabrina blinked and looked around.

"No, that's okay. Just put me down over there," she said, gesturing at the wicker furniture to their right.

"I want to look at your ankle. Open the door."

"You can look at it out here," Sabrina argued. She didn't want him in her house.

"Mrs. Compton. Open the door."

His tone, like that of yesterday, was clipped and cold, a curt order. Sabrina sighed out her anger and, reaching down, pulled open the screen door. The spring closure bumped it into Lawson's back while he waited for her to turn the knob of the solid inner door. Sabrina hoped it had hurt as she gave the inner door a quick shove. It opened easily, swinging inward on silent hinges, and in three steps Mitchell Lawson brought her into her own living room. He stood a moment as his eyes catalogued the quaint, old-fashioned furnishings. Then he carried Sabrina over to the mohair couch against the back wall and set her down.

"Let me take a look at that." He crouched before her and gently brushed sand from her leg.

"No, it's all right. I don't need—ow!"

Tears sparkled in Sabrina's eyes at the pain Lawson's gentle manipulation caused. She wanted to scream at him, tell him to leave her alone, but she couldn't force the words out through her clenched teeth, and she couldn't unclench them until the pain let up. She blinked her eyes clear and was shocked to see how swollen and discolored her ankle was already.

"Well, there's nothing broken," he said, smiling into her face, "you just gave it a good twist. Be okay in a few days."

"How the hell would you know?" Sabrina growled back. "You're a Special Agent, not a doctor."

She gave his title a mocking twist and he blinked at her before he spoke.

"I'm also a Pee-Wee Hockey and Little League Baseball coach," he said. "I've seen more strains, sprains and breaks in one season than most doctors do in a lifetime. I consider myself an expert." He stood up, towering over her. Sabrina resisted the urge to look up at him. "Have you got an elastic bandage, by any chance? I should wrap that."

"In the desk, I think," she answered, her voice tight. "In one of the bottom drawers, on the left."

She watched him open drawers and search among the papers and paraphernalia that had collected over the hundred-some years the desk had been in her family. She resented his intrusion there, as though the touch of his hands, the sweep of his eyes, would somehow contaminate the contents—the desk, the room, her whole life. She wondered how long it would be before he would start asking his prying questions, questions that chipped away at her very soul. He came up empty-handed after looking in all the left-hand drawers, and started in on the right ones. Sabrina opened her mouth to order him out of her house. His cry of victory cut off her words.

"Aha! I found it!"

He moved back to crouch before her, pleased success warming his cold blue eyes. He removed the metal butterflies that held the bandage closed and began winding the elastic fabric around her ankle.

"Now, if you keep it wrapped and stay off it for a few days, you shouldn't have any problems. I know it feels awful," he said, hearing her pained intake of breath, "but these things always hurt a whole lot more than they deserve to. Actually, from my observation, it seems that the more they hurt, the less serious the damage is. There." He rose and pulled an embroidered footstool over, setting her bandaged foot gently on the intricately worked surface. "Keep it propped up like this, and don't put any weight on it. A couple of aspirins should take care of the pain. Can I get you some?"

"No. It feels fine, I don't need any aspirin." Even Sabrina could hear the pain in her voice, and she winced at the unconscious betrayal, keeping her face turned from Mitchell Lawson's watchful blue eyes.

"Yeah, I can see you don't," he replied, his voice rich with irony. "Where are they, upstairs or down here?"

"Upstairs. In the medicine cabinet."

She hadn't wanted to tell him, but she knew he wouldn't leave until she did and she certainly didn't want him wandering the house on his own, poking into all her things while he searched for aspirin.

She stared at the archway through which he had disappeared, her lips pressed together in a tight line, wondering what he was doing, what he was prying his nose into up there. But he returned too quickly to have done anything more than get the aspirin bottle from the bathroom and a glass of water from the kitchen. Sabrina did her best not to touch his palm with her fingers when she picked up the two white pills he held out to her. Something about his nearness, the warmth radiating from his skin, the strength of his well-defined muscles made her unaccountably nervous. He disappeared while she swallowed the aspirin, and she could hear him moving around in her kitchen. She was just about to get up, despite the pain in her leg, and order him to leave, when he reappeared carrying a tray.

"I threw something together for you so you won't have to worry about getting up to eat," he said, setting the tray on another footstool, which he then slid close to her. "Tomato and cucumber sandwiches, you didn't have any lunch meat. And tea. For some strange reason, tea always seems to make people feel better."

He pulled an afghan from the back of a tall, wingback chair, a lacy ripple pattern in soft pink, beige and green that Sabrina had finished the last time she and Charlie had come to the cottage, late in May. He settled it over Sabrina's lap and legs, tucking it carefully around her injured foot. Then he stepped back and gave her a faint smile.

"Is there anything else you want, Mrs. Compton?"

"Yes." Sabrina looked up into his eyes. His smile faded. "I want you to leave."

He stared at her, his face still and watchful. Sabrina stared back, angry breaths lifting her chest as she poured all the venom she felt in his direction. Finally, he nodded and sighed. He walked toward the front door, turning in the archway to face her one last time. She could see the apology on his face, in his eyes, the sorrow he felt for having been the bearer of such news as he had brought, for the pain he had heaped upon the horror she had already suffered. She dared him to speak with a lift of her chin, to voice the pity he held for her. If he did, she'd fly at him with fangs and nails bared, ankle be damned. She didn't want his sorrow, or his pity. She didn't want his apology, either, or his kindness, and she didn't want him in her life. He could go to hell for all she cared. He could go to hell.

"Take care of that foot, Mrs. Compton," he said, softly. "Good-bye."

He turned and left the house, shutting the door firmly behind him. Sabrina stared for a long time at the archway where he had disappeared. Her body began to tremble until she couldn't stop shivering. She pulled the afghan up around her shoulders and leaned her head back on the stiff mohair upholstery, fighting tears she couldn't understand.

She lost the battle. She lay on the couch sobbing for she knew not what until at long last the tears slowed, and dried. The tea was lukewarm when at last she reached out for the tea Lawson had made. But still she drank it, remembering his words about how tea made people feel better. It appeared he was right. It did seem to help her relax, to feel less angry and resentful. And aware of her hunger. She was glad he had made the sandwiches, she didn't think she would be able to stand up, much less make dinner for herself. She bit into one, surprised at the clean, sweet taste, savoring the combination of fresh tomatoes and cucumber, slathered with mayonnaise and seasoned lightly with salt and pepper. She'd have to remember it, make it a part of her own culinary repertoire, even if it did come from Special Agent Mitchell Lawson.

She ate almost a complete sandwich and finished the tea before her lids began to droop. Late afternoon shadows deepened around her as Sabrina at last relaxed enough to fall asleep, regretting as she did so the rudeness she had shown to the tall, fair-haired FBI Agent. After all, the situation was not his fault. He had merely been doing his job. And she had seen in his face when he was leaving how difficult and distasteful that job could sometimes be.

Yet she was glad he was gone, glad she would not have to face him again. It was over, finally. Charlie hadn't truly existed, and the man he really had been was dead. That part of her life could be forgotten. Somehow she would have to find a way to go on, discover some meaning for the rest of her life. She would base it on truth, not lies or fantasy. And not on memories, either. She didn't have any that were real. Somehow she would have to find her own reality, one that wouldn't dissolve if a tall, fair-haired stranger came knocking on her door. Sabrina fell asleep with the sound of restless waves in her ears, and the memory of Special Agent Mitchell Lawson's strong arms carrying her across the shifting sand in her head. She smiled, though she didn't know it.

CHAPTER THIRTEEN

"Listen, Kelsey, if I knew, I'd sure as hell tell you," Mitch growled, exasperated. It was Friday, early in the evening. He stood in his third floor room at the Gaffe Island Inn staring out the sliding glass door at the darkening expanse of the Atlantic, totally unmoved by the alluring artistry of nature's maritime canvas. He barely saw the scenic view. Mostly, he just saw red. "I have no idea how much longer this is going to take. And I am *not* enjoying this little jaunt one bit, if you want to know, so stop your smirking. I can feel it through the phone. Has the background on the Compton woman come in, yet?"

"No, sir," Kelsey purred sweetly, making Mitch growl again. He knew she hadn't stopped smirking. "Dan Jeffers said he would take care of it personally, especially after he saw the picture you sent. This 'Compton woman,' as you seem determined to call her, is quite good looking, isn't she? Does she have a first name?"

"Of course she has a first name, not that it's any of your business!" Mitch turned away from the window and paced to the anonymous blond wood dresser. "Your business, Ms. McGuire, if you care to remember it, is to do typing and filing and telephone answering— in short, secretarial work. How about it? Care to try some?"

"Oh, I'd love to, Mr. Lawson. Except I'm too busy just now thinking up excuses to give to Mr. Henry as to why you aren't here tending to *your* business. Which is what he pays you for, I believe. Just as you pay me to be secretarial. Although, technically speaking, it *is* Mr. Henry who signs the checks. I have a feeling he'd sign them more readily, at least where you're concerned, if you actually showed some progress on that backlog beneath which your desk is hiding. Sometime this year, that is."

"I swear, Kelsey, if you weren't so damn competent, I'd fire you right now."

"Oh, really?"

"Yes. After I taped a few hours of your incredible voice, that is." Mitch dropped onto the comfortable double bed, loving the sound of Kelsey's purring laughter. "Has anything more come in on Biaggi?"

"Not much. Dan and I talked to everyone we could think of, called in just about every marker you had out there. No one's got a picture. I take it he's allergic to cameras, which is understandable in his line of work. And no one's even seen him, not for years. Does all the business end of things by pay phone and mail courier. The only ones who could identify him are his victims, they're the only ones who get to see him, not that it does them any good. Or us."

"Well, I knew it was a long shot."

"Rumor says that he's tied up on a 'big one' right now. He hit his target all right, but ran into some kind of snag. The payment won't be fulfilled until he clears it up completely. He is not, according to the same rumor, a very happy man right now."

"A big one, huh? DiGesare?"

"No one seems to know, not for sure."

"Damn, I was hoping *something* usable would turn up. Somebody somewhere knows the score, you can bet on that. If we could just find out what that bastard looks like. I hate the thought that I could pass him in the hall here, and never know it."

"I hate the thought that he *would* know it. You, unfortunately, Mr. Lawson, are not allergic to cameras. Besides, even if you were, you look so much like a cop you couldn't even fool a fool. You are being careful, aren't you?"

Mitch grimaced, well aware that behind Kelsey's casually worded question was the knowledge that he had not been in a field situation for over six years. Obviously, danger-honed reflexes were not exactly *sine qua non* for a desk job, and talents left un-exercised tended to rust. Badly. He sighed, long and loud.

"Have no fear, Kelsey, the same wondrous thoughts have also crossed this dinosaur of a brain. I'm not about to take any chances, not with retirement so close." Less than ten years. Mitch shuddered at the thought. He'd rather die, first. "And anyway, I'm really looking forward to fighting with the Chief when I get back. I love the way steam shoots out of his ears and his eyebrows form that inverted 'V' in the middle of his forehead. And I know he lives to make my life miserable. Wouldn't want to get hurt, and disappoint the old man."

Kelsey laughed. Mitch knew she was well aware that Oscar Henry was fourteen years Mitch's junior.

"Oh, you'll get your fight, Mr. Lawson, I can guarantee that. If you're not careful, he's just liable to head your way. He's that mad. Tell you what." Kelsey paused, then Mitch heard a sigh that sounded like liquid silk. "This is Friday. I'll give him a sob story and promise you'll be back by eight Wednesday morning without fail. That means you'll only be gone a week, not bad considering you had to follow 'The Compton Woman' to South Carolina, make contact, gain her trust, etc., etc." Mitch frowned at Kelsey's insinuating tone, but she spoke on before he could interrupt. "That gives you the weekend to finish up whatever it is you think is so important, and two days' grace just in case. And if you do get back a day or two early, it might take some of the wind out of his sails. I just wouldn't count on it, is all."

"Sounds workable to me," Mitch agreed, still frowning over the covert meaning in Kelsey's words.

"Dan and I will keep nosing around, send you whatever else we come up with. And the background on Mrs. Compton. Dan should have that ready later today. Anything else before I get back to secretarying?"

"Yes. Do me one favor, will you? Learn how to make decent coffee before I get back. That's a whole weekend, plus two days' grace. You should be able to handle that."

"You think so?" Kelsey said, laughing. "I wouldn't count on that, either."

Mitch hung up and lounged back on the soft double bed, eying the scant array of new clothing scattered on the companion bed beside him. Dark blue cotton slacks, two striped polo-style shirts and a navy windbreaker, exorbitant price tags still appended, to say nothing of the slacks and sweater he had on, plus extra underwear, and that little bit had set him back over three hundred fifty bucks. *We ought to do a Federal sting op here,* he thought, *really nail these tourists shops. How the hell do the locals make it?*

The worst part had been driving that damned midgetmobile all the way into Charleston, to find a shop where he could buy a new holster. After all, he couldn't very well walk around in his shirt sleeves with his shoulder contraption reflecting the sun's brilliant rays, could he? Although he'd been tempted. It would have given the local yokels something to talk about for a few months, and the shock and astonishment on their faces would have compensated him somewhat for the bite taken out of his credit card.

But the local cops were pissed enough at him as it was, so he'd grudgingly purchased a holster that let him tuck his .357 snug in his waistband and cover it with either shirt, sweater or windbreaker as he chose, even though he hated the feel. And the trip to the big city had been doubly worth it. He'd taken the toy car to the rental place, parked it on their counter—which hadn't been hard once he'd managed to unkink his body and stand upright like a normal human being— and driven away in something a whole lot roomier, incredibly less recalcitrant and at least sixty degrees cooler. This one, a nice, sedate dark blue, didn't glow in the dark, either.

Mitch yawned and glanced at his watch. Seven twenty-three. He'd run the electric razor over his face and go down to eat, maybe watch the stars come out through the bar windows, or from the terrace, and nurse along a couple of Scotches. And keep an eye on the other guests. Just in case. Then he'd turn in early, get a good night's sleep. He had a feeling he'd need it, since he had to face the Compton woman again tomorrow. Damn, but he had trouble now thinking of her in his usual cold, impersonal way, ever since he'd held her fragile body in his arms. He kept wanting to call her Sabrina. Maybe he really was losing his mind. First, he'd charged off on a case that should have been handled by the local boys, his precious ego all ruggled up. Then he'd let a pair of big, dark eyes and a whiff of haunting perfume distract him from his job. He should have kept at her yesterday until he'd gotten the answers he needed. Then he wouldn't still be stuck in this ridiculous place, with the 'Wrath of the Chief' awaiting his arrival back home. Mitch sighed, rose and cast one last hating glare at the out-priced clothes he'd bought before he headed for the bathroom, and dinner.

CHAPTER FOURTEEN

 Geoffrey Simmonds carried a heavily-laden tray in from the kitchen and set it on the table he'd placed between the couch and the wingback chair he'd pulled up.

"Who was that man I saw here earlier?" he asked, his tone teasing. Saturday had dawned overcast and humid, an airless, sticky kind of day that clung uncomfortably to every part of the body. Sabrina looked up from where she sat melting into the mohair upholstery, and frowned.

"What man? There wasn't anybody here."

"There most certainly was," Geoff insisted, pouring the coffee. "Outside on the porch. Kept looking back at the house as he walked away, like he didn't really want to leave. Saw him late last night, too." He took a bite of the ham, Swiss and tomato sandwich he'd brought from home, and grinned. "You have some long-lost relative with a shady past you're trying to keep in the closet?"

"What did he look like?" A cold chill ran down Sabrina's spine, puddled into a tiny, hard core of anger. She knew who it was, who it had to be. Damn him.

"I dunno. Tall, he seemed. Light colored hair. Couldn't see all that much, I'm not exactly right next door, you know, even though I'm right next door." He was right; although his was the closest house on this side of the road, two hundred yards was an appreciable distance. "Come on, eat something, or I'll go home offended," he urged.

Sabrina sighed, gave her friend an absent smile, and picked up a piece of her sandwich. He had considerately cut it into quarters. Special Agent Lawson's sandwiches hadn't even been cut in half.

"So tell, already," Geoff demanded when Sabrina's silence stretched. She swallowed her bite, took a sip of coffee, and shrugged.

"It must have been Mitchell Lawson, he's a Special Agent with the FBI. I told him I didn't want him back here anymore, I guess that's why he was sneaking around. He's the type that would that." She took an angry bite of the sandwich, her dark eyes glittering.

"An FBI agent? What do you mean? Why would an FBI agent be sneaking around your house?"

Sabrina didn't answer. Instead, she bit her lip and bowed her head. Geoff reached across the small round table and touched her hand.

"Sabrina? What's the matter? What's going on?" His canny eyes studied her a moment. "Is it something about Charlie? Something bad?"

"I guess you could say that," Sabrina answered at last, unwanted tears shining in her eyes when she looked up at her friend. "It seems Charlie wasn't really who he claimed to be. His real name was Tony DiGesare. He used to do money laundering for the Mafia in Arizona. From what Special Agent Lawson so kindly told me, I gather he also killed for them when he needed a little extra grocery money." The tears spilled over, streaked down her pale cheeks. "Seven 'hits,' isn't that what they call them? My Charlie... he killed people for money. I was married to him for over seven years and I never knew who he was. Or what he was."

"My God, Sabrina." Geoff moved beside her on the couch and put a comforting arm around her shoulders. "It isn't true, it can't be. I knew Charlie almost as well as you did. We were close. He confided in me, his hopes, his dreams, his fears. We were like brothers. There was never the slightest hint he could be capable of doing such things. He hated violence, you know that. Hell, he didn't even know how to get angry. It isn't true, it can't be. Charlie wasn't that kind of man."

"You're right," a deep voice said. "Charles Philip Compton wasn't that kind of man. But Anthony Albert DiGesare most assuredly was."

Geoff and Sabrina looked up to see a big, sandy-haired man clad in dark blue slacks and a blue and white striped polo shirt standing just inside the archway. He held an oversized slim black book beneath his left arm.

"Who the hell are you?" Geoff growled, rising, fists clenched, ready to do battle. Sabrina hastily wiped her wet face. "Who gave you the right to walk in here uninvited?"

"I'm sorry, I didn't mean to intrude. I didn't knock because I was concerned about Mrs. Compton's ankle."

"I'll bet." Geoff's caustic irony rang in the still air. He took a menacing step closer to the tall, solid man in the archway. Sabrina reached out and laid a hand on his arm.

"It's all right, Geoff. This is the man I told you about, the FBI agent. Mitchell Lawson. Agent Lawson, this is our—my—next-door neighbor and good friend, Geoffrey Simmonds."

"Mr. Simmonds."

Mitch stuck out his right hand, his blue eyes wary. Geoff Simmonds ignored the friendly gesture and turned to frown at Sabrina.

"It is not all right, Sabrina. If you told him not to bother you anymore, he has no right to come back here at all, much less walk in without permission. Permission that neither of us will give," he added, turning back to Mitch.

Lawson, obviously taking his cue from Geoff's belligerence, ignored the older man and directed his remarks to Sabrina.

"I am sorry to bother you, I know this is a very difficult time. But there are some things I have to ask you about your husband before I can leave."

"I don't know anything," Sabrina insisted. "I already told you that I had no idea Charlie was who he was, not until you told me. There's nothing I can help you with."

"You don't know that," Mitch contradicted. "You could know something that will help without even being aware that you do. You want the man who killed your husband caught, don't you, Mrs. Compton? What you tell me might make a difference."

Sabrina stared into those cold blue eyes, doubts flooding her. Did she want the killer caught? She had, desperately, just two days ago. Now she didn't know anymore. Charlie hadn't been any better than the man who murdered him, had he? Maybe he deserved what he had gotten. Was the death of a bad man as great a tragedy as the death of a good man? Should it cry out for the same vengeance, for equal justice? How was she to judge?

"She said she doesn't want to talk to you, Lawson," Geoff said, moving another step closer. "Now get yourself out of this house, or I'll put you out!"

"No. No, Geoff," Sabrina said. "It's all right, I'll talk to him. It has to be done sometime and I'd much rather get it over with. Do me a favor, okay? Will you get Agent Lawson a coffee cup before you go? I'd really appreciate that."

Geoff frowned his displeasure into her face, and in return Sabrina gave him a pale, sad smile. A moment later he nodded, turned away and strode into the kitchen to snare a coffee mug and bring it back to the living room. He plunked it down on the table, drank the last of his own coffee, and took the untouched half of his sandwich into his hand. He gave Mitch a hard look before he spoke again to Sabrina.

"Are you sure you don't want me to stay with you?"

"No, that's all right. I think this is something I have to do myself. Thanks, Geoff. I'll see you for dinner, though. At five-ish?"

"I'll be here," he promised. He looked at Mitch, still standing in the archway. "I won't be far away. You'd better not outstay your welcome. And you'd better think twice about any more nocturnal prowling from now on."

Puzzlement gleamed in Mitch's eyes as he moved out of Geoff Simmonds' way. He stood a moment watching the hostile older man stalk across the room and leave the house. Then he turned back to Sabrina. She held the coffee pot and his mug. She spoke before he could open his mouth and his thought vanished like smoke in a high wind.

"Do you take anything in your coffee?" she asked. "Sugar, cream?" Mitch shook his head and moved to the chair Geoff Simmonds had vacated. "You'll have to forgive Geoff. He and Charlie were very close friends. He's as upset by all this as I am."

Mitch sat, tucked the book he'd brought on the seat beside him and accepted the mug of hot coffee with a smile.

"It's obvious he thinks a lot of you, too. It's nice to have friends like that. How's the foot?"

"It's fine, it hardly hurt at all today. You were right about keeping it wrapped. I don't really need to be waited on like this. I guess Geoff just enjoys playing mother-hen. He doesn't get to do it very often, unless his grandchildren visit."

She smiled and shrugged, a tiny, tentative movement as if to apologize for talking about Simmonds. Silence fell. Mitch studied her pale face, the dark circles ringing her darker eyes. Sabrina toyed with the remains of the sandwich she could no longer eat, her hands trembling. Finally, she looked up at the man sitting across from her.

"It really is true, isn't it? What you said about Charlie?" Mitch nodded. "It's so hard to believe. I've thought about it constantly, ever since you told me, and I still can't believe that Charlie killed seven people. Not for any reason."

"People do sometimes change, Mrs. Compton. And remember, Tony—Charlie—he came to us, helped us put a lot of very evil men behind bars. He really tried to make up for what he'd done. Maybe it'll help to know that."

"I'm not sure it will. I'm not sure of anything, anymore. When I came home and found Charlie like that, I thought it was the worst thing that could ever happen to me. But I was wrong. Finding out that he wasn't who he said he was, that our whole life together was a lie..." She shuddered. "I just want to forget it. Forget Charlie, or Tony, whoever the hell he was, forget our time together, forget everything." She sighed, a tortured, ragged sound that echoed on the still heat of the early afternoon. Mitch sat silent as she struggled for control, not against tears but against the crushing weight of dark reality. He shook his head.

"Mrs. Compton," he said, but Sabrina held up a trembling hand, stopping him.

"No, it's all right. I'll answer whatever you ask, tell you whatever I can. Just please, when you're through, go away and leave me alone. Don't come back. Please. I don't think I can take much more."

"I really don't mean to hurt you, Mrs. Compton. I'm just trying to do my job."

"Your *job*?" Sabrina cried, her eyes flashing. "Why the hell did you wait so long? Maybe if you'd been doing your job earlier, Charlie would still be alive. I'd still have a husband I could believe in, a life I could trust. Isn't the Witness Protection Program supposed to *protect* witnesses? How the hell could they have found him?"

"I thought you might wonder about that," Mitch replied, picking up the book. "It was the first thing I wondered, too. Tony was well hidden, I saw to that personally. How did they find someone they shouldn't have been able to find? I got the answer, Mrs. Compton, from your husband's office."

Sabrina frowned at Mitch as she took the proffered book from his hand. She caught her breath in surprise when she looked at it, for duplicates sat on the bookshelf at home in Buffalo, and on the nightstand in the front bedroom upstairs. A sort of 'Who's Who' in the world of University Economics, it listed top professors from all over the United States and Canada, spotlighting with photos those who had made significant contributions to the teaching profession in the past year. Sabrina opened the elegantly bound 1988 book to page twelve, already knowing what she would see.

Charlie. Giving her a shy smile from the center of the page, an impressive list of credentials below heading an equally impressive write-up about the brilliant paper Professor Compton had presented at the International Economics Institute in San Francisco in June of 1988. Sabrina reached out tentative fingers to touch Charlie's picture as she studied his warm, comfortable face, looking for evidence of the murderer he once had been. She couldn't find it. Mitch Lawson's voice rumbled on in the background. Sabrina absorbed the meaning of his words without actually hearing them.

"Obviously, someone somehow stumbled across a copy of this book and recognized Tony, though he'd changed quite a bit in fifteen years. He probably felt safe after all that time, or figured the university community was insular enough that no one from outside would ever see it. I can't think why else he'd allow his picture to be published like that. It was like signing a death warrant."

"He was so proud of being singled out," Sabrina murmured, "you would have thought he'd won the Nobel Prize. It was all he could talk about for weeks. Such a little thing, a picture in a book. You wouldn't think it could cause so much pain, would you?" Slowly, Sabrina closed the book, idly fanning the pages with a melancholy air. The pages waffled and she frowned, staring down at the book in her lap. "It's torn. How did it get torn?" She looked up at Mitch.

"I supposed it happened when the office was ransacked," he said.

"What?"

"The man who killed Tony tore apart his office at the university about a week after the murder. At least, it's a pretty safe bet it was the same person, given the state in which he left your house. It'd be stretching coincidence quite a bit if the two incidents were totally unrelated. The police aren't sure if anything was taken or not."

"No one told me," Sabrina whispered, her eyes round with shock. "I had no idea. Why didn't someone tell me?"

"I gather you had left for California the day before. The police thought you'd be back in a week or two, and by the time they discovered you were staying longer, no one could locate you. And when you did get back, you left again right away." Mitch shrugged, and spread his hands in a helpless gesture. Sabrina shivered, wrapped her arms around her body, and shook her head.

"I don't understand this. They found Charlie—I mean, Tony. They found him and they killed him. Isn't that what they wanted? What were they looking for?"

"That's what I was hoping you could tell me. Whatever it was, it was pretty damned important. Biaggi never leaves a mess behind, he's too careful. And to take the chance that he'd be seen, or caught, in Tony's office—well, that's not like him. He never takes chances. I'd like to know just what was worth that risk."

"Biaggi?" Sabrina' eyes widened. "He's the one who did it? You know that? Why don't you arrest him, for God's sake? What are you waiting for?"

"Evidence, for one thing. Knowing in my gut that Vincent Biaggi killed Tony is one thing. Proving it is something else entirely. He's a consummate pro, Mrs. Compton. We've been trying to get him for years. So far, it's been a losing battle. We're not even sure what he looks like."

"I don't believe this. You have got to be kidding."

"Believe me, I wish I were. Can you think of anything at all Biaggi might have been looking for?

Something Tony kept hidden away? Something he was secretive about?" Mitch sighed when Sabrina shook her head. Then he brightened. "I know. What about a safe deposit box? Maybe here, at the bank in Gaffe."

"No. We didn't have any safe deposit box, Agent Lawson. Not here or in Buffalo. And Charlie didn't hide anything anywhere. There wasn't anything to hide." She rose, stepping gingerly on her still-sore foot, and sidled out from behind the table. Mitch rose and took a step toward her.

"The word on the street is that Biaggi still hasn't found what he was looking for, Mrs. Compton. I'd like to go through your husband's things. If I can find what Biaggi needs so badly, then maybe I can lure him out of hiding, trick him into making a mistake. That's one bastard I'd sell my soul to get off the street."

"All right," Sabrina agreed after a moment. "Charlie didn't keep much here, there are some papers in the desk there, and a few boxes in the spare room upstairs. I don't think you'll find anything, though, unless this Biaggi is interested in old economics test papers, or Charlie's research notes."

"Thank you, Mrs. Compton." They moved toward the archway. "You look exhausted. Why don't I let you rest this afternoon, and I'll come back in the morning? About nine-thirty, is that all right?"

"If I say yes," Sabrina lifted her chin and stared into his eyes, "will that keep you from sneaking around again like last night?"

She could almost see the questions that whirled in the cold blue depths of Mitchell Lawson's eyes. The blue deepened, grew colder.

"What are you talking about?" he asked. "I didn't come here last night."

"Don't try to deny it, Agent Lawson. Geoff Simmonds told me about my nocturnal prowler. He saw you, both last night and this morning, right out on the porch..."

Her voice trailed off, her breath stopping as Mitch's body tensed with alarm. He grabbed her arms and pulled her close, his fingers clutching hard at her flesh. Sabrina stared into a face suddenly grown grim and ruthless.

"The phone. Where's the phone?"

"It's behind you, on the table." Sabrina's voice shuddered with fear. "What is it, what's wrong?"

"Everything," Mitch barked, releasing her arms and turning to snatch up the antique telephone. "You're in great danger here, Mrs. Compton. Your friend Geoffrey Simmonds was wrong. I was not your 'nocturnal prowler,' as he put it. The man outside your house was your husband's killer, Vincent Biaggi."

CHAPTER FIFTEEN

 "Good morning, Mrs. Compton," Mitch Lawson said as he came through the garage access door into the kitchen.

Sabrina looked up from the table, where she sat over a half-finished plate of scrambled eggs and toast, and gave him a half smile. Mitch closed the door and walked to the stove, where he poured himself a cup of coffee.

"You look more rested today. You must have slept better, last night," he said.

"I took a sleeping pill," Sabrina admitted, shrugging. "I guess it helped, I didn't hear you get up. Is everything all right out there?"

Mitch nodded.

"Nothing to worry about, not a sign of anyone around who shouldn't be. I'll just take this out to Dan," he held up a second cup he'd poured, "so he won't fall asleep on his way to the Inn. Be right back."

Sabrina watched him leave, then turned back to her breakfast with a sigh. Mitch's assistant, Dan Jeffers, had arrived from Washington at one-thirty in the morning, to stand watch until Mitch relieved him at eight. She had lain wide awake until she heard his car pull up and Mitch go out to talk to him, her nerves jumping and her heart thudding in the darkened back bedroom. She knew that Mitch Lawson slept—or would when Dan Jeffers arrived—in the spare bedroom, and she could not stop thinking about it. Sleep was impossible. Her body tingled with the knowledge of his nearness. The thought of him in the room next to hers, the memory of his arms strong around her, the way he'd touched her cheek, the softness in his eyes when he'd said good-night made her shiver.

She lay still, staring at her closed door, hating herself, both fascinated and repelled by the attraction she felt for Mitchell Lawson. What was wrong with her? Charlie, her husband, her all-consuming love, had been dead just over two months, and now the man who had killed him was after her. How could she be feeling such things, aching for a strange man's lips, his hands on her body? What kind of woman was she? When at last Jeffers had arrived and Mitch had gone downstairs to meet him, Sabrina had taken one of the sleeping pills from the bottle in the bathroom. She woke at seven-thirty to find the bedroom across the hall empty.

The food tasted like sawdust to her. She ate only a few more bites before she gave up, scraping what was left into the garbage and quickly washing the few dishes she had used. She worked on, tidying the kitchen, waiting for Mitch to return. Finally, she could find no more to do. She dried her hands and moved toward the living room, pausing in the hall to look up the stairs.

What did he find up there? she wondered. Mitch had alerted the local police and called all over Washington to locate his assistant, then spent the rest of the afternoon and most of the evening sorting through the boxes in the storage room. He left only once, to go to the Inn for his clothes, waiting until Geoff Simmonds had arrived for their planned dinner so that Sabrina would not be alone. Geoff's eyes had glittered with determination when he'd learned of the latest events. He would stay to help protect Sabrina. But Mitch, returned from the inn, had ordered him to leave, turning aside the older man's objections, finally convincing him that he could best help by keeping watch from the safe distance of his own place and calling Mitch should he see anything suspicious. Mitch had insisted, once Geoffrey had gone, that Sabrina stay on the second floor where he was working. By the time she went to bed at ten-fifteen, he had not discovered anything remotely resembling the kind of thing someone would kill for.

Sabrina looked around the living room, struck deeply by the sudden unfamiliar feel of it, a room that only days ago had been her haven. Now it held disturbing memories—echoes of people who hadn't truly existed, the ghosts of those who really had. And the remembrance of cold blue eyes and a harsh, razor-sharp voice that had shattered her illusion of safety with two words. *Vincent Biaggi.*

Sabrina shuddered and opened the front door. Dark gray clouds lowered the sky to within an arm's length of the rooftops. Thirty feet away rolling surf pounded like pile drivers onto the sand. She shivered despite the mugginess of the fitful breeze as she walked across the porch and stood against the railing near the steps, inspecting the beach with frowning eyes. It felt wrong to her, as if something was missing or out of place. She could see two boats out on the ocean, sails gleaming white against the dirty sky, flying along with carefree abandon. She looked to her left, past the center of the shore's curving arc. People sat on the beach in front of the Gaffe Island Inn, though only a few brave souls had ventured out into the roiling water. She clutched the railing and leaned out, looked to her right to see Geoffrey Simmonds working around his house. She lifted her hand in response to his wave, then let her gaze move up to the cloud-filled sky. And realized what was wrong.

It was too quiet. The raucous scream of gulls was missing, the heavens devoid of their soaring, hovering presence. The sky was always dotted with birds, the air filled with the sound of their calls, yet today she hadn't heard one gull cry since she woke. There was no sound but the surf, and even that seemed muted, as if the ocean held its breath. What was happening? Why was it so quiet? Or was she simply building mountains out of molehills, seeing omens where none existed? Her heart began to thud. Sabrina leaned over the railing and again looked down the beach toward the Inn.

"What are you doing out here?"

Gasping, Sabrina spun, twisting her sore foot. She stumbled forward, and fell into Mitch Lawson's arms.

"Good lord, you scared me!" she said.

"You deserved it," Mitch replied, his arms staying around her longer than they needed to, the soft look in his eyes belying the harshness of his tone. "I told you not to leave the house, didn't I? What the hell are you doing out here?"

"Just looking at the water." Sabrina looked up at him then dropped her eyes. He let go of her arms, and she shivered, wishing she could kiss him.

"Damn it, Mrs. Compton, haven't you got any sense? Come on, let's get you back inside before something happens."

He took her arm again, this time his fingers tighter, angry-feeling on her flesh. Sabrina walked chastened at his side, limping slightly, glancing at the hard lines of his face in the dim hallway while he locked the door. She didn't speak until he escorted her into the living room and sat her on the mohair couch. The room felt stuffy and gloomy with the windows shut and the drapes pulled closed. Mitch snapped on the lamp on the end table beside Sabrina.

"I'm sorry," she said, breaking the silence that had fallen and keeping her eyes on her still-wrapped ankle. "I felt a little claustrophobic in here, I guess. All I wanted was some fresh air. I just wasn't thinking."

"It's all right, no harm done. I didn't mean to yell like that. I just don't want anything to happen to you, that's all." Mitch knelt and picked up her sandaled foot. "Let me check this, make sure you didn't hurt it again." He began unwrapping the elastic bandage.

"Did you find anything in the boxes last night?" Sabrina kept her hands in her lap, fingers laced tight together. She stared at Mitch's wind-tossed curls, wondering if they felt as soft as they looked.

"Not a thing. You were right, there were only old test papers and research notes. I thought maybe there might be something in those, but they all seemed pretty straightforward to me. Basic notes for his classes and the papers he wrote. Nothing even remotely suggestive or compromising to anyone."

"What will happen if you don't find whatever it is this man wants?"

Mitch looked up. Her heart lurched when their eyes met. Then he bent again over her leg.

"We'll worry about that if it happens. It has to be here, since it wasn't at the house in Buffalo or in Tony's —I mean Charlie's—office. Does this hurt?" He touched gentle fingers to her ankle.

"No, not much. It's a little tender, that's all."

"Good. Another couple of days, you'll be good as new." He began winding the bandage around her ankle again. "I thought I'd spend today going through the desk in here, if that's all right with you." Sabrina nodded, oblivious to the fact that Mitch could not see the motion with his head bent. "What about the desk up in the front bedroom? Did your husband keep anything there? Or in the trunk at the foot of the bed?"

He stood up, pulling Sabrina's eyes with him. She couldn't tear her gaze away from his face.

"I don't know," she admitted, her voice as soft as the dim light. "Probably. Charlie left his things wherever it was convenient. He wasn't very organized, for an economics professor."

"I'll start upstairs, then, if you don't mind." Sabrina shook her head. The silence stretched as Mitch stared at her, seeming as unable as she was to break eye contact. He reached out and traced his fingers down her cheek. "Don't look so scared, Mrs. Compton. It'll be all right, really it will. I won't let Biaggi get to you, I promise."

He turned and walked away, leaving a tender smile behind to keep her company. Sabrina watched until he disappeared through the archway, then leaned back with a ragged sigh, wondering what he would say if she told him she was much more terrified of him, of what his presence was doing to her, than of anything this Vincent Biaggi might do. She wished he would call her Sabrina, but was afraid to tell him to, afraid that the informality might melt away the shaky distance they maintained.

The day wore slowly away. Sabrina sat enveloped by a silence underscored by the faint roar of the ocean. An occasional slight scraping noise or dull thud from above her turned her gaze to the ceiling, and she wished she could see through the plaster into the room where Mitchell Lawson worked. It had been their bedroom, hers and Charlie's, a place of intimacy and privacy. Now their personal effects were being pawed through and scrutinized by a federal law officer, a man with sun-kissed curls and cold blue eyes. She wondered what Mitch thought of them, Sabrina and Charlie Compton, thought of them as a couple, as lovers. Or did he think of them at all, beyond the limits of his job? What reason would he have to bother?

She started dinner at three, stuffing two Cornish hens with a clam and shrimp dressing and putting them, covered with garlic butter, in a slow oven to roast. She made a salad, put a bottle of *pinot grigio* in the refrigerator to chill and set the table before returning to the living room. Mitch descended the stairs at four-thirty to find her back on the mohair couch, knitting and listening to a Benny Goodman record she'd placed on the wind-up Victrola. Sabrina paused in her work when she heard his step on the stair. She looked up, her heart filled with hope and apprehension.

"Anything?"

Her voice, barely above a whisper, blended into the music filling the room. Mitch shook his head and she sighed with disappointment, biting her lips as she bent her head to finish the row. If only they could find whatever it was that man was so determined to find. All Sabrina wanted was to get this over with, and get the disturbing Mitchell Lawson out of her life. She wanted to put the past behind her and build a future in its ashes. If that were possible. Ashes weren't exactly a good foundation on which to build.

"I suppose I'd better start on this monstrosity," Mitch said, patting the huge old roll-top desk. "I bet it's got a thousand cubby holes and hiding places. I'll probably be here until Christmas with my nose stuck inside this thing."

"Then maybe you'd better have a drink first," Sabrina said with a small laugh. "There's wine cooling in the fridge. I don't have anything stronger, Charlie and I aren't—" The words froze in Sabrina's throat. She pulled her stare away from Mitch's face and took a deep breath, letting it out with a ragged, painful sound. She shook her head, blinked her eyes, and spoke with slow precision. "I mean, I don't drink much."

"But you will have a glass with me, won't you?" Mitch asked, as though she hadn't tripped on her tenses, as though the ghost of her husband did not hover between them. Sabrina kept her eyes on the knitting in her hands when she nodded.

She had herself under control again by the time Mitch returned with two tulip-shaped crystal glasses filled with a cool, pale yellow liquid. She smiled her thanks, took the glass he offered and watched in silence as he sat at the other end of the couch. Her knitting lay on the cushion separating them.

"Something sure smells like heaven out there," Mitch said. He held up his glass. "To the chef. May she cook on forever."

Sabrina laughed.

"That's pretty brave, considering you haven't even tasted it."

"Nothing that smells that good could possibly disappoint," Mitch declared. He took a sip of the wine and smiled, his pleasure obvious. "I've been meaning to ask you about this place. There was no mention of it in the police report, even Detective Burke was astounded when we found out from your neighbor that you had a summer home. You should have seen his face, I thought his eyes would fall out." Mitch chuckled at the memory, but Sabrina's mouth tightened in anger. She turned her head away.

"It doesn't surprise me," she said, her voice dripping with venom. "That man is an absolute idiot. He has no business being a detective. If he knew his job even a little, and was willing to do it, this Biaggi would have been caught two months ago!"

Sabrina bit off her words, closing her eyes and pressing her fingers to her lips. The hand that held her wine trembled. Mitch waited in silence and sipped his wine as she fought her anger. Finally, Sabrina opened her eyes.

"I'm sorry," she said softly, toying with her glass. "I know Detective Burke did all he could do, that he really tried to find this man. I don't know why I feel like this. I'm just so angry at him, at that whole police department. They should have done *something*, they just should have."

"Don't apologize. Anger is a normal reaction. All victims need someone or something to blame. It's part of the recovery process."

"But I wasn't the victim." Sabrina frowned at Mitch. "Charlie was. He was the one it happened to. I wasn't even there."

"It happened to you, too, Mrs. Compton. You're what's known as a 'survivor victim.' That's what the experts call loved ones and friends who are left behind when someone is murdered. It's harder for the survivors than for the primary victims. At least it's over for them. But you have to live with what happened, learn to deal with the crime and assimilate in into your life."

Sabrina shook her head and took a sip of her wine.

"Do they make you take psychology during your FBI training? Or maybe in the Marshal Service? You certainly don't expect me to believe you learned that at Little League and Pee Wee Hockey practices."

"No, no psychology courses." Mitch rubbed his jaw, his fingers rasping over his late-day stubble. "I guess I just picked it up along the way. It's an occupational hazard in this business. We don't come in, usually, until a crime has been committed. To catch the criminals, we need to work with the victims. It helps, sometimes, to understand what they're going through." He finished his wine and set the glass down. "About the house, here. There was no mention of it in your husband's papers, no deed on record in his name."

Sabrina blinked at the note of authority that had crept into Mitch's voice. She stared at him a moment before replying, intrigued and a little frightened by the cold depths in the man, a hardness born, she supposed, from the work he did.

"That's because it's in my maiden name. I wanted to change the deed, have us both on it, but Charlie insisted that it remain mine alone. I inherited it from my grandmother when I was fifteen. It had been her mother's, built for her by her husband as a wedding gift. It's been owned by the women of our family for over a hundred years." She drained her wine and stared into the empty glass as she spoke on, caught in the past. "I don't know why Grandma didn't leave it to Mother, it wasn't like they were estranged or anything. I always thought they were very close. It should have gone to her first, and then me. I don't think Mother ever quite forgave me for getting the beach house. She'd always thought of it as hers, expected it would be one day. That it wasn't didn't make her last years any easier."

"So that's why this place hadn't been torn apart, too. Biaggi hadn't known of its existence, not until—"

"He followed me here," Sabrina finished, her voice scared. She felt her eyes widen. "Geoff said the man he saw was tall, with light hair like yours." Memories shifted, rose to the surface. Sabrina caught her breath. "There was a man like that, in Buffalo, in the park across the street from the house, and in the cemetery. I thought it was you, when I found out who you were. But it wasn't, was it? It was him!"

Fear enveloped her like a smothering blanket. She stared at Mitch. The room faded from her consciousness as she remembered again the feeling of being followed in California, the fleeting glimpses of a tall, lean figure that had frightened her into calling the police. Ever since he had killed Charlie, Vincent Biaggi had been following her. Why? Where did he think she would go? What did he want from her?

Mitch reached over and took the wine glass from her hands. His warm touch startled her, pulled her back into the reality of the room.

"Why don't I get us a refill?" he said, rising. "I think we could both use it." He gave her a reassuring smile and went into the kitchen. Sabrina gave him an A for effort, but she didn't feel reassured at all.

She picked up her knitting while she waited, too nervous now to allow her hands to lie idle. She gave Mitch a shaky smile when he returned, accepting the wine and taking a sip before putting it down and resuming her work. Mitch sat quietly beside her for a moment, watching as her fingers flew over the yarn. At last he shook his head.

"I keep trying to figure out what Biaggi is after," he said, his voice distant as though he spoke to himself and not to her. "It'd sure help to know what I'm looking for. Well." He shrugged. "Whatever it is, it has to be in this desk. That's the last place to search. Once I find it and let Biaggi know I have it, it'll be over, Mrs. Compton. You'll be safe."

Sabrina kept knitting, letting the silence lengthen. She knew Lawson's words were hollow. If he didn't know what he was looking for, he could very easily miss it. And even if he did find whatever this Biaggi person wanted, Lawson couldn't possibly know for certain the madman would leave her alone.

The music had stopped minutes before. The faint click of her needles and the even fainter whisper of the surf were the only sounds. Mitch let the silence stretch, then he sighed, set his half-full glass down and picked up the pieces of knitting that separated him from Sabrina. It seemed to her that he was stalling, and she wondered what was going through his mind as they sat together in the quiet air of domesticity that seemed to wrap the room. She knew it was crazy, but even with Charlie's ghost hovering close, and the madman Biaggi threatening outside the house, sitting in pseudo-connubial familiarity with this strange hard man felt right to her. She didn't want it to end.

"This is really beautiful," he said at last, fingering the yarn, his eyes tracing the intricate diamonds interspersed with triple cables. The yarn was blue, as pale as a late-summer sun-bleached sky, the pieces obviously the front and back of a man's winter-weight sweater.

Sabrina glanced up and tried to smile. She wasn't very successful.

"I was making it for Charlie. I only worked on it here, he used to call it his 'beach sweater.' I don't know why I'm bothering to finish it. I guess I just need something to do with my hands."

"It looks quite difficult."

"Not really, once you get used to the pattern. Of course, I keep having to get used to it all over again, every time I come to the beach, so it's taking me forever to finish. Charlie once said I must be part Russian, because this was obviously a five-year knitting project." Her voice faltered into silence. She added one more row to the sleeves, then looked up at Mitch. "Charlie was a big man, like you, though you're a lot taller. I'm sure this would fit you, all I'd have to do is make the sleeves longer for your arms. I've got plenty of yarn, I always overbuy. And blue is definitely your color, it'd be wonderful with your eyes and hair. Why don't you give me your address? I'll send it to you when it's done. I'd really like you to have it."

"Oh, I," Mitch stammered, obviously nonplussed by the offer. "I couldn't accept it, really. I..." His voice trailed off into a shrug.

Sabrina bit her lip and looked down at the needles she held.

"I'm sorry. I didn't mean to embarrass you. Of course you couldn't accept a thing like this. Your wife would never understand your receiving a handmade sweater from another woman. I know I wouldn't."

"My wife? What wife? I'm not married."

"You're not?" Sabrina looked up, her eyes wide with surprise. "But I... I thought—I don't understand. You said you coach Little League Baseball, and Peewee Hockey."

"Oh, that." Mitch picked up his wineglass and took a sip. "Those are my nephews, my sister

Bernadette's three kids. Hal died just over four years ago, so I play surrogate father whenever the mood strikes. It's just my luck they're all sports-minded."

"I'm sorry." Sabrina shuddered, remembering the death of her own father. "It must have been very hard for your sister, especially with three little ones. Was her husband also an FBI Agent? Or a Marshal?"

"Who, Hal? Not on your life. He was a computer analyst. He had leukemia. It didn't take long, but it was rather painful while it lasted."

"Life can be rather unfair, can't it, Agent Lawson?" Sabrina asked, her thoughts turning inward.

"Unfair doesn't quite describe it," Mitch agreed, his voice close to a whisper.

Sabrina sighed, regretting the morbid turn the conversation had taken. She wondered if Mitch was thinking about his brother-in-law. Or perhaps his investigation had taken him to Forest Lawn cemetery and a brown marble tombstone engraved with the words, *Our only child, lost before birth.*

Mitch reached over and touched her hand. Sabrina blinked, coming back from a place far distant in time and space.

"It's against regs, but I'd love to have the sweater, Mrs. Compton. On one condition." Mitch smiled, a mischievous gleam in his eye. "No more of this 'Agent Lawson' stuff. My name is Mitch." He touched her cheek, his eyes boring deep into hers. "Now finish your wine and lengthen the sleeves while I bury myself in your desk, OK?"

Sabrina shook her head.

"Mrs. Compton doesn't give gifts, Mitch," she whispered. "But Sabrina does."

* * *

Mitch's smile widened, and he nodded agreement. Then he rose, moved to the desk set against the archway wall and rolled back the lid before dropping into the old oak swivel chair. His back was to Sabrina and though he couldn't see her, he could feel her gaze on him while he worked. It was both a comforting and a disturbing sensation, and he found it difficult to keep his mind on his work. Something had happened between them, something he was not at all prepared for. He didn't understand it, and was certain he didn't want to. All he really wanted was to get this case over with as soon as possible and return to his nice, safe bachelor apartment in Washington, D.C. He worked on, not relaxing until Sabrina limped into the kitchen to put the finishing touches on their dinner.

He wouldn't let her serve the food in the kitchen, where the table stood against uncurtained windows. On so gloomy a day the lights would have to be on. They would be spotlit targets for anyone out in the dusk. He helped her set up a table in the living room, placing comfortable upholstered wingback chairs on each side of it, lighting two oil lamps for 'atmosphere' and cranking up the Victrola to provide background music.

They chatted casually while they ate, Mitch so vocally impressed with the savory Cornish hens and seafood stuffing that Sabrina blushed with pleased embarrassment. He told her about the shooting that ended his Marshal Service career and began his stint with the FBI. Unconscious references to her husband peppered her chatter. 'In The Mood' had been Charlie's favorite record. He loved to walk the beach most on dark and stormy days. He hadn't liked the taste of clams until she had mixed them into this stuffing. She loved to travel, but it had taken almost a major earthquake to get Charlie to leave his beloved economics texts, though he had enjoyed the few trips they had gone on. She always had fresh flowers in the house, even in winter, because Charlie loved the sight and smell of flowers. Charlie had discovered the wine they were drinking quite by accident, having absently picked up something quite different from what he had intended to purchase.

She seemed to grow more and more nervous as the dinner progressed. Mitch saw her hands trembling when she served the dessert, a sweet-tart lemon ice over ladyfinger sponge cakes. When Mitch complimented her on it, she once again spoke of her dead husband.

"I usually try to serve something light after a rich meal. Charlie always said it isn't good to—"

She froze, her eyes filled with desperate denial. The spoon clattered from her fingers onto the plate. She pushed away from the table and spun around, the momentum carrying her to the archway before she stopped. She stood swaying, her hands pressed against the sides of her face.

"I don't know why I keep doing that!" she cried.

"Doing what?" Mitch kept his voice calm, quiet. He rose from the table and walked closer to her.

"Talking about him. I don't want to talk about him. I don't even want to think about him, not anymore."

"It's only natural, Sabrina. He was your husband, you spent seven years with him. You loved him, and now he's gone. You need to talk about him. That's part of the grief process."

"But he wasn't real," she sobbed. Mitch put his arms around her. Her body felt like ice. "None of it was real. Charlie didn't exist, he was just a pretend person. I think about him and there's nothing there." The tears fell faster, garbled her words. "It's like a cruel dream, where everything is so perfect, then you wake up and find out it never happened. All I wanted was to have someone to love, someone to love me. That's all. And I thought I had it, I really did. And when it was over, when he was gone, at least I had the memories, something to hold onto, just one thing in my life that made sense and was real. But it wasn't. I never had anything at all."

"Oh, no, Sabrina," Mitch murmured, holding her close, stroking her hair. "You're wrong, it was real." She shook her head. Mitch raised her splotched face to his, his hands warm and gentle on her wet cheeks. "Charlie may have started out a pretend person, but he ended up real. Very real. From the moment he met you, he became real. And Tony DiGesare finally ceased to exist." He wiped the tears from her skin with his thumbs. "All that was left was Charlie, his warmth, his caring, the love he felt for you. That's what you did for him, Sabrina. That's why he was such a good teacher, why he could reach out and open his students' minds. Because you made him real. You two had seven of the most wonderful, loving, real years that anyone can ever be blessed with. The love you shared is very rare in this cold, indifferent world. And it will belong to you forever, Sabrina. Who Charlie used to be can't destroy it, and what happened to Charlie can't take it away. You created your own reality, Sabrina, a reality much more real than the rest of us ever find. A reality of love. True, complete and abiding love."

Sabrina's tears dried as Mitch spoke. His soft voice washed over her like a blanket of protection. She knew he was right, she could hear the ring of truth in his low whisper, see the depth of his conviction in his no-longer-cold eyes. She knew, from what he said, that he had read their letters in his search through their possessions. He truly understood the bond that had joined Sabrina to Charles Philip Compton for seven wondrous years. She sighed now as the burden of pain and despair beneath which she had struggled fell away, and she offered her gratitude on the platter of her dark eyes to the tall, fair-haired Special Agent as once she had offered herself to her husband. Mitch, too, had worked a miracle in her life. He had given her back her love to hold onto, and to build from.

"Thank you," she said, her voice trembling.

Slowly, Mitch's lips descended, touching Sabrina's with gentle desire. Her hands slid up, curled onto his shoulders, pulled him closer. His kiss roughened, inflaming her passion. Sabrina pressed against him, a soft moan echoing in her throat. Mitch's hands moved, searched, found her hair. His fingers twined amid the long, dark strands, taking possession of her in the misty gleaming lamplight. Sabrina could barely breathe. The kiss lengthened and she opened her lips to his. Her heart pounded in her breast. Gently, whisper-soft, Mitch's tongue touched hers in a loving caress.

The phone rang. Mitch and Sabrina jerked apart, startled by the abrupt intrusion, Sabrina's breath gasping in and out through her parted lips. She wondered if she, too, looked as confused and embarrassed as Mitch did. Then Mitch smiled at her and traced his fingers over her mouth.

"Go on, answer it," he said. "I'll pretend I'm domestic and start clearing the table."

Sabrina nodded and moved on uncertain legs to the telephone in the corner. She lifted it, keeping her back to Mitch who she could hear rattling dishes at the dinner table, and took the earpiece off the hook.

"Hello?" Even to herself, she sounded scared.

"Sabrina? Is everything all right there?"

"Oh, Geoff!" Relief surged through her, though what she had expected to hear she didn't know. "Of course everything's all right. Why wouldn't it be? We're just finishing dinner."

"Have you had the radio on?" Geoff knew she didn't have a television. The urgency in his voice made her frown.

"No. Why? What's wrong, what's happened?"

Mitch paused in the archway, caught by the alarm in her voice. He turned, his hands full of dishes, and met her wide, anxious eyes.

"We're in for a big one, Sabrina," Geoff said. "A hurricane. It's already destroyed half the Caribbean Islands, and it's heading straight for us!"

CHAPTER SIXTEEN

The radio reports terrified Sabrina. By Monday morning, Hurricane Hugo had leveled most of Puerto Rico, sliced across the eastern end of the Dominican Republic, wreaked total havoc in the Turks and Caicos Islands, and destroyed much of the beauty and almost ninety percent of the homes and businesses in the Bahamas. Then the storm, slowed by its passage over these tiny points of land that poked up through the waters of the Atlantic, seemed to pause as though considering its four options. It could continue to disintegrate slowly, dissolving into a tropical storm and dissipating before it hit the continental U.S. coastline, though its backlash would still carry torrential rains and cause serious flooding. It could continue straight on to hit Florida midway down its eastern shore after regaining some of its strength over open, shallow coastal waters, or veer into the Gulf of Mexico to inundate the western coast of Florida and the southern parts of Alabama, Mississippi, and Louisiana, perhaps reaching as far west as Texas. Or it could swing east out into the deep Atlantic, paralleling the coast while it built into a formidable adversary against which few man-made structures could stand, before the lure of land again pulled it onshore. All along both the east and gulf coasts, people watched National Weather Service bulletins throughout the night with bated breath, to find out what Hugo had in mind for them. Finally, on Monday at two a.m., the huge storm system rolled ponderously toward the east and moved slowly out into the Atlantic.

Waves of panic undulated all up the east coast. The storm had lost enough power over the Islands and Puerto Rico to teeter on the edge of downgrading to a tropical storm, raising everyone's hopes. Now, the longer it traveled over the ocean's deep warm waters, the more strength it would gather. Sustained winds were already being clocked at 112 miles per hour, close to its speed when it had devastated the Caribbean Islands. From the direction in which it now moved, it seemed certain that it would grow into one of the most powerful and destructive storms of the century.

Though most hurricanes tended to stay to the south, wreaking their havoc on those who lived in tropical, sunny climes, it was not unheard of for devastating storms to reach as far north as Maine. In 1955, Diane flattened the east coast from North Carolina to New England, killing 184. Five years later Donna hopscotched up from Florida to Maine, the first hurricane on record to hit both the South and the Middle Atlantic States as well as New England. Camille, in 1969, reached as far north as Virginia, causing billions of dollars in damage and killing 250 people, and in 1972, 122 died when Hurricane Agnes hit land in North Carolina, destroying the east coast all the way to New York. Through bitter experience, those living in America's coastal states had learned to both fear and respect hurricanes. To take one lightly, or ignore its power, often resulted in death. For most, evacuation was the only safe alternative.

The fact that Gaffe Island might stand in Hugo's path only added one more burden to Sabrina's already overloaded mind. She found it hard to concentrate on the likelihood of even more danger coming her way. Her anxiety had risen so high on Sunday night when Mitch Lawson had at last turned away empty-handed from the big old roll-top desk that, for the first time in three weeks, she had swallowed one of the tranquilizers her doctor prescribed after Charlie's death. She had woken screaming at three-thirty on Monday morning, assailed by hideous nightmares despite the sleeping pill she'd taken. The Agent's strong arms comforting her had taken away the images of blood and death, but they had also left Sabrina's nerves more tautly stretched than ever. She passed the remainder of the dark hours tossing, only half-asleep and haunted by the disconcerting memory of Mitch's lips warm on hers.

Mitch was still asleep when she rose with the sun, her eyes burning and her head throbbing, to pace the dim living room, feeling like a caged animal. Mitch had pulled the drapes closed and ordered her to remain indoors unless accompanied by either him or his assistant, Dan Jeffers, a short, blocky young man with dark hair, sparkling hazel eyes, and a tendency to smile too much. Mitch had also warned her to stay away from the bare kitchen windows, a dictum that prevented her from using the kitchen table. The band of high pressure pushed ahead of the hurricane's path had raised both temperature and humidity during the night. The house, with its doors locked and windows closed for hours, felt like a claustrophobic sweatbox. Sabrina endured the forced confinement for close to an hour before she rebelled. This was her home, her property. She would not be kept a prisoner in it.

She whirled, strode to the front door and pulled aside the translucent curtain. Leaden clouds stretched motionless across the heavens. The ocean looked sluggish and nasty beneath their ponderous weight. The deserted beach appeared cold and uninviting. No birds soared playfully over the water or picked through the nacre-studded sand. Fear flooded Sabrina. She bit her lip and backed away from the door, turning after a brief moment to walk down the hall past the staircase to the rear door where she pulled aside its curtain.

The street outside seemed as deserted and unfriendly looking as the beach in front. Palmetto trees clumped together diagonally across the road. Their fronds hung limp, wilted by the cloying humidity. A half-twilight reigned, the sun's brightness blocked by the sullen sky. Indistinct, murky shadows enshrouded the land. Even the air itself seemed filmy, conspiring with both heat and clouds to set a mood of evil foreboding. Sabrina shivered and decided she would stay indoors, as ordered.

She dropped the misty curtain and began to turn away. As her eyes swept one last time over the window, she caught a glimpse movement at the northern edge of the house. Quickly, she pulled the curtain back and peered out into the gloom of the day. There was nothing to see, no hint of motion anywhere, not on the ground or in the sky. Frowning, she stared to her right, searching what little she could see of the small porch and the dunes lining the curving road. All was still, quiet. A car appeared, sped down the road from her left to her right, heading for the north end of the island and probably the bridges to the mainland. Sabrina watched until it faded from view. Then again she let the curtain drop, her hands trembling.

She had seen something out there, she was positive she had. A quick, furtive movement, as though something, or someone, had begun to round the house and then swiftly pulled back when they saw the curtain in the door move. Or had her eyes merely been playing tricks on her? Sabrina paused at the bottom of the stairs and looked up, wondering if she should wake Mitch and tell him.

But tell him what? That the beach was too quiet, the air too still? That she couldn't stop shivering despite the heat? That she had seen some amorphous something where there was nothing to see? It was no wonder her imagination was out of control, considering the nightmares she'd had, the way sleep had eluded her. She wasn't about to make a fool of herself by climbing those stairs and waking Mitch Lawson with such a crazy tale. Being silly was one thing, being stupid quite another.

She went into the kitchen and took down a mug. Not until she lifted the coffee pot and began pouring the hot, freshly-perked liquid into the mug did she suddenly realize what she had seen. Relief flooded through her and she almost laughed. It had been Dan Jeffers, of course, patrolling the grounds, keeping watch while she and Mitch slept safe and comfortable in their beds. He'd been out there since eleven last night, alone and in the dark. It was just after six am now. That was seven long hours. The least she could do was bring him some fresh hot coffee.

Sabrina opened the kitchen access door and walked down the three steps into the garage, carefully balancing the full mug. Mitch had been adamant about staying out of bright lights, so she didn't bother turning any on. The main door was partly open, one of the four panels folded back to the outside. Very little light spread into the darkened addition. The single window centered over the horse stalls to her left added no more than a faint glow that just kept the darkness from being impenetrable. She stood a moment, letting her eyes adjust, moving when at last she could clearly make out the outline of the car to her right. She walked slowly down the car's length, trying not to spill any of the hot liquid, and edged around the back end to where the open panel gaped onto the brooding daylight. There she stopped and listened intently, hoping to hear Dan's footsteps. There was nothing but silence, ominous and total, broken at last by the sound of a car approaching. Sabrina stepped back into the shadows and let the red station wagon pass by, Her heart thudded in her chest. Her trembling hands almost spilled the coffee.

The echoes of the car faded and silence again clamped down. Sabrina nerved herself to step out of the garage, telling herself it was ridiculous to feel so frightened. It was broad daylight, for heaven's sake, at least as broad as it could get with thick dark clouds plastered across the sky. People were up and moving about, cars passing on the road. There was an FBI Agent in the house and another nearby out here. Nothing could possibly happen to her, not during the day. She was perfectly safe.

Still, she trembled as she turned to her right and edged around the narrow back porch. She glanced up at the back door, vividly remembering her arrival just five days ago, her desperate flight toward peace and solitude that somehow didn't exist for her anymore. She sighed and moved on, aware that many footprints marred the sandy soil she trod. More than there should be? How was she to know?

"Dan?" she called softly. Only the sluggish waves answered her. "Dan? I've brought you some coffee." Her thudding heart now overrode the ocean's pale voice. There was no reply from Dan Jeffers.

He must be at the front of the house, Sabrina thought. *That's why he can't hear me.* She felt loath to call louder, to advertise her presence outside the house. Mitch's voice echoed in her head, despite her conviction that she was safe: *Don't dare step out of this house unless one of us is with you.* She peered around the side of the house, saw nothing but sand studded with sparse sea-grass. No sign of Mitch's assistant. Looking to the left she scanned the dunes that separated her house from the McClellan's, the dunes among which she had confronted Mitchell Lawson. She saw only humped sand and wind-scoured rock, both lying dull and inert in the flat light. Chills traversed her spine. She took one last long look down the now-deserted dark ribbon of road and stepped around the corner.

She moved slowly down the length of the house, hugging the siding, her right shoulder almost brushing the wood. She glanced at the side living room windows as she passed them, one on each side of the old potbelly stove, and found the curtains still pulled tight. She caught not even the tiniest glimpse of the room. Once again she called Dan's name, silence her only reply. At last she stood next to the end railing of the front porch. She could go no further. Her feet teetered on the edge of the drop down to the beach. To gain access to the porch, she would have to go back around the house, walk in front of the kitchen windows, and use the steps that lead from there to the porch. Or go into the garage and through the house and open the front door.

She stood a moment watching the oily roll of the ocean, wishing she hadn't come out at all. She had only turned this way because she had seen the movement on this side of the house. But no one was here. Dan must have gone around to the other side while she was pouring the coffee. This whole thing was getting ridiculous. The coffee would be cold by the time she found him.

She turned to go back, sweeping her gaze down the length of the porch, thinking how funny it would be if Dan Jeffers suddenly appeared from around the opposite corner of the house. He didn't. Sabrina put her left hand on the railing, glanced down and saw something lying on the porch floor, near where she stood, covered with shadow. Something dark and long, rounded on the end closest to her, wedged between the glider and two large redwood chairs. Sabrina gasped and bent closer, stuck her hand between the upright pales of the railing. She touched the object, felt a sticky warmth coat her fingers. Beneath her hand she felt strands of short hair. The object moved beneath her touch, rolled to the side. A pale face emerged from the shadow of the glider. Dan Jeffers. A strangled cry escaped her lips, echoed on the still, menacing air. She snatched her hand back. It was covered with blood.

She screamed. The mug dropped from her right hand, thudded dully on the sand. Coffee splashed out to stain the pale soil as dark as the blood that oozed from Dan Jeffers' head. Staring at her bloody hand, Sabrina backed away from the porch, still screaming, visions of another body, other blood, superimposing over this fresh horror. Her movement brought her dangerously close to the twelve foot drop to the beach below. She turned, unsure of where she was, and found herself looking at the mounded dunes to her right. Her scream died, frozen in her throat. A figure rose from among the dunes, a man tall and lean, whose pale hair gleamed in the sickly light. Petrified with terror, Sabrina stared at him, unable to breathe, unable to scream, unable to move. His eyes bored into her, eyes as dark as the horror engulfing her. Time slowed, stopped. They stood immobilized, linked by blood and death.

His cruel lips lifted in a slow smile. The evil grin reached out, held her in thrall. Sabrina felt it wrap around her with an almost physical force, like a rope tightening, locking her into his power. The edges of her vision faded, turned black. She didn't see the dark blue Jeep that sped by, unheeding, not forty feet away.

He moved, took a slow step toward her. The motion snapped the bonds that held her frozen and she gasped. She threw up her arms. Her scream again rang on the dead air. She whirled and raced down the side of the house, ran for the gaping panel in a garage that now seemed a million miles away. Footsteps pounded behind her. She reached the corner of the house and swung around it, clinging to the siding with both hands. Her feet skidded in the sand and she almost fell. Her hand left a bloody smear behind on the wood. She raced on, too terrified to look back, to see where he was, and smacked into the edge of the back porch. But fear wrapped her too tight. She didn't feel the pain in her arm or the numbness that radiated down from her shoulder. She pushed away from the obstacle and ran on.

Agony lanced into her side, taking her breath away, and she stumbled as she passed the back door. At last she reached the end of the porch, able now to see the open garage door panel, a narrow dark slit that promised safety. Would she make it? Where was he? Were his hands even now reaching out to grab her, deny her sanctuary, take away her life? She could no longer hear his footsteps pounding after her. All that existed were the gasping breaths she forced into her overworked lungs. She plunged through the door into the garage, cracking her shins on the shiny chrome bumper as she caromed off the back of the Oldsmobile. She cried out in pain and fear. Her feet slid out from under her, throwing her forward onto the slanting trunk. Frantic, she pushed herself uptight. Hard hands grabbed her and she screamed again, twisting desperately in the unyielding grip.

"Sabrina! It's me, Mitch. What the hell's going on?"

The harsh sound of the deep voice shocked Sabrina, held the panic at bay. Her eyes flew open. She stared at him. Her racing heart and heaving lungs prevented her from speaking. She raised her hands, the dark blood shimmering dully in the dim light. The sharp echo of Mitch's indrawn breath reverberated over her harsh panting.

"Dan?" he asked, his voice intent, hard and angry.

Sabrina nodded, eyes riveted on the blood.

"In... the front... the... porch!" she gasped, not fully aware who it was who held her.

Mitch's fingers tightened on her arms, jerked her sharply. Sabrina blinked, focused on Mitch's face.

"Get inside, now! Lock the door and don't open it unless it's me. Stay away from the windows and don't turn on any lights. Understand? Now, get in there!"

He shoved her toward the kitchen access door and inched toward the open panel. Sabrina tripped up the three steps to the gaping door, pausing at the top to look back at Mitch. He edged up to the opening, then withdrew his gun from his waistband. Sabrina's eyes widened on the deadly-looking shape silhouetted in the oblong of light, then she turned, stumbled into the kitchen, and slammed and locked the door behind her.

CHAPTER SEVENTEEN

Mitch sidled around the house past the back porch, his gaze shifting from side to side, unheeding of the stones and shells that pricked his bare feet. There was no sign of movement, no sound but that of waves pummeling wet sand. His heart thudded as he paused at the corner, pressed tight against the clapboards, snugging the gun firmer in his hand. Why the hell had Sabrina been out here alone? And what had happened to Dan? Was he dead? He saw again the blood on Sabrina's hand and his teeth ground together. That bastard, Biaggi, it had to be him. If he'd killed young Jeffers, Mitch would never stop until he'd hunted him down and torn away Biaggi's life with his bare hands. Never.

Mitch took a deep breath and spun around the corner, .357 magnum extended and ready to fire. But there was nothing to shoot at, not a sign of the lean figure he had glimpsed from the bedroom window when Sabrina's scream had yanked him from a deep sleep. He debated searching the dunes but rejected the thought. Dan needed him more right now. He had to get onto the porch and take care of his assistant.

He turned and moved quickly but carefully around the back of the house, glancing in the garage as he passed to make sure Sabrina had closed the kitchen access door. Then he swung around the south side of the house and into a firing stance, swiftly scanning the barren expanse of sand-covered rocky cliff that separated Sabrina's house from that of Geoff Simmonds.

Satisfied no one was there, he scrutinized the deserted beach and the slowly rolling carpet of dull green water that stretched to the horizon. A car appeared on the road to his right, traveling toward him. Mitch lowered the gun out of sight and stood motionless, continuing to look for movement until the car had passed and the whine of its tires had faded. Then he moved forward as fast as caution allowed and rounded the front of the house, ready once again to do battle.

All was still and silent. On his left stood the house, tall kitchen windows reflecting the dull leaden gray of the sky. Eight feet to his right, the rock dropped twelve feet down to the beach. Straight ahead was the front porch, built to jut out over the edge of the drop-off. A short flight of four steps gave access to the porch from where he stood, and to the front door of the cottage, across from which fifteen steps led down to the beach. The remainder of the porch stretched to the north end of the house, ringed by a thick, waist-high wood railing.

The porch appeared deserted. Mitch ascended the three steps, his bare feet making no sound on the warm, damp wood. There, at the far end, he saw the huddled shape of his assistant. Again he stared around the still, ominously hushed beach, then moved quickly down the length of the porch to where Dan Jeffers lay. He pushed the redwood chairs up against the railing, knelt at the fallen man's side and laid hopeful fingers on his neck. His pent breath sighed out in relief when he felt the pulse, steady and strong despite the blood that leaked from a gash in Dan's temple to streak across his face and puddle beneath his head. *A lot of blood, too much for just one wound*, Mitch thought, though he knew that even minor scalp wounds tended to bleed freely. Mitch turned Dan onto his back. More blood, this time spilling slowly from wounds in his left shoulder and side. A large puddle stained the blue floorboards rust-red.

Mitch rose and went to the front door, rapping his knuckles on the window.

"Sabrina? It's Mitch. Open the door. Sabrina?"

He saw the curtain snick aside quickly, then the chain rattled out of its socket and the lock snapped free. The door swung inward on silent hinges. Sabrina stood in the opening, trembling, her face ashen, dark eyes huge with fear.

"He's alive," Mitch told her quietly, answering the question he saw in her eyes. "But he's hurt pretty badly. Stabbed, by the look of it. Call the police, Sabrina, and tell them we'll need an ambulance. And keep the doors locked until they get here, just in case." Sabrina gasped. Her lips trembled. Mitch gave her a small, reassuring smile.

"I'm not going anywhere, don't panic. I'll be right out here with Dan. Now, go make that call, then bring me some coffee, okay?"

Sabrina turned and disappeared into the house with neither a word nor a nod.

"This is what I was bringing to him," she said, her voice quivering, when she returned and handed a steaming mug to Mitch. She also gave him cloths with which to stem the bleeding, and a blanket to wrap around the injured man. "I thought I saw him near the back door, so I poured him a cup of coffee. But he wasn't there when I went out. I walked around the house, up to the porch. That's when I saw him lying here. And when I turned around—"

Her words choked off. Mitch laid a comforting hand on her shoulder.

"I know. I saw him, too. From the end window up in the bedroom. Biaggi, I'm sure. You were very lucky, Sabrina, that you got away. The next time I tell you to stay put, do it."

"But what does he want with me? I don't know anything." Tears trembled in her eyes.

"You'd have a hell of a time convincing Biaggi of that. Let's hope you never have to try. Now go inside and lock the door. And don't come back out until the police get here."

Mitch waited until he heard the lock snap closed and the chain rattle into place before moving back to Dan's side. He ministered to the savage wounds as best he could, his mind worrying at the oddness of the attack. Biaggi had had Sabrina, he could have snatched her away easily before Mitch could have even gotten downstairs. But he hadn't. He had let her get away, purposely, had merely been toying with her, scaring her. Nor had he killed Dan or lain in wait for Mitch. Why? What was he waiting for? Mitch had been so sure that Sabrina was the key to this thing, that it was something she knew that Biaggi was after. But he hadn't taken her away when he'd had the chance. Did that mean that it was the house itself he needed? Or was it both of them—Sabrina, and the house?

Mitch stared at his unconscious assistant, pushing aside the knowledge that the young man had a wife and two small children back in Washington. He brooded on the puzzling actions of his cunning adversary and sipped the coffee without tasting it, eyes and ears alert, his weapon in hand, ready to fire. His ruminations brought him no closer to enlightenment. Far to the south a siren wailed, drew slowly closer. Another joined it. And not quite as far to the north, though Mitch did not know, a pair of high-intensity field glasses kept careful watch on the increasing activity around Sabrina Steves Compton's summer cottage.

* * *

"Yes, Geoff, I have it on," Sabrina assured her worried friend. The muted voice from the radio on the desk warred with Geoff Simmonds' for her attention. Pressing the ancient receiver to her ear, she turned her back to the old, rounded oak box and gave her attention completely to Geoff.

"I haven't stopped worrying about you all day, Sabrina, not after what happened this morning."

"That was just an accident, Geoff," Sabrina began, repeating what Mitch had told her to say to curious neighbors who had gathered when the police cars and ambulance had arrived. Geoff's cynical snort cut her off.

"Sure it was. People get stabbed by accident all the time, especially when they're all alone. And haven't got a knife of their own."

"How did you know Dan was stabbed?"

"Mitch talked me, wanted to know if I'd seen anything. I won't pretend I understand what it's all about, but this nonsense is getting out of hand. The best thing that could happen is this hurricane. At least you'll be safe."

"Safe? What are you talking about?" She and Mitch had spent the hours since the ambulance left securing the storm shutters over the cottage's windows. But Sabrina had difficulty keeping her mind on the work, or the danger posed by the storm. She kept seeing the image of a tall, lean man rising ominously from the dunes a mere thirty feet from where she'd stood. The threat of a hurricane seemed minor in comparison.

"Haven't you been listening to the radio? The hurricane is headed straight for us. If it keeps to the track it's on now, the eye will pass over Myrtle Beach. Since that's only a hundred miles north of here and the storm is almost three hundred miles wide. We'll be in for a rough enough time even on the fringe. But they say this one is very unstable. It's changed direction four times just in the last three hours. There's a possibility it could swerve again and pass directly over us."

"That doesn't sound safe," Sabrina said frowning.

"What's safe, Sabrina, is that they're evacuating the island. They want everyone gone by six, that's when they're going to close the bridges and cut off electricity and water. Half the people have left already."

"But, why? I don't understand." Geoff's words made no sense to Sabrina, for she could not pull her mind away from the pit of fear into which she had fallen. She simply could not comprehend any danger greater than that which had stalked her on the dunes.

"For pity's sake, Sabrina," Geoff exploded. "That damned storm is a monster. The winds are almost a hundred forty miles an hour. That alone should be enough, but if it hits at high tide, even up in Myrtle Beach, the storm surge will wipe out Gaffe Island. Completely. Including us, even this high up. They figure that at high tide, the storm surge will be twenty feet or more. It'll roll our houses around like bowling balls. Even at low tide, the bottom half of the island will wash away. You've got to get off the island!"

"What about you, Geoff? Are you leaving?"

"I don't know yet. I've been boarding over my windows, and I'm pretty solidly built. Depends on what happens in the next few hours. If it won't hit at high tide, I may stick it out. But you'd better get off. Your place isn't as stable as mine, it's so old, and I doubt those hundred-year-old storm shutters you've been putting up will do a hell of a lot of good. Besides, considering what's been going on over there, I think a change of scene is for the better, don't you?"

"I suppose so," Sabrina agreed, sighing. It couldn't be as bad as Geoff was making it out to be. He was probably exaggerating to convince her to leave. "I'll talk to Mitch. He's the one in charge."

"You let me know, you hear? If Lawson decides to stay, you both come on over here. You'll have a better chance that way. Promise?"

"All right, Geoff. I'll talk to Mitch."

"Now."

"Yes. As soon as we hang up."

She said goodbye and stood staring at the telephone, shrouded in lamp-lit twilight even though it was only two-thirty in the afternoon. The wind had risen. Dark angry clouds churned across the leaden sky. Sabrina peered through a crack in the storm shutter at the roiling ocean. Its surface was strewn with white foam. Rain began to splatter down as she watched, driven sideways by the gusting winds.

She heard Mitch enter the bedroom but she didn't turn from the window. He had been searching for the mysterious object the killer was after ever since they had finished securing the windows. She knew from his silence that he had found nothing new. The trunk at the foot of the bed she once shared with Charlie creaked open. She heard Mitch begin to lift out the contents— blankets and old books, her ancestors' diaries, packets of letters, ancient photographs, ticket stubs and souvenirs whose meanings had long since vanished into the mists of time. After a moment, she went over to the desk and turned up the radio.

"Mitch, listen," she said, her quiet voice full of intensity and fear.

The warnings repeated, just as Geoff Simmonds had said them. Hugo, the strongest hurricane to ever hit the east coast, hovered out in the Atlantic like a menacing demon, twisting and turning as it slowly made its way toward land. If it did not change course, it would hit Myrtle Beach, or the area just to the north, at about five a.m., just in time for high tide. If it veered west earlier it could strike the Charleston Bay area around midnight.

Although low tide would make the storm surge less, the winds in the cloud wall close to the eye were the most dangerous of all. Damage from those winds would be extensive. Many buildings were expected to be leveled. All residents were warned to evacuate the area, to flee inland as far as they possibly could before securing shelter. At six p.m., the bridges linking the barrier islands to the mainland would be closed, and for safety all water and electricity would be shut off.

Sabrina stared at Mitch, who knelt surrounded by the memorabilia of four generations of Sabrina's family. He stared back, his thoughtful expression unchanging as the announcer spoke on about the approaching danger. The winds outside rose, rattled the shutters. Sabrina reached out and shut the voice off in mid-sentence.

"What do you think?" she asked, scarcely daring to breathe. If they stayed, would they be safe? If they left, would Vincent Biaggi follow them, stalk them until they could run no more?

"I think," Mitch said, nodding, "this is the best excuse I've ever heard for getting the hell out of Dodge. I've never been particularly partial to storms. Especially windy ones. How about you?"

Sabrina gave an embarrassed laugh and shook her head.

"I'm a coward. I hide under the bed when it storms."

"Good. Then it's settled." He scooped up the items he'd emptied from the trunk, dumped them back in, and shut the lid. "We can always finish going through this stuff when we come back. Tell you what." He stood up, stretched his arms over his head. "I doubt we'll be able to get a plane out of Charleston, I'm sure the airport's already closed, but if we drive over to Columbia we might just get lucky. It's only about a two hour trip. If we have to, we could always stay overnight and get a plane tomorrow."

"To where?" Sabrina shivered. She really didn't want to go back to Buffalo, to the house where Charlie had died. Especially not with Vincent Biaggi dogging her footsteps.

"I think D.C. might be a good choice, considering." Sabrina bowed her head. Mitch moved to her, enfolded her in a warm hug. "It's going to be OK, Sabrina. We'll figure out what he's after, don't worry. He's not going to hurt you. Trust me."

He placed a knuckle under her chin and lifted her face to his, his blue eyes piercing deep into her. Trust him... Sabrina didn't think she could ever trust anyone again, not the wholehearted way she had Charlie—or Tony, whoever he was. But at this point, what choice did she have?

Mitchell Lawson was all that stood between her and this sadistic killer. What did it matter that she knew almost nothing about Mitch, had no idea if he cared the least whether she lived or died? What did it matter that deep inside her there was a tiny, frightened child screaming with terror, who wanted to run before she was hurt again? She was caught in the midst of someone else's game, forced to play without any cards, helpless to stop the progression of events. That she would be steamrolled over as callously by Mitch as by Biaggi in the interest of winning the game, was a certainty she did not doubt. She was merely a pawn, and pawns existed to be sacrificed. That was their purpose.

Trust him. What choice did she have? Sabrina nodded solemn agreement, her eyes locked on his. She would, as far as she could, trust him. Mitch smiled and gave her a quick hug.

"Good. Then let's not waste any time. You pack up whatever you want to take with you, and I'll check with the hospital again, see how Dan's getting on. Then we'll make sure the place is all snug, and take off. OK?"

Traffic on the road outside had all but ceased by the time they left. Only occasionally did a car drive by, loaded with household goods. Mitch had called to find Dan Jeffers out of surgery, his condition listed as fair though the doctor told Mitch that he didn't expect any complications to arise. Dan was young and strong; within a week or two, he could be transferred to a D.C. hospital, where another week or so should see him released. The doctor expected Jeffers to make a full recovery unless the storm collapsed the building on top of them.

Sabrina toured the house, carefully choosing the items she wanted to keep safe from the wrath of Hugo. Two of her grandmother's quilts went into a suitcase, the sampler her great-grandmother had wrought, and the needlepoint silhouettes and crocheted antimacassars her mother had made. She added the sweater she wanted to finish for Mitch, the family Bible, the love letters and photos from the trunk in the front bedroom. At the last minute she zipped her great-grandmother's journals into an outer pocket. Her great-grandmother's hand-tufted chenille spread went into a second suitcase, along with her great-grandfather's pipe collection and some clothes for her. Mitch then lugged the cases down and put them in the Oldsmobile's huge trunk. Though Mitch had wanted her to ride with him in the rental car, Sabrina insisted on following him in the Olds. The car meant too much to her to leave behind. It was the closest link she had to her grandparents, to the happiness of life before sickness and death had invaded it. She'd never forgive herself if anything happened to the car.

She called Geoffrey Simmonds, told him that she and Mitch had chosen to leave and promised to call him when they arrived in Washington. She begged him to change his mind and leave also, then pleaded with him to be careful when he insisted on staying. The wind sounded like a howling banshee when she hung up and went out to join Mitch, who was methodically checking the storm shutters they had put up earlier. The savage winds yanked at his blond curls and he had great trouble keeping the ladder secure against the house. Sabrina could barely keep her feet beneath her as she leaned her weight against the metal rungs, steadying the ladder for him, her hair whipping in the wind, stinging across her face. Rain pelted down, and soon they were both soaked to the skin. Mitch insisted they dry off and change their clothing before leaving, seeing no value in catching pneumonia on their flight from the storm. It was ten minutes to five before they finally pulled away from the beleaguered cottage, Sabrina following behind Mitch on the now-deserted road to the bridge.

The driving was slow due to blowing rain that slickened the pavement and closed down visibility. Thick dark clouds draped a pall of eerie shadow everywhere. Sabrina could feel the big old car rock from the force of the wind, and her hands tightened on the wheel as if by sheer strength alone she could retain total control. When they passed behind the looming bulk of the Gaffe Island Inn, where Mitch had first stayed, Sabrina glanced up at the weathered old siding, wondering which room had been his. Had Biaggi stayed there, too, unknown and unrecognizable to Mitch? Her heart thumped at the idea, the thought that he could have been, most likely had been, that close all this time. She took a deep breath and looked through the windshield again, peering with squinted eyes through the rain-swept glass. Tension, the high winds, and the thud of old, ineffective wipers combined to make her head ache. She hoped it would not be like this all the way to Columbia. If so, she didn't think she would make it.

They left the Inn a quarter mile behind, coming at last to the first of the curves that would lead them around the northern tip of the island and down to the James Island Bridge. Palmetto trees clustered on the mounded rocks and dunes to the left, their fronds whipping violently. To the right, a narrow shoulder gave way to a series of tiered rocky ledges that slanted down to a tide-narrowed beach buffeted by foaming ocean. The area was undeveloped. No houses stood in view, no boats bobbed in the water, no cars moved on the road, save theirs. They might have been the only two people left on the face of the earth. Sabrina gasped as a particularly strong gust shoved at the car and instinctively pressed on the brake. The rain had lessened somewhat since they had left the cottage. She could see Mitch's car more clearly now, see his broad shoulders and fair head through her water-fogged windshield.

A muffled noise rebounded on the wind thrashed air, a tiny, sharp crack like thunder, so short that Sabrina wasn't sure she had even heard it, followed by a second crack. Mitch's head snapped to the right. His car swerved left. Then it jerked and began to wobble. The left front tire began to shred. The car veered back and forth, all over the road. Sabrina watched, helpless and horrified. Mitch slowly sank down out of sight. The front wheels slewed to the right. The car veered again, then plunged off the side of the road and crashed down the rocky tiers. It landed on its side, tires still spinning, its nose a bare few feet above the rapidly disappearing beach. The agonizing crunch of glass shattering and metal twisting vanished in seconds on the violent wind.

CHAPTER EIGHTEEN

Sabrina sat frozen, unable to breathe, her mind shocked into disbelief. What had happened? Then she gasped. Her hands left the wheel, pressed on her face.

"Mitch," she whispered.

The sound of her own voice released her. Her body moved of its own accord, her mind still immobilized by shock. Her hands dropped. One pushed the shifter into park, the other fumbled frantically for the door handle. All the while, silent screams of horror echoed in her head. They were alone out here. In half an hour the bridges would be closed, cutting them off from safety and help. What if she couldn't get him out of the car? What if he was badly hurt? Dear lord, what if he was dead?

The heavy car door finally swung open. Sabrina lurched to her feet, clinging a moment to the doorframe to steady herself against the buffeting wind, her gaze locked on the smashed car canted on the rocks below. She could detect no sign of movement, hear no sound but the mad howl of the wind, the roar of foaming waves and the growling chug of the Oldsmobile's motor.

"Mitch!" she screamed, at last letting go of the door. She prayed that he could hear her, would know help was near. "Mitch!"

She took a step forward, battling the wind.

Hard fingers clamped tight on her arm. They yanked her back and spun her around. A hard hand smashed across her face with stunning force. Pain exploded in her head. Her lungs emptied. She felt like a swimmer trapped underwater, unable to draw breath. She stumbled sideways, only to be pulled upright by another savage jerk. She was struck again, a vicious backhand blow on her right cheek.

Curiously, she no longer felt any pain. Her body flew backward from the force of the blow and her feet pulled out from under her. She smashed onto the pavement beside the car with a benumbing jar. Darkness swooped down and shut off her vision. Sabrina struggled to remain conscious, aware only that someone yanked and pulled at her arms. But she couldn't move. She seemed completely cut off from her body, as though the blows had detached her spirit from its fleshy abode. She lay limp, gasping for breath, her eyes closed. Rain pelted her face like sharp, stinging needles.

Then she was pulled to her feet. Pain returned with the movement, pulsating in her face, her hip and her shoulder. Her knees buckled and she moaned, gritting her teeth against the agony. Her wrists had been bound tight together. Her numbed mind couldn't wrap around the incredibility of what was happening. Her captor slammed her up against the car and put his lips close to her ear.

"In the car, bitch! Now!"

The cold inhumanness of the low growl shocked Sabrina. She tried to open her eyes She saw only a swirling mottled darkness that made her dizzy. Her stomach lurched. Her knees wouldn't lock. She reeled, almost lost her footing. The hard hands prodded her, shoved her toward the driver's door, forced her into the car and across the front seat.

"Down," he ordered, pushing at her. "On the floor. Move!"

Sabrina fell from the seat, her legs twisted and jammed with painful awkwardness beneath the dash. The man yanked at her arms then pulled out the lap belt and wound it around each arm individually just above the rope that cut into her wrists. Then he jammed the clip into the locking mechanism and pulled it taut, pinning her arms tight against the seat.

"Now, Sabrina Compton, it's just you and me," he said, his icy voice barely audible over the rising wind. He settled behind the wheel and shut the door, stepping on the brake as he shifted out of park. Sabrina lifted her head, trying to focus bleary eyes on the vague, blurred figure beside her.

"Head down," he said harshly, rapping the flat of his hand sharply on the side of her head. "Face to the seat and keep it that way."

Agony burst in her skull, echoes of pain that vibrated on until she thought she would faint. She didn't want to obey, but the pain defeated her. She dropped her head as ordered, cradled her face between her arms and desperately battled the darkness that threatened. The car moved. She felt it turn around on the road and pick up speed, bearing her away from the wreckage amidst which Mitch lay.

This isn't happening, she told herself over and over, her body trembling from shock, her face alive with pain, her hands slowly losing all feeling. *Please, God, let me be dreaming.* And for a long moment it seemed she was, dreaming and floating far above the place where her body had been beaten and crammed beneath the dash of a car. She lost awareness of herself, the man beside her, even the car and the howling wind that rocked it with alarming force as they drove along. She almost surrendered, almost let the darkness win. Then the car slowed, turned, crunched onto sandy gravel and stopped. The cessation of movement pulled her from the lulling lethargy. The engine died.

She didn't dare raise her head. Instead she turned her face until her cheek rested on her arms. Her vision was still blurred when she opened her eyes to see the man's misty figure open the door. He got out and walked away toward the front of the car. She blinked her eyes to try to clear them, wondering if perhaps she could somehow unbuckle the lap belt, maybe with her chin, and open the passenger door next to her before he came back. But she had no sooner thought it than he returned, climbed again behind the wheel and fired the engine. Slowly, the car moved forward into the darkness of what Sabrina recognized was her own garage.

He left the car again to fold closed the garage door. She heard the lock click shut before he turned on the garage lights. He took out the two suitcases Mitch had placed in the trunk only a short time before and laid them on the back seat. She heard the catches open, caught sight of the contents flying through the air. Soon the quilts, samplers, letters and books that Sabrina cherished littered the garage floor. He said nothing to Sabrina, working in absolute silence with his back to her. She lifted her head, very cautiously so he wouldn't notice, just far enough to see his jutting nose, the sharp slant of his cheek, the sand-colored hair that, unlike Mitch's, lay straight and fine on his head.

What was he looking for? What did he want with her? She longed to speak to him, scream at him, plead with him, but she was too terrified to open her mouth. She stayed silent and unmoving while time stretched out around her. The savage pain in her face had faded to a dull, insistent ache. Her hands and arms had gone numb, and she was losing feeling in her left leg, sitting on it as twisted as it was. The right side of her face was swelling up, she could feel that. But her eyes had finally cleared, though all she could see through the open driver's door were the tires lined along the garage wall and the contents of her suitcases being strewn over the dirt floor.

And then he was next to her, though she hadn't been aware that he'd moved, bending over her. The passenger door at her side gaped wide. He grabbed her hair and pulled her head up. Sabrina bit back a scream at the sight of the knife in his hand. He passed it slowly in front of her eyes, teasing her with the sharp, deadly blade, then swiftly slid it beneath the belt looped around her arms and sliced it apart.

The knife's tip bit into her flesh. Blood welled, trickled down her arm to stain the gray mohair upholstery. Sabrina, horrified eyes locked on her blood, did not hear him order her out of the car. He snarled, reached in and grabbed her. He hauled her roughly to her feet and half-shoved, half-carried her up the steps to where the kitchen access door stood waiting. He slammed her against the wall and held her there, pinned in place by a hard shoulder jammed into her back, while he sorted through the keys on her ring for the one to the kitchen door. Feeling had returned to Sabrina's legs by the time he found it and opened the door. She could bear her own weight again, though she wasn't sure she could trust it. He pushed her through the opening into the kitchen. She stumbled to a stop in the center of the room, flinching when the door slammed shut behind her.

He pushed the wall switch and the room flooded with light. Sabrina stood staring at the shuttered windows, knowing that no one would be out there to see the light through the cracks. There was no one to help her, not on a night like this. He could take down the shutters and kill her here, spotlighted in front of these windows, and no one would stop him. No one would even see.

"Move."

The one word felt like an icy finger tracing down her spine. She obeyed, shivering, stumbling toward the archway leading to the hall. She had almost reached it when he spoke again.

"Stop. Turn around."

She did. And saw him clearly for the first time.

Vincent Biaggi. Who else could it be? He stood staring at her, his eyes devouring her, eyes glowing with evil, dark with malicious intent. She understood now why she had mistaken him for Mitch. He was tall like Mitch, though leaner and harder looking, his strength concealed in slender, trim muscles. He resembled Mitch in a superficial way. They had the same color hair though Biaggi's was straight, a proud arching nose, lips that were thin and mobile and hands surprisingly large and square.

But up close Biaggi had a compact look about him, his face and body spare and narrow where Mitch was broad and solid. He was the most thoroughly evil man Sabrina had ever seen. He radiated malevolence, breathed out a frigid, sadistic air that froze her heart in her chest. Sabrina stood shuddering before him, watching his glittering dark eyes inspect and undress her, feeling as trapped and helpless as she had that morning outside the house. He wound his evil spell around her like an insidious web, pulling it tighter and tighter, using only his eyes. She could feel them caress her, those eyes, almost heard them order her to move. *Come closer, step nearer, near enough for my fingers to close around your throat.*

She almost obeyed. Just in time she pulled back and, with a tiny gasp, yanked her stare from his and looked at his hands. The hands that had killed her Charlie. Hands that now would kill her. She watched, fascinated, as they moved, unzipped the black windbreaker he wore. He withdrew, from a pocket in the lining, something small and oblong. Biaggi stared at it a long moment, at last looking at her once more. Then he smiled, a smile of pure, evil enjoyment. Again his hands moved, set the object on the table beside him. He turned it to face her, watching her face as though to savor her reaction.

Sabrina frowned, staring at the small brass picture frame, from the center of which she herself looked out, smiling. This was Charlie's picture of her, the one he kept on his desk in his office at home, in Buffalo. How could this man have it? Where could he have gotten it? She looked at him, her dark eyes genuinely puzzled. She opened her mouth to speak, to ask him. But she didn't. The answer was there, in his face, in the coil-taut poise of his body, the gleam of his eyes. It broke over her like an icy wave, shattering the tiny hope she hadn't even known she'd harbored—maybe this wasn't him.

But it was. It really was the man who had killed Charlie, who had come on a warm, bright summer day bringing darkness and death. This man had dragged Charlie from room to room, slashing at him, slicing him to ribbons as he shattered their home. He had tortured her husband for over two hours before finally blowing the back of his head away. And he had taken away only one thing from the ruins he had left behind, a thing that hadn't even seemed important or meaningful to Sabrina. A thing she had forgotten about long, endless weeks ago. Charlie's favorite picture of her, a small photo in an ornate brass frame.

Horror overwhelmed her. Panic surged in her breast. Sabrina gasped aloud. Her bound hands rose to fend off Biaggi. She shook her head and screamed. Adrenalin surged, prompted her to run, to get away. She spun, dashed through the archway into the hall and raced up the stairs, sobbing with terror. Her thudding heart obliterated the sound of Biaggi's pursuit. He caught her halfway up the flight and tripped her, slamming her down onto the steps, knocking her breath away. He knelt next to her, rolled her onto her back and began slapping her. Sabrina screamed again, twisting beneath his hands, hitting out at him with fists bound together, battering frantically at her tormentor. He ignored her blows. His hands roughened, moved faster, battered back at her until Sabrina no longer fought him, but instead used her hands to protect her face.

It was no use. Biaggi was stronger and faster. He simply knocked her hands aside and hit her again and again, savage, vicious blows that rocked her head from side to side. The side of her face hit the wall. The back of her head cracked on the edge of a step. Biaggi's hands swung, his face expressionless, until at last Sabrina collapsed. Her consciousness fled far away into impenetrable, silent darkness where Biaggi did not exist.

***

Biaggi rode the crest of his adrenaline high as he administered two final blows. Then he fisted a hand in Sabrina's shirt and pulled her close to his face. She hung limp, unconscious in his grasp. Blood trickled from the corner of her mouth. Her cheeks were scraped and bruised, raw looking. He studied her a moment, then laughed, a soft, mocking, indulgent laugh, before dropping Sabrina back onto the stairs. He watched as her body slid down to the bottom. Her head rapped on the stair edges. Her skirt bunched up beneath her crumpled legs. He stood and stared down at her a long time, waiting for her to move. She didn't.

Stupid bitch, he thought, his high dissipating. *You had to go spoil my fun.*

Then he descended the steps and grabbed her bound arms so he could drag Sabrina up to the second floor.

CHAPTER NINETEEN

 Sound penetrated first, wormed its way into the soft, comforting darkness. It grew louder and harsher, a pounding roar, a demented, whistling howl, bringing with it at the last pain—burning, searing, throbbing red pain.

The pain shifted as his consciousness deepened. It consolidated, settled down into his head and his leg— his right leg, the one with all the pins and metal in it. Mitch groaned, despairing, not wanting to think of what such pain in that leg might mean. Instead, he tried to figure out what had happened. Where was he? Why did he hurt like this? And what the hell was that god-awful noise?

He opened his eyes, but still could see nothing other than the redness of the pain. Groping with tentative fingers, he explored the space in which he lay, encountering puzzling shapes that gave him no edification. At last he raised a hand to where he hoped his face would be, and grunted in surprise. It was wet. Warm, sticky and wet. Damn, was he lying out in the rain somewhere? What the fuck was going on?

He must have lost consciousness then, for when once again he became aware, his hand lay on the ground beside him. Or in front of him, really, since he was on his right side. He didn't remember putting it there, the last he knew it was on his face, so he must have passed out and it fell. Carefully, without opening his aching eyes, he let his fingers explore the surface he lay upon. They encountered glass. And what felt like twisted metal. His mind cleared momentarily. A memory moved, came closer to the surface. He almost had it, could almost see and understand what it tried to tell him, but it eluded his grasping fingers and vanished beneath a dream of something cold and salty-tasting.

Water. It splashed on his face, eddied around the right side of his body, snaked up into his nose. He sputtered and coughed, half-screaming at the pain that erupted. Damn, that was real water! The shock of the discovery opened his eyes, and now he could just see through the red haze, recognized where he was, the danger that closed around him. If he didn't move soon, and fast, he would drown in the incoming tide.

Mitch gritted his teeth against the agony as he raised his throbbing head and levered his hands beneath him. He sat up an inch at a time, acutely aware of the glass shards strewn around him, the delicate state of his leg. *Please, God*, he prayed, unable to find more words for what was in his heart. If the leg wasn't broken, if the pins in his knee had not pulled out and if his hip wasn't dented too badly, then maybe he could get out of this. If it wasn't broken. If the pins were still there. If, if.

He succeeded finally in sitting upright and peered through the red haze. A car. He was in a car, one smashed and canted up on its right side. Above him hung the steering wheel, his exit blocked by the driver's door. The driver's window was mostly gone, its glass the jagged shreds littered around him, no doubt. Damn, he wished he could remember how this had happened. He knew it was important, more so even than escaping this shattered box before he became fish food. But he couldn't brood on it now, there wasn't time. Already the water level had risen a few more inches.

Mitch levered his feet beneath him with steely determination, taking most of the strain on his left foot, and reached up to where the door handle gleamed softly in the dimming light. Counting to three, he pulled the handle down and pushed up on the door with all the strength he could muster. It shifted, moved, raised up a few inches and crashed back with a solid thud, almost as if a force outside were pushing against him. Mitch again lunged at the door. It lifted, began to fall back, then flew open as the wind caught it in an iron grip.

Never one to look a gift exit in the mouth, Mitch hauled himself as quickly as he could up and out of the car before the wind changed its mind and imprisoned him once again. It took him less than two minutes, dragging an almost-useless right leg, to find himself halfway up a tiered, rocky cliff. The wind picked up and teased the car door, danced it upright then slammed it shut. He stopped and turned to watch the angry, red-tinted sea below slowly devour the wreckage he'd just quitted. Five minutes later the twisted metal was almost fully submerged.

The tide once again reached for his boot heels. Mitch turned and hauled himself all the way to the deserted, rain-swept roadway above. He sat at the road side breathing heavily, hunched against stinging, wind-driven raindrops, his pounding head resting on his left shoulder. He closed his eyes as his fingers gingerly massaged his leg. He kept his mind purposely blank, hoping the elusive memory would again return for him to snatch at.

It didn't. Rain beat on him. The wind pushed and pulled at his hunched form with impatient hands. The sea pounded on the rocks below and black clouds boiled in the sky above. Palm fronds across the roadway thrashed as though demented. Nothing else moved. No cars crept upon the road, no people struggled across the drenched dunes. Not even an animal sought shelter from the wild weather. And no memories rose, no enlightenment burst upon him. He still did not know where he was, how he'd gotten there, or what had caused the accident. Mitch sat waiting for strength to return and wondered at the absence of all living things, as much in the dark as when he'd first awakened.

Or, rather, as much as in the red, as he discovered when at last he again opened his eyes. The reddish film was still there, fainter now, but just as annoying. He raised a hand to his rain-slick face, tentative fingers questing over the source of the problem, his eyes. They seemed fine, at least they didn't hurt to touch, though the area around them no longer felt warm or sticky as it had in the car. Just wet. Then his fingers moved on, past his forehead to brush against his left temple. Pain shot into his head. Mitch gasped as fiery arrows darted into his eyes, wound down around his jaw and embedded pointed barbs deep into the pit of his stomach.

He pulled his hand away and saw, through the pain-tears he blinked away, fingers covered with red that quickly vanished in the drumming rain. Blood. That was what the red haze was, blood streaking across his face and into his eyes from a head wound. Warm, sticky blood had spread out like a veil over his eyes, a veil that was slowly clearing as the rain washed it away. He must have hit his head when the car crashed, probably whacked it into the window, shattering the glass and cutting himself. His fingers gently felt along the jagged edges of the wound, a long, deep, slanting gash from his cheekbone up his temple, over his forehead and into his hairline. It made sense that he hit his head, but somehow it didn't feel right. Somehow, he knew that the injury had happened before the accident, perhaps even caused the accident. But what had caused the injury?

He found no answer to his silent questions. In the end he shrugged them away. What did it matter how it had happened? That it happened was enough. He needed help right now far more desperately than he needed answers. Where the hell was everybody? It was inconceivable that in a world as crowded as this, he should find himself hurt in a place where not another living soul seemed to dwell. There wasn't a house in sight. He had no idea which way he should go to find help.

But he couldn't stay where he was. He knew he was bleeding rapidly, despite the driving rain that washed the evidence away, because every time he touched his head, his hand came away coated in red. If he didn't stop it soon, he would find himself too weak to move. And the storm appeared to be worsening. Already the wind felt stronger than when he'd first climbed from the wreck. He'd have to find a place to hole up, a place dry and warm where he could find a way to stem the bleeding and minister to his other hurts. Like his leg. Dark blood stained the thigh and knee of his slacks, too. It took a few minutes to nerve himself to move, but at last forced himself to his feet, barely able to stand against the power of the wind with only one leg to rely on fully. He knew it was no good by the time he took two limping steps. Without some kind of aid, he'd not be able to go anywhere at all.

Mitch swayed back and forth as he stood looking around in the murky twilight. Palmetto trees to his right danced madly. Their fronds whipped in total abandon. He'd have to be crazy to go near them. To his left, descending tiers of rock ended abruptly in a few yards at an angry, foaming sea. No help there. The wind shoved at him. He stumbled back a few paces and almost fell, his grunt of pain when he stepped on his injured leg drowned in the maniacal scream of the storm.

He again looked down at the rocks. If the wind grew much stronger it would blow him off the road, send him to a painful death on the very rocks he'd just scaled. He shook his head, not particularly pleased at the prospect of having his brains dashed out and his body battered into an unrecognizable lump. He turned away, intending to cross the rain-slick road to get away from the perilous edge near which he stood.

And he saw it. A board, wedged into the rocks about fifteen feet ahead of him, ten feet below the level of the road. A board about eight inches across, and five feet long, more or less. If he could get it, he could use it as a crutch and increase his chances of actually finding shelter of some kind. *If* he didn't slip and fall while climbing down and back up those slippery boulders with a leg that seemed increasingly reluctant to go along with the plans he made. *If* the board was strong enough and didn't snap in two the first time he leaned on it, or the second, or the third. *If* it wasn't wedged in too tightly for him to move. *If* he could wrestle it—and himself—back up to the road safely. *If* the wind didn't carry it away on him. *If* there really was a place of refuge within the limits of his strength.

A hell of a lot of ifs. It hardly seemed worth the effort.

But Mitch had never been a quitter, which was the main reason he'd been walking unaided on a leg the doctors had told him would need a brace, or a cane at the very least, before he'd managed to smash it up again along with his car. And so he lowered himself to his hands and knees and forced his pain-wracked body to crawl down over the tumbled rocks to where the board beckoned. It looked solid, and just about the right size. Mitch yanked it free of its perch and wrestled both board and his body back up to the roadbed with single-minded purpose. He crawled away from the dangerous cliff edge once he gained level ground, dragging the board with him, and collapsed on the far narrow shoulder with Palmetto trees shimmying above him.

When he regained consciousness, he again forced himself to his knees. He yanked off his green and black striped polo shirt, exposing the butt of the gun still nestled firmly in its waistband holster. He folded the shirt into a pad then lurched to his feet, draped the wadded fabric over the end of the board and cradled the board beneath his armpit. One final look around at the wild sky above, the deserted dunes and roadway, the rocks below stoically enduring the savage pounding of the sea, and he set off, moving downhill simply because it was easier, inching along with the aid of the makeshift crutch, hoping that he would soon find what he needed. Shelter. And answers.

He found both. A hundred feet away the road curved, a tight right-hand arc around which Mitch finally struggled, fighting the capricious wind with every step. Two hundred yards further on he raised his head and saw a building half-hidden by the slanting rain and the stormy darkness. It was large, three stories high, and as he drew nearer he realized it was a hotel of some kind. Deserted, from all appearances. The windows that he could see had been boarded over. There was no light anywhere.

A thought tickled his mind, teasing him with elusive meaning. Mitch puzzled over why this building seemed somehow familiar while he forced his aching body to continue on until he stood in the lee of the wind before the main double entry doors. They were made from thick oak and looked as though they had been standing sentinel for a hundred years. They were, of course, locked. Mitch's eyes blurred as he stared at the brass hardware, and he knew he was going to pass out again. Soon. He had to get inside. He prayed that whoever ran this place would forgive him. Then he drew his .357 and shot out the lock. He had barely enough strength to swing open one of the massive doors, but he persevered until he hobbled out of the rain and wind and into the lobby of the Gaffe Island Inn.

He recognized it almost immediately, though it was dark and filled with the rising howl of the storm. He recognized the ancient dory beached in the center of the huge reception area, the brass hurricane lanterns decorating the walls, the rich, worn oak counter behind which a blond reservation clerk had stood a few hours ago. In the wall behind the counter, the door to the manager's office stood ajar—a place where they might store emergency first-aid supplies.

He made his way across the nautical-patterned carpet into the office to find he was right. A first-aid kit in a cabinet on the wall held iodine and antibiotic cream, gauze, tape, aspirin, finger splints and smelling salts. He took out supplies as tiny pieces of his shattered memory began to come into view, attaching themselves to the memory of the Inn. He poured stinging iodine over his head and bandaged the wound with clumsy fingers, letting the remembrances flow however they chose.

The car had been rented, wouldn't the agency be thrilled. He'd stayed here on the third floor, giving the room over to Dan Jeffers when he'd arrived. The storm was a hurricane, that was why the place was deserted and boarded over. Dan Jeffers had been stabbed earlier, an ambulance had taken him away.

Stabbed? Mitch's heart thudded at the memory. Something had smashed through the car window, hit him in the head—a bullet! He'd been shot, that's why he'd piled the car onto the rocks. And why had he been driving the car in a hurricane? What was he—oh. That's right, they'd been fleeing the island, heading inland for safety, away from—

It burst upon him in full. Sabrina! She'd been following him in her own car. Where was she? There'd been no sign of her car at the accident and Mitch was sure she would not have left him. She would have stopped and gotten out to help him, leaving herself completely exposed to whoever shot him. Mitch knew, now, who that was.

Vincent Biaggi. He had her. Vincent Biaggi had taken Sabrina, had driven off with her in the antique Oldsmobile.

But where to? Off the island? Mitch didn't think so. No, Biaggi wanted something, wanted it desperately, something he was convinced Tony DiGesare had hidden away somewhere. What more perfect place than a summer cottage still deeded in his wife's maiden name? Mitch knew the hit man would never leave Gaffe Island without the thing he'd come for, and Sabrina was his key to locating the 'buried treasure.' He'd have taken her back to the cottage, where he would spend some sadistically enjoyable time 'coaxing' her to tell him where it was. That's where they had to be, at the cottage. So that's where he would go. He had promised Sabrina that Biaggi wouldn't hurt her. He had a promise to keep.

He tried to rise, but his body refused to cooperate. His vision blurred. The walls, the office chairs, even the desk behind which he sat, disappeared into a thick, black mist. Pain rose, jabbing at his head, his face, his knee. He couldn't breathe, but he didn't care. He had to get to Sabrina. Mitch reached out and groped on the desktop for his gun, sighing with relief when his fingers closed around it. *Ammunition,* he thought, fighting waves of shimmering darkness. He would need spare ammunition. There'd be some in his old room, among Dan Jeffers' things. He'd have to get up to the third floor and force open the door.

Again he tried to stand. Black shadows reached out and clamped him in their icy grip. His legs turned to rubber, refused to hold his weight. He lost all awareness of where he was and, with a despairing groan he didn't even hear, Mitch Lawson sank back into the old, dark-green leather chair. His body slowly relaxed as insatiable darkness absorbed his mind and transported him away into a barren and empty void.

CHAPTER TWENTY

"Where is it, Sabrina?"

The cold, malicious voice shivered into her. Biaggi's hands held her pinned against the headboard. Sabrina moaned and shook her head. Tears of pain and terror ran down her cheeks.

"Please, please," she choked, drowning in fear. "I don't know what you mean."

"Wrong answer."

Biaggi smiled gently, then laid the back of his hand across her already-torn and bruised face. Sabrina sagged to the left with a tortured groan as agony burst in her head. Biaggi pulled her up again, and shook her.

"The money, Sabrina. I want the money," he demanded icily.

Money?

She tried to speak, but little sound emerged through the pain. Sabrina frowned, blinking to bring

Biaggi's narrow, evil face into focus. Money, he wanted money?

"There's some," she gasped, "in-in my purse. And credit cards—"

He hit her again, twice. Sabrina's head fell forward as darkness again rushed in to take possession. Biaggi yanked her head up, away from the darkness, his hand fisted in her hair, and set his lips on her ear.

"Wrong answer again, sweetheart. Why don't I look some more while you think about it? Think about your face, Sabrina. About what it will look like in your coffin. Do you really want to be chopped up the way Charlie-boy was? You think about it."

He let her go and turned away. Sabrina slowly sank down, crumpling onto the pillows, barely conscious. She had first woken in the middle bedroom, the one she used for storage, the room to which Biaggi had dragged her after he'd beaten her on the stairs. She had lain huddled in the corner while he tore the room apart, listening to both his angry mutters and the wind's rising scream while she tried to make herself invisible.

But she couldn't. The madman had destroyed the room, even taking a knife to the mattresses on the twin beds. Then he had stalked over to where she lay and stood over her, staring down with evil, hating eyes, his wide, strong fingers toying with the sharp blade of his knife. She hadn't wanted to look at him, but the malevolent power of his eyes had drawn hers upward, until she lay shuddering, gazing into their demonic depths, unable to tear her eyes away while his slowly, almost tenderly, dissected every fiber of her being. She could almost feel her blood seep out from the wounds his eyes made in her flesh.

She'd moaned in terror when at last he moved, sinking to his knees and reaching out to touch her hair. Eyes still locked on hers, Biaggi had run his fingers through the black strands, pulling them across Sabrina's face until they nearly obscured her vision. His lips smiled, a gentle, even loving smile. But his eyes spoke of pain and death, and promised endless agony in words she could almost hear. Relief had shuddered through her when at last he'd stopped playing with her hair, but a moment later Sabrina wished he hadn't stopped, for now his hand moved on, caressing her breasts, gliding over her belly, sliding up beneath her twisted skirt to rest at the top of her thigh. Sabrina, hating herself for a coward but unable to hide her fear, whimpered and shook her head, pleading with tear-filled eyes and lips that moved soundlessly. *No, please. Please.* Not even the veil of hair over her eyes could keep her from seeing the sadistic enjoyment in Biaggi's face.

"He had good taste, old Charlie-boy," Biaggi had murmured softly.

Then his face had hardened. His hand had left her thigh to close around her arm and he had hauled her to her feet and shoved her ahead of him into the back bedroom she'd been using. Now she lay semiconscious on the antique counterpane, her blood marring its snowy whiteness, and listened to echoes of terrifying threats as her captor laid waste to her possessions.

He emptied the dresser and the two storage chests, flinging clothing and blankets about with mounting anger, slashing with his knife at the dresses, shirts and skirts in the closet. He emptied the bookshelf, tearing pages from the books for the hell of it, then stalked to the dresser and picked up the pieces of her great-grandmother's hand-painted china vanity set. Within two of the small, elegant bowls on the tray lay Sabrina's hairpins and earrings. Face powder filled a third. Rings hung from the delicate china hooks of the ring holder.

Biaggi opened the powder bowl and stared at the contents, his angered breaths wafting small puffs of whiteness into the air. He growled and flung the fragile piece of china across the room. It smashed into the headboard above where Sabrina lay, showering her with sharp china fragments and fragrant powder. Startled from her pained lethargy, she looked up as Biaggi hurled the rest of the china pieces at her. Screaming, she bent her arms over her head as the onslaught continued, her body now dusted with jagged glass shards, scattered jewelry and make-up. Her grandmother's silver hairbrushes smacked into her shoulder and arm. The matching hand mirror whacked her hip. Sabrina lay terrified and sobbing, unaware that Biaggi swiftly crossed the room toward her, knife drawn.

She felt the mattress sag beneath his weight and looked up to see him mere inches away, leaning one knee on the bed and raising the knife over her. Desperately, she tried to roll aside, force her pain-wracked, benumbed body out of the path of the blade. She managed only to move a few inches before the knife chopped down not six inches from her face, cutting open the pillow on which she lay. Over and over Biaggi jabbed at the bed, slashing pillows and mattress to ribbons, while Sabrina lay sobbing, frozen by terror at the center of his attack. Although she was sure that he meant to kill her, that the knife would slice into her at any moment, the blade never once touched her. At last Biaggi thrust the knife into its sheath, hauled her off the bed and shoved her down the hall into the front bedroom.

"Have you been thinking, Sabrina?" he asked with soft menace, pushing her up against the wall between the two front windows. He turned her around and held her in place, his hands fisted in her hair, one on each side of her face. His dark, malevolent glare probed deep within her. "Where is it?"

"What?" Her voice, a quivering, shuddering mass of fear, was barely audible above the roar of the wind outside.

Biaggi raised a brow. His hands tightened, pulled her head away from the wall and smashed it back again with savage strength. Sabrina screamed, the sound strangled by the agony bursting inside her skull. Lights flashed before her eyes and her knees sagged. Biaggi held her upright by the hands fisted in her hair, adding more pain to that which already devoured her.

"No more games, Sabrina," he growled. "I want the money Charlie-boy stole. Where is it?"

"I don't know, I swear I don't know!"

He snarled at her and again smashed her head against the wall. Pain gurgled in her throat. Sabrina feared she might vomit.

"No, don't, please! Don't hurt me anymore!" His hands tightened again, and Sabrina gasped. "Damn you! Don't you think I'd tell you if I knew?" she screamed.

That stopped him. Biaggi's eyes narrowed and he studied her intently, pondering her words. Finally, he nodded.

"Perhaps you would," he conceded. Then he smiled, and Sabrina's heart jerked in her breast. "But then again, maybe you're just stupid and stubborn, like your husband. Maybe all you need is more persuasion."

Sabrina moaned, the little strength she had left quickly vanishing. She hung in his hands, consumed with despair, wishing he would simply kill her and get it over with. What was the point of making her suffer like this? Surely he had to understand by now that she knew nothing, could tell him nothing. Why go on with this torture?

She opened her eyes, looked up at him and found the answer in his face. He didn't care if she could tell him anything or not, and he wouldn't stop hurting her even if she did. He enjoyed watching her suffer, took pleasure in the pain he inflicted. She was merely a plaything to him. The pain wouldn't stop until he'd had his fill of her. She wouldn't die until he wanted her to, no matter what he found in the house. Or when.

His smile faded as he watched comprehension slowly fill her eyes. After a moment, he leaned down and kissed her lips, a tender, gentle kiss of barely leashed passion. Then he laid his cheek on hers and whispered into her ear.

"You understand now, don't you, Sabrina? You will die. No one can help you, especially your federal boyfriend. He's dead, you know that, don't you? I shot him."

"No." She wanted to scream, but the word emerged as a despairing sigh.

"Yes. I shot him in the head. You know, Sabrina, you were right behind him. You saw it. He's dead, but you're not. Not yet." He kissed her again, and lifted his head to stare deep into her eyes. "You will be, soon. I can make it hard or easy, whichever way you want it. It's up to you, Sabrina. Think about it."

He let go of her and turned away to begin searching the room. Sabrina slid down the wall and curled onto the floor, unable to find enough strength to even sit upright. She didn't watch Biaggi. She couldn't bear to see the things she loved destroyed so heartlessly, and besides her right eye was almost swollen shut, making it difficult to see anything clearly. She wondered, idly, so full of despair that she barely had room now for fear, what else he would do to her before releasing her into death. It would be hard, she knew, for she didn't have the information he wanted with which to buy the easy way. But at least it would be over. Soon, he'd said—promised. Sabrina, like a woman drowning within sight of land, clung to the word with desperate hands. Soon, it would be over. Soon. Forever.

She jumped when he touched her. She'd forgotten Biaggi was there, her despair was so deep, her acceptance of the circumstances so complete. She felt almost as though she was dead already. He pulled her to a sitting position, propped her against the wall and caressed her face with deceptively gentle hands. He said nothing, letting his eyes speak for him until

Sabrina at last looked away. Tears fell down her bruised cheeks as he pulled her up to her feet, but despite her acceptance she cringed back against the wall, fearing the pain to come. Biaggi chuckled, and reached for her.

The lights went out. The room plunged into darkness. Sabrina screamed and lunged forward. Biaggi grabbed her, slammed her against the wall.

"What is it? Who's down there?" he growled.

"No one," she answered in a gasp. He leaned against her, his arm across her neck, choking her. She could hardly breathe, could barely get out the strangled words. "It's the storm, they've... cut the electricity. For safety. The water... will be out, too. Because... of the... storm."

The pressure eased on her neck. Biaggi took a step away from her, leaving her trembling against the wall. She could just see his outline limned by faint daylight shining through the heart-shaped cutouts in the storm shutters. He reached behind his back and pulled out a large, blocky object, then stepped closer to her. She could feel his breath hot on her face.

"I've got a gun," he said. He pulled the slide back, the deadly metallic sound vibrating beneath the wind's howl, and chambered a round before laying the cold length of the barrel against Sabrina's throbbing cheek. "If you so much as look sideways, I'll blow your face off. You understand?"

"Yes."

"All right. We're going downstairs. You be a good little girl and you'll get there alive. Now, move."

He grabbed her right arm in a vise-like grip and moved her toward the bedroom door, out into the hall, and down the stairs. Sabrina prayed that her weakened legs wouldn't buckle beneath her. He pulled her up at the bottom of the steps. Biaggi listened long and hard to the roaring wind that filled every nook and cranny of the house, his fingers tightening on her arm. Sabrina bit her lip as the pressure increased, fearing to make a sound. Finally, Biaggi spoke.

"Candles. Where are they?"

"We can't light candles, they're too dangerous in this kind of weather."

"Don't play games with me, Sabrina."

"I'm not. There are battery-powered lanterns in the cupboard beneath the stairs. They'll give more light than candles, and they won't start a fire."

"All right, show me. Go slow, and don't get cute."

He let go of her arm and fisted a hand in her hair, allowing her to take the lead down the dark hallway. He kept the gun jammed into the center of her back. Sabrina walked slowly in the blackness, hampered by Biaggi's nearness and the way he kept her head pulled back. She slid her bound hands along the wall beneath the stairs, searching for the cupboard door. She felt certain that in the dark she would miss it, that Biaggi would shoot her. Tears beaded her lashes long before she found the door latch.

"It's here," she told him, her voice shaking with relief. She swung the door wide. "There should be two lanterns on a shelf to the right."

He pushed her up against the wall, the gun tight against her head, and reached out. He fumbled around in the dark with his free hand until he found the lanterns. He took one down and switched it on. Bright light flooded around them for a space of six or seven feet.

"Here, hold this."

He gave her just enough room to turn and take the lantern from his hand. Then he took down and lit a second lantern, closing the closet door after inspecting the wet-weather gear that hung neatly on wooden pegs in the small space.

"Into the living room," he ordered, gesturing with the gun.

Sabrina obeyed in silence, pausing in alarm when a fierce gust shook the house. Biaggi prodded her with the gun and she moved on. He had her set the lantern on the telephone table just inside the archway, then ordered her across the room toward the mohair couch. Sabrina stopped, trembling, and stared at it. Just a few days ago Mitch Lawson had carried her in from the beach to this very same couch. Now he was dead, and soon she would join him.

Biaggi walked past her and set his lantern on the table beside the couch, slanting the shade to throw light full on Sabrina. She backed away from him, terrified, unable to see his face as he stalked menacingly toward her. She could feel his eyes on her, pulling at her, and of their own volition her feet stopped, held her motionless and vulnerable before him. She watched him tuck the gun away, out of sight, his stare still locked on her trembling body. Then he reached out, grabbed her arms, swung her around and threw her on the couch. In two strides he was beside her, kneeling over her, hard hands on her shoulders pushing her down, pinning her to the cushions.

Sabrina struggled, twisting in his hands, until his fingers closed on her neck and began to squeeze.

"Where is it, Sabrina?" he growled, half-shouting to be heard over the wind. "Where did old Charlie-boy hide it? Come on, sweetheart, tell Vince. Tell me where the money is."

Even had she known, she couldn't have said a word with his hands choking the breath out of her. Black spots swam before her eyes. Biaggi's gloating, evil face began to fade. Sabrina pulled at his arms, desperately trying to loosen his fingers. She barely heard the savage questions he shouted at her.

Then the pressure eased. Biaggi stood up and stared down at her, his face expressionless, his eyes as cold and hard as flint. Sabrina curled up on the couch and gasped for breath, her throat raw and burning, her hands raised to protect her face. Biaggi waited to speak until her trembling body relaxed and her gasping breaths slowed to a steady, painful rasp in her throat. Sabrina listened in silence, his every word a lance that pierced her through. She didn't look up at him.

"If you move, you'll wish you were never born. I guarantee that."

She nodded. He turned to the desk and began ransacking the drawers. Sabrina raised her eyes and looked at him. He had put her in the far corner. No matter where he was in the room, she would have to pass him to reach the archway. She looked down at the rope binding her wrists, at the flesh rubbed raw and bleeding beneath the coarse strands, and wondered if she could possibly make it. Off the couch, through the archway and the kitchen, into the garage and—what? Go where? In the middle of a hurricane? With her hands bound, pursued by a maniac armed with both gun and knife? If she could be sure he would shoot her, that she would die fast, she'd at least try it. But she didn't think he would shoot her, at least not to kill. It was obvious he had other plans for her.

Biaggi snarled, wrenching at a drawer that had stuck. Sabrina cowered back against the arm of the couch, terrified he would turn and take his wrath out on her. He kicked the desk twice and hit it with his fist, his voice rising to a shout of rage. Suddenly a sharp, insistent rap sounded on the front door.

"Sabrina?" a voice shouted. "Are you in there? Sabrina?"

Sabrina froze, her eyes wide and locked on the archway. Geoff. Before she could draw breath to scream, Biaggi was there beside her, his hand hard on her mouth. He pressed her back against the couch arm and held his knife at her throat, the tip pressing beneath her jaw.

"Not a sound," he breathed into her ear. "You do exactly as I say or I'll slit your throat. Understand?"

She nodded, terrified, watching his face. He lifted his hand from her mouth. The knife stayed pressed to her neck.

"Who is it?"

"A-a friend—a neighbor. He must have seen the light."

The knock sounded again, louder, more insistent.

"Sabrina! It's Geoff, are you all right? Sabrina!"

"H-he won't go away," she told Biaggi. "H-he knew I was leaving, b-because of the storm. He must have seen the light and thought something was w-wrong."

Biaggi turned his head and narrowed his eyes at the place where Geoffrey Simmonds still banged on Sabrina's door. Then he looked back at her. Sabrina gaped at the vile, malicious expression in his eyes.

"Then you'd better go talk to him," he said, using the knife to cut the rope binding her wrists. He pulled Sabrina to her feet, wound his arm behind her back and crushed her close to him, his hard fingers clamped on the back of her neck. He waved the knife threateningly in front of her eyes.

"Get rid of him, Sabrina. Carefully. One wrong word and I'll stick this between your ribs. And then I'll kill him. So don't fuck around, sweetheart. Just get rid of him."

"Yes," Sabrina agreed, shivering.

Biaggi smiled at her and dropped his hand, clamping iron fingers around her left wrist. He led her to the front door and nodded permission to slip the chain and turn the lock. She had to use only her right hand since Biaggi still held her left wrist in a crushing grip that made her wince. The light from the lanterns cast only a dim light into the hall, and she knew the shadows would hide most of the damage Biaggi's hands had done to her face. The board covering the door's window would hide Biaggi. Sabrina glanced at her captor for his consent then, as his nod, twisted the knob and opened the door, keeping her right hand on its outer edge.

"Good heavens, Geoff, what are you doing out in this? It's dangerous." She thanked God for the howling wind that covered the shaking of her voice.

"Sabrina, what the hell are you doing here? You said you were leaving."

"I was, Geoff, but I just couldn't. There's so much here, so many memories. I couldn't stop thinking about it. So I came back."

The wind gusted, rocking the door. She almost lost her hold on it.

"You know it's not safe, Sabrina. Come with me, to my place. We can ride it out there, together." Biaggi squeezed her wrist. Sabrina clenched her teeth to keep from groaning.

"I-I'm perfectly safe here, Geoff. The cottage has withstood storms like this before. You were crazy to come over here. Now, please. Go home while you still can."

"Are you sure you're all right, Sabrina? You sound funny." Geoff frowned, peering closer at her through the shadows.

"Of course I'm all right, Geoff. Don't be ridiculous. I'm just worried about you, that's all. I don't want you to get hurt."

Again, Biaggi squeezed her wrist. Sabrina gasped, covering it by pretending to have trouble holding the door against the wind. Geoff's frown deepened. His eyes shifted from her to the crack where the door met the frame and back to her. He narrowed his eyes at her and jerked his head toward the space between the door and the wall, as though asking if something was wrong, or if someone was hiding there. Sabrina leaned forward slightly, her voice pleading.

"Please, Geoff. If you don't go now you won't make it. We can compare notes on our adventures tomorrow over coffee, okay?"

"Sure, Sabrina, if that's what you want," Geoff agreed. "You just be careful, you hear?"

Sabrina nodded and tried to smile. She couldn't. It hurt her bruised mouth too much. Geoff started to turn away, pivoting on his left foot. Then he kicked out, smashed his right foot into the door. It slammed all the way open, knocking Biaggi into the wall and breaking his hold on Sabrina's wrist. Geoff caught the door on the rebound and slammed at it again with his foot, smashing it once more into Sabrina's captor. As Vincent Biaggi slumped to the floor, Geoff grabbed Sabrina's hand and yanked her out of the house.

CHAPTER TWENTY-ONE

 Geoff pulled Sabrina around the far corner of his house. The wind loosed its hold on them and she stumbled. Only Geoff's strong arms kept her on her feet.

"Are you all right?" he asked.

She didn't even try to speak. A nod was all she could manage.

"Stay here. Don't move."

Again, she nodded. She huddled against the siding and watched Geoff peer around the corner toward her house, then closed her eyes. She couldn't have moved even if Biaggi materialized out of the darkness to kill them both. Only a few minutes had elapsed since Geoff had yanked her from Biaggi's clutches, but it felt to Sabrina like they had been battling the demonic wind for hours—pushed back one step for every two they took, blinded by the driving rain, barely able hear or breathe. She'd expected

Biaggi's hard hands grab her at any moment. Tension and fear had shrunk her into an inert, quivering mass. Something touched her shoulder, and she jumped.

"No one out there that I can see," Geoff said, sliding a supporting arm around her waist, "not near the house, at least. Can't see more than a dozen or so feet in this storm, though. Come on, let's get inside."

He helped her though the back door, locked and bolted it behind them, then put her in a kitchen chair and brought an armful of thick terry towels from the downstairs bath. Sabrina sat huddled into herself, her head bowed and her arms clasped around her shivering body. Soft radiance from a hurricane lantern on the table glinted on the rainwater dripping from her hair and clothes. All she could think was, *Why? Why, Charlie? Why?* Geoff wiped the wetness from his face and arms, draped a dry towel around his shoulders and knelt beside Sabrina.

"It's all right, Sabrina," he said, enveloping her in a thick bath sheet. "You're safe, now. Was that the one Lawson told us about? Biaggi?"

Sabrina made a soft sound of assent as Geoff covered her head with another towel, gently pressing the water from her hair. Then he tipped her head up and began to wipe her face. Sabrina flinched and pushed his hand away.

"Don't. That hurts."

Geoff tilted her face to the light and drew in a sharp breath. Then he lifted her hands and stared at the raw abrasions that braceleted her wrists.

"Holy crap, Sabrina, what did that monster do to you? Are you all right?"

"I could use some ice. Do you think it's all melted?"

"Ice?" Geoff frowned at her, then drew in a breath. "For the swelling. Yes. Of course."

He heaved himself to his feet and crossed to a drawer. He took out a dish towel then opened the freezer door, assembling the ice pack while he spoke.

"How did this happen, Sabrina? I thought you were with Lawson, that he was protecting you. Where the hell is he?"

Sabrina pulled the bath sheet tighter around her and huddled into its warmth. Not that it helped. She didn't think she'd ever be warm again.

"He's dead, Geoff."

"What? How?"

Geoff knelt at her side again and gave her the makeshift ice pack. Sabrina pressed it against her face. Pain flared. She flinched. Her her breath hissed in as fire spread down her neck and up into her scalp. Then a soothing numbness began to spread and she felt herself relax until once again she could breath normally.

"I saw you both drive off," Geoff said, easing himself up into a chair beside her. "I thought you were safe. What happened?"

"Biaggi must have been waiting for us. He shot Mitch, his car went over the cliff onto the rocks at Lighthouse Point. I was right behind him, there was nothing I could do. When I stopped, Biaggi grabbed me and brought me back to the house."

Something shifted inside her at the thought of Mitch's death, his body at the mercy of the savage wind and rain. She felt her heart harden. An upwelling of hatred and anger burst through her like a geyser, bringing with it a cold warmth that stopped her shivering. She looked at Geoff and almost spit out her words.

"Do you think you killed him? Biaggi?"

Geoff considered a moment, then shook his head.

"I doubt it."

Sabrina felt a surge of relief wash through her. *Good. I want to be the one to kill him.* She pictured his blood on her hands and felt a bloom of satisfaction. Then she froze. The cold clamped down again. *Dear lord, what's wrong with me, wanting to kill someone, anyone? Even him?* She almost missed the rest of Geoff's words.

"Probably hurt him some, that huge old doorknob could do a bit of damage if it hit him just right. But I don't think it'll keep him down very long. This storm, though..." He frowned. "To be honest, I didn't think we'd make it back here, and it's getting worse every minute. That should stop him, at least until it's over."

Sabrina looked at the back door and shivered.

"Nothing will stop him," she said. "We can't stay here, Geoff. He'll kill us both."

"Sabrina—"

"No. He could be here any minute. We have to get out of here. Now!"

A violent gust shook the house before Geoff could respond. Something smashed into the front porch with a loud crack. Sabrina yelped, then winced and again pressed the ice pack to her face.

"Listen to that," Geoff said. "It's killing weather out there." Geoff grimaced as his words echoed in the dim kitchen. Sabrina would have laughed if she'd had the energy. Or could appreciate the dark humor. Geoff shook his head.

"Sorry. But we'd be crazy to leave the house."

"We have no choice, Geoff. He's coming."

"You may be right, probably are right," he added, forestalling her protest. "But there's no way we can walk anywhere, not in his wind. It's getting stronger by the minute. And my Midget won't be any help at all. We'd be blown off the road with the first gust, if we could get up the driveway, that is. I'm not sure even a heavy car like your Olds is any match for that storm out there. And where would we go? The bridge is closed. We're stuck here."

Sabrina stood up, paced to the counter and stood with her back to Geoff. She kept ice pack pressed on her injuries, wishing the numbness would spread down her neck to her chest and into her heart. She'd give anything not to feel the anguish and fear that enveloped her. Frigid water ran down the inside of her arm and she couldn't stop shivering. But it was worth the discomfort. She could now open the eye that had swollen shut, and the pain in her cheek and jaw had abated to a dull ache.

And he was right about the car. She'd teased him often enough about the MG's diminutive size, the trouble he had keeping the light car on the island's sand-slick roads under normal wind conditions. She stared at the plywood covering the huge window over the kitchen sink. She could feel her pulse race. Her breath quickened. A miracle—Geoff—had gotten her away from Biaggi, and she wasn't going to sit here like a frightened little lamb waiting for him to find her again. She had to live. She had to survive long enough to find the authorities and make Biaggi pay for killing Charlie and Mitch. She turned and looked at Geoff.

"Where's your gun?" she asked.

Geoff winced and she didn't blame him. Even she could hear the harsh loathing in her tone. Geoff rose and faced her across the gloom.

"You're not going after him, Sabrina. I won't let you."

"That's not what I intend. I'm not stupid, Geoff. But we need protection, and that rifle is all we've got. Because storm or no storm, he will come after us. Without that gun, we don't stand a chance."

Another strong gust shook the house and they both jumped. Geoff nodded.

"All right, I see your point."

Geoff gestured toward the front hall where the access door into the garage stood. Sabrina tossed the melted ice pack into the sink. She walked into the dark corridor, opened the door and felt her way down the four steps to the concrete floor. Geoff picked up the lantern and followed her into the large three-car space. His fire engine red MG Midget coupe sat in one bay. It looked like a miniature version of the real thing, especially standing beside the oversized catamaran that hogged the other two bays. Sabrina shuddered at the thought of braving the winds in it. Then she wondered if maybe it would be better—and easier—to die at the storm's hands than Biaggi's.

Geoff pulled the rifle off the wall, loaded it, and handed it to Sabrina. She clutched it with shaking fingers and studied the familiar mechanism. She was a good shot, she knew that from when Geoff and Charlie had taken her target shooting. But a man was a whole different proposition than a paper target. She was't sure she could aim a loaded gun at a man and pull the trigger. Even if it was Biaggi.

You can do it if you have to, she told herself as she watched Geoff open a box of ammunition and stuff his pockets with bullets. The garage around them echoed with the escalating howls of the storm. Something hard cracked into the siding and Sabrina yelped, her fingers spasming on the gun's stock. She was glad she hadn't yet threaded her finger through the trigger or she might have shot Geoff. Geoff looked at her, his eyes solemn.

"Probably a board torn loose from somewhere," he said. "We'll get a lot of that before this is over."

Or it's Biaggi, Sabrina thought. She gave Geoff a small nod of agreement because she knew he was trying to make her feel safe even though he looked as frightened as she felt. He reached over and gave her arm a reassuring squeeze then led the way back into the house. He threw the garage access door deadbolt behind them.

He paused when they returned to the kitchen. Then he shook his head and led the way into the den at the back of the house.

"Not so many windows here, and four strong walls," he said, referring to the open concept design that made one huge room out of most of the main floor. "Easier to defend. Plus there's an outside door over there in case we need it."

He nodded at the back wall as he set the lantern on the desk in the corner. It shed a soft glow halfway into the room, painting intimate shadows that caressed them with velvet-gloved fingers. Floor-to-ceiling teak bookshelves surrounded them, holding Geoff's eclectic mix of mystery, history, biography and astronomy. Sabrina stood in the center of the room, clutching the rifle and wishing they could light a fire in the fireplace. She felt cold to the core and couldn't stop shaking.

"So what's the plan?" Sabrina asked.

"Not a clue." Geoff shook his head and paced the room, in and out of the shadows, a lanky wraith in the darkness. "Just hunker down here for the duration and hope we get through to the other side, I guess. And pray we won't need that." He pointed at the rifle. The wind shrieked and again something hit the house a shuddering blow. Sabrina jumped and swung the rifle to the plywood-covered window beside the rear door. Geoff liberated the poker from the fireplace, brought it to her, then eased the weapon from her nerve-ridden hands.

"I think it'll be safer if we trade, don't you?"

He looked up as again the wind assaulted the house. Then he looked at her and smiled. The fitful light made the grin dance on his face. "Fasten your seatbelt, darlin'," he said, pitching his deep voice low and scratchy. "It's gonna be a bumpy ride."

Sabrina clutched the iron poker tried her best to smile at his imitation of her favorite Bette Davis line. She knew he was trying to lighten the mood, make their plight seem less dangerous. It didn't work, but she was grateful anyway. She was sure Biaggi was out there in the wind and rain, watching them like a spider, plotting the web in which he would capture them. She could feel his evil eyes probing the cedar siding, searching for her.

"I'm sorry you're involved in this, Geoff. It's not fair."

Geoff shook his head and grunted. Then he glanced at her.

"Why did he hurt you like this, Sabrina? What does he want?"

"I don't know." Sabrina shuddered. "Charlie stole something from the mob and they want it back. Biaggi thinks I know where it is."

"That's crazy, Sabrina. Charlie wouldn't steal, not the Charlie I knew."

"I don't think either one of us ever really knew him, Geoff." The howling wind almost swallowed her words, but she couldn't seem to produce more volume, get any more air into her lungs. "I can't stop thinking about it—that day, what Biaggi did to him. And Charlie never said a word, wouldn't give him what he wanted. Charlie knew I'd be next, that Biaggi would go after me. He *had* to know. But whatever he took was more important to him, meant more to him than I did."

"No, Sabrina. You're wrong. Charlie loved you deeply."

"But not enough." Sabrina's bitterness reverberated in the air. "He loved whatever he stole more."

"Sabrina, that's not—shit!"

Sabrina screamed. A huge crash reverberated above them. It sounded like the hounds of hell were trying to break through the roof.

Geoff kept both his gaze and the rifle pointed at the ceiling as they waited out the assault. Sabrina turned in a circle, poker ready to strike. She found nothing but wind-haunted shadows pressing back on her. Her stomach knotted and her nerves frayed with each passing second until she had to clench her teeth to keep from bursting into tension-generated tears. She was afraid if she started she'd never be able to stop. Then she thought of Mitch, his body lying in the smashed car on the rocks, pounded by the waves, and wondered if he would still be there when the storm ended, or if he would be swept out to sea and never be found. A moan vibrated in her throat.

"It's okay, Sabrina." Geoff gave her hand a quick squeeze, his gaze still intent on the ceiling. "We'll make it, I prom—"

Thud!

Sabrina grasped his arm.

"What was that?"

Geoff placed a finger on his lips. A gust of wind shook the house. Boards creaked. Nails screeched as something above them tore away. Sabrina looked up, her heart hammering in her chest. The wind died, a momentary gathering of strength. In the lull it came again. Sharp. Deliberate. Man made?

Thud... thud... thud.

On the wood covering a window somewhere in the house. The sound rolled on the wind, folded back on itself until they couldn't tell where it was coming from.

Thud... thud... thud.

Sabrina stared around the room, barely able to breathe. Geoff inched over and stood with his ear pressed against the glass in the room's outside door. Then he looked at her and shook his head.

Sabrina licked her lips and moved to the window behind the desk. She tried to look out, but the plywood left no gaps, not even a tiny sliver to peer through. She tightened her fingers on the poker until they ached and the muscles in her forearms began to spasm. It was Biaggi. She could see him in her mind's eye, circling the house, seeking a way in. She feared she might pass out. She concentrated on taking deep breaths. They rattled in her throat.

They stood in silence until Sabrina thought she would scream. Then Geoff eased away from the door and shook his head.

"It's just the storm," Geoff said. He walked over to the fireplace. "It's playing havoc with our senses."

"No. It's Biaggi. I know it is."

"Come on, Sabrina, think. He's not going to announce himself by knocking on a door or window. It was just a branch. Or a loose board, or something."

Sabrina stared at Geoff, then lowered the poker with a shuddery laugh. Her arms felt as though they were made of rubber. Or water.

"Yes. You're right. He—"

Again something hit a wood panel, a fist or a flashlight. *Or the haft of a knife*, Sabrina thought.

Thud... thud... thud.

It tumbled through the house from the front door and echoed through the den. Geoff swore, doused the lantern and left the room, heading for the front door. Sabrina followed, terrified to be alone. She looked at the poker, at the wicked hooked point at the end. She could do some damage to Biaggi with it, given the chance. *Please*, she prayed, *give me the chance*.

Wind-punctuated silence fell. Sabrina had never wanted to see outside so badly in her life. The walls closed in on her. She felt trapped, like a rat in a maze.

Or a spider in a web, she thought, a snare of Biaggi's devising. Then the bangs began again. Boards cracked, nails screeched. The wood panel over the front window shifted. Geoff pulled Sabrina close and pointed to the staircase that led to the open loft.

"Get up there," Geoff said. "Find a chest or something to hid in, somewhere he'll have trouble finding you."

"No. I'm not leaving you. This isn't your fight, it's mine."

"He killed Charlie and he hurt you. He's made it mine, Sabrina." She clutched at his damp shirt and he smiled at her. "It's okay. I'm damn good with this rifle. And he doesn't know I have it. That makes it an even playing field."

"Geoff, please—"

"Don't. It's okay. I'll be all right. And if I'm not, well, greater love and all that. Right? Now get up there!"

He shoved her toward the steps. More thuds rang out, but now they seemed to be coming from the kitchen area of the house. Then nails screeched nearby, pulling their attention back to the front of the house. Geoff again motioned her to move and she obeyed, pulling herself up by the railing until she reached the landing. She stopped and looked down. Geoff had moved forward to stand in the foyer between the front door and the den. He held the rifle at his shoulder, his body tense, his attention on the panels over the front windows. *Biaggi,* she thought. *Prying at the wood so he can break the window and get in.*

She reached the landing and stopped. Geoff was right. Since Biaggi had no idea they were armed, Geoff had a good chance of blowing him away as soon as Biaggi got a panel off a door or window. She looked up the stairs, wondering if there was an oasis of safety in the loft. One Biaggi couldn't find. She doubted it.

Then she shook her head. There was no way she was going to let Geoff face Biaggi alone. They were stronger together. There'd be no laying down of life, not if she could stop it. She firmed her grip on the poker and stood a moment, trembling, listening for the sound of the front door slamming open, the rifle going off, as she searched the dark shadows below for a hint of movement.

She'd started back down the steps when she saw it, caught it from the corner of her eye. Her feet froze. Geoff stood in the center of the living area, holding the rifle pointed at the front door. Sabrina saw the wood panel over the front door shift. It sank like a tired drunk and bared one corner of glass, a six-inch triangle of swirling darkness. Sabrina stared, but saw no other hint of movement, no indication of anything but wind-blown sand and debris. Where was Biaggi?

She eased down one step, then another. Three more. She crouched against the railing, poker held ready, intent on any sound, any movement that didn't feel storm related. Time slowed to a crawl. The howling winds receded from her consciousness. She felt trapped within a vacuum, untouched and untouchable.

Then everything exploded.

The wood panel tore loose and jammed into the window. Shards of glass spewed like lethal darts into the entryway. Geoff flinched and turned away, raising his shoulders and dipping the rifle barrel toward the floor. A shadow detached itself from the den behind Geoff and slithered forward.

"Geoff!" Sabrina screamed. "Behind you!"

Geoff staggered to the side as he twisted and swung up the rifle. Sabrina threw the poker at Biaggi. Both weapons fired at the same time. The flashes blinded Sabrina. She stumbled down the steps and lurched into the side table that sat at the bottom. Her fingers closed on a small glass vase. She clutched at it as she pushed away from the table, blinking, trying to clear her vision. Someone grabbed her arm. She screamed and swung her free arm, smashed the vase into flesh and bone. A roar sounded in her ears, and then she was free.

"Geoff! Geoff!" she shouted as she turned and stumbled toward the door. Glass shifted beneath her. Her feet skidded and she fell, slammed down on her back. Lights sparked in her eyes. She couldn't draw breath. The world began to recede.

A foot kicked her side and reality rushed back. Two forms struggled over her, locked in a deadly embrace, battling for possession of Geoff's rifle. Sabrina rolled away from the fight and forced herself to her feet.

"Geoff!" she screamed.

"Get out! Run!" he shouted as he yanked and twisted at the weapon. "Go!"

Biaggi lifted his head and glared at her. He lurched two steps closer to her, dragging Geoff with him. Sabrina whirled and yanked on the front door. Nothing happened. Then she realized it was locked. She twisted the lock knob and threw open the door.

Behind her she heard the sounds of fists hitting flesh, grunts of pain. Again Biaggi twisted toward her.

"Fucking bitch!"

Sabrina plunged through the door onto the deck that stood a dozen feet off sand that was now awash with wind-driven sea water. Rain pelted her face and body, feeling like glass shards driven into her skin. The wind tore at her, threatening to lift her up and toss her into the seething ocean below. She raced for the steps to her left. The deck bobbed beneath her feet and she almost fell. An agonized roar split the air. She clutched the railing and looked back.

Just beyond the front door the deck disintegrated. Boards leapt into the roiling air, tumbling like straw on a brisk breeze. Sabrina screamed and covered her head with her arms as deadly shrapnel cartwheeled around her. She felt the shock of impact as the debris pelted her, but her terrified mind could not absorb any pain from the blows. Then she was on her feet again, running, taking the six stairs two at a time, finally reaching solid earth.

Again the storm paused, held its breath for an eternal moment. A loud crack split the air. Sabrina stopped running and looked back at the house. Another shot rebounded into the air. Sabrina flinched at the bright flash that accompanied it. Then a figure appeared, outlined in the doorway. Hunched and swaying. Gripping the doorframe. It reached out to her, then slowly slid down and slumped onto the deck.

He stepped out from behind the body, rifle still clutched in his hand. He turned his head to the storm and Sabrina caught the silhouette of his hawklike nose, the faint gleam of stormlight on his pale hair. Biaggi.

She caught her breath and backed away, her heart breaking for Geoff. One step, two, three. Biaggi turned and looked at her, his face now in shadow. She could feel the smile that lifted his cruel lips.

"No!" she whispered and turned to run.

The edge of the sandbank crumbled beneath her feet. Sabrina screamed as she fell and rolled down the steep dune into the pounding surf below.

CHAPTER TWENTY-TWO

Mitch woke to pitch darkness inside and raging cacophony outside. It sounded like all the hounds of hell were loose, trying to get in to kill him. It didn't help that his skull felt like broken glass, or that the room slewed around whenever he tried to lift his head. He wasn't at all sure that he could get to his feet, and if he did he doubted his stiff, aching body would be very cooperative.

Shit, he thought, searching the desk drawers for a flashlight, *if I can't take getting grazed by a bullet, I ought to retire for real.* A fat lot of help he would be to Sabrina, even if he could get anywhere near her. And without a light, he'd be lucky to get out of the Inn's office.

He finally found a flashlight, an old-fashioned, heavy metal one tucked deep into a bottom drawer. It barely lit when Mitch clicked it on. Either the Gaffe Island Inn didn't have frequent problems with its electricity, or all the good ones had been taken during the evacuation. The dim bulb sent a sickly yellow beam out across the room, but at least it was better than no light at all. Mitch heaved himself up, grunting through clenched teeth with each movement, fixed the makeshift crutch board under his arm and hobbled out into the huge, oblong, echo-filled lobby.

Ominous creaks and groans filled the old hotel as Mitch made his way over to the narrow staircase, cursing the foresight that had prompted the authorities to shut down electric service to the island. If anyone ever needed an elevator, he did now. Why in hell was he addicted to top-floor-rooms-with-a-view? Idiot that he was, he'd actually requested to be put on the third floor without even considering he could be shot, banged up in a car crash, trapped by a hurricane, left with a pseudo-light that was fast fading and dependent upon a weathered teak board just to take a step. There had to be an easier way to earn a living.

It seemed to take forever to ascend to the third floor, though giving a conservative estimate and trying to be fair, Mitch figured maybe twenty minutes had passed. He had no idea what time it really was, his watch had been smashed along with the car, and with clouds darker than night boiling all over the sky it was impossible to tell. It could be high noon, though he doubted it. From what he remembered of the radio warnings, the bridges were to be closed by six, the water and electricity turned off at seven, and the hurricane to hit in full by ten p.m. And judging from what he could hear of the wind outside, he didn't think he'd slept through much of it.

He paused on the final landing to catch his breath, shooting the weak beam of light up the last contingent of steps. It barely reached to the top. The creaks and groans had notched up in pitch and become more threatening. It sounded as if nails were being wrenched from the roof tiles. Nervous sweat slicked his hands. Mitch forced himself on, toiling up the final twelve steps with fierce determination. A tremendous crash stopped his feet halfway to the top. Mitch listened intently and shivered at the echoes of tinkling glass that vibrated beneath the roar of the wind. It sounded louder now, the wind. Closer, somehow. It took more will power than strength to start climbing up again.

His room was near the end of the southeast wing, on the right side of the long, narrow unlit corridor. From his window, he'd been able to see Sabrina's house down the beach. He didn't, of course, have a key—he'd given it to Dan Jeffers to use—but he did have his gun. He'd simply shoot out the lock and let the department reimburse the hotel later. If the hotel survived the storm. From the way the building shook around him, he wasn't sure it would.

It took about ten minutes, Mitch figured, to navigate the inky corridor and reach his room, #327. He could have moved faster, but since there was nowhere to go until the storm was over, the only thing haste would accomplish was to further strain his injured leg. If he could avoid that, he might soon be able to forego the makeshift crutch.

Another loud crash, accompanied by a rending tear, reverberated in the darkness just as he drew his gun. He felt a breeze, cool on his bare skin, a nebulous swirling caress of air. He swept the flashlight beam around the ebony hallway, his heart now pounding more forcefully than his head. But he could see nothing in the dim yellow light, which only reached out about eight feet. He shook his head and hoped the building wasn't coming apart around him. Then he trained the light on the door to room 327, leaned on the board for support, and shot out the lock.

Dan Jeffers is a slob.

The thought flashed through Mitch's mind when he swung open the door and limped into the jumbled mess of the room. In the uncertain beam of his flashlight he saw clothing scattered around, a chair overturned and what looked like ice chips glittering on the floor. Ice chips? Curious, Mitch lurched closer to the sliding glass door that walled off the miniature balcony and realized with a shock that it wasn't ice glinting in the ray of dim light.

It was glass. Glass from sliding doors that had been boarded over. Now, a sheet of plywood thrust partway through the shattered panes, caught in swaying, twisted green curtains that kept it upright. Rain soaked the carpet in an ever-widening pool. The plywood shuddered with each gust, jerking in the force of the wind. The heavy traverse rod affixed to the ceiling sagged as Mitch watched. The wild wind swirled like a vortex in the confined space of the small room.

Mitch searched Dan Jeffers' things as quickly as he could, hampered by his injuries and the maniacal wind streaming through the broken glass. He went through the suitcase that the storm had dumped on the floor, the nightstand and dresser drawers, Dan's shave kit in the cave-dark bathroom, the slacks, shirts and jacket swinging in the closet alcove. He found what he sought in the left-hand jacket pocket—a spare box of ammunition for his .357 magnum, Not until his hand closed on the box did he remember that Dan's weapon had been in the glove box of the car he'd abandoned on the rocks. Damn. He'd feel a whole lot better if he had two guns against Biaggi, even if both were in one set of hands. He reloaded his pistol, then dumped the extra bullets into his pants pockets, pulled on his shirt and grabbed a towel from the bath to use as a pad.

He had his hand on the doorknob, ready to leave, when the plywood panel flew into the room with a grinding crash. It brought the rest of the glass with it and slammed into the wall not two feet from where Mitch stood. Rain poured in, driven sideways by the fierce wind that also sent lamps smashing to the floor and overturned the small bedside table. The bed nearest the gaping hole slewed around and banged into the second bed.

Mitch wrestled with the door, which was held fast by the wind's mighty strength. He couldn't pull it open. The board under his arm fell. Mitch let it go, concentrating all his meager energy on getting out of the dangerous room. A high-pitched screech burst in his ears, making him wince with pain. Turning, he saw the wall above the shattered glass doors disintegrate. Pieces of the ceiling and roof tore off and whirled away into the maelstrom. The storm was pulling the place apart. If he didn't get out, he could very well be sucked out of the room with the remains of the roof.

He wrenched at the door with panic-fueled strength, managing to pull it open just enough to throw himself through and onto the hallway floor. The wind slammed the door shut, almost catching his left foot. He'd lost the flashlight along with the board, but he didn't need light to see what was happening. His ears told him all he needed to know. This whole end of the Inn was coming apart, unable to stand against the rending force of the wind.

The last report he'd heard, before they'd left Sabrina's cottage, had clocked sustained winds in the wall cloud around the eye at close to 145 miles per hour. That had been at four o'clock. If it was ten now, that meant the hurricane had had about six hours over the warm, moist Atlantic to continue growing and strengthening. Maybe nothing could withstand this monster, but for Sabrina's sake, Mitch had to try.

He hauled himself to his feet and lurched down the hallway toward the stairs, clinging to the wall and ignoring pain in his leg that stabbed with every half-running step he took. The floor trembled ominously beneath his feet. He could hear, behind him, the echoing crashes and agonized screams of a building in self-destruct mode. He looked back when he reached the stairway, but in the darkness he couldn't see anything. The floor felt more stable here, just past the center of the structure. Obviously, the east side was bearing the brunt of the punishment. But Mitch was not about to trust in any lessening of vibrations. He wanted to be off the third floor and as close to the west wall as possible. He waited only long enough to catch his breath and for the pain to ease a bit in his leg, then he inched his way down the stairs. He clung to the railing, knowing that if he fell he might never get up again. The sounds of destruction faded as he slowly descended. At last he found himself in the center of the lobby, holding onto the side of the beached dory and listening for signs of the ceiling about to fall in on his head.

It appeared that it wouldn't, not for a while yet, though loud crashes in the restaurant to his left attested to more plywood panels being blown in through windows they were meant to protect. What he needed was someplace safe to hide, something that might not collapse if the ceiling did fall in. Mitch thought a moment, then groped his way across to the massive oak reception desk, felt his way around behind it and crawled beneath its sheltering bulk. He rested his aching head on a hard partition and thought about the cottage.

Could it possibly stand up under such a fierce, unrelenting onslaught? Or would it, too, disintegrate like his room had? Mitch remembered the files they'd amassed on Vincent Biaggi's handiwork, the state of his victims when at last he'd finished with them. He closed his eyes, wondering if perhaps it wouldn't be better if the cottage did collapse on Sabrina. Compared to what Biaggi would do, it was by far a kinder, and quicker, way to die.

* * *

He was beside her in an instant, pushing her down, forcing her head under crashing knee-deep waves. Panic-stricken, choking on salt water, Sabrina fought to gain her feet, to find air to breathe. But she could neither stand, nor get her head above the surface. The violent waves were too forceful, Biaggi too strong. Water filled her lungs. She could feel her awareness slip away, smothered by the foaming ocean. When at last Biaggi hauled her from the wild water and shoved her halfway up the steep dune, she was barely conscious. She lay gasping for breath, coughing up water, oblivious to the tight rope he again cinched on her wrists.

He gave her no time to recover but hauled her roughly onto the cliff edge, set her on her feet and prodded her ahead of him toward the cottage. Mauled by the wild wind, Sabrina fell over and over until at last Biaggi seized the rope around her wrists and dragged her behind him over the soaked, stony ground, up the porch steps, and into the house. Her body left a trail of water and sand on the carpet as he pulled her across the living room to the huge potbellied stove.

"A stupid move, Sabrina!" he shouted over the noise of the wind and the banging of the still-open front door. "All you did was get your friend killed." He tied her hands to a front leg of the heavy iron stove and took another short length of rope from his pocket. "You're going to pay for that, sweetheart. As soon as I find the money."

He looped the rope around her ankles and yanked it savagely, forcing a pained cry from her lips. He stood a moment, staring down with cold eyes at where she lay bound helpless at his feet. Her skirt was ripped and pulled askew, baring one leg almost to her hip. Half the buttons were missing from her torn blouse. She lay half-stuporous on her back, arms stretched out above her head, still shuddering in reaction to the near-drowning. She kept her eyes closed, afraid of what he would do if she looked up at him. There was no sound for endless seconds but the scream of the storm and the slamming of the door.

Finally, Biaggi turned away. Sabrina felt him move, felt the inhuman gaze leave her body. She cracked open her eyes and watched him wrestle the door shut, the wind now almost too forceful even for his strength. The battery lanterns threw weird shadows around the room as he finished his search, tearing apart the rest of the desk, knocking over tables and smashing lamps, emptying the bookcase and her knitting box, even taking his knife to the couch and chairs and laying open the ancient stuffing. She bit her lip to keep from crying out in protest when he slashed at her grandmother's delicate embroidery that covered the settee, terrified of the knife he held. Visions of Charlie's bloody body danced before her eyes. Biaggi's threatening words echoed in her head: *What do you want to look like in your coffin? Do you want to be chopped up the way Charlie was?*

She prayed that he would forget her. He didn't. He looked around the shattered room, then came and stood astride her. He ran his dark, hungry gaze down her body with gleeful anticipation. He said nothing, he only smiled—an icy, malicious smile that took her breath away. The wind outside screamed, howled. The house shuddered, but Sabrina didn't notice. Her eyes, her whole attention, were riveted on the knife Biaggi turned over and over in his fingers. Slowly, he sank down onto his knees, half-sitting on her abdomen. He raised the knife, his eyes tracing a path down the side of her face.

"No, please," Sabrina pleaded, barely able to force the words out through the terror that filled her. She shook her head, twisted her body, seeking escape.

Biaggi fisted his left hand in her hair and held her still. Sabrina froze at his touch, her eyes wide as the glittering blade raised even higher. Biaggi's arm plunged. Sabrina's heart stopped. The knife slashed down with stunning speed, swerving at the last second to become embedded in the dark pine floor about eighteen inches from her head. Bending close to her, Biaggi spoke for the first time in over an hour. The malignant tone, as much as what he said, pulled Sabrina's horrified stare from the quivering blade to his evil face.

"No more games, Sabrina, I'm tired of this. I want the money—now. Where is it?"

"I don't know." His hand tightened in her hair, and Sabrina gasped. Tears filled her eyes. "Please, I'm telling you the truth. I don't know about any money, Charlie never said a word about it. I didn't even know who he really was until a few days ago."

Biaggi's hand relaxed. The tension in his body eased. He straightened up, his eyes thoughtful. He didn't speak. Sabrina's terror deepened.

"What difference does it make?" she asked, her voice shaking. "He's already dead, isn't that enough?"

"It's a matter of principle." Biaggi played with her wet hair as he spoke, twined the dark tresses around his fingers, drew strands across Sabrina's face. "You don't take from those people and get away with it. That he's dead isn't good enough. They want their money back. It's a point of honor." His fingers dropped, began undoing the remaining buttons on her blouse. "Personally, I don't give a shit about their principles. But I accepted the terms of the contract. I don't get paid for Charlie-boy until they get their money back." He looked into her eyes and smiled. Sabrina gasped at the sadistic light in his eyes. "I don't work for free, Sabrina. I always get paid. If I don't find the money, then I'll take you instead."

He bent and kissed her neck, sliding his lips down the swell of her breast, his tongue questing beneath her bra. Sabrina moaned, the feel of his mouth on her body making her sick, his words slamming into her. Take her, what did he mean? How could Charlie have done this to her? Why hadn't he simply given Biaggi the damned money?

Biaggi's hands caressed her face, pushed her hair back. His lips lifted, met hers. Sabrina tried to pull away, to turn her head, but his strong fingers held her motionless, at his mercy. When at last he broke the kiss, he laid his cheek against hers and whispered in her ear.

"It'll last for weeks, Sabrina. Maybe months. Just you and me. I'll get my fee out of you, every last cent. I almost hope I don't find the money." He sat up and smiled at her again. "I may not, there's only the kitchen and garage left to search. Not much hope, is there? Unless Charlie-boy had a safe-deposit box in the Gaffe bank?"

Completely numb, Sabrina shook her head. Biaggi rose, his face hard and malignant, his legs still straddling her. The house again vibrated beneath the wind's savage assault. Biaggi glared at the shuttered windows. Then, without a further glance at Sabrina, he stepped over her, lifted the closest lantern and strode out into the kitchen, leaving her alone in the semi-dark, a darkness alive with ominous sounds and the echoes of Biaggi's vile threats.

For long minutes Sabrina lay motionless, barely aware of her surroundings. All she could think of was Biaggi's eyes, his mouth questing over her skin, his decision not to kill her but to take her with him. And Geoff, her friend, lying dead now because of her. Because of Charlie. Still, the wind would not be denied. It slammed at the house, wrenched at the siding, tore at the roof, pried insistently at the ancient storm shutters that denied it entrance. The house rattled, shook, seemed to dance on its foundation. Part of the front porch railing let go and smashed against the covered kitchen windows. She heard the steps to the beach, hammered at by both wind and water, collapse with an agonized roar. Frenzied waves tossed the loose boards into the air. The berserk wind caught them and slammed them against the front of the house.

One worked an edge behind the shutter over the living room window closest to the door. The rabid wind wrenched at the board, and the shutter pulled free of the house. The shattered railing outside the kitchen windows lifted, rammed into the eaves and broke away huge pieces of roofing tile. The insane wind, finding at last two weakened entry ports, howled in victory, then slammed and thrashed anew at the cottage. And the cottage, screaming and shuddering in protest, slowly surrendered to the insuperable force.

An ear-numbing screech split the air. Sabrina gasped and lifted her head. The noise seemed to come from the kitchen, echoing down from the roof. The house creaked and groaned in agony. Again, it quivered on its foundation. Terrified, Sabrina rolled to her side. She squinted into the darkness, searching the murky room—and saw the knife still rammed into the floor nearby. If she could somehow get to it, maybe she could cut the ropes binding her. Another anguished screech echoed in the darkness. The shutter on the front window lifted up and slammed back down against the house with stunning force. Sabrina, in a panic, twisted her body, pulling at the iron stove to which she was tied. But she hadn't the strength to move the ponderous mass, much less lift it to free her hands. Discouraged, she collapsed on the hard floor.

A tremendous roar reverberated through the room. The cottage shook like a leaf in a fall breeze. Sabrina looked toward the archway and saw a spray of glass shower into the kitchen. A second later, a sharp crack wrenched her attention back to the living room. The front wall disintegrated before her horrified eyes. Shattered glass and splintered shutters ricocheted about like bullets. Her mother's curtains bellowed in a deranged dance and tore from their anchors. Rain poured through the huge opening, accompanied by a hellish wind that tossed the room's contents around like toothpicks.

Chairs and tables tipped and spun across the floor. The slashed settee capered sideways then tipped over and slued around like a whirligig. Sabrina screamed, her terrified voice lost beneath the triumphant roar of the hurricane. The wind slammed into her. She felt her body skid sideways as it pivoted around the leg of the iron stove. The roiling air pummeled her with pieces of glass and shards of wood. The wind battered at her, sucking her breath away until she could no longer breathe. It wrenched at her body. Pain shot up her arms from her tethered wrists, pain darker and more smothering than the chaos around her. The last thing she saw, before the darkness whirled her far away, was the huge iron stove rocking perilously above her head.

CHAPTER TWENTY-THREE

She woke lying half on her side, her arms twisted up over her head. Rain splattered onto her face. She could hear the wind and feel it on her body, but it was too dark to see anything clearly. When she tried to move, every inch of her hurt. But at least she could breathe again, nothing seemed broken, and she wasn't dead. She felt grateful until she remembered that Vincent Biaggi stood between her and freedom. She wondered, then, if perhaps it would have been better to have died after all.

The wind seemed calmer, it didn't wrench at her anymore. And it sounded less virulent, though it still gusted with appreciable strength. Slowly, testing her bones carefully as she moved, Sabrina rolled over and looked around.

She appeared to be in a sort of triangular cave formed by the upturned settee, the mohair couch, and some tables and chairs the wind had jammed together.

The heavy iron stove had tipped over and slued around, carrying Sabrina with it, her hands still bound to a curving leg. It had been a miracle she hadn't been crushed beneath it when it fell. Her only view was out over the top of the stove's side, and all she could see was the wall against which it had once stood, its flue pipe still dangling between what appeared to be undamaged, still-shuttered windows, swaying uncertainly in the gradually lessening wind.

She looked again at her hands, at the tapering iron leg to which she was bound. It was just possible that she could wriggle the rope down and off the end of the leg. Her hands would still be tied together, but she would be free to move around. She worked diligently, fearing that at any second Vincent Biaggi would appear to cut off her escape. It seemed to take forever. Sabrina was trembling violently when at last the rope slid from the stove leg. She gulped air in relief, biting back the cry that rose to her lips, not wishing to alert Biaggi to her presence if he was, indeed, searching for her. Now all she had to do was get out from under all this furniture, make her way through her shattered house, find the road and someone to help her on the mostly-evacuated island, all with feet and hands tightly tied and without Biaggi seeing or catching her. The enormity of the task almost stopped her from even attempting it.

Almost.

But not quite. She hadn't come this far, survived so much, only to quit. Dying at another's hands was one thing when it felt worthwhile, when the cause of it made sense, was backed by love. But Charlie had lied to her, created a world of false security and taught her not only to trust in it, but to never even question it. He had left her bereft of a mooring, with not so much as the wreckage of their love to hang onto. Despite Mitch Lawson's comforting words about love creating its own reality, Sabrina knew now that love had had no hand in it, not from Charlie's end. She had merely been his cover, a protection he had coldly abandoned when it failed him. He could have saved her the pain and anguish she'd suffered already, the death she still might, had he cared. Had he truly loved her, he would have given Biaggi what he sought, the money he had come for. He would have protected her. He would have given his life for her, instead of for money. Love created nothing. Sabrina would never let herself trust in it, or anyone, ever again.

She inched her cautious way out of the cave and over the potbelly stove, her heart thudding. She scraped her shins on the rough iron surface but bit back the cry that rose to her lips. It was incredibly awkward tying to crawl over the huge rounded lump with her hands and feet bound, but she was afraid to try to move the precariously-positioned furniture, or try climbing over any of it. When at last she swung her feet onto the floor outside the pseudo-cave, she uttered a silent prayer of thanksgiving, head bowed and eyes closed in relief. The first thing she saw when she opened them again, in the almost non-light reflecting through the broken wall from gray clouds swirling in the sky outside, was Biaggi's wide-bladed, eight-inch hunting knife.

She stared at it, blinking, unable to believe what she saw. It was still there! Breathing heavily, she looked around the ruined room, searching for signs of movement, listening for any sound other than ocean and wind. There was nothing. It appeared, for the time being at least, that she was alone.

Hope surged in her body. She slid from her perch. Her weak legs collapsed beneath her and deposited her heavily onto the floor. She moved on a moment later, eyes and ears still alert, an awkward wriggle over to where the knife stood sentinel. She could still picture the way Biaggi had menaced her with it. Now it was hers.

It took a few minutes to disembed it. She had to wiggle it back and forth, coaxing it with care from the depths of the pine, for Biaggi's strength had driven it well into the wood. She hadn't the strength to merely yank it free, as he undoubtedly would have. Once it was free she cut apart the rope around her ankles, but she could not turn the blade to slice through the one on her wrists. The rope was too tight. It allowed her little movement and the blade was wide and long. She would only manage to cut herself, and she knew she was weak enough without spilling any more of her blood. But she had a weapon now, perfectly honed and deadly. If she moved slowly, quietly, and kept herself alert, she just might have the chance to use it.

Sabrina rose to her feet and edged toward the half-crumbled front wall. Escape was impossible that way. Half the porch had collapsed and the rest was littered with boards, roof tiles, glass and seaweed. Dim light reflected on water lapping not six inches from the crest of the drop off, and Sabrina surmised that the wind had driven the storm surge over the top to undermine the pilings holding the porch floorboards stable. There was no safety in that direction, not for her.

Taking a deep breath and seating the knife more firmly in her clenched hands, she turned and crunched her way slowly over the glass and wood strewn floor to the archway. The front door had held firm. The panel Mitch had nailed over its window was still in place. But rubble from the kitchen spilled out to half-block the hall, and Sabrina gasped when at last she sidled around the wreckage to the bottom of the staircase and peered into the ruin.

The entire front wall was gone, collapsed inward along with most of the roof. The glass-topped table had shattered. Its iron frame had tilted and twisted out of shape. The chairs were unrecognizable humps beneath the litter. Debris covered the counters, the stove and mounded all over the floor. She looked up. The skeletal fingers of broken ceiling joists reached into a dark void backed by now thinning clouds. Stars glimmered shyly in the deep blackness. Scarcely daring to breathe, Sabrina again peered around the room, searching among the piles of glass, plaster, wood and tile. Vincent Biaggi had been in the kitchen when the full force of the hurricane had struck. It was entirely possible that he was buried beneath the detritus. She fervently hoped so, though she could see no outline of a body, no sign of anything human in the silent darkness.

She edged back from the shambles of her kitchen. Away from the broken walls and roof it was dark, almost as dark as it had been before. The cottage groaned, its abused and twisted frame relaxing after the grueling effort of fighting the hurricane's fury. Sabrina sidled down the hall toward the rear door, jumping at every sound. She peered up the inky stairwell, but could distinguish nothing. A legion could be crouched on the steps and she'd not have seen them. The eerie silence after the demented howling of the wind totally unnerved her. She imagined footsteps echoing on the floor above her, thought she heard breathing in the darkness between herself and the door. Twice she whimpered in fear when the house creaked, and cried out loud when falling tiles smashed onto the littered kitchen floor. She made it as far as the cupboard beneath the stairs before she had to stop and take herself in hand again.

Then she moved on once more, keeping her back to the wall beneath the stairs and shifting her gaze from one end of the dark hallway to the other. Her hands clenched knuckle-tight the knife, holding it raised at chin level. The pounding of her heart masked other night sounds—the drip of water, the crunch of debris beneath her feet, the crash of tiles and plaster, the growl of the ocean. Not until she was within ten feet of the back door did she turn toward it.

A hard hand clamped tight on her left arm, just below her shoulder. Heart lurching, Sabrina looked into the darkness beneath the stairs and stumbled back to her right. The darkness moved with her, crowded her against the opposite wall, a tall, lean, menacing shadow that breathed death in her direction. It turned. Sabrina glimpsed an arching nose, caught the gleam of dim light on straight, pale hair. She screamed and struck out blindly with the knife.

She felt it hit him. Biaggi gave a stifled cry of pain. His fingers loosened, then clamped tight before she could pull away. Sabrina jerked the knife back and stabbed at him again. Warm, sticky blood splashed onto her fingers. Biaggi stumbled back into the darkness. His hand fell from her arm. She heard his body hit the floor with a heavy thump. She lost her hold on the now-slippery knife as she whirled and ran for the door. Her numb fingers fumbled with the chain and lock. She could barely breathe, she was so terrified that Biaggi's hands would again close on her at any second, despite the injury she'd inflicted. Not stopping to look back, she flung open the door and stumbled across the back porch.

She fell down the steps and landed on her knees in the gravel-strewn dirt. But she ignored the pain. She again surged to her feet and ran out into the road. It was completely dark, with not a light anywhere except in the eerily luminescent gray-clouded sky. Palmetto fronds hung limp, as though dead. Sabrina could hear nothing save her own gasping breaths. She blinked panic-induced tears from her eyes and looked up and down the rubble-strewn road, wondering which way to go. If there was help anywhere, where was it most likely to be? A palm frond dropped from a tree to her left with a loud crash. Sabrina gasped, whirled and ran to the right.

She had no idea where she was going. She merely ran, weaving around barely-seen obstacles, her fear intensified by the eerie silence and the curiously still sky above her head. Her sandals slid on the water-logged pavement. Her bound hands made both running and balance difficult. The road, masked by darkness, was almost impossible to see. When it curved, Sabrina lost her bearings and veered onto the unpaved shoulder. She lurched on, pain stabbing her side with every breath. She could feel her steps begin to slow as the pavement gave way to shifting, waterlogged sand. Then her foot hit a stone and skidded out from under her. She fell headlong, knocking the air from her lungs, scraping her elbows raw on the harsh surface.

She lay gasping for breath, trying to find the strength to rise and go on. But her body would not obey the frantic dictates of her mind. She had gone as far as she possibly could. She had reached the end of her endurance. Lowering her head onto her arms, she let hot tears overwhelm her.

A moment later, her head snapped up. A breeze had stirred the Palmetto trees beside her. Their rustling voices struck panic into her heart. The nether side of the hurricane. She had to move, get out of the open, or she would die. She forced herself to her feet but hard hands grabbed her before she could take a step.

Sabrina screamed and struck out, her bound hands curled into fists. The iron fingers tightened, shook her like a rag doll.

"Sabrina!" a deep voice ordered. "Stop, it's me! It's Mitch! Sabrina!"

He shook her again. Sabrina panicked as the words penetrated the fog of fear enveloping her. Mitch? It couldn't be, he was dead. It had to be Biaggi, trying to trick her.

"No!" She pushed at him, twisting to break his hold.

"Sabrina, it's Mitch! Stop fighting me, damn it! Listen to me!"

Sabrina froze and peered through the darkness, to search the face close to hers. "Mitch?" she whispered, too afraid to hope.

"Yes. It's me."

"Oh, thank God. I thought you were dead, Mitch."

"So did I, for a while, there," he said, holding her close. "Where's Biaggi?"

"I don't know, still in the cottage, I think. He-he tried to grab me. I had a knife, I stabbed him." Sabrina's voice choked off as she remembered the feel of the blade pushing into living flesh.

"Is he dead?"

She looked up at the grimness of Mitch's tone and shook her head. "I don't know. I heard him fall, then I ran. It was so dark, I couldn't see anything."

"Let's hope he is. We could use some luck right now." He caressed her face, unaware of her intake of breath as his hand slid over savage bruises he could not see. Then he sighed, looked up at the sky, and reluctantly loosened his hold on her. "Come on, we'd better get back inside. The storm isn't over, yet."

He kept an arm around her, guiding her along the curving roadway to the Inn, favoring his right leg. Sabrina caught her breath at the sight of the ravaged dark silhouette that stood against lighter colored clouds, clouds that once again had begun to slowly swirl around the sky. All three eastward-reaching arms of the structure had partially collapsed, the damage being most extensive to the southern ell. The southeastern end of the main building had also been torn apart. Mitch led her around to the west entry and groped their way across the lobby to the time-bleached dory. He sat her on its side, returning a few minutes later with a knife from the ruined restaurant.

"The storm's coming back, isn't it?" Sabrina asked, squinting to see Mitch in the dark as, working mainly by touch, he sawed through the rope on her wrists.

"Yes. We're in the eye now, that's why it's been so still out there. In a few minutes, all hell will break loose again." The rope parted, and Mitch let the knife drop to the carpeted floor as he pulled the strands from Sabrina's wrists. "But this time, it'll hit the door we just came in. Our best bet is to find somewhere on the other side of the building to hole up in."

"It didn't look very safe." Sabrina clenched her jaw as she rubbed at the raw flesh on her wrists.

"I know, but we haven't a whole lot of choice. The wind will hit this side of the building, so however unsafe the rest of this place is, it's still better than staying here. Come on, I'll—"

A loud crack cut off his words. A bullet hit the dory a few feet from where they sat and ricocheted into the darkness. Sabrina screamed and raised her hands to protect her head. Mitch grabbed her arm and pulled her away from the boat just as another bullet slammed into the wood where she had been sitting. They lurched through the darkness toward the stairwell, impeded by Mitch's limp. More bullets hit the dory, the floor, the lobby walls. Biaggi's malevolent voice echoed around them as they stumbled up the steps.

"I'll get you, Sabrina! You and your boyfriend! I owe you one, sweetheart, and you're going to pay! You hear me, Sabrina? You're going to pay!"

CHAPTER TWENTY-FOUR

"What are we going to do?" Sabrina asked, her voice nearly drowned out by the rising wind.

Mitch could just see her outline, for the fading bulb in the flashlight made little inroad on the thick darkness. They stood against the wall on the third floor, opposite the staircase. He hoped Biaggi didn't realize they'd climbed to the top story.

"I don't know," Mitch admitted, thinking hard. How much did Biaggi know of the layout of this place? Had he stayed here, too, perhaps only a few rooms away from Mitch himself? Or did they have the advantage of familiarity, an edge that might very well spell survival for them? Mitch frowned as he stared into the dark abyss of the stairwell. The cacophony outside blotted out any sound of pursuit. Even now, Biaggi could be inching up the stairs. Mitch grasped Sabrina's arm and moved her down the hall away from the steps.

"We can't stay here, and we sure as hell can't go outside," he said, his tone grim. "I'll find a place for you to hide as far from the west side of the building as I can, and hope Biaggi won't find you before the storm is over."

Sabrina didn't say anything, just watched him with big, frightened eyes. Mitch turned her into the center ell, the middle 'arm' of the E-shape the building formed. Far at the end they could see clouds through a gaping hole in the roof. He tried door after door along the hall, hoping to find one open. He didn't dare shoot out a lock as he had before. That noise would surely reverberate above the wind and alert Biaggi, tell him where they were. The longer he could keep him guessing, the better Sabrina's chances. If Biaggi were intent enough on his search, maybe he'd get caught in the open when the storm hit in full again. Mitch could only hope.

None of the doors yielded to his hand. Halfway down the hall debris began to slow their progress. Sabrina stumbled, Mitch's strong hand on her arm all that kept her upright. The wind rose higher, swirling in through the fallen roof to whip their hair around and yank at their clothing. Tiles and boards spun away into the black night. The building rolled beneath their feet as though they stood on a boat, not dry land.

An outer staircase had been built three rooms in from the end of each ell closest to the ocean to provide the inn's guests easy access to the beach. Mitch had hoped they could use those steps to gain access to the second or first floor and leave their pursuer searching the dark inner staircase and third floor while the hurricane ran its course. But the center wing ended in a pile of rubble where the outer steps and last three rooms had once stood. The wind tugged at a roof that continued to disintegrate. Truncated beams and ceiling tiles crashed down onto the water-logged carpeting. Rain slashed at their faces and the floor bobbled beneath their feet.

Mitch pulled Sabrina back to the Plexiglas-covered walkways that originally sat sixty feet in from the outer beach staircases. They linked the second and third floor ells together, so guests did not have to negotiate the entire length of one arm of the 'E' shaped building to reach the rooms along the other two arms. Mitch and Sabrina contemplated their remains in wind-punctuated silence.

The walkway to their right, the one that led from the center ell to the southernmost wing, had collapsed, leaving a gaping hole in the side of the building. The walkway to the northern wing still survived, though half the clear roof was gone. It was too dark now to be sure if it was still anchored securely to the walls or not. Sabrina looked at Mitch and indicated the narrow bridge with a tilt of her head. Mitch shook his head and turned away from the bridge, teeth clenched against his growing frustration, and retraced their steps back to the corridor that connected the inn's arms at their base.

Damn, Mitch thought, his heart pounding in his chest, *what do I do now?* He had to get Sabrina safely hidden away before Biaggi found his way to the third floor. He couldn't let that bastard touch her again.

He finally found a door in a small alcove on the inside wall of the northernmost arm, just after they had turned out of the base corridor. It surprised the hell out of him when the knob turned and the door opened. It wasn't a guest room, which probably explained why it wasn't locked. It wasn't perfect, considering it was on the side of the inn now being brutalized by the hurricane. But it was on an inside wall, not the dangerous outer wall of the wing. Since his choices were limited to this, it would have to do.

Sheets and towels filled the shelves lining the interior walls of the 5 foot by 6 foot room. A large industrial vacuum took up one corner. Two room cleaning carts occupied most of the remaining floor space. Still, there was room to secrete at least one person in the linen closet. Mitch checked and found a twist lock above the interior doorknob. He grabbed Sabrina and pushed her into the room.

"Get in there, and don't move until I come back for you." He had to shout to compete with the howling wind.

"No!" Sabrina's voice sounded panicky. She tried to push out of the room, but Mitch blocked the doorway. "Don't leave me alone."

"You can't stay with me, Sabrina. I can't see two feet in front of my face, the building is coming apart around us, and with this frigging wind Biaggi could be on us before we even know it. He's a trained killer, Sabrina, you know that, and I haven't been out in the field for six years. I sure as hell don't need a helpless civilian hanging around my neck. Not in these conditions. If you want to see the sunrise, do what I say. Understand?"

The dying flashlight lent just enough illumination for him to see the fear on her face. He knew how hard it would be for her to wait alone in the wind-haunted dark. He could also see suspicion lying beneath the fear and knew what it would cost her to willingly trust anyone again, even him. She shook her head, her lips open to speak though no sound emerged. A loud crash reverberated from the conference rooms diagonally across the corridor. Mitch's hands tightened on her shoulders.

"There isn't much time. I'll come back for you, I promise. Lock the door and stay put, understand? Don't move, no matter what happens."

"Please, Mitch, don't leave me."

She clutched his hand. He bent, kissed her swollen cheek and placed his lips beside her ear. He felt her shiver as his warm breath caressed her neck.

"I have to stop him, Sabrina. It'll be okay. Keep the door locked and he won't be able to get to you. Stay put, and let me do my job, okay? That's what I'm trained for, getting rid of scum like Biaggi. Please."

Sabrina gave him one last terrified look, then nodded and backed away from the door so he could close it. Mitch's heart twisted at the way she wrapped her arms around herself. She looked like an abandoned waif standing in the dark interior of the room. The last thing he wanted to do was let her out of his sight. But he knew he had no choice. He gave her a reassuring smile he wasn't sure she could see, then pulled the door closed. He pressed his ear against the wood until he heard the lock click in place. Then he stood a moment longer, listening to the roar of the wind. Somewhere far below, glass shattered. Much closer, something big and solid hit the side of the building with a wrenching thud.

Mitch turned off the flashlight and melted into the darkness of the northern-most wing. He trailed one hand on the wall for guidance in the dark as his ears strained to pick up anything human beneath the feral wind. He inched along, a bullet chambered in the gun he held, determined to find and neutralize Vincent Biaggi, no matter what it took. He wasn't ready yet to admit it to himself, but deep down Mitch knew that the stakes in the game had just gone higher. That bastard had hurt Sabrina, had beaten her black and blue. It was much more now than just his job. Now, it was personal.

* * *

Sabrina felt like she was suffocating in the linen closet. She could barely move, hemmed in by shelving and equipment. It was totally dark, not a flicker of light or shadow anywhere, as if all of creation had simply vanished into a black void. But it hadn't, she knew. The small space seemed to catch and magnify every sound outside the door. Her imagination ran wild. Was there anything left of the building out there? She kept her hands pressed to her lips to keep from crying out, but it was the fear that Biaggi might be near, that he might hear her, and not her hands that kept her mute.

How long she stood in the dark, huddled against the shelves, she wasn't sure. She lost awareness of the passage of time. It felt like she had been abandoned there for hours. Days. What if Biaggi got Mitch? How long would the bastard keep searching for her? What if he shot out all the door locks until he found her? A vibration thrummed through the walls, then the floor. Sabrina pushed further into the room. *Is the building collapsing?* she wondered. Would she be killed anyway? Would Mitch?

Mitch! Sabrina's head snapped up. He was out there alone, facing a monster, while she huddled like a coward in relative safety. This wasn't even his fight, for all his words about the FBI and training. It was her fight. Charlie had seen to that. It was Sabrina that Biaggi wanted. It wasn't right to let Mitch risk his life to catch this maniac. *He can't do it alone,* she thought. *They always have backup.* But Mitch's backup lay in a hospital bed. He had no one else. No one but her.

She turned and felt her way to the nearest cart, then began to pull out the contents. There had to be something she could use, something that might help. She found cleaning solutions and rags, sponges, a toilet brush—nothing she thought would be of much use. There was a large heavy bucket and two mops, but she couldn't imagine maneuvering something so unwieldy in the high winds outside the door. She was close to despairing when, in the very bottom of the cart, she discovered a metal box about the size of a loaf of bread. Her fingers fumbled a moment with the latch before the lid finally lifted. Inside Sabrina found small tools— a wrench, a few screwdrivers, pliers, other small hand tools she couldn't identify by touch.

She smiled with satisfaction as she picked up what felt like a Phillips-head screwdriver, pointed and sharp. She threaded it into her waistband. Then she grabbed a solid feeling wrench and stood up. The building shook again. A high-pitched squeal resounded in the small space. Sabrina cringed and pressed her hands over her ears. It seemed to go on forever before it finally stopped. Her breath rasped in her throat as she felt her way over to the door and twisted the lock open, wondering what she would find when she opened the door. If Biaggi was out there, she was ready for him. She hoped. She firmed her grip on the wrench, grasped the doorknob and turned it.

The wind shoved the door inward the moment she cracked it open. It hit her shoulder and threw her against the shelving. Linens cascaded around her. She almost lost hold of the wrench, but tightened her half-numb fingers at the last second. The pull of the wind sucked the breath from her lungs and pinned her against the wall. Rain pummeled her face, forcing her to close her eyes. She dropped to the floor and crawled out of the room. She felt the wrench in her hand clunk on the floor as she dragged herself by sheer will power down the corridor of the northern arm, away from the fury of the storm. She crawled a hundred feet before she collapsed, exhausted.

The thought of Mitch facing Biaggi alone pushed her back to her knees. She wiped the wetness from her bruised, aching face and looked back at where she'd come from. The outer wall of the arm where it joined the connecting base corridor, a few feet from the room in which she had hidden, disintegrated as she watched. Another screech rent the air as a huge section of roof tore off and whirled away into the ether, leaving the entire northwest corner of the building exposed. Churning pale gray clouds lent a semblance of light, enough for her to see the skeletal outlines of foreshortened walls and broken roof beams. Rain and wind surged in to savage interior walls and carpeting. There was no way she could get to the base corridor that connected the three wings. She was trapped in the northern arm of the inn.

Or was she? Sabrina turned and looked into the darkness down the ell's length. She couldn't see five feet in front of her, but she knew the walkway was down there. And though it had lost part of its cover, she could still use it to gain access to at least the center arm of the inn. If Biaggi and Mitch weren't in this northern one with her, they would have to be in the center ell, since the southern wing had been destroyed earlier. And if they were in this corridor with her, all the better. It was too dark for them to see her coming, and neither man would expect her to arrive on the scene, especially not armed. Maybe the element of surprise would prove the turning point for her and Mitch.

She pulled herself to her feet and began groping her way down the hall, listening for any human sounds beneath the noise of the inn's destruction. She couldn't see anything, the darkness was so complete, and she realized it must mean the ocean end of this arm was still intact. If so, she could use the outside staircase at the end to escape the inn—if the steps still stood, if the ocean didn't lap at the top landing and if the wind didn't blow her away. Not that there was anywhere to go even if she could get out. And she would not go anywhere without Mitch. She was through with running and hiding. She would no longer be a victim.

She neither heard nor saw any movement around her as she progressed down the corridor. It seemed that Mitch and Biaggi were elsewhere in the building. She would have to make it over to the central arm. A faint lightening of the darkness to her right announced the opening to the walkway. Sabrina paused as her heartbeat ratcheted up. Fear spread a cold heat though her, despite her resolve to be brave and resourceful. She listened a moment longer to the agonized death-screams of the inn, then braced herself to step out of the safety of the building. A noise stopped her feet—the crack of a gun riding the wind. The faint sound repeated twice after a short pause.

Mitch! Had he gotten Biaggi? Or had Biaggi shot him? It hadn't sounded nearby, not that the storm made it easy to tell how far away it had been, or even in what direction. But it meant that Mitch needed her, needed her help.

Sabrina peered again into the walkway, unable to see much despite the shadowy, vague light that reflected from the roiling gray clouds. Half the roof was gone and she could feel the strong winds that gusted and swirled along bridge's length. She couldn't tell how stable it was, but she had only two choices. She could wait here for whoever would come looking for her, Mitch or Biaggi, or she could take control of her life for the first time, and maybe affect the outcome of this fight. And if she died in the attempt, at least she wouldn't go out as a coward.

The bridge swayed when she stepped out onto it. Sabrina grabbed the railing for balance. The wrench clanged against the cold iron as she pulled herself along. The farther she went, the more the bridge undulated and the stronger the wind grew. She was terrified the structure would break apart beneath her feet. The clunk of the wrench marked every step and she began to count them in a failing attempt to keep fear at bay. She made it to the halfway point before the wind blew her off her feet and pinned her to the side of the bridge. The Plexiglas that remained, from her shoulders down, kept her from being thrown from the structure.

Loud cracks reverberated in the swirling air. A piece of the roof just ahead of her flew away. Then the wind loosed its hold on her. Sabrina clung to the railing, so weak and shaky from terror she could barely force herself to move.

But she did, the thought of plunging three stories to her death spurring her on. She peered toward her destination, the center wing, and gasped. Part of the bridge floor was missing. A gaping six-foot-long hole stood between her and safety. A strip of floor only three feet wide remained beneath the railing to which she clung. It didn't look strong enough to hold her. Above the hole the roof was missing, leaving a wall that ended at shoulder height. One strong up-gust of wind could lift her over the wall and into the abyss below. There was no way she could make it. She would have to go back.

Shock rippled through her when she turned her head to look back at the way she'd come. The bridge on that end had pulled partly away from the main structure of the building. It twisted around in the wind, sending shudders vibrating through the remaining parts of the bridge. Sabrina watched, frozen, as the back edge of the bridge separated from the hotel wall and crumbled inward. Debris spilled out through the gap into the windy darkness. Going back meant sure death. She had no choice but to continue on. *You can do this,* she told herself. *You have to. For Mitch.*

Sabrina edged her way past the missing floor boards one slow step at a time, her hands clenched tight on the railing, her toes jammed up against the wall. The wrench's clink marked her progress. The wind tore at her. The bridge shuddered and bucked. But she locked her gaze on the archway into the wing and concentrated on the solid ground and walls that awaited her. She moved on, inch by agonizing inch until at last she stretched out her left hand and grasped the edge of the opening. She took two more tiny steps toward the center arm before the bridge uttered an anguished wail and parted completely from the northern wing.

The floor beneath her dropped away and Sabrina's feet skidded down. She lost her grip on the railing. The wrench spun out into the darkness. She clutched the corridor opening with her left hand, her fingers digging into the decorative molding around the opening as her feet fought for purchase on the nearly vertical floor. She found it, lost it and, screaming, found it again. She pushed with her feet, pulled on the wall, and with one final, fierce effort threw herself onto the corridor floor just as the bridge separated totally from the hotel and dropped into the inky depths three stories below.

She rolled onto her back and for a moment lay shuddering, listening to the echoes of bridge's destruction. She could still feel the wind poke and prod at her and, afraid she would be sucked out into the night, she rolled to her side and climbed to her feet. *Get away from here,* she told herself as she forced herself to move. Her shaking legs did not collapse under her, which surprised her, and her strength seemed to return the further she moved away from the dangerous opening. The floor grew solid beneath her feet. The walls felt strong and sturdy. She moved on, searching for a recessed a doorway in which to huddle while she regrouped. She'd lost the wrench, but a touch at her waist assured her that the screwdriver had survived the ordeal.

She refused to acknowledge, or put into words, her fear that this was not a rescue mission, that those gunshots meant Mitch was already dead. The wind-scattered debris made the going tough as she stumbled toward the center of the wing. She couldn't see more than a few feet down the hall, and she feared she might stumble into the men unaware and unprepared. The wind's scream hid all sounds of anyone nearby—shots, voices, the movement of bodies inching down the corridor.

She paused in a doorway niche after she went twenty nerve-wracking feet and leaned shaking hands on the wall as she fought to still her panicked breathing. Should she take out the screwdriver, hold it ready to use? Or was it safer to leave it where it was and pull it only when necessary? She'd be totally helpless if she lost it the way she had the wrench. *I can't risk it*, she decided. *I'll leave it where it is. For now.*

She took a deep breath, stepped out into the corridor and froze. A tall figure stood in deep shadow fifteen feet in front of her. A man, but which one?

"Mitch?" she asked, her voice trembling, barely audible over the wind.

The shadowy figure did not answer. It moved closer to her with a sure-footed, predatory gait. Not Mitch.

Sabrina's heart thudded in her chest as she backed away from the menacing shadow. He held a gun in his right hand, aimed at the center of her chest. Her hand dropped, seeking the screwdriver. Biaggi waggled the gun.

"Don't move, Sabrina," he growled.

Sabrina froze. She knew he would shoot her if she moved, and she toyed with the idea of letting him. Mitch was probably dead, and she had no desire to be his plaything. At least it would be fast if she disobeyed him. But Biaggi didn't know she was armed—if you could call carrying a screwdriver being armed. But it was almost as good as a knife. And Biaggi was wounded, she could see the dark-stained white cloth bound around his left biceps. So he was weaker, now. Maybe there was still a chance, one fleeting second when she could pull the tool out of her waistband and drive it though his eye. Or into his heart. Avenge Charlie, avenge Mitch...

Then Biaggi reached out, captured her wrist and ground her bones together in his vicious grip. And all strategy flew from Sabrina's head.

CHAPTER TWENTY-FiVE

Biaggi yanked Sabrina close, then swung her arm behind her back and bent it up until she thought he'd break it. He raised his right hand, laid the side of the gun on her cheek. Its icy chill warred with the warmth that radiated from his lean, hard body. He bent his head and spoke into her ear, his breath hot on her face.

"You didn't really think you'd get away, did you, Sabrina?" He moved the pistol, slid it under her chin, pushed her head up and glared into her eyes. "You're going to pay for what you did to me, bitch. Long. And hard."

Sabrina thought of the screwdriver threaded in her waistband. Two moments, that's all she wanted. Two tiny moments. One to get the ersatz weapon loose and one to stab him with it. Her hand twitched. Biaggi shoved the gun into his waistband and captured her left arm with his right hand. He looked at the blood-soaked cloth wound around his left biceps then back at her as he pulled her arms together and clamped his left hand around both her wrists. Then he pulled his gun again, pivoted and began dragging her down the hallway.

Sabrina stumbled over the debris that littered the corridor, wondering how much strength the wound had sapped from him. It didn't seem like much to her, but it could be anger and adrenaline that drove him. Eventually he would tire, wouldn't he? How long could he hold her like this, his fingers so tight they almost cut off her circulation? She twisted her arms and yanked hard every time she tripped, hoping to sap his strength faster, but it didn't appear to have any real effect. He stopped once and stared at her for an eternity-long minute, and she knew he was well aware of her feeble efforts to gain her freedom. She doubted he knew the real reason she wanted an arm free, even though he held the pistol half-raised, pointed at her as though he debated shooting her. Or maybe hitting her with it. Then his lip lifted in a sneer and he once again began towing her down the hallway.

They were headed, she realized, toward the west corridor, to the steps that lead down to the lobby. Her heart stuttered. Did that mean Mitch really was dead? Or was Biaggi simply content with her, with what he would do to her once they left the Inn? *If the storm doesn't kill us first*, she thought. Once more she tried to pull away but Biaggi jerked her arms, forcing her onward.

Sabrina could see, thirty feet ahead, dark clouds boiling across the sky where the Inn's roof should be. Pieces of plaster and wood cartwheeled down the corridor around them. Something hard hit a glancing blow on her shoulder. She yelped and turned sideways, raising her left shoulder for protection. She lurched onto a jumbled pile of roofing tiles and broken beams. They shifted, wrenching her feet out from under her. She fell, her wrists pulling out of Biaggi's hard grip, and cracked her right side and her head on slabs of wood.

"Get up!" Biaggi's malicious snarl echoed above the wind.

Sabrina, dazed and winded, barely heard the growled order. Biaggi drew his foot back and kicked her shoulder. Sabrina screamed and looked up at him through wind-driven rain that half-blinded her.

"Up, bitch! Move it!" he yelled, shifting the gun to point at her head.

Now, Sabrina thought. She nodded and pushed herself to her knees, hunching over against the wind as her hand sought her waistband. Then her gaze fell on a three-foot length of board lying a foot away. She froze, staring at it. It would do more damage than the screwdriver. She imagined it in her hands, swinging it through the air, smashing it into Biaggi's head. He bent and jabbed her with the gun barrel, a sharp poke in her aching shoulder where his kick had landed.

Sabrina looked up at him and her heart sank. Even in the capricious shadows she could see his expression, the look in his eyes. He, too, had seen the board. He knew the desire that had surged through her, and he was looking forward to punishing her for it. And now she had lost the opportunity to draw the screwdriver. God, she was so stupid. Biaggi stepped back a few paces and gestured an order with the weapon: *Get up.*

Sabrina pressed the back of a shaking hand to her lips and half-turned away from Biaggi as she gathered herself to rise. Maybe she could still get at the screwdriver, if she could get her left hand out of his sight. She looked up to see where he stood and saw, beyond him to his right, the corner where the central hallway joined the spine of the "E." The darkness shifted, and Mitch appeared. Sabrina's eyes widened with shock. Mitch had his head bent against the wild wind. His limping gait looked unsteady on the rubble-strewn floor. Sabrina knew he didn't—couldn't—see them.

Movement near her pulled her back to Biaggi. He spun away from her, dropped into a crouch and swung his gun toward Mitch, who teetered on a shifting pile of litter.

"Mitch!" she screamed.

Her voice disintegrated almost instantly in the turbulent maelstrom. And yet somehow Mitch seemed to hear her cry. Mitch looked up; Sabrina yanked at the screwdriver, but it had twisted in her waistband and she couldn't free it. Mitch raised his gun and fired just as his feet slipped in the rubble. The shot went wide. He fought for balance, twisting to the side as Biaggi fired back. Sabrina saw Mitch's body jerk. His legs buckled and he crashed onto the littered floor.

She screamed. She yanked again and the screwdriver came free from her waistband. Biaggi took a step closer to Mitch, gun aimed at his head. Sabrina ran at Biaggi and swung the tool with all her strength. He turned and raised his injured left arm to deflect the blow. The screwdriver plunged deep into the underside of his forearm. The point burst out through the top. Blood sprayed into the air as he jerked back a few steps and stared at the screwdriver impaled in his arm.

Then he roared with rage, raised his gun and fired at Sabrina. The impact lifted her off her feet and sailed her across the corridor into the wall. Her body exploded. A strange numbness spread throughout her in undulating waves. She couldn't breathe, couldn't hear. Time slowed to a crawl. For an endless moment she stood against the wall, pinned in place by shock and the wind, her eyes seeing but her mind not comprehending what happened only a few feet away.

Mitch clawed himself to his knees and fired four shots at Vincent Biaggi before the man could turn away from Sabrina. Biaggi spun, staggered. The huge pistol dropped from his fingers as he crumpled onto the rain-soaked carpet. Mitch grimaced in pain, bent double and sank down atop a pile of rubble. Sabrina's numb legs folded and she slid down the wall, leaving a dark red trail behind on the wallpaper. She hit the floor with a solid thud, moaning as suddenly pain erupted, blotting out the ferocious sound of the wind. Agony engulfed her and the darkness deepened. Her body canted sideways, and she rolled face-down onto the sopping, rubble-strewn carpet.

* * *

The hospital released her five weeks later. She sat beside Mitch in the back seat of a car chauffeured by Charlotte's local FBI agent, a rangy, brown-haired, hazel-eyed man named Ned Costello whose lazy drawl grated on her nerves. The savage bruises on her face and body had faded to yellow and the swelling had abated. The cuts and abrasions, as well as the rope burns on her wrists, were healing well, with minimal scarring. Her left arm, wrapped in a sling, was bent at the elbow and covered in plaster that rose to encase her shoulder.

Sabrina massaged the thin, lifeless-looking fingers that stuck out of the hard shell, trying to work some warmth into them. Her ravaged shoulder and arm would need a lot more than time to mend from the shattering impact of Biaggi's bullet. The wound would stand as a permanent reminder of the ordeal, one Sabrina did not need. She had been lucky, the doctors said, after telling her that she probably would not regain total use of her arm, that she had not died. An inch or two lower and the bullet would have severed the aorta. She'd have bled to death in mere minutes. Sabrina wondered how long it would be before she began to feel lucky.

She glanced at Mitch, who looked out at the destruction the hurricane had wrought in the beautiful old southern city, his face devoid of expression. Much of the devastation still remained—trees torn and uprooted, houses and buildings missing roofs and walls, shattered windows still boarded over, huge piles of rubble from the on-going clean-up set awaiting removal. He didn't look at her, seemed unaware of her solemn stare. Sabrina dropped her gaze to look at his leg which she knew was bandaged beneath the blue-gray slacks he wore. There had been two operations to repair the damage both the accident and Biaggi's bullet had wreaked. He had discarded his crutches only two days ago. The cane he was forced to use lay propped against the seat between them.

Sabrina sighed, turned her head away and closed her eyes. *Does he remember?* she wondered. Did he think about those last few hours when they were trapped on the third floor of the Inn, trying desperately to stay alive until the storm ended and rescue could come? Were they burned into his memory, as they were into hers?

It had been his hands that had pulled her back to awareness, back to the wind- and rain-scoured corridor three stories above the solid earth. She had been floating, her spirit cartwheeling, rejoicing in its freedom. There had been no pain, no suffering. She had even forgotten that she had a body, or a life to live out in lonely isolation, a life devoid of love, of sharing, of trust. She was content to simply float, forever.

But he touched her, turned her over, and brought pain and reality roaring back into her being. She heard his voice, calling her name, through the agony that wrenched at her. She gasped, opened eyes that barely focused and remembered Biaggi.

"Mitch! Oh, God, Mitch! He'll kill you! He'll—"

"Shhh, it's all right." He smoothed back her hair. His face looked grim in the shadows, his eyes dark, cold and very, very angry. "He's dead, Sabrina, I shot him. Don't think about him, anymore. He's dead, I promise you."

The wind gusted, whipping pale, wet curls around his head. His shirt was gone—he'd wrapped it around the wound in his thigh. He leaned down and pulled her blood-soaked blouse apart. Sabrina watched his jaw clench as he inspected her shoulder, and though she wanted to turn her head and see it for herself, she kept her eyes on his face. She knew would learn more that way. She watched him draw in his breath and brace himself to meet her eyes, and she knew he would lie to her. She was right. When he did shift his eyes to hers, the truth was there, beneath the casual air he feigned, the half-smile on his lips. It was bad.

"It's not so bad, Sabrina. I've seen worse, believe me." He leaned back and looked around the corridor. Rain slashed into Sabrina's face. She scrunched her eyes shut, shielding them with her right hand. Another large chunk of the roof above them let go with an anguished screech. Shards of plaster pelted them. Mitch leaned over Sabrina, protecting her with his own ravaged body until the danger had passed.

"Damn, it's not safe here. I've got to find us some shelter. I'll be right back, Sabrina."

He crawled off into the darkness, dragging his injured right leg. Sabrina shut her eyes and waited in pain and wind-wrapped silence. Would he come back for her? Or would Biaggi be waiting to finish the job he'd started? Two shots reverberated in the boiling air and Sabrina gasped. *No, no, not again*, she prayed, tears filling her rain-blinded eyes. *Please, not again.*

Then, somehow, he was there beside her. Mitch. She cried out when he touched her face and she knew he could read her fears, see them in her eyes though she didn't speak a word.

"Don't panic, Sabrina, it was only me. I shot out a lock so we can get under cover. I told you he was dead, remember? He can't ever hurt you, or anyone else, not ever again."

Sabrina nodded, hoping, praying that he was telling her the truth about Biaggi. Mitch smiled and wiped the rain from her face.

"You're going to have to help me, Sabrina. I can't walk, there's no way I can carry you. It's not far, but I can't do it alone."

He slid his left arm under her back, lifting her a few inches from the floor. Sabrina stiffened. Pain caught in her throat, preventing her from crying out.

"Put your arm up around my neck and hold on." Mitch waited patiently until she found the strength to lift her right hand and loop it around his shoulders. "Now, I'm going to slide you back a few inches at a time, as carefully as I can. You'll have to help by pushing with your feet. Do you think you can do that?"

"I'll try," Sabrina said in a whisper. She wasn't sure he heard her, but she hadn't energy enough to speak louder. She tightened her hand on his neck and dug into the sopping carpet with her heels.

It took an eternity to gain the room, an eternity that lasted close to five agonizing minutes. She was covered with sweat within seconds. Her breath came in heavy pained gasps by the time they reached the threshold. Mitch had pulled the pillows from the two double beds onto the floor. Sabrina moaned in relief when he laid her down on their comforting softness. The room, completely enclosed by walls and ceiling, felt warm and dry. Sabrina let herself drift, hoping only that they were far enough away, that the storm would not eat its way to the shelter they had found. She didn't think about rescue, she couldn't even imagine the storm ending. And then Mitch was beside her again, pulling her blouse away from the savage wound.

"I hate to do this, it's going to hurt, but I've got to stop the bleeding."

Sabrina looked at her arm, lying lifeless on the floor beside her.

"I can't move my fingers," she told him. "I can't feel my arm at all."

"Don't worry about it." He pulled a sheet from the closest bed. "It's the trauma, bullet wounds always feel numb. It doesn't mean anything."

She knew he was lying again, but this time she was grateful for it. She watched him tear up the sheet and make two thick pads which he then bound to the front and back of her shoulder. She clenched her teeth, but she could not stop the moans that pushed up from deep within, or the hot tears that rivered down her temples. All she managed to do was keep herself from fainting. Mitch wiped her face with gentle care once he'd finished binding the wound. He took her right hand in his and held it tight.

"You're quite a woman, Sabrina Compton. Not many would be as brave as you."

"I bet you say that to all the women you're caught in a hurricane with." She gave him a faint smile. Her body began to shiver.

Mitch covered her with the blankets and spreads from both beds. He placed two chair cushions beneath her feet, to elevate them. And he kept her talking despite the drowsiness that tried to close her eyes, going over the things that Biaggi had told her, speculating on where Charlie could have hidden the stolen money, telling anecdotes about his field experiences. The powerful storm slowly moved on. The wind gradually dropped. The rain began to soften until at last it ceased.

Sabrina succumbed to fatigue, pain and loss of blood just as dawn broke on the horizon. Her eyes closed and, though she could still faintly hear Mitch's voice, she could no longer move or respond in any way.

"Damn it, Sabrina," he cried, clutching her cold hand in his barely warmer fingers. "Come on, don't give up. You've come too far to let him win. Damn it, wake up." She tried. All that moved were her lips, parting in a small silent gasp that Mitch obviously didn't see. "Please, Sabrina," he pleaded. She could feel his breath, warm on her face, his hand smoothing back her hair. It felt wonderful, gentle and comforting. "Please, don't die on me. I couldn't take that, not when I've just found you. Please, my sweet, hang on. It won't be much longer. It'll be light soon, people will find us. Please, don't leave me. Don't die, my sweet."

He pressed his lips to hers, lips that almost vibrated with his desperate effort to keep life in her. The kiss shivered through Sabrina. Her heart thudded so heavily she was sure he could hear it. She wanted to respond, tried to respond, to kiss him back, mold her lips to his. But the lethargy held her too close and darkness wrapped itself around her even as she yearned for the light. She relaxed in Mitch's careful embrace, and knew no more until she woke two days later in the hospital.

Their tires bumped over the temporary repair on the bridge, and she looked up to find they had already crossed James Island and were now swinging around the northern end of Gaffe. They passed the place where Biaggi had shot had Mitch the first time, sending him off the road and onto the rocks. Sabrina watched him turn his head and stare at the ocean that had almost claimed him. He said nothing, and she wondered what was going through his mind.

But she didn't ask. The tension that now held them miles apart had been building since she'd first seen him a week ago in the hospital. Sabrina felt as awkward and uncomfortable around Mitch as he appeared to feel around her. She couldn't seem to find words for what was in her mind, her heart, and Mitch avoided looking at her as much as he could. They'd never been alone once help arrived, one or the other surrounded either by doctors, local police, Marshals or FBI agents. The only one who seemed happy that she'd survived was Dan Jeffers. He'd stopped in to say good-bye before leaving for D.C., his knife wound healed enough to allow him to travel.

It wasn't real, she thought as she watched the devastated landscape out the car window. *I must have imagined it. Dreamed Mitch's solicitation and caring, his desperate urging not to die.* After all, she had been weak and in shock. It stood to reason that the whole incident, especially the kiss, had been mere hallucination. Now that Vincent Biaggi was dead and the case almost at a close, Special Agent Mitchell Lawson had dismissed her from his mind. There were still questions unanswered, questions that probably would never be answered, but they were not important anymore. It didn't matter that whatever had been stolen was still missing. It didn't matter that her life had been shattered irreparably. The killer had been eliminated, the whys and wherefores discovered. His job was done. It was time, now, to move on to another puzzle. Sabrina Compton no longer held any value.

One more unknown sin from her past she had atoned for with loss.

The road curved, bringing the half-skeletal remains of the Gaffe Island Inn into view. Sabrina's body tensed, panic rising despite the fact that Vincent Biaggi was dead. Memories crowded close—too close. Her sharp intake of breath echoed clear in the car. Mitch turned to her for the first time since they'd picked her up from the hospital.

"Are you sure you want to do this, Sabrina? It's not necessary. My men have been all over the cottage. If there was anything there, we'd have found it."

"I don't care what's there or not," she replied, her voice shaking. "I just want to see it. I have to. I need to."

Mitch sighed, nodded and again turned his head to stare in stony silence out the window. Brilliant sunlight glittered on deep green water and sparkled on white sand. Sails rode the waves like waving hands. Gulls stitched the foamy sea and marshmallow-studded sky together with carefree, gliding arcs. The air smelled fresh and clean, tinged with a tang of salt. Were it not for the denuded Palmetto trees, eroded dunes and shattered houses, it would have been impossible to believe that anything violent or destructive had ever visited this enclave of peace and tranquility.

They pulled up outside Sabrina's cottage and Ned Costello came around to open her door and help her out while Mitch, still silent, climbed from the car on his own. She stood staring at the cottage, amazed by the odd sense of deja vu that thrilled through her, as though she once had known a similar place, not this particular one. She felt no sense of welcoming like she had only weeks before. And strangely, now that she was here she felt no desire to go in, much less stay.

She moved first to stand in the open garage doorway. The roof had partially collapsed, half-burying her grandfather's precious car, though much of the debris had been cleared already, baring dents and scars to the brilliant light. A dark-haired man in jeans and a red T-shirt picked up the warped books and ruined letters Biaggi had strewn over the floor and dumped them in a large green receptacle. Sabrina turned her head and caught a glimpse of pale blue half-hidden behind the tires still lining the inside wall. Charlie's sweater, the one she had offered to finish for Mitch. Like her marriage and her life, it too had come to nothing.

She left the garage and walked to the back porch steps. Mitch stood at the bottom, waiting for her, leaning on the cane. She could see in his body, in the lines on his face, how much it hurt him just to stand upright. And how much it embarrassed him to show such weakness. The still-raw scar that marked where the bullet had creased his head stood out in stark relief in the bright sunlight. His eyes looked tired and old. For the first time, Sabrina wondered about his age. She feared that, whatever it was chronologically, his was a job that aged the spirit prematurely. Then she wondered how old she looked in the merciless sunshine. She gave him a sad smile before she mounted the steps and entered the house.

Sabrina was surprised to see how much clean-up work had been done under the federal agents' auspices. The front living room wall had been repaired and the windows replaced, though the front porch still sagged in jagged pieces. A temporary door had been placed over the kitchen archway, complete with a stout lock to keep unwanted intruders out of the main part of the house. That door was open now, though work was no longer being done in the remains of the kitchen. It was obvious to Sabrina, when she peered through the opening, that the kitchen-garage addition would have to be razed and completely rebuilt.

Mitch stopped her when she started up to the second floor, placing a warm but firm hand over hers on the railing.

"Don't push yourself, Sabrina. There's nothing to be gained by going up there, except maybe more nightmares. Whatever happened up there, it's over. Let it be. Please."

She stared up at the hallway, knowing he was right. There was no reason for her to go up there other than to relive the things Biaggi had done to her, the hurt and anger she had felt at Charlie for allowing it to happen. What good would reliving it do? It wouldn't change it or make it go away. It wouldn't make Charlie's love real, or worth remembering.

"All right," she said with a sigh, stepping down off the stairs and walking into the living room. She hadn't really wanted to go up there, anyway.

The living room actually looked half-civilized. The curtains were gone and the front wall was raw-looking in its newness, but the men had replaced the iron stove beneath its vent pipe and moved what furniture had not been smashed into a semblance of order. Warm, sunny days had allowed the couches and chairs to dry out, so they were usable despite the shredded state of their upholstery. Sabrina walked to the windows and stared out at the sparkling ocean, her gaze shifting to Geoff Simmonds' house. It appeared completely undamaged. The boards on the windows had been removed, but there was no sign of life around the place.

"Poor Geoff," she said, her voice, her whole being, full of remorse and guilt. "He tried to save me, you know."

"Yes, you told us," Mitch replied quietly.

"His house looks fine. He always said it would withstand a big blow. He should have stayed in it. He'd still be here if he had."

She turned from the window, suddenly exhausted, and moved to the lumpy mohair couch. She sat blinking tears from her eyes, her head bent into her hand.

"Are you all right?" Mitch asked.

Sabrina shook her head. She didn't think she'd ever be all right again.

"You were right, I shouldn't have come here today. I should have gone to the hotel." She took a deep breath and raised her head and saw a large cardboard box set on the now-rickety coffee table. It was nearly full of various small items. A half dozen things sat on the table next to the box. "What's this?"

"I told the men to gather anything that looked personal, or valuable. Jewelry, pictures, that sort of thing. I thought maybe you'd want to take it back with you."

Sabrina looked at him, touched by the sensitivity of his perception. He had perched awkwardly on a slashed armchair. She could tell his leg was bothering him.

"Thank you," she said with a smile. "That was very thoughtful." She looked back at the table. There, among the water-stained pictures and her great-grandmother's silver hairbrushes, lay a large, gold filigree locket. She reached out her hand and picked it up.

"We found that in here, Mrs. Compton," Ned Costello said. He'd been with them both the entire time, though Sabrina hadn't paid him much attention. "On the floor, in the corner. It was pretty badly soaked. I hope it's not ruined. It looks rather old."

"Yes, it's supposed to be." Sabrina stared a the lovely piece and relived her wedding day, the day Charlie had draped 'his' grandmother's locket around her neck. She pressed the catch. The locket sprang open to reveal the pictures Charlie had so lovingly, as she'd thought, placed within.

They were ruined, stained and crinkled by their wet treatment. Sabrina's lips trembled as she ran her thumb over the once-slick surface of Charlie's smiling face, trying to straighten it. Her breath caught in her throat.

"There's something in here, behind the picture," she said, looking up at Mitch.

He rose and, leaning heavily on the cane, came to sit beside her. He took the locket from her hand and pried out the stiff oval photo. There beneath the picture, snugged into the filigree frame was a flat silver key with a five-digit number engraved on its head.

"What is it?" Sabrina asked, her heart thudding.

"A safe-deposit box key, it looks like. To which bank, I wonder?"

Mitch pried the key loose. He glanced at Sabrina, whose face had gone white. Then he pulled Sabrina's picture from the other side of the locket.

Beneath it lay a folded square of paper. It was faded by time and its immersing in water, but the writing was still legible—Charles Philip Compton's neat, precise accountant's script. The name of a bank, the number of the safe-deposit box the key fit, and the name the box was rented under.

"Oh, dear lord," Sabrina whispered. "That was why Charlie didn't tell him." Mitch frowned a question at her. "I was wearing the locket that day. If Charlie had told him, Biaggi would have waited for me to come home and then killed me, too. Charlie was trying to protect me. No matter what Biaggi did to him, he stayed silent. All the torture, all that pain. Hours of agony, for me. To protect me. Because he loved me." Tears spilled over, ran down her pale cheeks. "He really did love me."

CHAPTER TWENTY-SIX

Early December snow fell softly, dusting the ground with powdery whiteness. Sabrina, in the front seat beside Donald Bradley, who drove, shivered slightly, wishing she'd been able to button her coat. Despite the weight she'd lost and not yet regained, the coat was still too form-fitting to close over the bulk of the cast.

Donald maintained a silence that felt strained, though there was little enough to talk about on the short drive. He had been uneasy around her, as had Anne, ever since they had discovered the truth about Charlie, about who he'd been, what he'd done. It wasn't for lack of trying. They'd both been kind, sympathetic and solicitous, and totally shocked to learn their dear, meek friend had once been not just a criminal, but a murderer. Yet, somehow an estrangement had grown between them, an awkwardness filled with pensive eyes and unvoiced questions. They treated Sabrina differently, as though she had changed.

Well, perhaps I have, she thought as they pulled into a parking spot. *I certainly don't feel the same.*

Donald Bradley got out and came around to open her door and help her out. The coat slipped from her cast-encased shoulder; with a gentle smile reminiscent of past innocence, he slid it back in place. Then he took her arm and guided her over the slick sidewalk into the Goldome Bank on Delaware Avenue, just north of Sheridan Drive.

It was an impressive structure of white stone with tall pillars flanking the entryway and intricate carving over the door. *This is the way a bank should look,* Sabrina thought, pausing in the foyer for Donald to open the inner door for her. It was not like the modern buildings most institutions favored nowadays, though this was not an old edifice by any means. It had merely been designed to look and feel like a solid, dignified doyenne graciously bowing to the masses that passed by, and through, its portals. It succeeded admirably.

Mitchell Lawson was waiting for them, standing with two other men near a desk to the right of the door. Surprised to see him there, Sabrina walked slowly toward him, her heart racing in her breast. She hadn't seen him for a month, not since he had escorted her in awkward silence back to Buffalo to set in motion the complicated procedure for opening Charlie's safe-deposit box. Her gaze slid over the two men with him —one with myopic eyes hidden behind thick lenses and a short, slight body clad in an off-the-rack brown suit, the other not much taller but huskily built, dressed impeccably in a conservative custom-made dark suit that echoed his fashionably-styled dark hair. But her barely-curious glance didn't linger. She might not be able to bring herself to meet Mitch's thoughtful, intense gaze, but she also couldn't keep her eyes far from his tall, imposing figure. She gave him a slight smile and a tiny nod of greeting, wondering what she could—should—say. Before she could speak Donald Bradley removed a paper from his pocket and handed it to Mitch.

"I think you'll find this is in order," he stated, his tone somewhat curt. Sabrina knew he'd been singularly unimpressed by the F.B.I. agent when they'd met a month ago, and the fact that he blamed Mitchell Lawson for Charlie's death and Sabrina's injuries showed clearly in both his face and tone of voice.

Mitch didn't respond to the implied challenge in the lawyer's words. He merely opened the paper, bowed his head and gave it a quick scan. Sabrina wondered if anyone else saw his chest and shoulders rise in a silent sigh on seeing that it was, indeed, in proper form. *It has probably been an even more frustrating wait for him than for me,* she thought. The intervening Thanksgiving holiday added days to the time it had taken Bradley, as executor of the estate, to obtain the necessary court order to allow him access to the safe-deposit box. Then, once the order was secured, they had had to wait until the State sent a representative to preside over the opening. Legal machinery might grind on relentlessly, but it didn't do so quickly. And Mitch could not put this—put her—fully behind him, she knew, until all the i's were dotted and the t's crossed.

Mitch nodded his satisfaction and handed the paper to the dark-haired man, who he then introduced as Glenn Tyson, the manager of the branch. While Tyson inspected the official-looking seals and deciphered the legalese of the myriad typed words, Mitch introduced the man with the glasses: Simon Nizialek, an auditor with the New York State Tax Department. He most definitely looked the part— underfed, underpaid, nervous and self-important. Nizialek shook Sabrina's hand with fussy precision, repeating the procedure with Donald Bradley as his bright, bulging dark eyes noted every detail of their persons. Sabrina felt herself analyzed, categorized and hung in a niche all in the space of a few seconds.

Nizialek took the court document from the bank manager, scrutinized every detail while those around him watched, then he turned and retrieved his briefcase from beside Glenn Tyson's desk.

"Well, suppose we get this thing open and see what your husband put into this mysterious box of his, Mrs. Compton," he said, and cleared his throat. From his tone, it was obvious he heartily disapproved of the public's deviousness in salting away taxable monies. "It will take more than enough time just to sort the contents, much less ascertain a correct value, and I'm sure we all have other duties to attend to today."

Bank Manager Tyson's energetic stride led the way across the marble floor, followed closely by Nizialek and Donald Bradley. Sabrina, wishing she could simply go home and forget about the safe-deposit box, matched her pace to Mitch's and gave him a sideways look.

"Such a lot of fuss for something I don't even want," she murmured.

"Red tape, rules and regulations," Mitch replied with a wry grin, gesturing at the small group waiting impatiently for them at the entrance to the vault. "Guys like these eat it up. Bankers and lawyers are bad enough, but tax men!" He shuddered. "God forbid you should get something worth a dime and not pay the taxes on it."

Sabrina didn't smile, though she knew that was Mitch's goal.

"Mr. Nizialek can take the whole thing with him, for all I care. It's blood money. I don't want it. I don't even want to touch it."

Glenn Tyson made a great show of rereading the court order and carefully checking Donald Bradley's identification before producing the release forms for him to sign. While they waited through the formalities, Mitch touched Sabrina's shoulder.

"How's the arm?"

"It's fine," she said with a small smile. "The cast should come off in a couple of weeks. I hope."

"It's been a long haul," Mitch commiserated, nodding.

"How's your leg doing?" She watched his eyes as she had in the Inn, and she knew he would lie to her again.

"Great. I'm practically back to normal. Jasen, he's my sister's oldest, he thinks it's terrific that I've got a metal knee now, too. He calls me the semi-bionic man."

Sabrina laughed softly, not wanting to deprive him of that small victory, and looked over to where the signing-in ceremony was just concluding. It hurt to see lines of strain etched deep into Mitch's face, the residue of constant pain that lurked in his eyes. He still limped heavily, for all his careless words, and still relied on the cane he so very much detested. Sabrina knew that both of them would carry permanent disabilities as unwanted reminders of the unforgettable.

The bank manager gestured them into the vault, where he produced the master key for Charlie's box. Donald Bradley stepped forward, withdrew the key that Sabrina had found and inserted it in the lock. Sabrina turned her head, not wanting to watch. She heard the keys turn and the box slide smoothly from its frame. Glenn Tyson pulled it free and carried it to a small table.

"I'll leave you to open it," he murmured, clasping his hands. There was an odd note in his voice, and Sabrina realized that curiosity ate at him. He wanted nothing more than to see the contents of that box. She watched him leave the vault and wished she could change places with him. She had no desire at all to see what the bank manager longed to glimpse. Donald Bradley touched her arm, bringing her back to the room where three men stood around the table, waiting for her attention.

"Do you want to open it, Sabrina?" Donald asked, holding out the key.

Sabrina looked at the box on the table. Its smallness surprised her. Though perhaps eighteen inches in length, it was only five inches wide and stood a mere three inches tall. Certainly there couldn't be much in it, even if it were all in big bills. Not the kind of money Biaggi said Charlie had stolen. She frowned a silent question up at Mitch. He frowned back, his eyes as confused and wondering as she felt.

"How much did Biaggi say Tony took, Sabrina?"

"Eight hundred thousand, I think. How could it possibly be in this? It's too small."

Mitch shrugged with both shoulders and lips. "We'll never know unless we open it, will we?"

I don't want to know! She had said that once before, when she had first met Mitch. Now the words again burst within Sabrina, filling her eyes with tears. She almost said them aloud, biting them back at the last second. Had she the strength, she would have turned and run from the room, from the bank itself. Her right hand, clenched on the table beside the box, trembled visibly.

Mitch seemed to hear the cry, her silent plea for ignorance in which to hide from the world, from the cold, unfeeling cruelty of reality. She could see his eyes absorb the pain that spilled from hers, blotting it up as though he could take it all upon himself. Her lips began to quiver, and she shook her head.

"You have to know, Sabrina." His soft voice and compassionate gaze made inroads deep into places she didn't want anyone to come ever again. "It won't be completely over until you know it all. You have to know."

"No!" she whispered. Panicked, she pushed at him, at the pieces of him that had invaded her space. Mitch drew back, stumbling a bit, his eyes sad and hurt. Afraid she would begin screaming, or physically hitting him, Sabrina turned away from the table, and pressed a shaking hand to her lips. "No," she repeated, louder, firmer. "I don't!"

"Well, *someone* had better open this thing," Simon Nizialek snapped, his mypoic eyes icy. "I certainly haven't time to waste on emotional nonsense!"

"Then you open the damned thing, if it's so important," Sabrina cried, whirling to face him. She trembled with rage. "Go ahead. Open it. You're the only one who cares what the hell is in it."

The state tax official glared at her, then reached out and snatched the key from Donald Bradley's hand. He jabbed it in the lock, twisted it sharply, and lifted away the box's lid. Despite her abhorrence and the panic surging in her breast, Sabrina could not pull her stare away from what she did not want to see.

She thought it was empty, at first. Stunned, she moved closer to the table and peered into the shadowed interior of the narrow shallow box. Then she saw it, in the back corner. A small black velvet pouch lying atop a folded piece of paper. Nizialek reached for the tiny bag, but Mitch forestalled his hand with an authoritative gesture. With careful precision, as though he knew what he would find, he drew out the bag, opened the drawstring and poured the contents into his large, broad hand.

Diamonds. Brilliant, flawless, glittering like stars in the overhead lights, they ranged in size from three to six carats each. Sabrina stared, entranced by their beauty, barely hearing the tax agent's grumbled complaints about the inconvenience this would cause him. Now he'd have to go to the expense of having them appraised. The paperwork would be enormous, it would take months. Mitch gently took Sabrina's hand, turned it over, and tipped some of the sparkling gems into her palm.

Sabrina stood mesmerized by the unexpectedness of the find and the size of the blue-white stones. She ran the fingers of her left hand over the diamonds, counting them aloud. Ten glittered in Mitch's hand. Seven nestled in her cupped palm, flashing liquid silver as they refracted the overhead lights. They were so large she had trouble holding them in her small hand. Simon Nizialek jotted copious notes in his file, then opened the velvet bag and took the gems one-by-one from first Mitch, then Sabrina, checking her count, his ferret-eyes intent as though he feared she would slip one into her pocket, or beneath the cast. Sabrina glanced up at Donald Bradley, who looked dazed. He shook his head, disavowing all prior knowledge of Charlie's cache. At last Sabrina looked again to Mitch, who stood reading the paper that had been folded beneath the bag.

"I don't understand," she said. Nizialek continued to take the diamonds from her hand and make notes on each. She ignored him. "Biaggi said Charlie took money, he was looking for money. Where did these diamonds come from? Where did he get them?"

"This explains it, in detail." Mitch laid the paper on the table, turning it so Sabrina could read it. "A very thorough man, your Charlie. He kept a record of everything, like the efficient accountant he was. See, here," he indicated with a broad finger the top three lines, "these are the places where he bought the stones, and how much each one cost. Never more than two stones from any one place. That way, no one would get suspicious. A very carefully thought-out plan. Look at the dates." His finger moved again. "It took him three years to buy them all. Three years of embezzling the money—a lot more than Biaggi said, too, close to two million—and turning it into diamonds. I guess when he figured he had enough, or maybe when he thought they were about to catch on, he came to us."

Sabrina stood completely still, staring at the writing on the paper, caught in echoes of the past. It was so like Charlie, her wonderful Charlie, to carefully document his every move, even if illegal. Hesitantly, she touched the ink with trembling fingertips. It was like touching him. He seemed so close, she could swear he was in the room with them. If she lifted her head, she would see him smiling at her as he used to do when he was filled with a delicious secret. His eyes would be sparkling with excitement, and the tiny dimple in his cheek would flash on and off. All she had to do was lift her head. Very deliberately, Sabrina kept her head bent, her gaze on the paper.

"There are twenty-five stones listed here," Simon Nizialek said, furiously copying the list into his file. "But there were only seventeen in the bag."

His tone sounded like an accusation, his glance at Sabrina a confirmation of his belief that beneath his very nose she had somehow spirited eight diamonds away, to avoid death duties. Mitch's lip lifted in a sneer. Again, he touched the paper. He spoke directly to Sabrina, ignoring the tax man.

"See? He'd been selling the stones off, one-by-one," he explained, moving his finger down a few lines. "The first was two years after he came here. He'd bought it for seven thousand dollars and sold it for eight thousand five hundred. The next one he sold eighteen months later. And so on. Eight diamonds in fifteen years."

"What do all these names mean, and the amounts after them?" Sabrina asked.

"I think those are the people he gave the money to."

Surprised, Sabrina raised her head at Mitch's quiet, solemn tone. But Mitch didn't look up at her. He stared on at the paper, his mind far away. Sabrina could almost see the memories that deluged him.

"The families of men hit by the Mob. Delgado and Henderson, they were federal agents. I worked with Delgado, off and on, until he was killed." Sabrina looked down at the paper. Beside the name Delgado was the date, 8/3/78; after Henderson, Charlie had written, 12/26/83. "They were contract killings, both of them. Mob-style executions. Delgado had three kids, his oldest was a girl about thirteen or so. Henderson had a two-year-old, and one on the way. About four months after the killings, both widows received anonymous checks in the mail. Cashier's checks, drawn on local banks. No note, no name, no indication of any kind who had sent them. I'm sure when I check, I'll find the amounts tally." He slid his finger over the two numbers: $9,673 and $11,892. Then he moved it down to tap beneath another name.

"Grady," he continued with a sigh, "I remember that name, I think he's D.E.A. Or was; he died in '84. Right?"

Sabrina looked at the date: 3/2/84. She nodded, a strange, lightheadedness beginning to creep over her. This Charlie was a man completely unknown to her, as completely opposite to Tony DiGesare, who himself had killed for money, as he was to the Charlie she had lived with for over seven years. The amazing thing was that they had existed side-by-side, the two Charlies. One her childlike, absent-minded husband, who was innocent and naive and trusting and kind, who had no idea there was any world other than his academic ivory tower. The other was a man who used stolen blood money to systematically atone for murder, a man experienced, cunning and realistic, who dared not trust another soul, not even his own wife.

Which Charlie had come first? Which one was truly real? Sabrina looked again at her husband's writing, at the dates on the paper, and she knew. Mitch's words had been more than right. In loving Charles Philip Compton, she had created not only a life of beauty and meaning, she had created Charlie himself, the sweet, gentle, good man who had fulfilled her so completely. It was that other man, the secret one, the one she had never known, who Charlie himself had created. It was that one who was truly real, for whom she was just a cover. It was that one who had almost gotten her killed. The real Charlie. Mitch's voice came to her from a far, and lengthening, distance.

"That's poetic justice for you, using the Mob's own money to compensate the families of their victims. I wouldn't have thought old Tony had it in him—a sense of honor, twisted though it was, and a conscience. It's hard to believe. But I guess its true. According to what's here, he'd been planning this whole thing for at least three years before he came to us."

"A point of honor," Sabrina said, her voice fragile-sounding in her ears. She could barely breathe. "That's what he said, Biaggi, that it was a point of honor. Honor among thieves, and murderers."

She couldn't stop shuddering. She could feel the blood drain from her face and she feared she would faint. Mitch looked up at her and abandoned his post. He limped to her side. The touch of his hand, his arm strong around her waist, pushed back the threatening white mists. She could breathe again, though her shaking continued and her legs felt too weak to hold her upright. Donald Bradley brought a chair from the corner and set it behind her.

"Sit down, Sabrina," he urged, his face dark with concern. "Please. I won't be much longer. You just sit and relax for a few minutes."

"No," she replied, shaking her head, her voice breathy and tremulous. She couldn't seem to control it. "I can't stay here. I can't. I want to go home. Please, Mitch." She turned her eyes to his still, watchful face. The mists closed in on her, again. "Please. Take me home."

But she knew, even as she said it, that she had no home, not anymore. Her perception of the world, and the people in it, had been shattered. It would take long, long months to rebuild it into something that could stand against the winds of reality. And right now she feared she would not have the strength to even make the attempt.

Mitch nodded. His lips moved, but she couldn't hear his words. He wavered, his face receding into the distance. Sabrina shook her head. She looked at Donald Bradley, but she could barely see him. He bent and pulled the chair close as her legs collapsed. The last thing she remembered was Mitch lowering her onto the seat and kneeling beside her, cradling her head on his shoulder. Then the mists enfolded her and whirled her far away from lies and murder and diamonds sparkling brilliantly in the vault's overhead lights.

CHAPTER TWENTY-SEVEN

"Yes, Kristin, I promise," Sabrina said with a laugh, hugging the child's thin body. "I will bring my famous chocolate chip cookies on Monday. With pecans," she added, echoing the child's reminder, "not walnuts."

"How many?" China-blue eyes wide, Kristin Malak's pale face shone with excitement. Sabrina rose from her knees and bent over the child, placing her hands on the arms of the wheelchair.

"You can eat one for every step you take." Kristin's impossibly-huge eyes seemed to grow bigger, rounder. Again, Sabrina laughed with delight. "Kristin Malak, you are a true con artist. I have a feeling you've been practicing secretly, and you'll end up with the biggest tummy ache this side of Candyland."

"I will, Sabrina," Kristin promised. "You'll see. I'll eat dozens and dozens!"

"Then I'd better get home and start baking, hadn't I?"

She kissed the seven-year-old's cheek and gave her another quick hug, looking back for one last look and a wave when she reached the therapy room door. She always hated leaving. It would be so much easier to simply live at the hospital. Even after all this time, it was hard to go home alone.

"Well, what sneakiness have you two been up to today?"

Sabrina turned to see Joyce Petrie, the head physiotherapist, leaning against the corridor wall, her arms crossed, a smug smile on her broad, dark face.

"You'll see on Monday," she answered with a teasing lilt to her tone.

"You have really worked wonders with that child, Sabrina. We had gotten no cooperation from her at all. We had almost given up on her walking until you started volunteering. What's your secret?"

Sabrina glanced through the window in the therapy-room door. Kristin, who had been injured in the car accident that had also killed her father, was busily playing a board game with a boy a year older who had lost a leg to cancer.

"It's no big mystery," she said, looking back at Joyce Petrie. "I simply get them hooked on my chocolate chip cookies, then threaten not to bring any more. They'll do anything I ask."

"Sure. And it has nothing at all to do with the fact that you just love them to pieces, does it?"

"Uh-uh," Sabrina replied with a confirming shake of her head as they walked together down the hall toward the outer door. "It's the cookies, I swear."

"How are you doing? Is the arm any better?"

"It's a great weather barometer, I can tell you that," Sabrina admitted with a rueful laugh, rubbing her shoulder. "But outside of a few aches when it rains, it's been fine. It's really hard to complain about a stiff arm when I see what these kids are going through. I don't know what I'd do without them, they give me so much joy."

"I'd like to see them—or us—get along without you. It was certainly our lucky day when you came through that door, Sabrina."

"No, it was mine, Joyce. I'll see you Monday."

Spring sunshine warmed the air outside. Sabrina breathed in the vibrant smells of new life as she walked across the parking lot to the Rambler. She would never have become involved with handicapped children had it not been for the lengthy and oftentimes painful therapy sessions she had undergone. And while she was not quite grateful for all that had happened, she knew that had Charlie not been killed and his murderer's bullet not shattered her shoulder, she would never have seen the children.

Children on crutches and in wheelchairs. Children born with physical defects or victims of abuse and accident. Children who struggled daily with the same pain, bewilderment and fear that she struggled with, but who had not the life experience needed to overcome and survive. And yet, in many ways they were stronger than she would ever be, for they merely accepted, did what had to be done, received each little gain with unbridled joy and each setback with stoic submission. And then began anew. She had gained much more from the children than she could ever give to them, for they had taught her how to live again. How to live, how to love, and how to trust.

She drove up Delaware Avenue with the windows open. The fresh breeze blew her dark hair around her face. When she reached Delavan, she turned into the entrance to the cemetery and drove to Charlie's grave. Though it had been a year and a half since Vincent Biaggi had stalked her, and she knew very well that he was dead, she still avoided the lovely, tranquil lake where she had first seen him. Nightmares, she had learned, had a habit of clinging close. There was no point in tempting those that had faded to return. It was hard enough to stand before the brown headstone and hold onto only the good memories. It was hard enough to remember her Charlie, the one she'd created.

The workmen had been there, as they had promised. The words she'd given them had been carved into the face of the marker, below the name 'Compton': *In Loving Memory of Anthony Albert DiGesare*. They stood out in sharp relief in the bright late-afternoon sunshine. It had taken her more than a year to come to terms with the man she had married, and the truce was shaky at best. But there was a peace of sorts embodied in these words, and in the letters she had written to Charlie's mother and sister, who he had named in his will. An acknowledgment of the convoluted twists and turns that had made up Charlie's character. She had also learned from the children that you can't go on until you make peace with yourself.

Her eyes lifted and she read again the words that Charlie had had carved into the stone so long ago: *To live in the hearts of those we love is not to die*. A tiny smile curved her lips and a warm feeling settled over her. She understood, at last, what the words meant, what Charlie had been trying to tell her. Love creates and empowers. Love is both living and life. Love is the only reality.

"Good-bye, Charlie," she whispered. "I love you."

She drove toward home, knowing deep inside that the healing would continue, gradually. Someday, in the not too distant future, she would be whole again.

The doorbell rang at four-thirty. She was staring into the freezer, trying to decide what to make for dinner and finding that nothing appealed, and she welcomed the interruption. Thinking it was most likely the paper carrier, she grabbed a few dollars before opening the door.

It was not the paper carrier.

"Mitch!" Her heart leapt into her throat. She had trouble catching her breath. "I don't believe it! What are you doing here?"

Yes, what? Memories reared, and fear abruptly crowded into her heart, her lungs. Mitch smiled and shook his head.

"Don't panic, Sabrina. It's a social call, not an official one."

"Please, come in," she said, with a relieved sigh. "It's really great to see you."

"It's been a long time, hasn't it? You're looking good. The shoulder okay?"

"Good enough. Come on into the kitchen, I'll get us some coffee."

He sat at the small oblong oak table and watched her measure coffee, pour water into the top of the coffee-maker. She set cups and saucers, spoons, sugar and a small cream pitcher on the table. The machine on the counter began to hiss and steam. When she sat opposite him, the delicious aroma of brewing coffee filled the air.

"What brings you back to Buffalo? Another case?"

"In a way." Sabrina felt herself flush beneath his intent gaze. She looked over at the dripping coffee as he spoke. "It wasn't easy to find you. I didn't know you'd moved."

"There were too many memories in that house." She shrugged. "I couldn't get past them, not living with them every day. Besides, that place was miles too big for just me. I spent too much time cleaning the darned thing."

"And your arm? What's the final verdict on that?"

"I've got about seventy percent movement back, which is around forty percent more than they thought I'd get. And I don't have to watch the weather reports, anymore. That's a plus."

"Yeah," Mitch agreed. He rubbed his right leg. "I know exactly what you mean."

Sabrina rose and poured the coffee.

"So, what are you doing here?" she asked as she sat again. "I didn't think I'd ever see you again." She sipped her coffee, noting the changes the last sixteen months had wrought. Gray was now noticeable in his sandy hair. His skin showed more lines, especially around his mouth. He seemed to have lost some of the sparkle in his blue eyes. He looked, somehow, lost and lonely.

"Are you kidding? You had to know I'd turn up someday. You owe me a sweater, remember?" Sabrina laughed, and nodded. "Actually, I'm here on a permanent basis. I retired from the Bureau six months ago."

"What?" Shock dropped her jaw. Sabrina stared open-mouthed at him. "Why?"

"I don't know, I guess I just lost my taste for the job. It wasn't fun anymore, hadn't been for quite some time, actually." He took a sip of coffee, his eyes pensive. "And I kept thinking about this city, how much I liked it when I first saw it. It has a real homey feel, you know? I guess I just wanted to be where I could feel comfortable. So, I retired and moved here. I've been here for a month."

"But isn't your family in Washington? Your sister and your mother? Your nephews?" Mitch nodded. "Won't you miss them? I don't understand how you could just pick up and move away like that. What will you do here?"

"Oh, I'll keep busy. I'm a businessman, now. I bought out some guy who wanted to move south. Don't look so shocked, I didn't wander that far from the fold," he said with a laugh. "It's a security agency. You know—guards, dogs, security systems, all that good stuff. No point in wasting all my expertise, is there?"

Sabrina smiled and shook her head. Some of the old sparkle had come back when Mitch spoke of his business.

"You really do like all that 'good stuff,' don't you? You should see yourself, you look like a little kid with a new toy."

"I feel like one," he admitted. He stared into her eyes and his smile faded. Sabrina's heart began to thump. "I stayed away purposely, Sabrina. To give you time. It almost killed me, I had the phone in my hand a dozen times a day, every day. But I knew you needed space, so I didn't call. And I didn't write. For as long as I could."

Sabrina looked down into her coffee, her mind in a whirl. She wanted to speak, but she had no idea what to say. So many words vied for attention, she couldn't single any of them out.

"I care about you, Sabrina. More than I've ever cared about anyone. You're gutsy and honest and brave, the most truly genuine person I've ever known. When I thought you would die in that damned inn, it felt like a part of me was dying, too."

"Really?" She glanced at him. "I thought I had dreamed it, the things you said, the way you kissed me. I didn't?"

She looked up. Mitch's eyes caught hers and would not let go.

"No, you didn't. I love you, Sabrina. That's why I'm here, bag and baggage." He reached across the table, folded his warm, strong fingers around hers. "We're not kids, we don't have to rush into anything. I don't even know how you feel about me. But I thought we could just take it slow, and see what happens. There's a lot of rough memories to get around, and that won't be easy. But I'd like to try. I have to try, because I can't imagine my life without you in it. I just can't."

Sabrina smiled, and nodded. She thought again of the words Charlie had put on the gravestone, and her hand tightened on Mitch's. Love created reality, and reality meant life. She was ready for life now. She was ready to let love create her world anew. She looked deep into Mitch's eyes, and knew it would not take long.

SUSAN'S BOOKS

For readers who love suspense and paranormal suspense, available in both print and kindle format:

Tangled Webs
Proof of Identity
Sins of the Past
Piece By Piece*
Obsession*

For writers of both fiction and creative nonfiction: Write It Right Workbooks available from Amazon Kindle:

Volume 1: Character
Volume 2: Setting
Volume 3: Story
Volume 4: Point of View (POV)*
Volume 5: Plot*
Volume 6: Dialogue*
Compendium I: Volumes 1, 2, 3: Character, Setting, Story
Compendium II: Volumes 4, 5, 6: POV, Plot, Dialogue*

Write It Right Workbooks available from Amazon Print:

Workbook I: Volumes 1, 2, 3: Character, Setting, Story
Workbook II: Volume 4: POV,
Workbook III: Volumes 5, 6: Plot, Dialogue

*Coming soon, by summer 2014